S0-BHU-456

THE CROOKED PATH

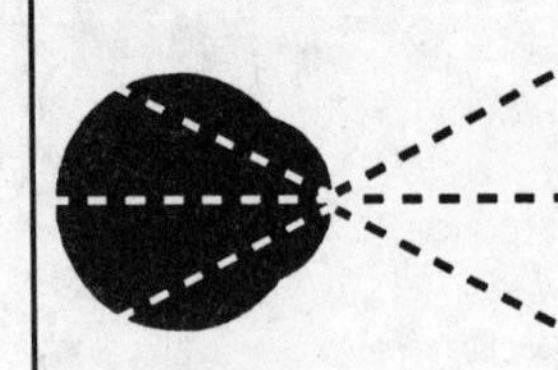

THE CROOKED PATH

IRMA JOUBERT

THORNDIKE PRESS
A part of Gale, a Cengage Company

Farmington Hills, Mich • San Francisco • New York • Waterville, Maine
Meriden, Conn • Mason, Ohio • Chicago

Scripture quotations are from the King James Version.

Thorndike Press, a part of Gale, a Cengage Company.

Thorndike Press® Large Print Christian Historical Fiction.
The text of this Large Print edition is unabridged.
Other aspects of the book may vary from the original edition.
Set in 16 pt. Plantin.

LIBRARY OF CONGRESS CIP DATA ON FILE.
CATALOGUING IN PUBLICATION FOR THIS BOOK
IS AVAILABLE FROM THE LIBRARY OF CONGRESS

ISBN-13: 978-1-4328-4633-6 (hardcover)
ISBN-10: 1-4328-4633-7 (hardcover)

Published in 2018 by arrangement with Thomas Nelson, Inc., a division of HarperCollins Christian Publishing, Inc.

Printed in the United States of America
1 2 3 4 5 6 7 22 21 20 19 18

CAST OF CHARACTERS

Lettie Louw
Annabel de Vos
Klara Fourie
Christine le Roux
Fourie siblings
Boelie
De Wet
Klara
Irene
Romanelli siblings
Marco
Antonio
Lorenzo
De Vos siblings
Annabel
Reinier
Pieterse siblings
Gerbrand
Pérsomi

Children born to:
Lettie and Marco Romanelli: Isabella, Leonora
Klara and Antonio Romanelli: Cornelius, Lulu, Marié
Christine and Gerbrand: Gerbrand
Christine and De Wet Fourie: Anna, Lulani
Annabel and Boelie Fourie: Nelius, Lientjie

GLOSSARY

biltong — lean meat, salted and dried in strips

boccie — Italian game of bowling

Boer — inhabitant of the Transvaal and the Free State in the time of the Anglo-Boer War; a white, Afrikaans-speaking person

braai — to grill or roast (meat) over open coals; barbecue

bushveld — a subtropical woodland ecoregion of southern Africa that encompasses most of the Limpopo Province and a small part of the North West Province of South Africa

bywoner — subfarmer, sharecropper

Great Trek — an eastward and northeastward migration away from British control in the Cape Colony during the 1830s and 1840s by Boers

Great Trek centenary — one hundred–year celebration of the Great Trek. A reenactment of the trek began on August 8, 1938, and culminated in a symbolic ox-wagon trek from Cape Town to Pretoria.

Jacobus Hendrik Pierneef — South African landscape artist, generally considered one of the best of the old South African masters (1886–1957)

koesister (also koeksister) — plaited deep-fried dough, soaked in syrup

matric (matriculation) — the final year of high school; the qualification received on graduating from high school

oom — uncle; also a form of address for any older man

ouma — grandmother

oupa — grandfather

pap en wors — Pap (pronounced *pup*) is porridge made from mealie meal. It's a traditional side dish, especially in the northern parts of South Africa, and is often served with *wors,* a traditional sausage.

rainbow sandwich — a multilayered sandwich made with carrot, spinach, beet, and goat cheese spreads

rusk — a hard, dry biscuit, a traditional South African breakfast meal or snack, typically dunked in coffee or tea before being eaten

tannie — aunt; also a form of address for any older woman

Tukkies/Tuks — informal name for the University of Pretoria or its students

Van Riebeeck's Day — celebrated annually on April 6 until 1994, in honor of Cape Town founder Jan van Riebeeck

Voortrekkers — Dutch pioneers who journeyed to the Transvaal in the 1830s to escape British rule; also, an Afrikaans youth movement, similar to the Boy Scouts and Girl Guides

Wits — the University of the Witwatersrand, in Johannesburg

"I stand with outdated maps in my hand . . . alone, without recommendations in the vast desert."

— YEHUDA AMICHAI, HEBREW POET, 1955

■ ■ ■ ■

Part One: Stepping Out

■ ■ ■ ■

Chapter One

What she was looking at, was definitely not what she wanted to see.

Lettie stood facing the full-length mirror in her mom's bedroom. Her heart, which had been overflowing with joy only this morning, lay heavy in her chest. From this moment, she vowed, not a single cake or dessert or sweet would cross her lips, ever again.

It was De Wet's fault, for speaking to her this morning. Or perhaps her mom was to blame, for making all those cakes and tarts. Or Annabel, for showing up when she did, flaunting her athletic figure.

Or maybe, just maybe, she herself was to blame.

Whatever the case may be, she was drawing the line.

This morning at the school fair De Wet — drop-dead handsome De Wet — had casually leaned on the table where she was working.

"Hello, Lettie. Who would have thought a smart girl like you knew how to make pancakes?"

"I'm just selling them," she said, embarrassed. He was tall, and when she looked up at him, his green eyes twinkled with mischief.

"Well, they picked the right person to look after the money. It's a lovely day, isn't it?" he made small talk. "I say, what are the chances of a flop or two for a broke fellow?"

She found him three and added a generous sprinkle of cinnamon sugar.

"Thanks, you're a pal," he said cheerfully.

As he turned to leave, Annabel fell into step beside him, chatting easily.

Lettie felt a sharp pang in the region of her heart. Then it dawned on her. Why had De Wet asked for two pancakes?

Lettie and Annabel had been friends for as long as they could remember. Lettie's father was the only doctor in town, Annabel's father the only lawyer. Annabel's mother had decided early on that Lettie would be a suitable playmate for her daughter.

Lettie lived with her mom and dad in their home in Voortrekker Street. The front room was used only when the minister came to call. They spent winter evenings and Sundays in the big kitchen with the table in the center of the room and the AGA stove, where her mom was always busy. In summer, when the bushveld was dry and hot, they sat on the back porch. Wire mesh kept out the flies and mosquitoes — except when someone forgot to shut the door properly. The house always smelled delicious, because Lettie's mom liked to surprise Lettie and her dad with a treat when they came home.

Annabel lived in a big house farther up the street. It had a semicircular front veranda, with pillars and four steps, and a bell beside the heavy front door that Lettie had to ring when she went over to play. A housekeeper in a neat uniform would open the door. Inside, thick carpets lay on the polished floors. The girls' games were confined to the veranda, so they wouldn't mess up the house. Annabel's mom was a tall, thin woman with pitch-black hair. She was very strict and always carried a drink in her hand. Annabel's dad was a big man with a florid complexion, thinning hair, and spectacles. He was hardly ever home, because he worked hard at his law firm. Lettie saw him only at church.

Lettie didn't like playing at Annabel's

home, so they mostly played at Lettie's home.

When they were in Form II, all the children from the surrounding farm schools came to the town school and lived in the hostel. That was how Lettie got to know Klara and Christine.

Christine's father was an important man. He was the Member of the Provincial Council for their constituency. But Christine wasn't important. She was just their friend.

Lettie took an immediate liking to Klara and Christine. She would have loved to be Klara's best friend, but Klara and Christine were already best friends. Lettie didn't have a best friend. She and Annabel would never be best friends.

Lettie had always been her daddy's dearest little sweetheart and her mommy's pretty little darling. Lettie's mom and dad were both short and stout and friendly. Lettie took after both her parents. She had always been a happy child.

But halfway through Form II she began to take notice of her friends' looks.

Klara was continually tucking behind her ears the unruly chestnut curls that kept escaping their plaits. She had rosy cheeks and lovely green eyes. She was athletic and had a beautiful singing voice. There wasn't an ounce of fat on her body.

Christine was small, with blonde curls and blue eyes. She always looked slightly startled — not afraid, but uncertain, rather — and she battled a little with her schoolwork. Klara often helped her. Christine was as pretty as a china doll.

Annabel was tall and slim, with shapely legs and golden skin. She was very good at sports and she was clever. She usually wore her long dark hair in a plait but, whenever possible, she would allow her shiny, silky tresses to cascade down her back. Her eyes were dark and she plucked her brows in neat arches, just like the movie stars. Her lips were full and her teeth pearly white.

Annabel was a stunning beauty, Lettie realized.

All the boys liked Annabel.

Klara's brother, De Wet, was one year ahead of them at school.

All the boys were in love with Annabel and all the girls were in love with De Wet — even the matric girls, despite the fact that he was their junior. De Wet was good at everything. He was a superb athlete and played in the first rugby team even though he was only in Form III. He was at the top of his class every year and he sang the male lead in the operetta. What was more, he was friendly to everyone, including Lettie.

He even remembered her name.

But it was that sharp pang in the region of her heart that had brought her face-to-face with herself in her mom's full-length mirror.

She was short and plump. "It's just puppy fat, you'll outgrow it," her dad always reassured her. But she was nearly fifteen.

She leaned closer to the mirror and took a critical look at her face. Her skin didn't look like Klara's, or Annabel's. "Your complexion is a bit oily," her mom said, "that's all. It means you won't have wrinkles when you're older." But at fifteen, getting older was of no concern to Lettie.

To crown it all, she wore glasses.

In front of the mirror in her mom's bedroom that particular night Lettie resolved never to eat cake or dessert or sweets again.

Her resolve didn't last long.

But the butterflies that fluttered in her tummy every time De Wet was near did not go away. The feeling was more amazing than anything she had ever felt before.

When Lettie was in Form IV, her dad dropped her at the school gate with her suitcase, her biscuit tin, and her blanket roll for Voortrekker camp.

"Here, Lettie!" Klara waved her over. She and Christine were standing next to the truck.

De Wet and his friend Braam were loading the suitcases and bags. De Wet jumped from the back and came to where she was standing. "Hello, Lettie, can I take your case?" he asked.

"I could've brought it over myself," she stuttered.

"Not on your life!" he said, laughing. His eyes sparkled, and his light-brown hair fell across his forehead.

The butterflies threatened to come fluttering out of Lettie's bright-red ears.

Annabel arrived in a uniform that was too short, and her hair wasn't tied back. She looked lovely as usual.

"De Wet! Braam!" she called out, pointing at her big suitcase and blanket roll.

Lettie pushed her glasses higher up her nose, envying Annabel's nerve.

That night they sat on the ground around the big campfire, Klara between Lettie and Christine.

Annabel crossed over to the other side of the fire. Lettie saw Annabel bend down and say something to De Wet. She saw De Wet laughing up at her and moving over to make room. She saw Annabel squeezing in between De Wet and Braam.

A dull ache lodged in her throat. The smoke from the fire stung her eyes, so she had to look away.

All weekend Annabel trailed after De Wet.

And all weekend De Wet looked like the cat who had got the cream.

During the last term of the school year, Lettie studied harder than ever. She reread all her assigned literature. She even read the newspapers so she could join in the conversation when Klara and Annabel were discussing politics.

On the last day of term she was awarded a prize for best achievement in Form IV. But she wasn't elected a prefect, and neither was Christine. When Klara and Annabel were called to the stage, Christine moved up to sit next to her.

Klara was appointed head girl, and De Wet, who, as the outgoing head boy, was also on the stage, stepped forward, put his arm around his sister's shoulders, and congratulated her with a kiss in plain view of the entire school.

Christine sighed beside Lettie. "What other boy would kiss his sister in front of everyone? Lettie, isn't he just the most adorable boy in the whole world?"

Lettie nodded. But her heart swelled inside her body, so that there was hardly any room to breathe.

In 1938, the friends boarded a train to join in the Great Trek centenary celebrations. They were met at Pretoria station and taken by bus to the campsite where thousands had gathered.

"My legs are like jelly after the long trip. I'll stand for a while," said Annabel when they realized the bus didn't have enough seats. But when two boys moved to make room for her, she sat down between them.

And when they arrived and the girls had to carry their luggage to their tents, Annabel made no move, just stood looking around. "I'll find a few strong men to help us."

"I can carry my own case," Lettie protested.

"Never!" said Annabel. "You'll see how keen these gallant young men are to help us."

And she was right. Annabel tilted her head slightly, shrugged her shoulders despondently, and gave some boys a poor-me smile. They immediately came over. "Can we help?" one of them asked.

Annabel looked up in mock surprise.

"Really? But . . . these cases are terribly heavy!"

One boy stepped forward and picked up the biggest of the suitcases. "Oh, this is nothing," he said.

"Gosh," said Annabel, "you must be very strong!"

The boys fell into step beside Annabel. All the way to their tent Annabel laughed and joked with them. Christine and Klara talked between themselves in low tones. Lettie followed in awkward silence.

Inside the tent, Annabel turned to her. "See, Lettie," she said, carelessly tossing her hat onto her blanket roll, "that's how you treat boys . . . men. They're a bit like goats. If you stroke their egos, they'll eat out of your hand."

The next day Klara announced a simulated battle between two groups on horseback. Her brothers, De Wet and Boelie, would take part.

De Wet would be riding his horse. Lettie drew a deep breath.

After breakfast they walked up the Lyttelton Hill to get a good view of the event.

"Gosh, we should have brought umbrellas. This sun is vicious," said Lettie. She could already feel her skin turning crimson.

"Don't be such an old lady, Lettie." Annabel sighed. "A little sun will do you good. You're as pale as a white mouse."

The event Lettie had been looking forward to suddenly seemed less enjoyable.

At exactly half past nine the order came: "Charge!"

From all around came the sounds of small arms discharging. The riders advanced, sheltering behind trees and shrubs. There was the deafening sound of exploding bombs. Here and there a rider jumped off his horse, firing as he advanced.

Christine had both hands pressed to her face. "What if they kill each other?" she asked anxiously.

"Heavens, Christine," Annabel said, "do you really think they'd use live ammunition? You'll believe anything, you know!"

Then Lettie saw him. De Wet was leaning forward, his tall figure pressed against his horse, the reins tight in both hands, charging straight at the enemy.

"Look, over there in the clearing!" Klara shouted. "Look at him go!"

Lettie kept watching until he disappeared behind a clump of trees.

Then she exhaled slowly. Surely no other man on earth could be that perfect.

■ ■ ■ ■

"Where's Annabel?" Christine asked when they were sitting by the fire later that week.

"Oh, she's around somewhere," Klara said.

"Shouldn't we go look for her?" asked Christine.

"No, leave her," said Klara.

Someone played a few chords on an accordion and they began to sing the well-known trek songs: *"Die sweep het geklap en die wawiele rol . . ."*

Lettie's eyes kept searching for De Wet.

The concertina joined in. *"Aanstap, rooies, die pad is lank en swaar . . ."*

There were too many people around the campfire. She couldn't spot him among the others.

In time a delicious languor took hold of Lettie. "I'm sleepy. I think I'm going to turn in," she told the other two.

"We won't be long," said Klara. "Tomorrow it's the main event and we don't want to be tired."

Slowly Lettie found her way between the tents. She heard the voices lagging behind the accordion: *"Liewe maan, jy seil so langsaam . . ."* In front of her the hill rose undisturbed, firmly embedded in its age-old rock foundation. Overhead the stars were bright in the firmament.

She was filled with happiness, with a joy too deep for words. It was a wonderful, wonderful camp, after all. She leaned against a tree, felt the hard, rough bark under her fingers. She belonged to the best people on earth. She was proud to be an Afrikaner.

She closed her eyes. Her heart was filled with warmth. She was in love, and it was . . . marvelous.

She carried on, making her way between the tents in the bright moonlight.

Then she saw them. The girl was in the man's arms. The man's hands were sliding over her back, pressing her against his body. His head was lowered, his lips locked over hers.

The girl was tall, the man even taller.

It was Annabel.

And De Wet.

Time stopped. The moment froze.

Quietly Lettie turned and chose a roundabout way back to her tent.

Her heart was cold as ice and heavy as lead. She put on her nightdress and spread out her blankets.

The ice around her heart began to melt. She curled into a ball and pressed her face into her pillow.

She lay without moving, pain like a solid crust around her heart. She told herself not to cry, begged herself not to cry.

She missed her mom.

Shortly afterward she heard Christine and Klara enter.

Christine whispered, "Klara, he *was* kissing her. I saw it with my own eyes."

"Oh, it doesn't mean anything," Klara whispered back. "A boy will kiss any girl who throws herself at him. And you know what Annabel is like . . ."

But De Wet wasn't like other boys, was he? Lettie's heart, her entire being, cried out.

She lay motionless on her small island of blankets while her two friends quietly spread their own blankets and shook out their pillows.

She thought of Christine.

She knew Christine was also in love with De Wet. The icy hand around her aching heart gripped a little harder. Pretty little Christine was also in love. And she was also in pain tonight, feeling the same agony.

After a while she heard Klara breathe deeply and evenly.

Much later, when Annabel came in noisily and prepared to go to bed, Lettie was still awake. “Are you asleep?” Annabel asked as she unrolled her blankets next to Lettie.

Lettie ignored her. She didn’t want to talk about the truth, which was that Annabel was Annabel, and she was Lettie Louw, and a man like De Wet Fourie would never be hers.

Chapter Two

"I want to be a journalist. I've made up my mind," Annabel announced one morning before school as the four friends walked to their classroom. "I'm going to Tukkies next year."

"A journalist?" Christine asked uncertainly.

"Yes, Christine, someone who writes in the papers, you know?" Annabel replied, rolling her eyes. She turned to Lettie and asked, "What are you going to do?"

"Study medicine," Lettie answered without hesitation. "At Wits, I suppose, where my dad was also a student."

"Wits! An English university!" Annabel exclaimed. "And medicine! I'm not sure it's a suitable career for a woman. It's so . . . masculine." She shrugged. "But I suppose it's okay for you."

"I think Lettie will be a wonderful doctor," Klara said. "She's certainly clever enough, and she'll be good to her patients."

Annabel raised her eyebrows skeptically and turned to Christine. "And you, Christine, what are you going to study?"

"I don't know." Christine was quiet for a moment. "Actually, I'd like to work with sick people too, help them, you know?"

"Don't be silly," Annabel said. "You couldn't even pass the Voortrekkers' first-aid course!"

Lettie noticed Klara's hand resting briefly on Christine's shoulder. For a fleeting moment she wished that Klara could also be her best friend. She also wished she could attend Pretoria University because . . . well, because De Wet was there. But her dad believed that Wits had the best medical school, and Lettie believed her dad knew best.

Throughout 1940, World War II was eclipsed by Lettie's new surroundings: the big city of Johannesburg, university, her life at the women's residence, the English lifestyle and viewpoints all around her. Lettie felt ill at ease, completely out of her comfort zone.

Her classes were interesting and stimulating, and she coped with her studies easily. "But we've learned nothing that's directly applicable to medicine," Lettie told her dad at Easter, the first time she went home.

"Just you wait," her dad said, laughing.

"Have you worn the evening gown we bought before you left?" her mom asked.

Lettie fished for an excuse. "No, Mom, first-years don't attend functions."

The wireless had plenty of news about the war, as did the papers, the lampposts, even the cinemas. In the corridors at the dormitory and between classes there were heated discussions about the war — almost everyone at Wits had a father or brother or boyfriend fighting up in North Africa.

"There must be twice as many girls as guys at varsity," said Lettie's roommate. "I don't know where we're supposed to find partners for the spring ball."

Lettie wished there were no such thing.

But that night she dreamed De Wet came to fetch her for the spring ball. In a daze she floated across the dance floor in her sleek new gown. In the small hours of the morning, the dream dissolved.

Lettie spent the night of the ball in her room, studying. The elegant dress her mom had bought for her at Miss Pronk's shop at the beginning of the year hung unworn in her wardrobe.

▪ ▪ ▪ ▪

During the October vacation, Lettie met Henk when Klara brought him home from varsity.

"Is he your boyfriend?" Lettie asked when she and Klara got a moment alone in the Fouries' kitchen. Annabel — no coffee maker — had remained on the veranda with Henk, Christine, and De Wet.

"Well, yes, I suppose so," Klara said vaguely.

"But . . . are you in love with him?" Lettie asked. Henk wore spectacles and had a captivating Cape accent.

"I don't know," Klara answered, pouring boiling water over the coffee grounds in the bag. "Lettie, I don't really know what it feels like to be in love."

"Are there butterflies in your stomach every time you see him?" Lettie asked. Despite the passage of time, the butterflies still appeared every time De Wet spoke to her.

"Butterflies?" Klara thought for a moment. "No, not really. I just get a kind of . . . warm feeling, in my heart."

"Oh, well," Lettie said hesitantly, placing coffee cups on a tray, "that might work too."

They joined the others for a game of cards around the big dining table covered with Klara's mom's starched white tablecloth. After drawing lots, Lettie and Henk and De Wet were placed on the same team.

"We'll take you down in the first round!" Annabel exclaimed.

De Wet laughed easily. "You're welcome to try, Miss Big Mouth. But Lettie is on our team, and none of you girls can hold a candle to her." His green eyes were dancing with mirth.

"I'm no good at cards," Christine said anxiously. Klara squeezed her hand.

"We're going to munch you like a corncob." De Wet boosted his team's ego. "Lettie, you're our captain. Play the first card!"

The further they drew ahead, the more elated De Wet grew, winking at Lettie when she made a clever move and whistling through his teeth when he trumped the other team. The better they played, the more miffed Annabel became. Finally Klara doused the threatening inferno her brother had ignited and surrendered.

"That's enough, you win," she said. "Our team will see to the coffee. You three pick out some music."

At the end of the vacation, Lettie took three things back to Johannesburg: a huge tin of biscuits (despite her firm resolve to go on a hunger strike), another new ball gown (despite having told her mom she had never worn the previous one), and the memory of one of the most wonderful nights of her life.

Because, although she told herself over and over again that De Wet had simply been friendly, that his flirtatious behavior was all part of the game, her fluttering heart refused to pay heed.

During the Christmas vacation of Lettie's second year at Wits, she visited Klara at the Fourie farmhouse. As she boiled water for coffee, Klara told her that Christine had enlisted and joined the troops in Cairo.

"Why? What was she thinking?" Lettie asked, placing rusks on a plate.

"I made her promise to write to you. Perhaps she'll explain." Klara shook her head. "Christmas is a sad affair this year."

Lettie sensed Klara's loneliness for her best friend. "Will Henk join your family?"

"Yes." Her tone lacked enthusiasm, and her eyes darted to the servants' quarters off of the kitchen, where a young Italian prisoner of war was lodging with them.

"What's he like, the Italian?" Lettie asked.

Klara blinked. "Who? Antonio?"

"Antonio Romanelli!" Lettie sang the name. "It's melodious, don't you think? I heard him singing earlier. What a voice. And handsome too."

"He's the enemy, Lettie." But Klara blushed.

"Yes, it's too bad he's not one of our own people." She placed coffee cups on a tray. "Why is he here?"

"He's been assigned to help Boelie build a dam on the Pontenilo. Or maybe it's a bridge. I don't ask. Papa is of two minds about his presence." She waved away the topic while her cheeks were still pink.

"How's De Wet?" Lettie asked as casually as possible.

"Fine," Klara said. "He's busy on the farm, but he's nowhere near as handy as Boelie. We see a movie now and again. Annabel usually goes along. I'll let you know the next time we go. It would be nice if you could come too."

Of course, Annabel. That night Lettie was sucked into a deep, dark vortex. By morning, her perspiring body was tangled in the sheets. She knew De Wet wouldn't spare her a second glance after all these years. And yet she fell prey to his charm every time she saw him — the natural charm he turned on everyone he encountered.

Lettie rose and poured out her heart to her mom while they drank coffee together.

"De Wet is a wonderful man, sweetheart," her mom agreed, "but there are many other wonderful young men your own age, thousands of them, in fact. Maybe not all of them are as tall and well built and handsome as De Wet, but the right man will show up, you'll see. Sometimes life takes strange turns, but in the end every pot finds its lid."

It seemed she would have to set her sights on Mr. Personality, Lettie thought. Even if he did turn out to be as short and chubby as a pot.

WAAF Camp
Cairo
24 December 1941

Dear Lettie,

It's Christmas Eve and strange to be so far from home. But apart from being homesick, I'm perfectly fine, really.

Lettie, you're nearly a doctor, so there's something I want to ask you. Actually on behalf of a friend. She doesn't have anyone to ask, so I offered to write to you.

My friend's boyfriend is a soldier over here. She doesn't work with me, but I sometimes see her at meals. She wants to know how one gets pregnant. I suppose you find it strange that we should be asking a question like this, but your dad always told you things and you're studying to be a doctor and everything, so you probably know the answer.

Lettie lowered the letter. It was quite incredible, she thought, that two young women, both of age, living in the midst of a world war, could be so ignorant of the most basic facts of life.

She picked up the letter and read on:

My friend also wants to know something else. If a girl is pregnant, is there a way not to be pregnant anymore? Or is the baby already alive? She doesn't mean she wants to kill the baby if it's already alive, she's just wondering at what point the baby becomes a real person in one's tummy.

You probably find these questions absurd, Lettie, but my friend is really anxious to know. I think she might be asking on behalf of another friend of hers, someone I don't know in person. We didn't know who to ask, so we're asking you.

I hope you have a wonderful Christmas — you and your mom and dad.
All the best.

Your friend,
Christine

When she had read the letter, Lettie sat motionless for a long time, thinking. It was not the letter she had hoped to receive from Christine. Was there any possibility that the "friend" might be Christine herself? Lettie immediately dismissed the thought. She knew Christine well enough to know she would never go that far with a boy.

Besides, Lettie knew Christine was madly in love with De Wet. Or could homesickness have driven Christine into the arms of another man?

No, impossible, Lettie decided. Besides, Christine would have been honest with her or, at the very least, confided in Klara. They had always been close. And she felt sure Klara didn't know about any such thing.

Lettie got up, took a writing pad from the top drawer of her desk, and began to answer Christine's letter. She did her best, though it wasn't easy putting the information Christine was asking for on paper. She imagined Christine blushing as she read the letter. Christine would probably consider the entire chain of events a gross sin. Lettie smiled to herself.

She sealed the envelope and addressed it. On the back she printed *PRIVATE AND CONFIDENTIAL.* Then she put the letter next to her dad's doctor's bag so that he would mail it the next day.

In April of Lettie's final year at university, the war in Europe ended. Christine was expected home any moment, with a baby. Klara said the father was Gerbrand Pieterse, a bywoner from her family's farm who had also been stationed in Cairo during the war. He would not be coming home.

"How has his family taken the news?" Lettie asked. Her heart felt heavy for Christine, for the child.

"About the baby?" Klara asked. She shrugged. "It's a boy. Christine has named him for his father."

Antonio, the young Italian prisoner of war who had lodged with Klara's family while the bridge and later the new church in town were being built, had returned to Italy. All over the country there were celebrations to welcome the returning soldiers. Lettie's varsity chums and her colleagues at the hospital where she was doing her practical work were in a festive mood.

Mr. Personality had still not put in an appearance. "Give it time," Lettie's mom said. "He'll turn up." In the meantime Lettie worked hard to stay at the top of her class. She had to make her mark somewhere at least.

Lettie spent her July vacation working at the hospital in Joburg. She had a small, chilly room on the south side of the staff quarters. When Klara paid her an unexpected visit, she slept on a hospital mattress, which they stowed under Lettie's bed by day.

Lettie didn't see too much of Klara, who had actually come to visit her fiancé, Henk. Late at night, after Klara came back from a date with Henk, and in the early mornings, before Lettie reported for duty, they lay on their beds chatting. Klara had plans to come teach at a nearby school.

Tuesday evening Henk invited Klara and Lettie to his flat to listen to music. He bought fish and chips, which they ate from the newspaper wrapping.

"Not very hygienic," Lettie said, "this newsprint, I mean."

"Well, don't eat the paper," said Henk. He had mischievous eyes that always looked amused.

As they were lying in the dark that night, Lettie said, "Henk is one of the nicest guys I know, Klara."

"Ye-es, he is, isn't he?" Klara replied sleepily. "It was a nice evening, but I'm exhausted. Sleep tight."

Thursday evening Klara asked, "Lettie, do you have an evening gown?"

"More than one," Lettie replied. She didn't mention that they had never been worn. "Why?"

"We're going dancing tomorrow night."

"You're welcome to wear one of my dresses, but I'm afraid you'll drown in it." Lettie laughed. "Besides, it'll be much too short."

"No, silly," Klara said, "you'll be wearing it yourself. You're coming along."

Lettie was silent for a moment. "With you and Henk?"

"And one of Henk's colleagues. I haven't met him, but Henk says he's a nice chap."

"Klara . . . ," she said uncertainly.

"Oh, come on, Lettie," Klara urged. "The four of us will be going together. We'll have a good time. You can't say no!"

"Fine," Lettie agreed quietly, but her heart began to race. Was she really going to a dance — in one of her ball gowns?

The next afternoon, while Klara was taking a bath, Lettie spread her three brand-new gowns on the bed. Which one should she wear? She stroked the delicate blue dress of her first year and gave a slight smile. In her mind she heard Annabel say, "Lettie, it's so old-fashioned! It's so . . . 1940!" On the other hand, all her dresses came from her first three years. After that her mom had understood that Lettie didn't need new gowns. Or perhaps it had just become too difficult to get hold of fabric.

"Which one are you going to wear?" Klara asked behind her. "Oh, that dark-green one is stunning!"

The evening was a fairy tale. Lettie glided across the floor of the town hall in a bubble, the music flowing through her body. Her partner was a bit awkward at first, but after a while he lightened up and began to laugh heartily at his own jokes. They danced well together.

The best parts of the evening were the two dances she had with Henk. He was a good dancer and a fun companion.

Back at the doctors' quarters, she and Klara chatted until the early hours. "When do you plan on getting married?" Lettie asked. "December?"

"I don't know," said Klara. "I suppose so."

"You don't sound very excited," Lettie

ventured.

"I haven't given it much thought," said Klara. "We'd better go to sleep now. You're on call tomorrow."

"Henk is really handsome, Klara," Lettie said after a while.

"Hmm," Klara said dreamily, as if she was too sleepy to reply.

But before Lettie fell asleep, she heard Klara toss and turn, heard her friend curl into a ball on the mattress beside her, heard her smothered sigh.

The next morning Lettie was rudely awakened by the shrill sound of her alarm clock. She got up, switched the kettle on, and went to the bathroom. She was unaccustomed to dancing. Her feet ached and her eyes smarted from lack of sleep. It would be a long day ahead.

When she got back to her room, Klara said, "I'm going to break off my engagement tonight."

Suddenly Lettie was wide-awake. Her hands flew to her face. "Klara? Are you sure?" she asked. "Have you thought this through?"

"Yes, I'm sure," Klara replied. "I think I've known for a long time what I must do, but I just haven't been able to drum up the courage to do it. We've been together so long, Lettie, and I do love him, but I know now I can't marry Henk. I know it."

Lettie took the coffeepot and two cups from the shelf and measured two scoops of coffee grounds into the bag. "Is there someone else, Klara?" she asked, pouring boiling water over the coffee. "The . . . Italian? Antonio?"

Klara shrugged.

"That's what I thought." Lettie nodded.

"There's nothing between us, Lettie. He's gone back to Italy, to the girl he's been engaged to since before the war. They'll probably get married soon. He wrote to her while he was here and he regularly received letters from her." Klara gave a mirthless laugh. "I know her name. I even know her handwriting."

Lettie poured the coffee. "But he made you realize Henk isn't the right man for you? Sorry, I forgot to buy milk."

"You know, Lettie," Klara said somberly, "if Antonio had asked me to go to Italy with him, I think I would have packed my belongings there and then. I don't know that I'd even be willing to move to Johannesburg for Henk. I do know that I don't love him enough to marry him."

Lettie was quiet for a long time, then she

asked, "When are you going to tell him?"

"Tonight," Klara replied. "I must talk to him tonight. I'm going home tomorrow."

Poor Henk, Lettie thought. *Poor, poor Henk.*

When Klara came in late that night and lay down on her mattress, Lettie pretended to be asleep. She didn't want to hear what Klara had to say.

She couldn't help thinking of Henk. She knew what it felt like when the force of your own love was just not enough for the other person.

The next morning she helped Klara carry her luggage down to the parking lot. "Thanks, Lettie, I've enjoyed talking to you," Klara said awkwardly, her eyes sad.

"Do come again, if you can stand sleeping on the hard hospital mattress," Lettie said, trying to put her friend at ease.

"Thanks." Klara nodded. "But . . . in a year or two you'll be joining your dad's practice, won't you?"

"Yes," Lettie said, glad to change the subject. "My dad wants me to take over. He's in his seventies, you know."

"That's . . . very old," Klara said, surprised.

Lettie smiled. "My parents weren't young

when I was born. My dad was nearly fifty and my mom forty-five. Here's Henk now."

Just before Henk parked, Lettie said, "Klara, are you sure you're doing the right thing?"

"Yes, I'm sure."

When Henk got out of his car, Lettie noticed he looked slightly pale. He glanced briefly at the two of them. "Can I take the luggage? Is this everything?" he asked cordially.

"That's the lot, Henk, thanks," said Klara, not making eye contact either.

As they were about to leave, Lettie said on the spur of the moment, "Come for coffee, Henk. Anytime you like."

The grayish-blue eyes behind the lenses looked straight at her for a moment. He smiled slightly. "Thanks, I will," he promised.

He looked away quickly. But not before she saw the misery in his eyes.

And so the long wait began.

She knew Henk would come for coffee. She had seen in his eyes that he was glad she had asked. He would simply turn up one evening and say, "Come, Lettie, let's go have that cup of coffee you promised me."

Maybe they would talk about Klara — yes,

they probably would, because it would still be on his mind. And she would listen — she was a good listener.

Later they would mention Klara less often, and start making their own conversations. They would discuss his job, or where she would be doing her internship the following year.

Maybe they would go to the movies.

Or out dancing again.

At the end of the vacation, she returned to her room in the women's residence at Wits.

She knew Henk would find her there. He had once asked her the name of the res where she lived.

But the phone call or knock on the front door never came.

She didn't see him again until December, just before the start of final exams, when she bumped into him on a city tram and he introduced her to the pretty petite brunette hanging on to his arm.

That night Lettie resolved to forget about Henk. He would no more notice her than De Wet would. Henceforth, she decided, men would be colleagues, maybe friends. Nothing more. Because men caused pain, intense pain — especially handsome, friendly men.

Lying in her narrow bed on that warm night, Lettie made a decision. From now on she would focus on her career. She would become the best doctor she could be. She'd go back to the bushveld and take her father's practice and help their people. In time, the name of Dr. Lettie Louw would be on everyone's lips. That's how she would be remembered.

Because she knew: no man would ever look at her the way they looked at Annabel or Klara or Christine.

A light breeze stirred the curtains in the small hours of the night. She felt the breeze touch her, smooth her nightgown over the full curves of her body.

She cried herself to sleep.

■ ■ ■ ■

Part Two: Love and War

■ ■ ■ ■

Chapter Three

Marco Romanelli was the eldest of three boys. He lived with his parents and two brothers in a village in the north of Italy, high in the Alps, near the French and Swiss borders.

The village was isolated. The winding road leading there was steep, with sharp curves, and strangers seldom stopped there.

The Romanellis' house was in the center of the village, on the square. Marco's parents, Giuseppe and Maria, occupied the only bedroom. Marco and his brothers, Antonio and Lorenzo, shared a small room at the back of the house. There was only one other room, with an open fireplace, a wooden table and six chairs, a stove, and a small oven. There was a big oven outside, but in winter, when the snow was heaped against the houses and the occupants had to tunnel their way out like moles, Maria cooked inside.

In front of the house was a patio, where Giuseppe and his friends sat on Saturday afternoons playing chess. And talking. And pouring wine from a jug, taking small sips from clay goblets.

Maria bustled in and around the house all day, cooking and baking and cleaning, hoeing and planting and sweeping, knitting sweaters and patching trousers and darning stockings. She sang while she worked and spoke to everyone.

Giuseppe was a sculptor. He carved figures from the white marble found in the quarries around the village. He was a quiet man, and when he did speak, he took his time. Giuseppe had always struggled with words. They got stuck in his thoughts, and it required great effort to force them past his unwilling tongue. But he was a good listener and knew exactly what was going on around him.

Marco and his brothers had a great number of uncles and aunts, like Tia Sofia and old Luigi with their shameful grandchild, Tia Anna with her sharp nose, the uncles in the vineyards and the orchards and the stone quarries, the aunts stirring pots and working in the vegetable gardens, at the washtubs and sewing machines.

The only other people Marco Romanelli

knew were the villagers: Father Enrico, who was also the schoolteacher; the Baron of Veneto, who lived in a stone villa high on the cliffs above the village; and the doctor, who was the smartest man in the village.

And of course there was Gina Veneto, the baron's utterly spoiled, pesky young daughter. She looked like a doll with her curly hair and blue eyes, but when the Romanelli boys didn't want to play by her rules, she would run to tell her father.

Some Saturday afternoons the doctor would bring his gramophone and records to the patio in front of the Romanellis' modest home. He would put a record on the turntable, position the wide mouth of the horn so that everyone could hear, carefully wind up the gramophone, and lift the needle very slowly over the edge of the record.

That was how Marco Romanelli was introduced to the voices of Enrico Caruso, Tito Schipa, and Beniamino Gigli, to the deep bass of Ezio Pinza and the warbling soprano of Amelita Galli-Curci.

Marco Romanelli instinctively knew it was heavenly music.

Shortly before his sixteenth birthday, Marco, who was smart, became a boarder at the senior school in the bigger neighboring town. All three of the Romanelli boys were intelligent. It was the early thirties, the time of the depression, but the doctor helped with the school fees, as did one of Marco's uncles. Even the baron lent a hand. Two years later Marco's brother Antonio also enrolled at the town school, while Marco moved on to the university in Turin.

In Turin Marco studied languages: Italian and Latin, of course, as well as French, German, and English. Besides languages, he studied music and music history. Though he loved music, his first love was literature, in which he could lose himself.

Marco had no interest whatsoever in politics. When Italy invaded Abyssinia on October 3, 1935, he barely registered the event. He was oblivious of the aircraft spraying mustard gas on villages in that distant African country. When the other students discussed politics, he turned a deaf ear. "Marco lives in a world of his own," said his fellow students.

But something else happened to Marco that year. In fact, it struck him head-on and knocked him out of his dream world, populated by old books. The name of that something was Rachel Rozenfeld.

A year earlier Mr. Rozenfeld had opened a shop in Marco's village. The villagers were glad because they had been dependent on the provisions the railway bus brought from the big town once a week.

Mr. Rozenfeld, his plump wife, and their two daughters came from Lithuania, where conditions had become unbearable. Jews had no rights there. Just like in Russia, where they had been before, the Jews were being persecuted at every turn.

During the day Rachel worked in her father's shop, while her younger sister attended Father Enrico's school.

When Marco came home from Turin during the long vacation, he saw Rachel Rozenfeld, with her shiny black hair, sparkling dark eyes, velvety skin, and apple-red cheeks. When she laughed, her teeth gleamed white, and her voice was like mountain bells.

No Dante or Janvier, no Rainer Maria Rilke or William Shakespeare — no master of world poetry could have described her beauty.

He also noticed the soft curves of her young figure.

That vacation Marco Romanelli lost his heart to Rachel Rozenfeld.

At dusk on warm summer evenings, the young people of the village liked to walk up the path, across the Ponte Bartolini, over the level terrain where the boys played soccer on Saturdays, past the centuries-old bell tower without its bell, to the castle ruins. Only the thick stone walls stood firmly where they had been planted centuries before.

Marco strolled quietly at Rachel Rozenfeld's side. Though he didn't look at her or touch her, he was intensely aware of her presence. Over them, the castle's shadows loomed.

Marco listened to Rachel's voice, nodding as she told him how Tia Sofia grumbled about the prices of everything she bought. "But you have to take her the way she is. She's really a good person, you know, Marco?"

"Yes," said Marco, licking his dry lips. How did a man say to a beautiful girl . . .

"I'm so sorry for their grandson. The boy always seems afraid someone will kick him," said Rachel. "Do you know what he looks like?"

"Yes," said Marco. How could he tell her he liked her? Would it be easier to write the words on paper?

"And old Luigi is strange," Rachel chattered on. "Do you know what he did the other day?"

It wasn't something he could write on

paper. He would have to tell her himself. He would have to be careful, assess her reactions, adapt to the situation. But he had no experience in that kind of thing. Except for his mother, he didn't really know any other women. He didn't know how women thought.

"Marco?"

"Yes, no, I don't know," he said, bewildered.

Rachel stopped and turned to him. "Are you listening to me?" she asked, smiling. Her lips were slightly apart, full and shiny.

He stopped too and looked down at her. She was gorgeous. "You're beautiful, Rachel Rozenfeld," he said.

Her smile froze. She seemed startled.

He ran his hand over his hair. What was he doing?

Her dark eyes came alive. "Marco?" she whispered uncertainly.

A warm affection welled up inside him, almost overwhelming him. Unable to stop himself, he reached out and gently touched her cheek. "I . . . You're lovely, Rachel."

She shook her head, bemused. "Marco," she said again, her voice stronger now.

"I like you, Rachel," he said simply, shaking his head slightly. "I like you the way . . . a man likes a woman. I think you're" — he shrugged — "beautiful."

She frowned, her expression earnest, her eyes cautious. "I'm Jewish, Marco."

For a moment he didn't know what to say. He had not been expecting that reaction. But he looked at her velvety skin as the last rays of the sun bathed her face in gold. "I know," he said.

Her shiny teeth gently gnawed at her lower lip. "And you're Catholic."

He nodded and looked away, over the blue-tinted valley unfolding beneath them between the toes of the mountain. Where was she going with this?

"Marco, look at me."

When he looked at her, her eyes revealed an ancient sorrow. "I know we are from different religions, Rachel, but it's too late to think about it now. I've found you, and I want to get to know you better," he said.

She shook her head. "My parents . . . your parents? Marco, it's . . . A friendship can't work at . . . *that* level."

He nodded. She was so much older than her fifteen years, he thought, so much more mature than the giggling young girls at university. "You may be right, Rachel," he agreed quietly. "But no matter how much I would like to respect our parents' wishes, in the end we have to lead our own lives. Over the past months I . . . well, I've learned to love you. It's not something I can stop doing. Or *want* to stop doing. I want us to try, just try."

Her hands flew to her face. She pressed them to her rosy cheeks. Her eyes were wide and dark, fixed on him.

"You don't have to say anything right now," he said softly. "I just want you to know how I feel. Come, we must head back. It'll be dark soon."

They walked back in silence, new knowledge hovering between them.

The vacation was almost over. Twice more they crossed the bridge and walked up to the old castle. Now Rachel was the quiet one, with Marco trying to bridge the awkwardness between them. He had spoken too soon and frightened her, he feared.

But at dusk on the last day before he would be returning to university, Rachel appeared in the small back garden of the Romanellis' home. "Can we take one last walk?" she asked shyly.

Marco's heart pounded. Joy threatened to engulf him, but uncertainty about what she might have come to say quelled every trace of excitement.

They walked to the ancient bridge across the Bartolini River. She stopped to gaze down the narrow gorge carved into the cliffs by melting snow and rainwater over many centuries.

"Rachel?" Marco asked softly.

She kept gazing down the gorge. The road to the village was visible only in parts. "See how crooked the road is that leads to our village," she said, almost matter-of-factly.

"Even a crooked path has to lead somewhere, Rachel," he said earnestly.

She turned to him, her eyes wide and dark. "I wish it could work, Marco," she said despondently, "but . . ."

She gave a deep sigh.

He clutched at the straw. "Because . . . you feel the same about me?" he asked.

She hesitated, then nodded. "Yes, Marco, I feel the same."

Joy flooded him, made his head featherlight, lifted his feet up to the crumbling walls of the castle, to the peaks of the Alpine cliffs that towered majestically over them. "That's enough for me, Rachel," he said. "For now, it's enough."

In 1938, Marco began to teach at Father Enrico's little school in the village. He took the senior classes for Latin, math, English literature, and music so that students no longer had to leave the village to attend senior school. The villagers were pleased that more children were being given the opportunity to be educated.

Marco and Rachel walked nearly every day at dusk.

The people saw them and whispered. Then they shrugged.

The year also brought the Anschluss, with Hitler unceremoniously annexing Austria into Germany.

"It's just the beginning," exulted Lorenzo, Marco's youngest brother. "Germany and Italy will show the rest of the world, wait and see."

Marco frowned. "You're talking as if you support Hitler's actions," he said.

"Of course I do. The Germans are systematically taking back what was stolen from them after the Great War. Hitler is Europe's strong man and Mussolini is the smart one. Together they are invincible," Lorenzo gushed.

That night sleep eluded Marco.

Lorenzo's words hung like a sword over his head. Mussolini was dogging Hitler's footsteps. Hitler was half a step ahead, with Mussolini following like a goat being led to slaughter.

And there was no greater anti-Semite on earth than Hitler.

In the last days of 1938, Marco adopted a serious expression. And Rachel Rozenfeld's laughter was silenced.

Mussolini's racial laws became more and more radical. The most recent one forbade any Jew from marrying an Italian.

"Marco?" Her voice was pleading.

"We'll make a plan, I promise," he said, gently pushing the dark hair back from her face.

When Germany invaded Poland on September 1, 1939, the homes in the Romanellis' village grew quiet. Because the people knew. They had lived through the Great War and survived it. Many of their loved ones had not.

The Rozenfeld home grew even quieter. They had experienced anti-Semitism before — first in Russia and later in Lithuania. Mr. Rozenfeld's shoulders grew bony.

Rachel still unlocked the shop door each morning. But she jumped whenever she heard a strange noise.

It was quiet, like before a storm. The people were waiting.

Six months later the thunderstorm broke over Europe. Germany launched its blitzkrieg, and the Deutsche Wehrmacht stormed in. On April 9, Denmark and

Norway were issued an ultimatum to accept the protection of the Deutsches Reich immediately. Denmark surrendered. Norway was overrun and flattened by Nazi tanks.

The war seeped into the homes. The lowing winds blew it in through the front door when someone came in from outside. It oozed through the floorboards and the closed shutters. At night at the scrubbed tables around the pots of steaming polenta and *spezzatino* and the bottles of home-brewed wine, the war washed over the words of every family's late-night conversations, pouring into the hearts of the homes.

Early in May, Hitler's armored divisions began to crawl westward over the plains of northern Germany. A sea of German tanks rolled in. Wave after tidal wave hit the Dutch towns, breaching their military dykes. Holland fell apart before the onslaught. The blitzkrieg rolled through Gelderland, over Utrecht, until it reached Amsterdam and then continued toward Belgium.

On May 15, the Netherlands surrendered. On May 28, Belgium caved in.

British, French, and Belgian troops were trapped on the coast at Dunkirk and were saved by a sea full of fishing boats.

The rumors about the persecution of Jews in Germany and Austria intensified every day. And though the villagers were fond of Mr. and Mrs. Rozenfeld and their two daughters, the village was no longer a safe place for them.

On a Saturday afternoon that summer, Giuseppe Romanelli and Baron Veneto and Father Enrico and the doctor were at their chessboards, the younger men were playing boccie on the square, and the boys were kicking footballs on the level field on the sunset side of the village.

Maria shook out the carpets and spread them in the sun. Tia Sofia was arranging thin tomato slices on a wire rack, and the women of the village were stewing fruit and vegetables, carefully sealing them in hot jars. You never knew what was coming.

Two figures walked up the mountain. They were walking hand in hand, because it was common knowledge: Marco Romanelli and Rachel Rozenfeld were in love — may the Holy Mother of God protect them.

Near the castle Marco spread the patchwork quilt on the grass and Rachel unpacked the basket: bread, goat's milk cheese, and jam. Biscotti and apples, a jug of wine. She sank down on the blanket beside him. "The sun is lovely, Marco," she said, leaning back, closing her eyes, and turning her face to the light.

"The days are lovely," he said. "We must enjoy every moment."

"Because winter is on its way," she said, her eyes still shut.

"Yes," he mused.

She rolled onto her side, resting her head on her arm. "Tell me something interesting — a story, perhaps? Please?"

Marco looked down into her dark eyes. Today he had to speak, he knew he had to. Stories of castles and princesses were nothing but fairy tales. Today they had to speak about a plan of action.

He just didn't know how to do it.

He drew her closer. A breeze came up. "The most interesting stories are true stories, things that really happened," he said absently.

"Oh yes, tell me," she insisted, moving into the crook of his arm.

"Did you know the unification of Italy started right here in our province, in Piedmont? Italy consisted of nine separate states, but then Cavour came. He was born here in Piedmont, and . . ."

She began to laugh. "Marco! We're having a picnic! Don't be a teacher and drag up history. Tell me a real story." She nestled closer to him.

"Rachel, it's not easy to tell you a story if you're so close to me!"

She laughed softly. "Your problem," she teased.

He sighed. He had to get past the storytelling. He had to talk to her. But he knew her by now, and a story would have to be told. "Fine," he began. "A count and a countess had two sons. And then . . ."

"Tell me where they lived."

"In a castle, a very big, beautiful castle high on a mountainside. The castle was in Spain, but I think it looked a lot like our castle here."

"A castle built of stone, fine." She nodded, content. "It must have been long, long ago."

"Oh yes, our castle is from the Middle Ages as well. Anyway, the eldest son, who would later become the Count di Luna, was strong and healthy. But when the youngest son was just a baby, a gypsy cast a spell on him, and he was weak and sickly."

"Why did she do such a terrible thing?"

"I don't know. She must have had a grievance against the king," he said. With his index finger he traced the contours of her face. "You're lovely, you know?"

"Marco! The story!"

"Very well. The old count had the gypsy

captured and burned at the stake."

"Like a witch?" Rachel frowned.

"They must have believed she was a witch. But just before she died, she made her daughter, Azucena, promise to avenge her death. That night Azucena stole the little brother. In the woods outside the castle Azucena made a big fire. When the guards went to investigate, they found a child's bones in the ashes. The old count refused to believe that they belonged to his little boy. On his deathbed, many years later, he ordered his eldest son, the Count Di Luna, to find Azucena.

"Now, Count Di Luna was in love with Leonora, a friend of the Spanish princess. But she, in turn, was in love with —"

"No, no! First you must describe what she looked like."

He looked down at Rachel and brushed the dark curls out of her face. "I think she must have had rosy cheeks, and black curls that framed her face, and the loveliest dark eyes in the whole world. She was really, really beautiful."

Rachel laughed happily. "Fine, now the story. She was in love with . . . ?"

"Leonora wasn't in love with the count; she was in love with the troubadour Manrico. One day the count saw her running into Manrico's arms and he challenged the troubadour to a duel. Leonora tried to stop them, but in vain. The fire of jealous love is a deadly fire."

She frowned, puzzled, then sat up. "Oh no, Marco, now the count is probably going to kill the troubadour. I said I don't want to hear another sad story, like the one about the princess locked up in the castle . . . What was her name again?"

"Clothilde. She was the daughter of King Victor Emmanuel, the king of Piedmont."

"I don't want to hear another sad story like the one about Clothilde."

"No, this one is . . . different. Listen. Besides, it's also the story of a well-known opera. I would like you to know it."

She lay back in his arms. "Okay, but I don't know what a troubadour is."

"Rachel, I can't tell the story if you keep interrupting with questions!"

"A troubadour?" she insisted.

"A troubadour was a writer and performer of songs and poems. Remember, the story takes place in the Middle Ages, when troubadours moved from one castle to the next."

"Manrico the troubadour?" she reflected. "Sounds good. Carry on with the story now. Did the troubadour win?"

"Well, they were both wounded in the

duel, but Manrico felt as if he had won. Something we didn't know, though, was that Manrico was Azucena's son."

"The daughter of the gypsy who was burned at the stake, who swore she would avenge her mother's death?" Rachel made certain.

"That's right. And though Azucena was old by now, she still hated the count whose father had caused her mother's death. She had told her son, Manrico, the story. She had also told him how she had kidnapped the count's little boy, planning to burn him, but had thrown her own child into the fire instead —"

"Oh no, what a wicked old woman! Marco, is this a nice story?"

"Rachel!" he said in exasperation.

"Fine, I'll listen. Carry on."

"She told him she had raised the old count's son as her own."

"So Manrico was in fact the old count's sickly little boy? Which would make him Count Di Luna's brother?" asked Rachel. "It's a very complicated story."

"Yes, it is. At that moment a messenger arrived with the news that Leonora, who believed that Manrico had died in the duel, had decided to become a nun and spend the rest of her life in a convent. She was taking the oath that very night. Manrico hurried off to try and stop Leonora.

"In the meantime, Count Di Luna and his helpers were planning to abduct Leonora from the convent. However, when Leonora and the other nuns walked by, Manrico grabbed her and took her away with him."

"And they lived happily ever after?" asked Rachel.

"Not really," answered Marco.

"Then I don't want to hear the end of the story," she said firmly. "It's like that story of Romeo and Juliet you told me the other day. It upsets me, Marco. Why are the lovers in the stories always so dumb? It's not logical."

Marco sighed. "Stories aren't always logical. That's why true stories are better, like the story of Princess Clothilde."

"No, the truth is too sad."

"Sometimes we have to face the truth," he said earnestly.

"Like . . . now?" she asked softly.

"Yes, Rachel, like now. We have to talk," he said urgently, almost pleading.

"I know." Her voice sounded distant, thin. Resigned. "We have to go away, don't we? We have to go now."

Marco nodded slowly. "It would be better. Just for a while. Maybe to Switzerland, it's not far. I'll help you, I'll —"

"We'll be okay on our own."

"No, we've spoken about this. I'm going with you, to see that you find a safe place where you can stay for the duration of the war."

"Couldn't we just hide in our house? Not open the door, keep the windows shut? You could bring us food at night."

"No, it wouldn't work, and you know it."

She gave a deep sigh. "I know. I'm just so tired of . . . leaving." She shook her dark curls back and smiled bravely. "You'll have to tell me the end of Leonora and Manrico's story another day. It's not . . . story time anymore."

He wrapped his arms more tightly around her.

"This war won't last forever, Rachel. Hitler will be defeated, I know it. And then you'll come back here and we'll find someone to marry us, both the priest and the rabbi. What do you say?"

"Do you really think it's going to happen one day?"

"Yes, Rachel, I know it's going to happen," he said firmly.

But a cold fist was clenched around his heart.

■ ■ ■ ■

The rumors increased. Ugly rumors about the persecution of Jews in Germany and Austria, and in Poland and Czechoslovakia and Hungary.

"I'm going with you," Marco told Mr. Rozenfeld one evening. "We'll try to find you somewhere to stay in Switzerland or France."

"Your place is here, Marco," Mr. Rozenfeld said wearily. "We'll manage."

"I'm coming along," Marco said firmly. "When I'm satisfied you're safe, I'll come back to the village and my pupils. When the war is over — and I'm sure it won't take long — I'll fetch you."

"Very well then," said Mr. Rozenfeld.

The following week the Rozenfelds boarded the railway bus, taking all their belongings with them. Marco went with them, carrying only a backpack.

A week later, when the railway bus returned up the hill to the village square, the Rozenfelds were on it, bag and baggage.

"France isn't an option. The Jews are leaving in droves. And Switzerland has closed its borders," said Marco, running his hand over his dark hair. "They have been flooded by refugees from France and Italy, Germany and Austria, and countries as far away as Poland and Russia. Only the wealthiest can still buy their way in."

Worry had etched deep lines into Mr. Rozenfeld's ruddy face. Mrs. Rozenfeld shook her head, dazed, and Rachel's usually rosy cheeks were pale. Her younger sister, Ester, had eyes puffy from crying.

The next morning Rachel unlocked the shop door as if they had never been away. The women bought flour and coffee and darning cotton, because supplies at home were low.

Life went on, the way it had for centuries.

On June 10, 1940, Mussolini declared war against England and France.

When the French capitulated, the villagers in Italy threw up their hands in dismay. It was a good thing the Rozenfelds hadn't gone to France, they told one another. Where the red and black swastika was raised . . .

The rumors about the fate of Jews grew in magnitude, now also including Jews in France, Holland, and Belgium. Jews were living behind barbed wire in ghetto camps, like livestock.

"We must hide you," Marco urged Mr. Rozenfeld. "If only one of the houses had a secret room, a cellar, even . . ."

But the homes in the village were small and simple. Only the baron's villa had a wine cellar. And everyone knew about it.

A garrison of soldiers, Mussolini's Blackshirts, pitched camp on the outskirts of the village, on the sunset side, in the shadow of the old Roman bell tower.

That night Maria said, "Marco, Papa and I talked. The Rozenfelds have to get away at once. It's become too dangerous."

"I know." Marco gave a deep sigh and ran the fingers of both hands through his thick hair. "I just don't know where to take them."

She looked at him earnestly. "You do realize, Marco, don't you, that associating with them could put you in great danger?"

Marco's expression was every bit as serious. "I know, Mama, I know." He turned to his father. "But I also know there's no other way."

Giuseppe nodded. He understood.

"I'm worn out thinking," said Marco. "I wondered . . ." But he didn't say what he had wondered.

"Th-th-the m-m-mountain," stammered Giuseppe.

Maria turned her head sharply in his direction. "Giuseppe?"

"It's what I also thought," Marco said, nodding, "but I'm not sure."

"It's cold up there, and winter is coming," Maria protested. "You can't —"

"N-n-no other p-p-place," said Giuseppe.

"Papa is right," said Marco. "It's the only solution."

"But it's dangerous and —"

"Mama, I know the mountain like the back of my hand. I grew up on the mountain. Papa taught us. There are many caves where you can survive a cold winter if you know what you're doing. A man, an entire family can vanish up there and wait out the war."

Maria pressed both her hands to her face. "Oh! This war!"

"It won't be long." Marco comforted her, putting his arm around her shoulders. "It's just a temporary arrangement, until everything returns to normal."

Giuseppe nodded. "G-g-go," he said.

Marco bent down and kissed his mother's cheek. "I'm going to speak to the Rozenfelds," he said and walked through the door.

The next morning, for the first time since the Rozenfelds' return on the railway bus, Rachel didn't unlock the shop. The doors and windows of their home remained shut as well for an entire week.

Marco quietly left for Turin and returned with bags of supplies. At night the women brought pickled vegetables and dried tomatoes, olive oil and polenta flour and wine, and Marco and Giuseppe carried the heavy bags up the mountain, to an unknown destination.

The last evening Marco said, "I'm just up there, Mama." He hugged his mother tightly. "From time to time I'll be coming to the village to fetch provisions. At least once a month, I think."

"Papa will bring extra blankets as soon as we get them," Maria said through her tears. "He says he'll leave them in the second cave, you know where it is. He says . . . you'll manage."

"Yes," said Marco. "Papa knows the mountain better than anyone else."

"Go safely, and come back safely," Maria said, crossing herself.

That night the Rozenfeld family disappeared. Along with Marco Romanelli. The darkness swallowed them, and the next morning the mountain had wrapped itself around them.

Chapter Four

The ascent was painfully slow. Step by step they felt their way up the mountainside. It was a dark night. The stars were distant in the pitch-black sky.

Marco led the way, holding Mrs. Rozenfeld's arm, virtually dragging her up the mountain. The narrow path wound up the steep incline. They frequently stopped to rest. At times they were forced to crawl on all fours.

The plump little woman at Marco's side leaned heavily on him, gasping and panting. "I can't go any farther," she sobbed after a while.

"We must get to the first cave under cover of darkness," Marco said. "Once we're there, we can stay for the rest of the night."

The rope around Marco's waist stretched tight every time someone behind him stumbled. "I can't see a thing," Ester complained.

"It's crazy, climbing these cliffs in the pitch dark."

"It's the only time it's safe. We can't risk being seen by the garrison's men," Rachel said behind her. She was panting as well. "The moon will be up in a while. Then it should be easier."

"It'll probably only be a half-moon," Ester grumbled.

When they stopped to rest, Marco handed out chunks of cheese and chocolate, and sometimes a few raisins. "Drink enough water, even if you don't feel thirsty," he said.

In the small hours the moon made its timid appearance over the mountaintop, its pale glow a source of comfort rather than light as they struggled on.

They reached the first cave just after sunrise, after walking for almost ten hours. Even at night, Marco and his father had done it in less than four hours. "We'll spend the day here, then go on," Marco said.

"Won't we be safe enough up here?" asked Mr. Rozenfeld. His face was pale, and he was mopping his brow despite the cool breeze. "My wife . . . I don't think she can stand another night's walking."

"This cave isn't safe. The goatherds sometimes come up here," said Marco. "And the young boys exploring the mountain know about it. But we can rest here for two days before continuing."

Almost a week after they had left their home, they reached the cave Marco had picked out. He had been there only once before — about five years earlier, when he and Antonio had stumbled upon it by accident. "I think we must be the first humans ever to enter this cave," Antonio had exclaimed at the time.

The last day had been the hardest. It was the only day they had climbed in the daytime, as not even an experienced mountaineer would risk descending the steep cliffs after dark.

Marco took Ester down first, firmly attached to a rope. "Why are we going all the way down again?" she complained.

"We've come a long way east, moving diagonally, first up, then down again," said Marco. "Now we must go down this ravine. The cave we're heading for isn't much higher than our village, which means it won't be quite as cold as it would be farther up the mountain."

Marco returned to fetch Mr. Rozenfeld. "My wife won't make it," he said, pale and perspiring. "She's afraid of heights."

"I'll blindfold her," said Marco.

But when he went back up, Mrs. Rozenfeld flatly refused to go down the steep cliffs. "I'd rather die up here. At least I won't be dragging you into oblivion along with me," she said.

It took a lot of persuasion from Rachel and many reassurances from Marco to finally get her to climb down. "You'll have to bury me here," she said when they were all together again, "because there's no way I'm going back up these cliffs."

"This gorge is our salvation," said Marco. "The cave I have in mind is up ahead, hidden in another gorge, its mouth completely concealed. No one will find us there."

And it was true. They were right in front of the cave when Ester cried out, "Here's another cave! You'd never guess!"

The mouth of the cave was a cleft in the rocks, no more than three feet high. Ester crawled in on all fours.

Despite the bright sunshine, the cave was dark inside. The floor, sandy near the mouth, sloped slightly upward to a reasonably level rocky ledge. The roof was too low for Marco to stand up straight, but the Rozenfelds had no trouble.

The cave was deep enough to allow them to create some kind of privacy. "I think we should make a screen to divide the cave in two," Marco proposed when everyone had taken a good look around. "You can all sleep at the back. The front part can be our kitchen and living area. I'll sleep in the front."

"To protect us from the wolves at night," Rachel teased.

"Don't joke. There are bound to be wild creatures up here," Marco warned. "That's why the goats sometimes disappear."

"I'm more afraid of Nazis than wolves," Ester said firmly.

During the next three weeks, Marco, Rachel, and Ester made the journey five more times to fetch the supplies Marco and his father had stored in the first two caves: warm clothing, blankets, pots and kitchen utensils, lamps and candles, a medicine chest filled with herbs and ointments and syrups. There was food as well: bags of polenta, dried pasta and flour, bottles of oil and jam, fruit and vegetables in jars, pickled meat and congealed fat, salt and sugar and coffee, even a little wine. The villagers had opened their hearts and their hands. On the last trip they brought Marco's books and his violin.

Life in the cave began in earnest.

Rachel took over the housekeeping, arranging everything and organizing their daily routine. Water had to be fetched, and as much wood as possible — enough to see them through the long winter.

The nights were already freezing. Marco was glad of the warm coats and caps the Rozenfelds had brought from Lithuania. They would need them when winter really set in.

They fashioned a screen of twigs to separate the front section from the back of the cave. They built a second screen to serve as a kind of door at the mouth of the cave, using small twigs and pine needles to make it as airtight as possible. They hoped it would keep out the worst of the cold at night.

"We must have a fireplace where we can cook our food," Rachel said.

"Maybe just outside the mouth of the cave — over there, in the corner of that crevice," Marco said. "The fire will be sheltered against the wind and the smoke will be outside. But we can only light a fire after dark, or the smoke may be noticed. The people who live on the mountainside are wary of mountain fires. If they see smoke, they're sure to send out a search party to find the fire."

Life in the cave began to take on a fixed rhythm: peaceful, almost domestic.

By day they did the usual chores; they swept, fetched wood and water, prepared food. They read a lot. Mrs. Rozenfeld's eyes were too poor to read, so Marco or Rachel or sometimes Mr. Rozenfeld read to her from Marco's books. "We should have brought more interesting books," Rachel said.

Every morning Mr. Rozenfeld ticked off the day on the calendar so they would always know what day and date it was. "Why is it important?" asked Ester.

"We must know," her father replied.

They made music nearly every day. Mr. Rozenfeld also played the violin, and Marco taught the Rozenfeld girls the finer points of the instrument he loved so much.

One day, during what the girls jokingly called their "music lessons," Marco spoke to them about opera music. "When I was at university in Turin, a group of us once took the train to Milan, to La Scala opera house," Marco remembered with a smile. "It was a wonderful experience. We saw *La Traviata,* with Tito Schipa in the role of Alfredo."

"*La Traviata* — the fallen woman?" Ester asked, amused. "What's the story about?"

"It's set in Paris, around the beginning of the eighteenth century —" Marco began.

"Ester, you don't want to hear these opera stories!" Rachel said firmly. "Marco has told me one or two, and they're the dumbest stories you can imagine. And the music is awful — the kind the doctor used to play on his gramophone."

The evenings were harder. They were reluctant to use the kerosene and candles, saving these for winter. Marco would persuade Mr. and Mrs. Rozenfeld to tell stories: the Russian folk tales they'd grown up with, stories from the time when Russia still had a czar, sometimes stories they themselves had heard from their grandparents. They spoke about the Russian pogroms, the persecution of Russian Jews in the previous century, which had forced their parents to move to Lithuania.

Rachel and Ester told Marco about their school in Lithuania, about the things they got up to when they were younger. "Oh, I never knew about that!" Mrs. Rozenfeld said, shocked. "How daring!"

The stories made the nights a little shorter.

But after a while Ester became irritable, pacing up and down like a caged animal, her frustration barely contained. The next time Rachel asked her to do something, Ester came undone. "You're not my boss!" she shouted. "Do your own dirty work!"

That same evening, when Rachel dished up unleavened griddle cakes and a dollop of jam for supper, Ester cried, "I refuse to eat this again! It's the fourth time this week we're expected to eat these rocks! There's a lot of other food."

"Ester, we're in this together." Mr. Rozenfeld tried to calm her down. "Rachel is making provision for winter."

But Ester stormed off to sulk on her sheepskin in the dark back room.

One evening after supper Marco and Rachel were sitting outside on their own. The night was icy and clear, the moon not yet up. The sky was black velvet, the stars bright and incredibly close. Marco and Rachel, wearing their coats and caps, huddled together under a single blanket they had wrapped tightly around themselves.

"It's actually . . . wonderful up here," Rachel said dreamily. "Not as cold as I had feared, just a bit nippy."

"Wait until winter really sets in. We'll need every ounce of energy just to survive," Marco warned.

"What a pity everyone can't enjoy it," Rachel mused. "Mama . . . I'm worried about her. She's listless, not interested in anything. She always used to do the cooking, but now she doesn't even lend a hand."

"It must be very uncomfortable for her,"

Marco said.

"And Ester is totally impossible. I don't know how we're going to get through the winter with her."

"Ester has just turned fourteen," Marco said calmly. "She's a typical teenager."

"But she's so selfish, and so ungrateful." Rachel frowned.

Marco smiled. "Fourteen," he said again. "One of our biggest enemies is boredom. We have so little to stimulate us. I think it's part of Ester's problem."

"There are enough chores she can help me with," Rachel said. "And you try to teach her, but even then she's stubborn."

Marco laughed. "It's not exactly a young person's idea of fun," he said. "But enough about Ester. We have a moment alone, you and I. Let's not waste time talking about other people."

Winter arrived. The wind roared down the ravine, howling like hungry wolves around the cave day and night, tugging furiously at the flimsy twig barrier at the cave mouth.

"The wind isn't all bad," Marco said philosophically. "If it blows like this, the smoke won't be noticeable, so we don't have to wait for nighttime to make a fire."

"I'm afraid we're going to run out of

wood," Rachel said hesitantly.

"Let's divide the wood into six piles for the six winter months," Marco suggested. "By the end of March we should be able to go out again. Probably sooner, but by then it should be safe."

"End of March!" Ester groaned. "We're going to die in here."

"That's enough, Ester," Mr. Rozenfeld said firmly. "Think of the alternative and stop complaining."

They began at once to sort the wood into piles. After a while even Mrs. Rozenfeld came to help. Some of the wood was still green. Mr. Rozenfeld arranged the greener pieces around the sides of the cave to dry out.

Sometimes the wind would change direction without warning and a flurry of smoke would blow into the cave, making their eyes water and leaving everything smelling of smoke.

Marco punched a few holes in a tin can and they filled it with hot coals. It brought a little comfort during the freezing nights.

At the beginning of October the first snow fell. Some days thin snowflakes gently sifted down. Other days brought sleet and snow crystals blustering through the ravines.

On rare occasions the weak winter sun

would break through the gray cloud masses.

Their world diminished to the cave and its immediate snow-white surroundings.

As one interminable, tedious day followed another and the dark, icy nights grew longer and longer, Ester became increasingly difficult, Mrs. Rozenfeld increasingly tearful, and Mr. Rozenfeld more silent and more reserved.

Only Rachel seemed cheerful. But when they were alone, she said, "Marco, please tell me the winter will pass?"

Marco gave an exhausted smile and stroked her face. "Summer always comes again, I promise," he said. His expression grew serious, and his voice was very deep when he said, "Rachel, I can't tell you often enough how much I love you."

"Tell me again why," she said, snuggling against him.

"Because you're brave and hardworking and smart and . . . just lovely. Because you're Rachel. There's no one else like you in the whole world." He shrugged. "I just . . . love you."

"And I love *you,* Marco. You're the most wonderful person I've ever met. I can't believe what you're doing for my family. I don't know how to thank you. Alone we would . . ."

He stopped her words with his lips and wrapped his arms around her. "It's enough for me to have you with me every day," he said simply.

In the first spring days of 1941, when the snow began to trickle down the mountainside, slowly turning into streams, Marco went down to the village.

The sun was still feeble, but the icy winds had abated. Rachel and Ester draped the skins and blankets over the rocks outside the cave. Everything smelled of smoke and mildew.

Four days later Marco returned with the first news from the outside world they'd had in months. "Italy is fighting in North Africa now. They plan to invade Egypt and other parts of the Mediterranean coastline," he told them.

"Why would they want to do that?" Ester asked.

"Something to do with the Italian commercial fleet and military security in the Mediterranean," he explained. "At the moment Britain controls both exits from the sea, the Suez Canal and Gibraltar."

"You sound like a schoolteacher again," Ester grumbled.

Marco laughed. "You asked," he reminded

her. Then he looked at Mr. Rozenfeld. "People seem to think the war in Africa will soon be over. Italy will be no match for the British forces."

"As long as Hitler doesn't decide to come to the aid of the Italians in Africa." Mr. Rozenfeld sighed. "Then there'll be trouble."

"The Deutsche Wehrmacht is already there," Marco said cautiously.

Mr. Rozenfeld shook his head. "Then it's going to be a long battle," he said. "Did you bring us a new calendar?"

Marco nodded. "Here it is, in my bag," he said, handing Mr. Rozenfeld an envelope. "My two brothers have also left for the front — for North Africa," he added.

"Oh no, Marco!" Rachel cried and her hands flew to her face.

"Lorenzo went to war?" Ester cried, dismayed.

Marco nodded. "Apparently the commander of the garrison unrolled a large notice one morning and nailed it to the church door. The villagers were very upset — they say it borders on heresy!"

But the Rozenfelds weren't Catholic, and they didn't quite understand what he was saying. "What did the notice say?" asked Mr. Rozenfeld.

"That all men between the ages of eighteen and thirty were being called up for military service," Marco answered.

Rachel drew a sharp breath. Her dark eyes widened. "Surely that includes you, Marco."

"Yes, it does. The notice also said Mussolini would send garrisons of armed soldiers to every remote corner of Italy to make sure every able-bodied Italian man joined up."

"If you fail to report, you'll be contravening the law, Marco. It's a criminal offense," Mr. Rozenfeld said.

"I know," said Marco.

Ester began to cry. "Will this war never end?" she sobbed.

Only Mrs. Rozenfeld gazed at them stolidly.

At dusk Marco and Rachel had a moment alone. Marco said, "They're expecting heavy fighting in the desert. Both sides seem to have thousands of troops deployed there."

Rachel turned her head to meet his eyes. She took his hand and asked softly, "Is that where Antonio and Lorenzo are now?"

He nodded slowly. "Yes, in the desert. In North Africa."

One bright summer's day they heard Ester shriek outside the cave. Marco whirled around. Had something happened to her?

Had she seen someone? Marco and Rachel rushed out, with Mr. Rozenfeld on their heels.

"Look what I found," Ester cried when they reached her, laughing and pointing.

Two goats stood a stone's throw from the mouth of the cave, their sharp hooves on the loose stones, their beards moving rhythmically as they chewed, their large eyes gazing calmly at the cave dwellers.

"Ester, where did you find the goats?" and "Where on earth did they come from?" Rachel and Marco chorused.

Ester waved her arms excitedly. "I was looking for wood, so I walked down the cliff, that way. I sat down to rest and I looked down the valley, and then I heard a noise. At first I thought it was a baby crying. But then I realized it was a goat, and I thought it would be nice to have a goat, because we would have milk and we could make butter and cheese and everything! So I went to look for it and I found her and another one. I think it must be her baby, though he's already quite big." She paused to take a breath.

"And how did you get them here?" Rachel asked, still astounded.

"I put the rope I had taken for tying up the wood around the goat's neck, but she didn't like it and wouldn't budge. So I just walked ahead, calling, 'Come, goats, come,' and they came. And now they're here."

"Very good, Ester," said Marco, smiling.

"What a stroke of luck!" Rachel said. "Well done, little sister."

"They're my goats now," Ester said firmly.

After that, Ester milked her goat every morning, brought the milk into the cave, then headed off with the pair in search of grazing. "Don't go too far," Marco warned almost every day, "and be careful of the sheer cliffs — for your own sake as well as the goats'."

Rachel churned butter with a wooden ladle her father had carved for her. "How do I make cheese, Mama?" she asked.

Listlessly Mrs. Rozenfeld explained how to go about it. "But I don't know if it'll work. We don't have the proper supplies," she said. "I'm going to lie down. I don't feel well."

Rachel poured the curdled milk into a frayed cloth, tied the corners together, and hung it up for the moisture to drain.

All summer long the cave dwellers had milk with their polenta, and butter and a kind of cheese with their flat bread.

The days began to get colder. Winter was coming, and the green pastures higher up the mountain were hidden under a blanket of snow. "We'll have to slaughter the goats," Marco said late one afternoon.

"You're not killing my goats!" Ester screamed, wrapping her thin arms around the goats' necks. "They're *my* goats. You leave them alone!"

Even after Mr. Rozenfeld had spoken to her earnestly, she remained furious and bitterly unhappy. "Murderers!" she shouted at Marco and Rachel.

When the first snow fell outside the cave a week later, Marco took the goats some distance away from the cave, slit their throats, skinned them, and cut the meat into chunks. Inside the cave Rachel and Mr. Rozenfeld rubbed salt into the smaller cuts, let them cure for a day wrapped in the freshly slaughtered skins, then hung them up to dry in the wind. Marco dug a shallow hole in the frozen earth a short distance from the cave mouth, wrapped most of the meat chunks in cloths, placed them in the hole, and filled it up with snow, marking the place. "It should last us through the winter," he said. "There are thirteen pieces, which means we can take out a piece every week and cook it."

Mr. Rozenfeld worked for days, rubbing salt into the skins and drying them in the feeble sunlight that occasionally broke through the clouds. Then he worked the skins until they were soft. They attached the two skins to the screen at the cave mouth to stop the wind and cold from entering the cave.

At first Ester flatly refused to eat the meat, but after a week or two she spooned some of the sauce over her pasta. "Ugh, it's terribly salty!" She shuddered.

"Yes, we might have been a bit heavy-handed with the salt, but at least the chances of the meat going bad are virtually zero," Marco said philosophically.

Day broke without any sign of the sun. Only their inner clocks made them realize it had to be daytime.

Marco rose from his sheepskin and moved the screen away from the cave mouth. The night's snowfall had completely sealed off the mouth of the cave. *At least it made the cave a little warmer,* Marco thought. He picked up the shovel and began to work the snow away so they could reach the fireplace. A narrow corridor now connected them with the outside world. Marco wrapped his coat around him and went outside.

The day was gray and dark, the clouds low and murky, the cliffs overhead and the gorges below covered in a thick layer of snow. He scooped up a bucketful of clean snow, crawled back inside, and replaced the screen in front of the cave mouth. He was glad of the feeble light that trickled in. It would save their candles.

"We can make a small fire," he said. "It's cloudy and misty outside. No one will notice the smoke."

He opened his diary. December 25, 1941. The Rozenfelds carried on with their small lives in the belly of the mountain, as they had been doing every day for the past two months. As they would be doing every day for the two months that followed.

Only Marco realized it was Christmas.

Early in spring Marco went down the mountain. "Let's cut your hair before you go," said Rachel. "You'll frighten the people with your wild hair and dark beard. You look like a caveman."

"That's exactly what I am." Marco smiled, stroking her long dark hair.

"Please bring me an apple," said Ester. "I have such a craving for an apple."

Two nights later Marco arrived at his parents' home. Giuseppe immediately lit a lamp, and Maria fell into his arms. "You must be careful when you come down in the dark," she said, heaping his plate with polenta and pork knuckles. "If you slip and break something, no one will find you."

"I *am* careful, Mama. This is delicious." He didn't add that it was his first proper meal in almost two months. In the cave their supplies were at rock-bottom. They had run out of a lot of things, even before Christmas. They'd had no meat since the wolves discovered their hole in the ground two months earlier.

"Papa has the supplies ready. A lot of it is in the first cave already," said Maria.

"I noticed when I came past. Thanks, Papa."

Giuseppe nodded wordlessly.

There was a moment's silence, then Maria asked, "Marco, how are you really doing up there in the mountain? You're nothing but skin and bones. Do you have enough food?" Her voice sounded tired, and the lines on her face were proof of her anxiety for her three sons.

"We're doing okay," Marco said slowly. If one considered the alternative, it was true. "Our supplies are very low, but we got through the winter. It's almost summer, so conditions will improve. It's just . . . Mrs. Rozenfeld isn't well. She's been out of sorts and she has a bad cough. And she's very depressed."

"I've put in some chest drops," said Maria. "And try to get hold of those herbs we used for Tia Anna's chest, remember? It's good for fever as well. You brew it like tea, simmer it very slowly."

"I remember." Marco nodded.

"And Rachel?" asked Maria.

"Rachel is well, Mama. She's strong. And very, very lovely."

Before the sun rose he disappeared back into the dark belly of the mountain.

We are wasting away, Marco thought as he sat looking at Rachel and Ester. They had hitched their dresses up above their knees and bared their arms, trying to absorb as much of the summer sun as they could. Under their sleeveless vests their shoulders were bony, and their knees looked big and knobby compared to their thin white legs.

How much longer could they last? The supplies he managed to bring from the village were meager, and Rachel couldn't save anything for the winter to come. But Marco was responsible for these people, for the two old parents in the cave dealt so many hard blows, for the two young girls whose lives still stretched ahead.

No goats appeared in the summer of 1942.

Marco noticed that their conversations were changing, becoming smaller, less intense, restricted to essentials: what to eat, where to find dry wood, who should sweep the fireplace or fetch water, whether to light the candle. But especially: What are we eating?

Earlier, on hearing that Jews all across Europe were being herded like cattle into camps, they had wondered how many others were hiding from the soldiers. "I think people are hiding in back rooms and in lofts and behind secret walls," Rachel had said.

"Or in tombs," Ester had added dramatically. "The Germans won't look in tombs."

"We're really blessed to have this cave," Mr. Rozenfeld had said. "At least we have a measure of freedom."

And now all they could talk about was food. Earlier they had hoped for peace. They wondered if humankind would ever learn. Now they could only live day to day. Day to hungry day. They led a primitive existence. They had too much time to think and brood. Time was their greatest enemy. Marco knew he must do something to change this.

But for the life of him he could not think what.

■ ■ ■ ■

"I must go back to the village one last time before winter comes," Marco said one cold evening at the beginning of October. "I hope I can get supplies. The war . . . The villagers don't even have food for themselves."

"I'm worried about the winter," said Rachel. "Mama's cough isn't getting better."

"I'll try to get some more medicine," said Marco. "I just hope the doctor has supplies, that the army hasn't requisitioned everything."

"Bring wool, if you can find any, so we can knit sweaters."

Four days later Marco returned, shaking his head. "The shops in Turin are just about empty," he said. "And what the people do manage to buy, they have to lug thirty miles back to the village. The railway bus is no longer running."

Rachel looked dismayed.

"Did you bring me an apple?" Ester asked anxiously.

Marco shook his head. "There are no apples, Ester. What grows in the orchards and fields and gardens is confiscated by the soldiers. The villagers steal their own apples and tomatoes and the last of their vegetables at night to put food on their tables."

"I have such a craving for an apple," Ester said quietly.

That night when they were alone, Rachel said, "Marco, how will we get through the winter? We don't have enough food."

"We'll just have to be more careful," he said.

"More careful?" she asked, shaking her head. The implications of her words were clear: *Look at us.* "And the war? Do you think it will last much longer?"

Marco sighed. "No one knows," he said, "and you can't believe what the papers and the radio say. They boast of the victories of the Italian forces. But the doctor's son, Pietro, who's a journalist in Rome, tells a different story — which he's not allowed to write, of course."

They sat in silence for a long time. Overhead the stars were visible in patches between wispy clouds. The night around them was silent and freezing. They huddled together, sheltered from the bitter world.

Then Marco spoke. "Just before I left, the baron came to tell us he had heard on the radio that a major battle was about to take place in Egypt. The soldiers have dug themselves into the sand and are ready for action. One of the heaviest artillery barrages in the history of warfare is expected, according to the radio. At a place called El Alamein."

"El Alamein. Are . . . your brothers still there?" Rachel asked, rubbing his stiff shoulders.

"Yes," he said, "that's where Antonio and Lorenzo are."

The third winter in the cave became the worst one. The days were short and dark and freezing; the nights were long and filled with terrifying dreams. Outside the cave the wind howled and gusted furiously. It snowed for days on end. The sun vanished completely.

Their world diminished to the dark confines of the cave. Every day they cleared the snow from the cave mouth and replaced the screen in front of the small opening. They were extremely careful with the kerosene and candles.

But it wasn't the cold or the dark or the musty air that tormented them day and night during that third winter in the cave. Nor was it Mrs. Rozenfeld's hacking cough or the nightmares that kept them awake. It was hunger.

Hunger became their faithful companion

by day and by night.

One day Mrs. Rozenfeld developed a high fever. One moment she would be burning hot and the next moment freezing. Her once plump figure, now wasted away, shivered and shook inside the thick coat under the warm duvet. The next minute she was pouring with sweat, gasping for breath. She sat up anxiously and gazed at them with wild, frightened eyes.

They fed her medicine, but she couldn't keep it down.

Mr. Rozenfeld, despondent, sat apart from the rest of them in the gloomy cave.

None of them slept that night, nor the next day and night.

Early the following morning Marco found Rachel just outside the cave mouth, huddled beside the dead fire in the freezing cold, her neck drawn into the collar of her coat. He knelt beside her and put his arm around her shoulders.

She burst into uncontrollable sobs.

He opened his big coat and held her to him, stroked her back and her hair. She wasn't wearing her cap.

"I think Mama has pneumonia, Marco. She's going to die and there's nothing I can do," she sobbed.

"You're doing what you can." He tried to

comfort her, but he knew there were no words to make it better.

When her sobs subsided, she raised her head and looked him in the eye. "I can't go on, Marco."

Carefully he wiped her tears. How terribly thin her face had become. "You can, Rachel. One can always go on. You're just exhausted. Try to rest. I'll sit with your mother."

"We're all going to die in this cave," she said hopelessly. "We don't have enough food for the winter."

"We'll manage, Rachel, I promise."

"Do you . . . really think so?" she asked.

"I know we will," he said, against his better judgment. "Try to get some sleep. You need your strength. Lie down on my sheepskin at the front of the cave."

But there was no question of sleep that day. Mrs. Rozenfeld's condition rapidly deteriorated. By eleven that morning there was a rattling sound in her throat. She managed to raise herself slightly and stare at them with unseeing eyes before she gave a deep sigh and sank back on her tangled bedding, lifeless.

"Mama?" Ester put out her hand, but she didn't touch her mother.

Marco took Mrs. Rozenfeld's hand, and

his fingers closed around her wrist. He looked up at Rachel and shook his head.

Rachel bent down, hesitated a moment, then gently closed her mother's eyes.

Mr. Rozenfeld sank to his knees beside his wife, rested his head on her thin body, and remained like that without moving.

Ester jumped to her feet. "No! No!" she screamed and stormed out of the cave. They let her go.

After a while Marco went in search of her. The icy landscape outside the cave was perilous. He found her in the next gorge where, two summers before, she used to leave her goats at night. He sat down beside her and gently put his arm around her shoulders. She turned and clung to him. "Now I have no one," she sobbed.

"You have your father and Rachel. You still have each other," he said gently. "And I'm here too. You've got me."

But she kept shaking her head. "You and Rachel are together, and Papa is . . . gone."

"You're Rachel's only little sister. No one can take your place in her heart or her life," said Marco. "And I don't have a sister, you know? After the war, when Rachel and I get married, you'll officially be my sister too. But I already consider you my sister — if you'll let me."

She thought for a while. "Okay," she said. "Just don't take my place in Rachel's heart."

Marco smiled. "I could never, Ester. No one can take your place. You're unique."

He felt her nod. "Fine," she said. "And Papa?"

"Your papa has lost his lifelong partner. It's . . . tragic. I think we should give him time to come to terms with his loss. I think he was expecting her to die. That's why he's been so quiet the past few weeks. Just love him, and Rachel too. You need each other now."

Ester gave a deep sigh and one last sob. She wasn't really crying anymore. "You know what, Marco, I also knew Mama was going to die. I've known it for a long time. I don't think she wanted to live any longer. She didn't even speak to us anymore."

Marco remained silent.

"She said we'd have to bury her here, remember?"

He remembered. A lifetime ago. Could it be that only a little more than two years had passed?

Ester sat in silence for a long time before she asked, "Do you think we're all going to die?"

"No, Ester, I don't think it for a moment. We're going to survive. The war will end.

Sooner or later all wars come to an end. Then we'll pick up the pieces and carry on with our lives."

"You told us in one of your history lessons about a war that lasted eighty years. If this war lasts that long, I'll be ninety-five when it's over!"

He laughed softly. "Do you remember which war it was?"

"No, Marco, I never listened. You know how I hate history."

"Hmm," he said. "It was the Dutch War of Independence, from 1568 to 1648. But that was centuries ago. No war lasts that long today."

"Yes, sir, if you say so." After a while she drew a deep breath. "I'm sorry if I'm a bit . . . difficult at times. I don't really want to be that way."

"You're not a *bit* difficult at times, Ester. Sometimes you're impossible. But we'll survive that as well."

"I'm not all that bad!"

He gave a slight smile and got to his feet. "Come, let's get back to your father and Rachel," he said, holding out his hand to help her up.

Under the snow the soil was rock hard, and Marco didn't have a shovel. The wind was icy, and there was very little strength in his emaciated body. After a while he stepped back and shook his head — he certainly wasn't going to be able to dig a grave.

He fetched the handsaw and removed a few branches from the nearest fir tree. If he could stack them over the body, it would hopefully keep the wolves away at night.

They wrapped Mrs. Rozenfeld in the cloths they had used for the meat. "Can't we just put Mama's coat on her?" Ester sobbed. "It's so cold."

"Your mama doesn't feel anything, Ester," Marco said softly. "And I think she'd want you to take her coat, now that you've outgrown your own. Yes, I know for sure that if she were here now, she would say, 'Ester, put that coat on.' "

Ester averted her face and clung to Rachel.

Mr. Rozenfeld laid his wife in the shallow grave. "Her suffering is over," he said, his voice choked. "Marco, will you please say a prayer?"

Mother of God, help me! Marco thought. *How do . . . Jews pray?*

But he prayed from his heart to God in the wide heaven above them. They stood around the open grave, motionless, dazed, exhausted, unwilling to take their final leave.

At last they piled branches on top of the body and covered everything with a thick layer of snow.

That night Rachel slept in Marco's arms for the first time. All night long she lay with him under his blankets, huddled against his body.

"Maybe it would have been better if they had taken us to a Jewish camp," Rachel said one evening in the new year. They had each eaten a spoonful of thin porridge made from flour. "At least there would be food."

"We don't know what the conditions in the camps are like," Marco said earnestly.

"Food isn't the most important thing in the world," Mr. Rozenfeld said softly. "At least here we have each other. In the camps the men would probably be separated from the women."

"I want us to stay together. I want to be with Papa," said Ester.

"As soon as it stops snowing, I'll go down to the village," Marco said. "My tracks would be visible in the snow if I went now."

Later that night, lying in his arms, Rachel whispered, "I didn't really mean it when I said I want to go to a camp. This time in the cave is precious to me, Marco. It's something we'll always have — the knowledge of this time we spent together. And . . . even if something happens to either of us . . ."

"Nothing is going to happen to us, Rachel," he said and held her more tightly. She was so terribly, terribly thin.

". . . even if something happens to either of us," she continued, "the other one will always have the memory of this time we had together."

Marco made the trip down to the village before he was sure it was safe. They had run out of supplies, including flour to make porridge. "We can stretch it for three days," Mr. Rozenfeld said, his eyes unnaturally bright and deep in their sockets.

On the lower reaches of the mountainside close to the village, Marco saw two soldiers on foot, clearly patrolling the area. He waited until late at night before he crept down to the village.

It was his youngest brother, Lorenzo, who opened the back door to his soft knock. "Marco!" he exclaimed before turning and softly calling, "Mama! Papa! Come, Marco's here!"

When he opened the door wider, Marco noticed at once: Lorenzo hung between two crutches, his right leg missing. "Lorenzo?

You're here?" he said, holding out his hand.

"Yes, well, as you can see, half of me stayed behind on the battlefield, but at least my head is still in place. Come in."

He looked up and met his parents' eyes, which registered shock and disbelief. He knew he was painfully thin. His coat hung loose on his frame. His face was gaunt and gray, his hair long and unkempt. He had come home hungry.

He ate, wolfing down the food and washing it down with hot coffee. "We don't have any food left," he said. "It might have been better for them in a Jewish camp."

"No," Lorenzo said firmly. "Pietro says there are terrible rumors about conditions in the Jewish camps."

"I can't stay. I must get back as soon as possible," Marco said. "It's too dangerous. There are spies everywhere. Even if you brought supplies here from another house, they'd be suspicious."

"We didn't expect you so soon," Maria said uncertainly. "We don't have much, but I'll give you what we have. We haven't been able to harvest anything from the gardens yet, and we seldom get any supplies from Turin these days. But we have some ham Papa smoked last week, and I made cheese the day before yesterday. We still have flour and oil and salt. The sugar is finished, but one can do without it," she said, scurrying around. "Papa will take some more provisions to the second cave as soon as possible. Come in about a week. Oh, Marco, I'm so happy to see you!"

She took the last bag of dried tomatoes and the last two bottles of pickled olives from the back of the kitchen cupboard. "The vitamins and oil will do you good," she said.

Within an hour he was on his way back up the mountain. He had eaten. He was feeling stronger.

The minute he arrived, they ate — carefully, their hands trembling. Then Rachel began to stack the food into small piles.

"Next week I'll go again, to the second cave. My father will leave food there. Lorenzo will slaughter a goat and cure the meat. We'll have enough to see us through."

"I hope they'll use less salt than you did with my two goats," Ester remarked before glancing up quickly. "Why is Lorenzo home?"

"Lorenzo was at El Alamein. He says it's a hellhole in North Africa, with nothing but sand and sun, where the generals play their chess game and the enemy lies in wait behind every dune. He was wounded in the leg." He did not tell them that Lorenzo had lost his leg.

"Wounded!" Ester cried. "How serious is it?"

"It's serious, but he's at home recovering. It's been six months since the battle of El Alamein," said Marco.

"And Antonio?" Rachel asked softly.

"Tonio was taken prisoner. He's somewhere in South Africa, but he's not in a camp. He's building a bridge. He writes that he's doing well, that he's stationed with good people."

"Does he have enough food?" asked Ester.

"Yes, he gets good food. But . . . things aren't looking good for Italy. The army is retreating from North Africa," Marco said. "There are rumors that the Allies want to invade Italy. I truly don't know how much longer our armed forces are planning to hold out. It's stupid. The war is choking our country to death. Our men are being ripped apart on the battlefield, thousands of women and children are starving in the towns. And if the Allies invade Italy as well . . ."

Mr. Rozenfeld gave a deep sigh. "We're far removed from the war here, surrounded by the mountains. Out there the soldiers are battling to survive in the trenches. I know, I was in the trenches myself during the Great War. Men intent on destroying each other, while actually they're destroying themselves." He paused, then added, "Centuries of progress seem to have resulted in nothing but self-annihilation."

"It's definitely better up here in the mountains, even if we are always hungry," Ester said, nodding.

"Yes, it's better here," said Marco, but his anxiety did not subside.

He did not tell the rest of them that on his return trip he had twice noticed foreign soldiers in the mountains — even as far up as the second cave.

That summer they lost all perception of time. They had no calendar. It was no longer important. They had no idea of the time of day. They had stopped winding their watches a long time ago. They had no idea what day of the week it was, nor what month. They measured the passing of time by the sun. Sometimes it was warmer, sometimes colder. Sometimes it was overcast and dark, and they ate earlier than usual.

They had to go farther afield in search of wood. They had to be more and more resourceful when hunting for edible plants and bulbs.

Marco could no longer go down to the village. It was too dangerous. At times he would still venture to the second cave for flour and salt. They caught hares and birds in traps. They dug out bulbs and boiled infusions from leaves, which they drank.

They survived, and day and date were unimportant.

"Our crooked path is going round in a circle now," Rachel remarked to Marco late one night.

He drew her stick-thin body closer. That way they both felt a little warmer, and not only physically. "But it's a good circle, isn't it?" he asked.

"It is," she said. "If you think about it, we are lucky."

One morning — it was growing chilly, even by day, so they knew that winter was close — Ester's bloodcurdling scream raced up the ravine, bounced off the cliffs, and echoed back down.

Marco's blood ran cold. Ester had gone in search of wood. He had warned her over and over to be quiet, careful. It was quite possible that the soldiers could come up to where they were. That scream . . .

The three of them stormed out. "Hide!

Hide!" screamed Ester — and the mountains repeated, *Hide, hide . . .*

Rachel was already running down the mountainside. "Rachel, slow down!" Marco cried. But she kept running.

Then Marco saw them. Three soldiers in Nazi uniforms stepped out of the trees. One had Ester in a firm grip. A second raised his rifle and aimed it at Rachel. "Halt! At once!" he shouted.

Rachel froze.

"You two up there, come down slowly, with your hands in the air!" the soldier bellowed. When Marco and Mr. Rozenfeld seemed to hesitate, he raised his rifle higher. "At once! I have the two girls in my sights. I won't hesitate to shoot the Jewish pigs."

Slowly Marco raised his hands. "Come," he told Mr. Rozenfeld. "Our time in the mountain has come to an end."

Chapter Five

"May we just fetch our things? Our coats?" Marco asked when they were standing in front of the soldiers. They were no more than boys, he realized, children who should still be at school.

The soldier with the sparse Hitler mustache pressed the barrel of his rifle against Marco's chest, while the red-faced one prodded Rachel in the back with his weapon. "Keep your hands in the air," he bellowed nervously.

"Our hands are in the air," Marco said in German as calmly as possible. "Please allow one of the girls to fetch our things. Or the old man. We won't survive without our coats."

The soldiers glanced uncertainly at each other. One of them nodded at Ester. "Fetch your coats!" he ordered. "But only your coats!"

"Bring our coats, and our caps, gloves,

and sweaters," Marco said in Italian.

"What are you saying?" one of the soldiers roared. "Speak German!"

"She doesn't understand German," said Marco. "I told her to bring our coats and caps."

"Don't try anything. If that one tries something, we'll shoot the rest of you on the spot. Tell her!" the man with the mustache shouted.

"She won't try anything," Marco said calmly.

Like a frightened deer Ester scampered up the ridge on her skinny legs. When she came hurrying back, slipping and sliding down the mountainside, she was laden with coats. "I brought the two griddle cakes Rachel made last night," she whispered as they began to walk. "And our mugs and plates. I didn't know what else."

"Good thinking," said Marco.

For two days they struggled down the mountain. The second day Mr. Rozenfeld couldn't go on. "Leave me here, Marco," he said dully.

"We're nearly at the bottom," Marco said, firmly grasping the old man's arm.

"And when we're there?" the old man asked.

Marco did not reply. What could he say?

At the first village they were bundled into the back of an army truck and trundled down the mountain. "Where are they taking us?" Rachel asked in a small voice.

"I don't know," Marco answered. "Probably to some . . . camp."

Mr. Rozenfeld sat bunched up, his neck drawn into the collar of his coat, his head and shoulders drooping. Ester was huddled against Rachel, one hand clinging to her sister's arm while she ate the last scrap of griddle cake with the other. Her teeth bit into the dry, rock-hard cake, and she swung her head from side to side in an attempt to tear off a piece.

Their temporary dwelling was an army tent they shared with a Jewish family from Milan. More Jews from the northern and northwestern parts of Italy arrived daily.

For the first time in many months they had news from the outside world. They learned that it was the end of October 1943. Mussolini had been defeated at the beginning of August.

Marco gave the man who told them this an incredulous look. "Mussolini is no longer in control?" He wanted to make sure.

"Not in most of Italy," the man answered. "Do you know that the North African front surrendered in May?"

"We don't know about anything that happened after April," Marco said.

"Well, the Germans were also forced to retreat. They got a beating in the desert," the man said with satisfaction. "And then the Allies came across and landed in Sicily."

"The English forces? On Italian soil?" Marco repeated.

"The English and the Americans," the man confirmed. "The government sent Mussolini packing, and sometime toward the end of July King Victor Emmanuel threw Mussolini in jail and appointed Marshal Badoglio prime minister."

"Badoglio? Who's he?" Marco frowned.

"The new prime minister, you heard the man," Ester cut in.

"He's a military man and a true fascist," said a young man named Josef whom Marco had met.

"Anyway," the older man carried on, "Badoglio negotiated in secret with the Allies and on . . . er . . . sometime in September Italy surrendered."

"We surrendered unconditionally on September 8," Josef corrected him.

"Surrendered?" Marco asked. "So there's peace now?"

"That's what you'd think," Josef continued. “But when the English landed in the south of Italy, the Germans immediately occupied the northern parts and German special forces paratroopers rescued Mussolini from prison and made him head of the pro-German Repubblica Sociale Italiana.”

Marco shook his head. “So here in northern Italy we are in a socialist republic, still ruled by Mussolini?” he made certain.

“Actually, under German rule, Mussolini is nothing but a puppet,” Josef replied.

“He’s always been one,” said Marco.

“It has radically changed the destiny of the Jews,” the older man said. “Before the German occupancy a month or so ago, no Jews were sent to camps. But then they let loose the SS and the Nazi dogs to sniff us out and arrest us.”

“So the years we spent hiding in the cave were unnecessary?” Marco said, dismayed.

“And Mama died in vain?” Ester asked uncertainly.

“No,” Mr. Rozenfeld said softly, “your mother has been spared this humiliation. She would never have survived it. She rests where there is peace.”

That night, when Rachel lay in Marco’s arms on the thin mattress under the rough blankets, she said softly, “Our years in the cave weren’t pointless, Marco. I was with you every day. It was hard, yes, but it was also the happiest time of my life."

More Jews arrived every day. After a week in the tented camp, everyone was loaded onto trucks and taken to the station. They boarded the waiting train, up to twenty people crammed into a compartment meant for six.

"I hear we're going to Trieste, the city in northern Italy with the largest Jewish population," a man said.

"Where's that?" Rachel whispered.

"It's a seaport in the northeast," Marco answered, putting his arm around her thin shoulders.

"I think they're sending us to La Risiera di San Sabba, near Trieste," another man said.

"Is it a military camp as well?" Marco asked.

"It used to be a warehouse, before the Great War," Josef answered from the side. "Evidently the Deutsche Wehrmacht changed it into a camp at the beginning of the war, actually a kind of police detention barracks."

"How do you know all this?" an older woman asked sharply.

"I have a friend who lives in Trieste. He

works in the industrial district, and that's where the camp is," Josef answered, sounding impatient.

"That fellow seems a real know-it-all," Rachel said softly to Marco.

"Careful what you say," he answered, smiling. "Have you seen the way he and Ester are eyeing each other?"

"Oh no, Marco!" Rachel said, dismayed.

He laughed softly. "Your baby sister is growing up. She's no longer a little girl."

But Rachel frowned and shook her head. "She's sixteen. She's too young," she protested.

"I hear three thousand Italian soldiers were killed there awhile ago by SS officers and the Ukrainian guards," a third man joined in.

Marco felt Rachel draw a sharp breath. He stroked her arms and said out loud, "I don't think we should listen to rumors. Let's see for ourselves what the situation is."

"I agree," said the older woman with the sharp voice. "Stories lead to nightmares — and we have enough of those already, thank you very much."

La Risiera di San Sabba was an unobtrusive building at the docks, in the heart of the industrial district. They were herded down a long corridor, ending in a large courtyard. "Line up!" a stout man roared. "Families together."

Quickly Marco repeated the order in Italian.

The anxious groups tried to organize themselves. Men stood around uncertainly, women grabbed and let go, children cried, and somewhere a dog began to bark hysterically.

"Where's the man who can interpret?" the officer asked on the megaphone.

"That's you!" Josef nudged Marco. "Go talk."

Eventually Marco and the Rozenfelds were given a number for a small, dark, windowless room. Five beds with thin mattresses were stacked in a corner. The rough walls were covered with faint sketches — relics of previous inhabitants.

They set up the tiny room as comfortably as possible. "We can use the extra bed for storage," Rachel said.

"Not that we've got much to store," said Ester, taking their four plates and mugs from the bag.

But soon a young man and woman and their baby moved in with them, and they had to reorganize. The Rozenfelds pushed three beds against one wall and gave the new arrivals two beds against the opposite wall, with a narrow gap between them.

An hour later they had to line up again. They stood for hours in the bitter cold. After a while Mr. Rozenfeld's legs gave way, and Marco and Rachel held him upright. "I can't anymore," he whispered hoarsely through dry lips.

At last they were each given a pair of coveralls made of coarse striped fabric, with a big yellow Star of David on the sleeve. "These are our work uniforms," Marco interpreted to the dejected assembly. Even the children were provided with coveralls.

"It looks like the men's pajamas in the movies." Ester giggled when they were back in their room. "And it's terribly scratchy. I'm glad Papa sleeps in a nightshirt and cap."

"This is all I have now," Mr. Rozenfeld said.

They were divided into work teams. The men worked in the rubber factory nearby, Rachel joined the seamstresses, and Ester worked in the kitchen. The guards, they soon found out, were common criminals who treated the prisoners brutally.

Besides Jews, the prisoners included Communists, Gypsies, and a number of Slovakian and Slovenian citizens.

Life inside the high walls surrounding Risiera di San Sabba began to acquire its own rhythm. When the bugle sounded at dawn, the prisoners shuffled quietly into straight lines for the morning roll call, where their names were carefully ticked off. The names of those who had fallen ill the day before or during the night were struck from the roll and the rest were given a ladle of runny porridge for breakfast.

The mornings and evenings were bitterly cold. The men rubbed their hands together to work up a little heat, and the women wrapped their coats more tightly around themselves. Marco was grateful for the warm Russian coats and caps the Rozenfelds had brought from Lithuania.

The rations were meager, but after their years in the cave, they had grown accustomed to eating very little. They worked long, hard hours, and at night they lay together on their three narrow beds, whispering. Some nights the baby would whimper, and sleep wouldn't come.

Ester went around with shining eyes. In the early mornings she sat beside Josef, leaning against a low wall in the courtyard, eating her porridge, and in the evenings she disappeared until the bugle sounded, when she would hurry back to their room. Five minutes after the bugle had sounded the guards would search with spotlights, and anyone found moving would be punished.

One night Ester did not return to their room. Rachel lay awake all night. Marco had to physically restrain her from opening the door and going in search of her little sister. "She's with Josef." He tried to calm her down.

"But . . . she would never do something like that!" Rachel said. "We weren't raised that way, we . . ."

With his finger, Marco stroked her cheek in the dark. "It's no different from us, Rachel," he said softly.

He felt her stiffen. "It is!" she said firmly. "We're adults, we're engaged, and we've known each other for years. She met the man less than a month ago. She —"

"Let her be," said Mr. Rozenfeld from the bed next to theirs. "It may be the last scrap of joy she'll experience in her young life. Tomorrow we may all be dead."

Rachel drew a sharp breath. "Papa, don't say that!" she whispered.

"Death holds no fear for me anymore — just deliverance," Mr. Rozenfeld said slowly. "I'll be with your mama again."

They lay in silence on their beds, his words like heavy blankets suffocating them.

"I wish Ester was here. I'm so worried," Rachel whispered in Marco's ear awhile later. "And I'm worried about Papa as well. He seems to have lost hope."

Marco enfolded her in his arms. "Ester will be fine," he whispered back. "Grant her some happiness."

His own anxiety went further than Mr. Rozenfeld, but he didn't tell Rachel that. He knew Josef had a quick temper and an even quicker tongue.

Today the guards had taken one of the other wise guys aside. The youngster wasn't at roll call tonight. Marco knew his name would not appear on the list tomorrow morning.

More and more people arrived at the camp and were squeezed into every available space. San Sabba could accommodate a maximum of three thousand prisoners, but by now there were more than five thousand.

The camp authorities began to send away groups of Jews by train. "To Poland," someone said as they were sitting in a circle slurping their evening soup. They ate slowly, to make the food last a little longer.

"I heard one of the guards mention Auschwitz," another man said.

"Auschwitz? Have you heard of such a place?" Josef asked skeptically, looking at Marco.

Marco shook his head. "No, I doubt it's the name of a place. It's probably just the name of the camp."

"What does it matter what a camp is called?" said Rachel. "I suppose all camps are the same."

Josef shrugged. "It can't be any worse than here," he said.

"No, it *is* worse. I hear they're killing Jews on a large scale," the first man said. "They load them onto trucks and gas them with exhaust fumes — truckloads of them."

"They bury them in mass graves. I've heard it as well," the second man confirmed.

"Well, I think it's absolute nonsense," Marco said firmly. "After the Great War, the League of Nations was formed by all the Western countries to maintain a degree of order, of . . . civilization, even in times of war. Not even the Nazis can ignore it."

"Or the rest of the world will declare war against them?" Josef scoffed.

"I believe every word I hear about those pigs," the first man said, leaning into the circle and lowering his voice. "Let me tell you: Just after the Italian surrender was announced in September, the Nazis sent an entire commando of SS dogs to Lake Maggiore and arrested a lot of our people in Licino, Stresa, Baveno, and Pallanza. Those people simply vanished, just like that, off the face of the earth. But — and listen to this — fishermen discovered a large number of bodies in the lake. Something smells fishy, wouldn't you say?"

The people in the small circle didn't look up. They slurped the last of their soup, got up quietly, and went to their rooms.

Josef got to his feet as well and motioned with his head in the direction of his room. "Come," he said brusquely to Ester and walked away.

Rachel watched them leave, a worried look on her face. Then she turned to Marco. "I don't like that fellow," she said quietly.

Marco shook his head and did not reply.

Early in 1944, *Sturmbannführer* Christian Wirth became the camp commandant at San Sabba. He was a harsh man with a thunderous voice, and soon he became known as "Christian the Terrible."

The guards, Marco noticed immediately, were as afraid of him as the prisoners. "You must be careful," a guard said to a column of men winding their way in the dense fog to the factory in the early morning. "He was in charge of Operation Harvest Festival at Lublin in November last year. More than forty thousand Jews were killed in two days — just because one of them had refused to toe the line."

"I think he's talking nonsense," Josef said loudly to Marco.

"I'd be careful," Marco said quietly. "Wirth seems the kind of person who would do something like that."

From the continuous stream of new arrivals at the camp they heard that the Allied Forces were gaining ground all over Europe — first in Russia, and now there was a rumor that England and America were planning to invade and liberate France.

"Italy is being shot to pieces, destroyed from below by the Allies, from above by the Nazis," one old man said somberly. "Our houses and our synagogues are nothing but blackened ruins, and centuries-old cathedrals have been shot to pieces."

More and more trains left every week — for Poland, they heard. Early in the morning the people were lined up, names were read out, and they filed out the courtyard and through the long corridor and disappeared.

One morning near the end of the winter

of 1944, the names of Marco Romanelli, Rachel Rozenfeld, and Ester Rozenfeld were read out as well.

Josef's name wasn't read.

Neither was Mr. Rozenfeld's.

From the corner of his eye Marco, saw Ester begin to move. With a swift movement he grabbed her and covered her mouth with his hand. "Stand still and be quiet!" he whispered urgently. "Cooperate, or they'll shoot you without thinking twice."

Without time to say good-bye, without travel papers or any form of identity document, Marco, Rachel, and Ester — three numbers on a typed list — walked to the station, heading for an unknown destination.

Hefty men in Nazi uniforms were waiting on the platform. Their dogs were barking, straining at their leashes. "Line up!" the commander bellowed.

It was no longer necessary for Marco to interpret. Everyone was familiar with the commands. "Where you're going," the man thundered, "you'll get first-class treatment. It's a good labor camp, one of the best, with recreation facilities. You're the lucky ones."

"It sounds good," Rachel whispered. "Marco, what do you think . . . Papa . . . ?"

He shook his head. "I don't know, Rachel. He . . . does good work in the factory offices . . ." But he didn't believe himself. And he didn't believe a word the Nazi officer had said about the camp where they were heading.

The officer read out every name on the roll. Then he looked up and asked, *"Wieviel Stück?"*

A corporal answered smartly, *"Fünfhundert und zwölf Stück! Alles ist in Ordnung!"*

They were hastily bundled into ten cattle trucks waiting at the platform. The doors were shut and bolted from the outside. Inside, the people were squashed together.

The train did not move. After a few minutes, someone whispered, "What's going on?"

Nothing happened.

Almost soundlessly, people in the crowded truck began to clear a little space for themselves, their only view through the narrow chinks between the wooden slats.

Night was falling by the time the locomotive began to blow and pump and inch forward. The train moved slowly all through the night.

Outside, the moon was bright. Marco sat pressed up against the rough wooden boards. Rachel and Ester leaned on each other, half on top of him. They finally managed to fall asleep, but for Marco sleep would not come.

Slowly the moonlit landscape moved past. What awaited them at the end of this journey?

Sometimes the train stopped for a long time in the open country, seldom at a station. Through the parallel slats of the cattle truck he gazed at the tall, dark cliffs. *I will lift up mine eyes unto the hills, from whence cometh my help,* Marco thought. Looking down into the dark hollows of the Adige Valley, he told himself, *The eyes of the Lord are in every place.*

The names of the last Italian cities disappeared behind them as they passed one brightly lit station after another. "I'm so thirsty," Ester mumbled. "Marco, is there no water?"

Marco stroked her hair. "Try to sleep, Ester," he said softly.

She curled up and began to cry softly. She did not ask again.

When the sun rose on the second day, the train was steaming and puffing over the winding Passo del Brennero, the centuries-old pass through the Alps that forms the border between Italy and Austria. "I must get water," Rachel whispered.

"Look outside," Marco said, his finger pointing through a crack. "It's the Brenner Pass, built by the Romans in the second century." He was trying his best to distract them. Ester had been crying all night, while Rachel had clung to him with a kind of desperation. "At first it was just a track for horses and mules, of course, later for mule wagons. Round about 1860 the railway line was built."

"I see," said Rachel.

Below them lay green hills where cattle grazed peacefully. *He maketh me to lie down in green pastures: he leadeth me beside the still waters . . .*

"This is also where Mussolini and Hitler met at the beginning of 1940 to sign the Pact of Steel," Marco carried on resolutely.

"What does it matter?" Ester asked. "Isn't there any water at all?"

But the single bucket of water that had been in the truck at the beginning of their journey had been finished within the first hour.

"They'll bring us water soon," said Marco.

"Who? The guards?" Ester asked bitterly.

And she was right. While the freezing cold had been their worst enemy during the first long night, thirst now descended on the wagons. When they stopped, people begged for water. Women and children squeezed their hands through the slats, pleading for a handful of snow, but no one responded. The soldiers on the platforms chased away any person who tried to approach the train.

Children kept whining while the old people simply gave up, lying in defeated heaps.

By the second night it grew quiet. Occasionally someone would still groan or cry softly, tearlessly. Fear about what was waiting ahead dominated the thoughts of the survivors, hunger pushed up in their throats, thirst filled their bodies, made their tongues thick. Sleep eluded them.

Through the cracks they recognized Austrian names: Salzburg, Vienna. Then the names of Czechoslovakian towns and cities. Finally the peculiar spelling of Polish names. During the fourth night the cold was unbearable, the world outside covered with pale white snow.

They had stopped trying to communicate with anyone on the outside. After four days and four nights without food or water, they no longer had the strength.

Marco tried to prepare Rachel for what was waiting. "It's possible we'll be separated, men and women. Just see that you survive — that's what's most important."

She gave him a serious look. "You too, Marco Romanelli," she whispered past her parched tongue.

"I will," he promised. "I'll wait for you, Rachel. When the war is over — and I know it can't be long now, the Allies are getting the upper hand everywhere — when the war is over, you're going to be my wife."

She nodded slowly and pointed upward, through the crack above their heads. "Marco, look at the stars."

He looked up. The sky was black velvet, the stars glittering diamonds — unchanged for centuries. "Remember the words of King David: 'When I consider thy heavens, the work of thy fingers, the moon and the stars, which thou hast ordained; what is man that thou are mindful of him?' Yet God is always near." He was silent for a moment before adding: "I suppose it's in your Torah as well."

Rachel nodded again. "I . . . think so," she said uncertainly. "These are our stars, Marco. They've come all the way with us, no matter how crooked our path may have been."

They sat in silence, relishing their closeness.

By early morning the train slowed down and stopped. Marco looked outside. They were in open country. In the dim moonlight he saw a landscape carpeted with snow as far as the eye could see, interspersed with a few sparse trees rising like silent, dark skeletons.

After a long wait the train slowly began to puff and jerk again. Inside the carriage, no one looked up anymore.

At first light the train blew off steam and jolted to a halt. They had entered through large gates to arrive in the middle of an open area — *Birkenau,* the sign said.

"I think this is the end of our journey," Marco said quietly.

Chapter Six

Each day was exactly like the one before. In the morning a siren wailed, and the numbers lined up for a bowl of thin porridge. Day after day the starving people wasted away, dying a slow death. They were fed a daily ration of thin soup, a handful of rice grains, and half a slice of bread until they could no longer get up. Those who were strong enough pushed others out of their way for a sip of water and pounced on any crumb that happened to fall.

By day they worked long hours in the snow, wind, driving rain, or blazing sun.

At night they lay on their thin mattresses.

Sometimes the smell of burned hair and flesh shrouded the camp like a dense fog. "The corpses are being cremated," the inmates whispered.

More prisoners kept arriving at the camp — disheveled, petrified creatures, staring blankly with eyes that had seen too much.

On arrival they were stripped of their possessions and squeezed into any available space.

On a warm summer's day at the end of June 1944, a group of Jews from the camp Fossoli di Carpi arrived at Birkenau. More than five hundred children and elderly people were immediately separated from the rest and taken away. "Straight to the gas chambers," the people whispered.

"But the Allies are so close!" the new arrivals protested.

"How close?" asked Marco.

"They invaded Rome on the fourth," a young man said. "The Allies are close to the Gothic Line. The province of Modena is a battlefield, but the English are gaining ground."

"And they've landed in France, in Normandy," his friend said. "The Allies crossed the English Channel. They're in France this very moment. I believe they've driven the Nazis out of Paris."

"So they've finally launched their second front," someone said excitedly.

"Rome, Paris — Berlin will be next!" someone else cried.

The news lifted the spirits in the camp and became a burning hope for the future.

■ ■ ■ ■

It was high summer now. It had been more than three months since Marco's arrival in Birkenau, three months since he had last seen Rachel. Slowly Marco climbed up to his bunk. If he sat up, his head touched the ceiling. But he preferred the top bunk. It was more private, and no one scrambled past him at night to get to the slop bucket in the corner of the cell.

He took off his coveralls and stretched out his tall, aching frame. It was stifling in the cell with its four tiny windows high up in the walls. By morning the air was thick and stale.

The folds of the gray blanket scratched his bare shoulder.

There was a rustling sound.

He frowned and rolled over.

The rustling sound was there again, like paper.

He raised himself slightly and felt under the blanket.

Between blanket and mattress he found a scrap of paper, folded tightly.

His hands trembled. He unfolded it slowly. Could it . . . ?

It was too dark. He couldn't see.

He lay awake until the early hours, the tightly folded paper clutched in his fist. When at last he fell asleep, he dreamed of Rachel, her figure soft and full as it used to be, her hair blowing in the wind, her cheeks rosy, her laughing mouth turned up to him. When he woke, he was pouring with sweat. The paper was still clutched in his fist. It was pitch-dark. No stars were visible through the narrow windows.

Rachel! His entire being longed for her. If only he could hold her one more time . . .

Eventually he could make out the paper was a letter, but it was still too dark to read the words.

Dawn broke at last. He saw Rachel's round letters. They turned into words:

I am fine. Sister and I in good health. We work in the gardens. My love keeps me strong. There will be a future after this.

Emotion such as he had not experienced for weeks welled up inside him. Rachel was alive. She was well.

He looked at the letter in his hand, but the words were swimming.

He blinked again and again. He read and reread, burned the words into his heart. At last he raised the scrap of hope to his mouth and slowly chewed the paper, as if it were sacramental bread, before swallowing it.

All through the day he was filled with joy.

In the night longing began to gnaw at him again.

The next morning he tore a page from his notebook. His head was resting on his rolled-up coat, which served as a pillow. He took a blunt pencil stub from its pocket. His hands were trembling. He could almost feel her presence.

He formulated the words with care, choosing those that would let her know he got her letter.

> I am fine. I am healthy. My love grows stronger every day. The future is waiting.

He hid the letter in the same place he had found the one addressed to him two nights before.

All day long his heart rejoiced. There was a future waiting after this hellhole where they were imprisoned. He knew it.

That night he searched his bed, but his own letter was still where he had left it. He must be patient. Whoever smuggled in Rachel's letter couldn't manage to come every day.

A week later the letter was still there.

When two weeks had passed, he destroyed the page. He felt he had lost all chance of contact with his Rachel.

The days and nights dragged on interminably, indistinguishable from one another.

One early morning in a series of identical early mornings, a new trainload of Jews arrived at Birkenau from northern Italy. "Today is August the fourth," said an elderly man from Trieste as they ate together.

August the fourth? Marco thought. How unimportant days and dates had become.

"Conditions in Italy are appalling," another man said.

"For non-Jews as well?" Marco asked quietly.

The man nodded. "For everybody. The towns have been blown to pieces, our currency is worthless, children walk the streets begging for food, people are even killing their . . ." He fell silent. "It's . . ." He shook his head.

Marco turned away, the runny porridge sticking in his throat. *My family, my brothers, my father,* he thought. *And . . . Mama?*

Would peace never come?

Their workday was fourteen hours. As long as the sun was shining, the prisoners got no rest. That day was even longer than usual, longing and anxiety eating away at his reserves. At nightfall he drank his thin soup and enough water. He didn't stay to talk to the others, to listen to the new arrivals' news. His mind refused to accept any more information. His aching body wanted to rest.

His hand felt around under the blanket, as usual. He searched every night, though two months had passed since he discovered the letter. It was something he looked forward to every day, a scrap of hope in a hopeless existence.

Then his fingers touched it.

His heart jumped, his stomach churned.

He clambered from his bunk and rushed outside. The sun had gone down but there was still plenty of light.

On this day, this specific, endless, hopeless day, the letter was there.

He turned his back to the men sitting in a small circle just outside the door, talking. Slowly he unfolded the paper, his eyes caressing the familiar handwriting.

> Sister gone. Like Mama. Heart aches. I see the stars at night. I remember.

Marco drew a deep breath and closed his eyes.

No. No.

He looked at the note in his hands.

It was true. Ester was gone. Ester was dead.

She was only seventeen. She would never eat the crunchy apple she had craved.

And Rachel was all alone. In body and in soul.

His heart reached out to her across the high walls and the barbed wire. She was so near, only a few hundred yards away. Yet she was so incredibly far.

Maybe she was watching the birds circling in the sky high above the camps at this very moment. Yet she was unreachable.

No, he told himself, *she's only a letter away.*

And she's alive.

The future is still waiting after all.

The days were getting colder when Marco was sent to work in the synthetic rubber factory. It was a long walk, but at least he worked indoors by day. The snow fell steadily all night long.

After a week or two the smell of the hot rubber began to irritate his chest. He soon learned to stifle his impulse to cough.

More and more Hungarian Jews arrived at the camp. Most of them were immediately transported to an unknown destination.

Rumors of the gas chambers grew stronger. "Those aren't just burning corpses we smell," people whispered.

With the new arrivals came the news that some weeks earlier there had been an attempt on Hitler's life. "But he's alive?" the people asked.

"Unfortunately, yes," came the reply. "But it's only a matter of time. The net is closing around Germany."

Deep in December, close to Christmas, Marco figured, a letter was waiting for him one evening.

> I am well. I know you are there and you are waiting. That is why I am able to carry on. All my love.

He sank down on his knees. "Mother of God," he murmured, "you are here, and that is why I, too, am able to carry on. Please take care of Rachel, even though she's not your child. I love her deeply. And be with my family at Christmastime . . ."

Then he was overcome by emotion.

One day the flood of prisoners dried up, the trainloads of people vanished like smoke in the air.

"The Nazis are no longer in control," the men told each other.

The guards were restless. They screamed at the prisoners, sounding anxious. "They know the end is near," the people whispered.

More and more people disappeared. The two bunks below Marco were empty, the lumpy mattresses and thin blankets claimed by others in a desperate attempt to keep the cold at bay.

"It won't be long now," the men told each other. They needed the reassurance more than the dry lump of bread they were given every day.

Less than two weeks after the previous letter, Marco found a new scrap of paper under his blankets. His heart jumped with joy as his trembling fingers unfolded the letter.

The handwriting was not hers.

> I regret having to write this letter. She is gone. It was a short illness, but she had no reserves. We gave her coat and cap to a young girl. She had no other possessions. The coat was very good. She spoke your name before she left us.

The letters on the paper did not make sense. The coat had come all the way from

Lithuania.

Then the words sank in. The realization filled his entire body, his scrawny legs gave way, his heart burst apart, darkness descended on his mind.

Someone picked him up where he was lying in the snow and dragged him inside. He woke in a strange bed, one of the bottom bunks without mattress or blanket.

He didn't feel the cold. With enormous effort he hauled himself up to his own bunk. Sleep eluded him.

So this is how it ends. "All is vanity," says the Preacher.

That night Marco Romanelli coughed up flecks of blood while his heart bled dry and died.

The next morning and all the mornings that followed he got up, ate his daily bread, worked by the sweat of his brow, coughed. Every night the blood was there.

By day he suppressed the coughing bouts until the guard had done his rounds. Then he bent double, coughing until he felt his chest would burst and flecks of foam plastered his lips. When he wiped his mouth, the back of his hand was covered in bloody mucus.

His mind was dull, his eyes dim, his heart empty.

His body was cold cold cold.

One early evening the planes appeared. "The Russians!" someone shouted. Sirens wailed, people screamed and ran, guards barked orders through megaphones.

Then the bombs came down — like huge hailstones, ripping the earth apart. An outbuilding was hit and went up in flames.

The planes departed as suddenly as they had come.

The evening was filled with the screams of people, the hysterical barking of dogs.

All night long the lights remained on as trucks roared and orders were bellowed over loudspeakers.

Marco was aware of the scrambling around him, below him.

He lay motionless and ice-cold on his thin mattress, his emaciated body wrapped in his old coat, the thin blanket drawn over his head, unaware that cell B8 was being evacuated, its inmates loaded into the back of covered trucks.

"We're burning the camp!" a guard roared at the cell door. "Everyone out!"

The words did not reach his feeble body, his exhausted brain. His chest seemed about to rupture from violent coughing fits. He no longer tried to suppress them.

Sleep engulfed him, merciful and pitch-black.

At sunrise no sirens were wailing. Marco closed his eyes — he could not go on.

Sometime during the day he was dragged from his bed and taken outside. The camp was silent, the kitchen doors and gate wide open.

They propped him against a wall in the pale sunshine. "Eat, Marco," someone said. "The guards have left everything. Have some food."

Around him men were opening tins: meat and fish and sweet canned fruit. They ate like savages, choking, throwing up, eating some more.

The stronger ones filled their pockets and draped blankets around their shoulders before setting off through the gate.

Someone helped Marco to one of the lower bunks and covered him with blankets. "Here's bread, Marco, and water. And a slab of chocolate," the man said. Then he too left.

It grew quiet.

Several days and nights passed before the tanks arrived. The soldiers spoke Russian. They took him along.

Days and nights merged into one. He was

in a bed. Occasionally someone fed him or gave him a drink of water. Each coughing fit ripped his chest apart. He vomited blood. No one cleaned it up.

"He's Italian," someone said in Russian. "Sometimes I hear him mumble."

"What's your name?" they asked.

Marco did not answer.

"We must send him to Rome," a voice said one day, speaking the language of Milton and Shakespeare and Wordsworth. *What are the classical poets doing here?*

"What's your name?" the voice insisted . . . *What's in a name . . . ?*

If only it weren't so terribly cold.

He became aware that his bed was shaking. The pain was unbearable. He sank into darkness.

The train rocked and jolted, carrying his aching, starving body back along the winding route.

Occasionally the mist dispersed. The periods of daylight grew longer. The pain remained, as did the battle for breath.

He found out he was in a military hospital in Rome. The staff spoke mainly English. "What is your name?" they asked.

"Marco Romanelli."

"Romanelli?" The voice sounded puzzled.

His eyelids were too heavy to open. "I'm . . . not . . . Jewish . . ." His lips were too tired to continue forming words.

It was the end of July 1945, he found out. The Russian tanks entered Birkenau at the end of January. He had spent nearly six months in a Russian military hospital. He had been transferred to Rome a month ago.

Hitler took his own life on April 30, he heard a voice say. Germany surrendered on May 7.

At the end of April, communist guerilla fighters caught and hanged Mussolini and his lover, Clara Petacci, in a public square. A crowd gathered to watch as the body was hung upside down, someone else added.

"Only Japan is still fighting," a male nurse told him. "I honestly don't know how we're going to get food into you. If you don't eat, you'll never get strong."

But even the thinnest soup came back up.

"Let me . . . go home," Marco pleaded.

The doctor shook his head. "You won't survive the journey and with the roads the way they are . . . Besides, you're being fed intravenously. No, first you must get stronger."

On August 6, an American plane dropped an atom bomb called Little Boy on the industrial city of Hiroshima in Japan. More than one hundred thousand people died, and a dense cloud of smoke hung over the city. "They'll have to surrender now," the male nurse said, pleased. "Don't move. You're so full of holes already, I fear today I'm not going to find a vein for this needle."

Three days later the second American atom bomb, Fat Man, was detonated over the Japanese city of Nagasaki. "Now Japan will have to accept America's conditions for peace," the nurse with the broad American accent said. "No one argues with America!"

"I want to . . . die at home . . . please," Marco told the doctor the next day. The doctor, a young man with dark circles under his eyes, turned wearily and walked off without a word.

Early one morning a few days later, a man in a smart suit stood at Marco's bedside. "Do you recognize me, Marco?" he asked.

Marco nodded slightly. It was Pietro, son of the village doctor, who worked as a journalist in Rome. "Pietro," he said almost inaudibly.

Pietro nodded. "Someone called me yesterday," he said. "I've come to fetch you. We're going home."

He huddled in the passenger seat of the

small car, shivering in spite of the bright sunlight. They kept driving, hour after hour. He dozed off, wrapped in a dark haze or a dim white fog. When he surfaced, his entire body ached.

He did not speak. He had no idea of his surroundings.

But just before sunset, when they reached the steep, winding road that led to the village, Marco whispered, "I'm going home."

"We're almost there," Pietro said beside him. "Before the sun goes down, we'll be home."

It was twilight when they rounded the last bend. A group of boys ran from the village square to the doctor's home.

The villagers heard the car and came out of their houses.

Pietro drew up in front of Giuseppe and Maria Romanelli's home and got out.

Exhausted, Marco opened the passenger door, struggling to get his legs out. He tried to stand, but his legs gave way and he fell back onto the seat.

Cautiously the people approached. They stopped, stared in horror.

Pietro bent down and hooked his arms under Marco's armpits. "Come, let me help you up," he said, carefully pulling him out of the car.

Lorenzo appeared. "Marco?" he asked.

Marco gave a slight nod.

He leaned with his left side against Pietro's shoulder while Lorenzo draped Marco's right arm over his shoulders.

Only then did Marco notice Lorenzo's crutches.

He was shocked all over again. It had completely slipped his mind that his lively, active younger brother was on crutches. "Half of me stayed behind on the battlefield," Lorenzo had said a long time ago.

Somewhere deep inside a sliver of emotion detached itself. *I can still feel,* Marco thought dimly. *I'm still alive.*

They half dragged, half carried him across the patio to the small house. The pain in his chest was unbearable, the cold and exhaustion overwhelming. Then he knew nothing more.

He became aware of a warm hand on his cold cheek. He was surrounded by a dense white fog and struggled to emerge from it.

"Marco? Are you awake?" he heard his mother say.

He forced his eyes open. Her face swam into focus. Her hands were cupped around his face. "Marco," she said.

"Mama," he whispered, almost inaudibly.

But she heard him.

She turned and reached behind her. "I've made you some soup," she said huskily and produced a bowl. "I'll . . . help you," she said.

He tried to stop her. He knew what would happen. "No, you must eat, just a few mouthfuls," she said.

But it was no use. He forced himself to swallow the thin soup, his stomach cramped violently, and everything came back up. Wearily he closed his eyes. "Never mind, just rest," his mother said. She cleaned up the mess and pressed her warm lips to his cold forehead.

He was never alone. When he opened his eyes, his father was sitting at his bedside, quiet and rock-steady, as always. Or Lorenzo, with a book in his lap. He would get up and moisten Marco's dry lips or cover his ice-cold body with a sheepskin.

Or Antonio. "Tonio? You're back too?" Marco asked softly.

"Yes, Marco. We're all back home."

Back home.

He slept for days and nights, or a day and a night, or maybe only an hour or two. At times he awoke. Lorenzo would be standing at the small window, looking out.

He would hear his mother's voice in the

front room. "I'm worried sick. He can't keep anything down," she said. "Doc's medicine doesn't help. I don't know what else to do. Even my homemade barley soup comes up."

"Cat gut," he heard Tia Sofia say. Tia Sofia — a voice from his childhood. "You must slaughter a cat and place the warm guts on his stomach," she said.

"I don't know about that," his mother said.

"Or the fresh stomach contents of a young goat," Tia Sofia suggested. "It always works."

"I think we'll just follow the doctor's advice," his mother replied. "But we must be patient. Doc says the damage was done over many years."

An unusual calm descended on Marco. The women's chatter was familiar. *Something always remains,* he thought. Warmed by the thought, he went back to sleep.

When he woke again, his mother said, "I've strained some potato soup through a cloth. I'm going to feed it to you one spoonful at a time every half hour. Yesterday's water stayed down. It should work."

At the hospital they gave up. But a mother never gives up, even if it means she has to trickle a spoonful of soup into her son's mouth every half hour all through the night, night after night.

Drop by drop, spoonful by spoonful, day by day, Marco's condition improved. A week later his father carried him out to sit in the sun. "The sun gives energy," his mother said.

Antonio joined him, fit and strong from the healthy diet down in South Africa, his skin darkened by the sun. Antonio sat down and fed him his three spoonfuls of soup. "Before you know it, you'll be back on your feet," he said. "There's peace. Your life is waiting."

Marco drew a sharp breath. "But . . . she's gone, Tonio."

Antonio nodded and laid his hand on his brother's arm. "Yes, Marco."

"She was so hopeful." His voice faded. He was exhausted. But he desperately wanted to talk about her, his Rachel. Because her death was still an open wound. "The last time I heard from her, she was filled with hope. It was . . . just before Christmas. Someone had smuggled a letter in."

He leaned his head back and closed his eyes. Antonio gripped his hand firmly. Everything hurt. "Tell me," said Antonio.

"She was so brave," Marco said, his eyes still closed. He moved his hand slightly and his fingers gripped Antonio's warm hand. "Even when her sister died."

"I'm . . . sorry," Antonio said softly.

They sat together for a long time. Somewhere in a tree a bird called its mate.

At last Antonio said, "Come, take another sip, before Mama gets cross."

Marco opened his eyes, met Antonio's gaze. They smiled and nodded.

. . . before Mama gets cross . . .

They were brothers.

As Marco began to regain his strength, he had a lot of time to notice things. Everything was not as it used to be, he soon realized. The men were still bringing in their heavy bushels of fresh produce from the vegetable patches and fields and orchards, the reddest tomatoes, the fattest grains of wheat, the sweetest grapes. And the village women canned peaches and green beans and dried tomatoes and sultanas while dishing out advice on how to get him fit and strong again. Father Enrico called to tell him his classroom was waiting.

But within the walls of their home and at the table in their front room, the tension mounted. And they — and the entire village — knew why.

Gina Veneto, daughter of the baron, was

Antonio's fiancée. They were engaged before the war came, and Father Enrico had blessed their engagement.

But Antonio had been away a long time. He'd spent three years in North Africa before being sent to South Africa as a prisoner of war. During that time Lorenzo had come home, injured, and his childhood friend Gina had been there to support him in his hour of need.

The villagers understood. They just didn't know whether it was right of them to understand.

One night when Antonio began to speak, it was Marco's turn to listen. "Maybe they were always meant for each other," Antonio said. "Remember how they used to fight as kids? They could never leave each other alone."

"But . . . she's *your* fiancée, Tonio, and Lorenzo is your brother."

Antonio nodded slowly, earnestly. "I remember Lorenzo once saying, 'All's fair in love and war.' He seems to have meant it quite literally." There was no bitterness in his voice.

Marco was silent for a while. Then he asked, "Tonio, was there a girl down in South Africa?"

Antonio glanced up quickly. Then he nodded. "Yes, there was. But it didn't really come to anything."

Marco waited.

"It's different there, Marco, everything is different: the language, the food, the customs, the people, their faith. Especially their faith. They're not Catholic. It's just . . . too weird."

Marco nodded. About faith he understood. He understood perfectly. "And now?" he asked.

"Now I'm going to break off my engagement to Gina. I must — it's not working. When I'd just arrived, before you came back, I was angry, but not anymore. Next week I'm going back to Turin to complete my studies. Then I plan to carry on with my life."

They sat in silence for a while, then Marco asked, "What's her name? The girl down south?"

"Klara," Antonio said softly. "Her name is Klara."

Winter set in and temperatures dropped. The wind howled around the corners of the houses and the first snow began to fall. As the cold gripped Marco's body, the coughing started up again. "We're moving your bed to the living room, near the stove. It's warmer than the back room," Maria decided one morning.

Lorenzo and Antonio had returned to the university in Turin to complete their studies. Giuseppe removed the mattress and bedding from the bed and carried the bed to the front room. He moved the rough wooden table and chairs and the cabinet with the crockery and food stores out of the way and placed the bed against the wall.

It was still hard to eat, but if he really took his time, he kept the meat and vegetable broth or softly boiled polenta down.

One weekend in October the brothers came home. "Goodness, Marco, you look much better!" Antonio exclaimed, surprised. "One of these days you'll be round as a ball and we'll have to put you on a diet!"

Maria smiled, pleased. "He's eating solids," she said, gently laying her rough hand on Marco's bony shoulder.

"I've been taking short walks," said Marco. "When the wind dies down and it's sunny outside, I walk across the square, to the doctor's house. But these days there's rarely any sun."

He had not yet ventured as far as the boarded-up store of the Rozenfelds.

That night, when their parents and Lorenzo were asleep and Marco was in bed in the front room, Antonio sat down on the upright wooden chair at his bedside. "I'm going away, Marco," he said.

"Away? How . . . away?"

"I'm going back to South Africa."

"South Africa?"

Antonio nodded. "It's a wonderful place. People call it the land of milk and honey. Cattle and sheep and goats graze on the open plains, the views go on forever, and there's sunshine all year round."

"Just a few months ago you said it was too different, too weird."

Tonio waved it off. "It's a prosperous country, with a strong economy. Here in Italy . . ." He shook his head. "There's no money here, Marco. The war has ruined our country. I can't see myself making a living here as a young architect."

Antonio was going, Marco thought. Far away, thousands of miles. They might not see him again for years. A tight fist clutched at his heart.

Then he remembered something else. "And?" he asked.

"And . . . Klara's brother was here, in Italy. He came to see me at university. He . . . there's a chance it could work out, Marco. I think she might be waiting for me."

Marco frowned and looked at his brother.

Antonio's expression had softened. His gaze was deeper, more intense — happier. Marco's own heart contracted with a sudden, sharp longing.

"Then you should go," he said.

In the spring of 1946, Marco was back in his classroom at Father Enrico's little school. He began with only a few lessons every day. He did not have the energy to do more. He worked without a salary. No one had money — including the government. But his classroom was bursting at the seams with young people keen to learn English: Wild boys who had been kicking balls when the war broke out were sitting in front of him with slicked-down hair, eyeing the girls. Tall young men with deep voices, who had lain in the trenches and seen bombs explode, now wanted to complete their education.

By day Maria worked in her vegetable patch. Giuseppe helped her, doing the hard digging and carrying heavy buckets to water the seedlings. In the evenings he still chiseled and carved out his marble statuettes. But he couldn't sell them, not even to people abroad, because no one had money. During the long winter that would begin its onslaught in six months' time they would have to sustain themselves on the produce from their own little garden.

At the beginning of May 1946, Marco read in the paper that La Scala opera house in Milan would reopen on the eleventh with a concert by the soprano Renata Tebaldi. The conductor was Toscanini. La Scala had been rebuilt after being badly damaged by bombs in 1943. "Oh, Papa, if only we could go!" he said.

Giuseppe Romanelli nodded and laid a heavy hand on his son's shoulder.

"One day you'll go. There will be other concerts," Maria said.

That summer Gina Veneto married Lorenzo Romanelli. The village provided as much of a feast as was possible. Antonio sent photos of his own wedding to a strange girl, Klara, in a distant country. Maria put up the photos on the wall in the front room. The villagers came to see. "Pretty girl," they said. "Shiny hair, rosy cheeks — there's obviously enough food over there."

Marco studied the photos and took in the full cheeks, the soft arms, the feminine curves. He remembered how dreadfully thin and cold his little Rachel had been when she had clung to him during their last night together, her skeletal silhouette as she had walked away from him the next day on her way to the women's camp. In the photograph Antonio looked happy. Marco's heart was an aching void.

In summer Marco perked up and was able to teach a full day. His pupils were eager to learn.

But in winter the cold reentered his body, the coughing fits resumed, and the medicine the old doctor prescribed upset his stomach. They moved his bed back to the front room, close to the stove. He stayed there day and night, but the cold remained, and the thin layer of fat he had accumulated in summer soon disappeared. He lay on a sheepskin to prevent the formation of pressure sores on his hips and back. What strength he had gained quickly seeped out.

From South Africa, Antonio wrote:

Over here it's hot — sweltering at times. The sun is bright, we're anxious for rain, it's very dry.

Strange to think about Christmas when it's so hot. It's the only time I miss the snow.

Klara and I are very happy. It's wonderful over here, Mama and Papa. I miss you both, and I think of you every day and pray the Holy Mother of God will hold you in the palm of her hand. But I am blessed to have a wife who loves me.

At work I am doing well. The firm of architects I work for was awarded a big contract for a luxury hotel complex just outside Pretoria, where Klara and I live. They have put me in charge of the project. I'm truly excited. Klara and I would like to buy a house of our own, and with this contract we should be able to afford it. Nothing fancy, but our own.

I share your anxiety about Marco's health. Sometimes I wonder whether he should come here. The bushveld is warm and dry — hot, even in winter. It would be good for his chest.

"No," Maria declared. "No, it's too far." And she stirred the steaming *fagioli* on the stove with an almost aggressive vigor.

Early one morning shortly after Christmas, Maria summoned the doctor after yet another bad night.

"I think Marco should go to the hospital in Turin," the doctor said, shaking his head.

"No," Maria said firmly. "People die in the hospital. I'll nurse my child back to health myself."

The doctor prescribed penicillin, a new miracle drug from Turin. The village women offered advice, proposed ancient remedies.

By the spring of 1947, Marco was back in his classroom. Klara had given birth to a baby boy.

Consider my proposal,

Antonio wrote in June.

> It's winter in South Africa now, but even now I don't wear a coat when we spend a weekend with Klara's parents in the bushveld. The people who live there don't own coats. I really believe it's the only thing that will save Marco.

"Don't own coats?" Maria Romanelli repeated, incredulous.

Giuseppe nodded earnestly, breaking out of his typical silence for his son's sake. "We m-m-must th-th-think." His stutter was as pronounced as ever.

"No!" said Maria.

"F-f-for Marco," Giuseppe continued.

Maria closed her eyes and shook her head.

That night Marco lay on his narrow bed in the back room. He couldn't face another cold winter, coughing until he lay exhausted like an old man on his sheepskin. He couldn't keep losing everything he struggled to gain.

Wherever he went, the memory of what was, what might have been, followed him like a blind dog refusing to stray far from its master's feet. He was lucky to be able to live with his parents. He was showered with more love and attention than he could have wished for. But a deep longing for his Rachel followed him wherever he went, waited for him at every street corner, was there at the sight of every young girl.

His mind knew she was gone. His heart was desolate and distraught.

He wrote a short letter to his brother in the distant sunny land.

Are you serious, Tonio? What are my chances of finding work? Do you think I would find my feet? And what about the language? And the Church?

Six weeks later, at the height of summer, when the days were long and Marco could feel the strength returning to his warm body, his brother's reply arrived:

Yes, Marco, I am serious.

I enquired at the local school in the bushveld town where Klara grew up. It's not too far from Pretoria, where we live. They would love to offer Latin as a subject, and they'll welcome you with open arms. You can also teach English. Everyone here speaks English, but I must warn you: the people of the bushveld speak an English that would make Shakespeare turn in his grave! You could definitely make a huge difference.

Please think carefully. I know it would break Mama's and Papa's hearts, but you're young. Here you won't merely survive, you can have a good life and make a complete recovery.

Marco thought about it long and hard, weeks on end, weighing everything.

Early in September, shortly after the birth of Lorenzo and Gina's baby boy, when the first cold showed its dark, cloudy face, Marco spoke to his parents and his brother.

"No!" said Maria.

Lorenzo put his hand over hers. "Mama, wait," he said quietly. He turned to Marco. "Antonio and I have spoken," he said. "The future looks promising in South Africa. There's a strong economy even in these times."

"And . . . the sun shines every day," Marco said softly.

"G-g-go." Giuseppe spoke the final word.

■ ■ ■ ■

Thus Marco Romanelli came to find himself aboard an Italian ship in the port of Genoa on a cold day at the beginning of November 1947, waving good-bye to his brother on the quay far below. Only Lorenzo was there to see him off, balancing between his crutches, waving and waving his white handkerchief.

Maria and Giuseppe Romanelli had said their farewells at home. Alone. Because the country where Marco was going was far, too far. He would not be coming home again.

Just as Antonio would not be returning either.

Maria had given him a marble statuette of the Madonna and Child Giuseppe had made for her when Marco was born. "So you may remember, Marco, you will always be our firstborn," she had said.

The ship's band played a rousing number.

The horn sounded. Slowly the ship drew away from the quay. Lorenzo waved with both arms.

The paper streamers that connected the ship with the land began to snap.

Lorenzo's figure diminished and vanished

among a sea of waving handkerchiefs, and the city faded into the distance. As the sun set, the last Italian mountain disappeared from view.

Marco Romanelli would not be accompanying his father to a concert at La Scala opera house after all.

He wiped his eyes with his damp handkerchief. Then he turned and slowly made his way to his cabin in the belly of the big ship.

Part Three: Intersections

Chapter Seven

January 2, 1947, was Lettie's first day as a qualified doctor at the Pretoria General Hospital. She worked long hours, just as she had during her internship, and sometimes, especially over weekends, she was thrown in at the deep end. She spent the occasional Sunday with Klara and Antonio, and she shared in their joy about the baby Klara was expecting.

The little boy was born that winter. Lettie went to see Klara in the Moedersbond Maternity Home, next door to the General Hospital. Klara lay tucked under blankets in a pale-green bed jacket with lace frills at the neckline. Her cheeks were rosy, her eyes shiny. Klara had never looked so beautiful, not even on her wedding day.

"Family names are not an Italian tradition," Klara said, "so we've decided to name our son after my father and grandfather, Cornelius."

"He's awfully small to carry such a big name," Lettie remarked, looking at the wrinkled little face in Klara's arms. She stroked the tiny cheek with her forefinger.

"Small or not, we're naming him Cornelius," Klara said firmly. "He'll grow into the name."

A month later young Cornelius Johannes Romanelli was baptized in the church in Klara's hometown. Lettie put in a weekend's leave and drove to the bushveld for the occasion.

The whole family was in church on Sunday: Klara's brothers, Boelie and De Wet; their sister, Irene; and the siblings' parents and grandparents. Annabel and her parents also attended, and Christine, with little ginger-haired Gerbrand clinging tightly to her hand.

De Wet held the child's other hand. When mother and child had returned from the war, De Wet erected a protective barrier around them both. His marriage to Christine marked the day Lettie finally buried her unspoken love for him. She had stood up with her childhood friends in an awful pink gown, feeling like a smiling frosted pudding.

Klara and Antonio stood side by side at the baptismal font, Antonio with his arm around his wife's waist. Klara's ouma carried the baby to the font. When they sat back down after the ceremony, the baby still in Klara's arms, Antonio leaned over and kissed his son's small face. *So Italian,* Lettie thought, amused. *Afrikaner men don't kiss their sons.*

After the service, with everyone admiring the baby, Lettie couldn't help noticing that Klara had gained quite a lot of weight during her pregnancy. *If Klara has another baby, she'll end up looking like me,* Lettie thought. Yet Antonio still seemed madly in love with her.

A big feast was waiting at the Big House on the Fouries' farm.

"It was a beautiful ceremony," Lettie said, congratulating Antonio. "I'm sorry your parents couldn't be here."

"De Wet took a lot of photos," Antonio said. "As soon as he has them developed, I want to send my parents a few. They're very proud of their first grandson."

The baby was sleeping peacefully in his woven basket.

"Fortunately Antonio's brother Lorenzo and his wife are also having a baby soon," Klara said. "They live in Turin, not far from Antonio's parents."

"My mother would have enjoyed today,"

Antonio said in a subdued voice.

"We're planning a visit," said Klara. "But it's very far. Antonio will be away from his work for a long time. We can't afford it right now."

"Maybe it's better they weren't here," Antonio said after a while. "The ceremony wasn't exactly . . . well, Catholic."

That spring Lettie began to spend more time with Klara and Antonio, especially on Sundays. She and Klara rekindled the friendship they had in their schooldays, and the years at university during which they had grown apart faded into the background. Lettie got to know Antonio and came to realize he was a wonderful man.

"I think my brother is seriously considering coming to South Africa," Antonio said one Sunday when Lettie joined them for lunch.

"To the bushveld?" asked Lettie. "To our town?"

"Yes, the climate will be good for his chest," answered Antonio. "I spoke to the school principal when we were there for Cornelius's baptism, and they'd be happy to offer him a job. Marco is teaching in Italy, but he's not earning a salary."

"He could teach Latin and English," said

Klara. "Come along, Lettie, I think Cornelius is awake."

In the bedroom Lettie said, "Klara, you've lost a lot of weight. I didn't notice it at first, maybe because of the bulky winter clothes. You do know you shouldn't be dieting while you're breastfeeding, don't you?"

Klara laughed. "No, no, I'm not on any special diet. And I have more than enough milk for the little man, just look at these sturdy little legs. Here, hold him while I fetch his diapers from the clothesline."

Lettie held the solid little body. She was used to working with babies in the hospital, but they were usually newborn, or sick. This little chap was healthy and beautiful.

"He's lovely, Klara," she said when Klara came back inside and took the baby from her. "Tell me, how did you manage it?"

"Having such a lovely little boy?" Klara asked, surprised.

"No, losing weight without following a special diet. Or are you just naturally slim?"

"Oh no." Klara smiled, deftly pinning on a dry diaper. "It's hard work. I wasn't happy with the way I looked after Cornelius's birth so I decided to watch what I eat. I've been avoiding sugar and starch as far as possible, and I try to stay away from fatty foods."

"What happens when people invite you

for lunch or supper, or when you go home?" Lettie asked. "My mom cooks rich food, and there are always cakes and desserts."

"So does my mom, especially if she wants to impress people. But I try to pick meat or vegetables that haven't been cooked in butter. Or I pick a few tomatoes and a cucumber in the garden. Tomatoes and cucumbers aren't fattening."

"And if you get hungry?" asked Lettie. She seemed to permanently crave something to eat.

"Oh, I'm never really hungry. It's usually just a case of wanting something to chew on. Then I'll eat an apple, that's all. And I exercise. I try to take a walk every day. I put Cornelius in his stroller and take a brisk walk up and down the hills. He loves it!"

That evening Lettie spent a long time staring at the mirror in the ladies' bathroom at the doctors' quarters. If Klara could do it, she could too. If she ended up resembling a rabbit, at least it would be a skinny rabbit.

The next morning Lettie took her tins of rusks and biscuits and beef biltong edged with yellow fat to work. At teatime she took everything to the tearoom. "Help yourselves, there's plenty," she said.

"Goodness, Lettie," said the doctors, "what a treat! Thanks!" They helped themselves to her mom's delicious rusks and biscuits. They carved her dad's fatty biltong in thick slices and dived in.

After teatime she took what was left to the nurses' canteen. "I have something for you," she said cheerfully.

"Dr. Lettie!" they cried. "Thank you, you're a star!" And they dived in as well.

"I'll fetch the tins tomorrow," she said over her shoulder. "Make sure they're empty."

When the vendor rang his bell in the street, she slipped out and bought tomatoes and cucumbers and apples. And a bunch of carrots and a head of lettuce, for good measure.

As she was working over Christmas, Lettie couldn't go home, but at the end of the year she left the General Hospital and prepared to take over her father's practice. She returned home in time to attend De Wet and Christine's New Year's Eve party on the farm.

Her father collected her at the station and drove down the deserted main street, turning left into Voortrekker Street. To the left was the church, flanked by the old vicarage with its wide veranda. Across the street lived Oom Wessie. His front door opened virtually onto the sidewalk, and his entire backyard was taken up by an enormous vegetable garden. At the side of the road young boys were herding cattle back to the stables for the night. Tomorrow morning, when they had finished milking, they would drive the cows and calves back to the common.

A twilight calm descended on the town as the sun set behind the tall steeple of the church.

Lettie drew a deep breath. This was her world. She knew the bushveld air, the early-evening smells and sounds. She was glad she had decided to come back.

Her father turned right into an untarred street and stopped behind their home. Lettie got out and opened the gate, then returned to the car, which her father pulled in and parked. She shut the gate and went up the three steps to the back door. Inside, she smelled her mom's green bean stew.

Over the past few months she had lost pounds and pounds, and for the first time in years — since Form II, she thought — she felt good about herself. Her friends hadn't seen her for months. First she had worked the night shift and then in the emergency room. She'd had no free time to spend with friends.

Her parents had been shocked by the sight

of her. "Lettie, are you ill?" her dad had asked when he fetched her at the station.

At home her mom clapped her hands together. "Child, are you eating enough?" she cried.

Lettie laughed. "I'm fine, I just watch what I eat," she reassured them. "I wanted to lose weight. I feel a lot more . . . attractive."

"You look lovely," her mom admitted, "but don't lose any more weight."

Well, I'm not sure about lovely, Lettie thought an hour later as she admired her new navy-blue dress in the mirror. She had bought it the week before and it had cost her almost all her savings, but she really wanted to look her best tonight. She wanted to lose more weight. She felt good.

When Annabel honked at the gate just after eight after promising to pick Lettie up at seven, Lettie went out with more confidence than ever before.

"What's happened to you?" Annabel asked, clearly surprised. "Did you play doctor at a prison camp?"

Lettie gave her an indulgent smile. "No, I simply decided to shake off some excess baggage," she replied and got into the passenger seat. She turned to the back and addressed Annabel's younger brother. "Hi,

Reinier, how's varsity?"

When they arrived at the farm, De Wet was the first person to see her. "Lettie, you look wonderful," he said sincerely. "What's come over you?"

"A hunger strike," said Annabel, linking her arm with his. "Tell me, how's life treating you?" And she led him away toward the barn.

Outside the barn, the fires were burning high. Inside, there were lanterns, and hay bales to sit on. The band had not yet begun to play, and everyone was gathered around the drinks table.

Klara and Christine came from the direction of the kitchen. "Hello!" Klara called out. "Lettie, you look . . . wow!"

"Oh, Lettie, you look so pretty!" Christine cried, equally surprised.

Lettie felt as if the world were unfolding in front of her. "You're the one who inspired me, Klara," she said, somewhat embarrassed.

Christine took Annabel's hand. "You look beautiful too, Annabel, as usual," she said, "but doesn't Lettie look good?"

"Yes," said Annabel. "Now we must just do something about the hair and the outfit."

"The dress is lovely, so elegant," Klara protested.

"Yes, but the color doesn't suit her. And the dress is . . . ye-es, elegant, but better suited for a woman in her thirties."

Klara's brother Boelie came in from outside. "Boelie," Annabel called and hurried away in her flowing sea-green creation.

"Don't mind her," said Klara and took Lettie's hand.

"I won't." Lettie smiled.

"Come along," said Klara. "I want to introduce you to Antonio's brother Marco."

Chapter Eight

Marco Romanelli was tall, even taller than Antonio, with the same straight nose, thick eyebrows, and dark hair falling over his forehead. But he was painfully thin, and his face had a grayish, unhealthy pallor.

"How do you do?" he said, extending his hand. His voice was the same deep tenor as his brother's.

Lettie took Marco's outstretched hand. His clasp was firm, but his hand was skin and bones. "I'm pleased to meet you," she said in English.

"Lettie is one of our best friends and she's going to be your doctor," Antonio told his brother.

"A female doctor?" Marco said, surprised. *"Ex Africa semper aliquid novi."*

"Out of Africa always something new," said Antonio, casting an amused glance at his brother, as if to say, *I may have been away for a while, but I still know my Latin.*

"Plinius the Elder," Lettie added.

Both brothers turned to look at her, and she noticed their astonished expressions. Then Marco smiled and nodded. "You're right, both of you," he said, but his eyes remained fixed on Lettie.

"When did you arrive?" she asked.

"Beginning of December," he replied. "The heart of summer. The weather is so . . . warm here."

"You're going to boil, just you wait, man from the Alps." Klara laughed.

"I see the meat is done," said Antonio. "Can I dish up for you?"

"That would be nice, thank you," said Marco.

As the brothers walked away, Lettie said, "Goodness, the man is thin!"

"Awful, isn't it?" Klara replied. "He eats the tiniest portions, as if he can't hold down more than a few bites. And he gets so tired! The first three weeks he slept almost night and day. Since we've been here on the farm, he seems slightly better. But it's the coughing that really worries me."

"He must have suffered damage to his lungs." Lettie nodded. "I suppose Antonio is delighted to have his brother here."

"Oh yes. Antonio chose to come here, but I know he misses his fatherland and especially his family. When we picked Marco up at the station, Antonio was in tears. And Christmas . . . it was very touching. I'm really glad Marco is here."

"And will he be teaching?"

"At the high school, yes. I do hope his health improves. He must get healthy and strong again. Please look after him when we go back to Pretoria."

"I will," Lettie promised. "He's officially my first patient. I'll take good care of him."

On Monday Lettie went to the surgery with her father. Her rooms were ready. Her mom had made new drapes and a bedcover, and her dad had put up a brass sign that read *Dr. Lettie Louw.*

She put down her brand-new doctor's bag (a Christmas gift from her dad) and opened the curtains. It was already sweltering. The day was going to be a scorcher.

When she turned from the window, the receptionist, Mrs. Roux, was standing in the doorway. "Your first patient has arrived," she announced and stepped aside.

Marco looked even taller and thinner than he had at the party. "Please come in," she told him.

Antonio appeared behind him. "Sorry we're so early, Lettie," he said, smiling, "but

Klara and I are leaving today. I have to be back at work tomorrow. You probably haven't had time to find your feet yet."

"Don't worry," said Lettie. "I'm quite at home around here. This is where I grew up. Please take a seat."

The two brothers sat facing her — two figures carved from the same block of marble by the same sculptor — one in radiant health, the other pale and emaciated.

"Marco came to South Africa to get well. It's the main reason he's here," Antonio began awkwardly. "He can be a hard nut to crack, but I want him to come and see you every week so you can keep an eye on his progress."

Marco sat calmly, watching her with a slight smile that reached his eyes. When Lettie glanced at him, he said in an amused tone, "Actually, I'm the elder brother, you know!"

"And you allow him to bully you like this?" she played along.

He nodded, pretending to be serious. "It's terrible. But if it means I'm going to be fussed over by an attractive young lady, I'll allow it."

Was he making fun of her? His expression was friendly, and he seemed quite serious. "You're a flatterer, just like your brother," she replied. "Tell me, what are your symptoms?"

"Antonio is in a hurry," Marco remarked. "Please go, Tonio, you have a long drive ahead. I'll manage. I know exactly what's wrong with me. I'll walk back to my lodgings. It's not far." Again with that slight smile.

Antonio got to his feet. "Very well," he said. "Lettie, promise you'll make sure he visits you every week."

"I promise."

The two brothers spoke to each other in Italian, Antonio waving his hands and talking earnestly. Marco nodded and smiled, then laughed and gave his brother a pat on the shoulder. Antonio put his arms around his brother. They kissed each other on both cheeks and said a few more words before Antonio hurried off.

"Good, now we can be properly introduced," Marco said, sitting back down.

They spent the next half hour talking, Lettie writing, Marco waving his hands in the air.

He was different from his brother after all. His voice was more intense than Antonio's, and at the same time softer. He spoke perfect old-fashioned English with an enchanting accent. And his eyes held the hint of a smile even when he was being serious.

She forced herself to focus on nothing but the medical facts. She questioned him in great detail, and he answered as comprehensively as he could. She paid special attention to his diet during the past seven years. The picture became clearer.

"Fine," she finally said. "Now will you remove your clothes, please, and lie on the bed?" She drew back the curtains around the bed.

"Everything?" he asked dubiously.

"No, no," Lettie said. "Shoes and socks and shirt will do."

When she picked up the stethoscope, she noticed a slight tremble in her hands. *It's just because he's my first patient here,* she told herself.

She examined him carefully while he lay stretched out on the bed. "Marco, you're . . . very thin," she observed.

"Yes," he agreed.

"We'll have to do something about that," she said. "I'll do some research on special diets, and I'll speak to Aunt Gertie at the boardinghouse." She listened to his heart and lungs and said, "She can be quite strict with her lodgers, but she has a good heart. Fine," she concluded, stepping back, "you may get dressed now."

"My chest?"

"It's quite congested. We'll keep a close watch on it. I'm going to prescribe a tonic to build your strength, as well as a cough mixture. Does your chest hurt when you cough?"

He shrugged. "A little."

"The medicine will help. Look after yourself and don't catch cold. The pharmacy is next door to the surgery."

"Is it possible to catch cold in this place?" he asked, putting on his shoes.

"You'll be surprised," Lettie replied.

Late that afternoon, as they were driving home, Lettie said to her father, "Marco Romanelli was my first patient this morning."

"I saw him," said her father. "The man is nothing but skin and bone."

"How he survived on what he was fed is a mystery," Lettie said. "I don't think any of us around here know the true meaning of the word *hunger.*"

Christine paid Lettie a visit in her first week at the surgery. She wanted Lettie to see Gerbrand.

"This sturdy little chap?" Lettie said, smiling at the boy, who was watching her with suspicion. "What's wrong with him?"

"He was never . . . er . . . vaccinated

against smallpox as an infant," Christine said uncertainly.

Lettie frowned.

"I was in Egypt during the war . . . ," Christine began to explain. "Then, just before Christmas, De Wet said . . ." She reached out with her hand and stroked the little boy's hair.

"Never mind," Lettie said. "It's good that you've brought him. I'll fetch the vaccine."

"I'm afraid it's not going to be easy," Christine said anxiously.

During her two-year internship at the hospital, Lettie had dealt with plenty of small boys. "Don't worry, it's child's play," she said, kneeling in front of the boy. "Your name is Gerbrand?" she asked, smiling.

The boy glared at her.

Ten minutes later Lettie said, "Well, not quite as easy as I had thought. But I think we're friends again. Did you come to town with your dad?"

"Yes. But . . . er . . . I also wanted to see you," Christine said softly.

"What's wrong?" Lettie asked.

Christine brushed a strand of hair out of her face. "I . . . think I'm pregnant."

"Chrissie, that's wonderful!" Lettie exclaimed. "Get up on the bed, let's take a look. Are you late this month?"

"Ye-es."

"How late?" Lettie asked, handing Gerbrand a toy car from the cupboard.

"Four months," Christine answered.

Lettie looked up, startled. "Four months! Have you seen a doctor?"

Christine shook her head helplessly.

"Well, don't worry," Lettie reassured her. "We'll make sure everything is right."

The little redhead appeared at her side. "Don't hurt my mommy," he said.

Lettie smiled. "I won't, I promise."

He narrowed his eyes, then turned his attention back to the toy car she had given him.

"Tell me, Chrissie, why didn't you come in before now?" Lettie asked, following the routine procedure.

"I was . . . afraid," Christine said very softly.

"There's nothing to be afraid of," Lettie said. "Everything sounds normal, everything looks right. You can get dressed. I suppose De Wet is over the moon?"

"He . . . doesn't know," said Christine.

"Well, then you're going to tell him — tonight," said Lettie. "He'll be ecstatic."

"You think so?"

"Of course," Lettie said firmly.

That night as she lay in bed she thought

of her friend. It must be wonderful for a woman and her husband to know they were going to give birth to a little person.

She rolled over and tried to sleep.

But sleep didn't come.

Lettie began to look forward to Marco's weekly visits. Sometimes they chatted awhile before she examined him. He had a habit of leaning closer when he was listening, looking her in the eye, occasionally nodding, his gaze seeming to reflect her words. His bony hands with the long fingers usually lay calmly folded on the desktop between them.

He asked about her practice, her patients.

"They're mostly children, sometimes women," she answered. "I have only one male patient. Fortunately he comes regularly, to maintain the balance."

Marco smiled. "Not always voluntarily," he said.

They spoke about the school where he was teaching. "It's . . . very strange," he said. "The children are completely different here, the routine as well. And yet, in a strange way, it's the same."

"Can you handle it? I mean, are you strong enough to stand in front of a class all day?"

"I get very tired," he admitted. "But most

afternoons I'm able to rest. I've been excused from sports coaching this term. It's just . . . the coughing that bothers me at times."

"We'll try a different cough mixture," she said. "We'll have to see what works."

During his next visit he spoke of his love of reading since childhood. "Any kind of book, but mostly historical nonfiction. It gives you access to a different world, Lettie. It's probably the one thing I missed most when I was . . . in camp. That, and music."

"How many languages do you speak?" she asked.

"I don't speak them all, but I read quite a few," he answered vaguely.

"And what are you reading at present?"

"I usually read two or three books at the same time, but the one I'm enjoying most at present is a collection of Leonardo da Vinci's writings. I consider him one of the most remarkable minds that has ever lived," he said. "Did you know that, among other things, he sketched a type of helicopter at the beginning of the sixteenth century? The design was highly impractical, but the idea was sound."

Lettie nodded. "He was from your part of the world — from Florence, wasn't he?" she asked.

Marco gave her a surprised look. "You know that?" Then he smiled. "Yes, he was born in the town Vinci in Tuscany, some way south from where we live. But he worked in Milan for a long time, for Ludovico il Moro. That's our part of the world. It's . . . er . . . Not everyone knows where Da Vinci was born."

Another time he told her of his love of music. "I miss good music," he said, speaking of his landlady. "Aunt Gertie's radio is on all day, but it seems she mostly listens to Afrikaans serials. And the music is . . . well . . . not my type of music."

Lettie laughed. "It's probably *boeremusiek* — local instrumental music. My father has a wide variety of classical records. You should come and visit sometime. My dad would love to play you his collection."

"Thank you," he said, nodding. But like most unspecific invitations, it remained hanging in the air.

On a warm Friday afternoon at the end of February, Marco said, "Lettie, these weekly visits are a waste of your time. I'm in better shape than I've been in years."

She smiled and shook her head. "And the cough?" she asked. "I need to monitor your lungs on a weekly basis. Besides, Antonio paid in advance, so you'll just *have* to come, whether you want to or not."

"It's not that I don't want to come," he hastened to assure her. "It's just that I hate wasting your time."

"I'm not all that busy," she said, still smiling. "Besides, winter is imminent, and we must make sure you don't fall ill."

"The way Aunt Gertie's feeding me, you'll have to put me on a diet soon." He smiled, taking off his shoes.

"Hmm," Lettie said after a while. "Looks good. You gained three ounces this week. Let's take a listen to your heart and lungs."

The following Wednesday night the sound of the phone shrilled through the house. The operator kept ringing until Lettie's father picked up. It was a sound Lettie had grown up with. The sound of the phone in the dead of night meant there was an emergency somewhere. In the past she had rolled over and gone back to sleep, but now she jumped out of bed and got dressed.

"Who is it?" she asked, nearly colliding with her father in the passage.

"Neels Fourie called," he replied. "It's his father, Oom Cornelius. Doesn't sound good. He can't breathe. You don't have to come. It could turn into a long night."

"I'm coming," Lettie said, already at the

back door, thinking of Klara's father and grandfather on the farm.

In the car her father said, "He's very weak. I've been expecting the worst for some time. But you never can tell."

They drove on in silence. Lettie looked at her father's hands on the wheel. The hands of an old man who shouldn't be called out in the middle of the night anymore. "You must teach me to drive so I can take the midnight calls," she said as the old Hudson crossed the Pontenilo bridge Antonio helped to build so long ago.

"There's no need. I can do the night calls," her father said. "It doesn't happen all that often."

"Still," Lettie insisted.

When her father stopped at the Old House where Klara's grandparents lived, De Wet's car was parked outside. Inside, all the lights were on.

They were too late, Lettie realized the minute they entered the sickroom. "He's asleep," said Klara's ouma, but it was clear that she knew.

Lettie turned and went to the kitchen. "Let's make coffee," she told the old black woman who stood wringing her hands in front of the stove.

"Cornelius . . . ?" she asked softly.

Lettie shook her head.

The old woman fell to her knees and covered her head with her apron. Somewhat awkwardly Lettie put her hand on the woman's shoulder. The next moment De Wet was there. He knelt beside the old woman and spoke to her gently. "It's better this way, Siena. Oupa won't have to fight for breath any longer. He's at peace now."

"The Lord has come to fetch him," the old woman said in a muffled voice.

De Wet looked up. "Siena and Oupa grew up together," he told Lettie. He got to his feet. "Will you make coffee, Siena, please?" he asked.

"Leave everything to me," she said, getting up with an effort. "Where's Ouma?"

"I'd like to attend the funeral," Marco told Lettie on Friday afternoon. "I didn't know the old gentleman personally, but he's family nonetheless."

"I'll be going as well, for Klara's sake," said Lettie.

"Do you think we could go together?" asked Marco. "I'm not sure how things are done in your church."

"Of course you can come to the funeral with us," Lettie said. "And there isn't much to do. Wear a dark suit and tie and sit quietly."

He smiled. "Sounds irresistible," he said. "A black suit and tie on a February afternoon. It's hot, or haven't you noticed? And sitting quietly during a service of which I don't understand a word sounds like fun."

"It's high time you learned some Afrikaans," Lettie said. "You're in Boer country now. Come, get on the scales and we'll see how you came along this week."

"I'm reading an Afrikaans book," he said as he took off his shoes.

"Does it make sense?" she asked.

"It's a children's book I borrowed from the library, the story of Pinocchio. Fortunately I know it. And there are pictures as well."

She laughed. "Do you read it at bedtime?" she teased.

She was constantly amazed at how easy it was to talk to Marco, even to joke with him. She who had always been struck dumb in the presence of any boy or man.

Suddenly, for no good reason at all, she was looking forward to the funeral. *It's absurd,* she thought, *it's . . . improper.*

She needed a new dress anyway, she decided that evening. She didn't have a black dress. She'd been steadily losing a pound or two every week. Early Saturday morning she found her way to Miss Pronk's dress shop. She chose a black dress, draped over the chest, with a narrow waist and a full skirt that fell in soft pleats.

"My goodness, Lettie, who would have thought you could look so striking!" Miss Pronk said, pleased. She was a tall, thin woman with hair piled high on her head and a nose like a quarter pound of cheese. "You were always such an awkward, chubby little thing. Just look at you now . . . beautiful, yes, gorgeous." Miss Pronk tugged at the dress and touched Lettie's neck. "Your mother's pearls would add the finishing touch." Her gaze fell on Lettie's hair. "And go to the hairdresser's. A new style is what you need."

Lettie shook her head and paid. "Thank you, Miss Pronk," she said. "I'll come back next month for one of your pretty frocks."

"Remember the hairdresser's!" Miss Pronk called after her.

Lettie laughed and waved over her shoulder. *What a strange lady.* But she'd been running her tiny "boutique" for donkey's years.

Back on the street Lettie had second thoughts about her hair. She'd worn it long since junior school. And she didn't have a lovely mane like Annabel's or Klara's. Her hair was too fine. Why not try something new?

On an impulse she walked into Ellen's hair salon. Two ladies were waiting. She was on the point of leaving when Ellen saw her. "Lettie!" she called out. "Sit down. What brings you here?"

"Do you have time?" Lettie asked, suddenly unsure. Should she really have her hair cut? What if she looked silly? She was so used to wearing it in a French roll.

"Of course I have time, dear," Ellen said, producing a comb from her ample bosom. "What are we doing today?"

"I'm . . . not sure. I just feel it's time for a change. Do you think I should cut my hair shorter?"

Ellen removed the hairpins and ran her fingers through Lettie's hair. "You have lovely hair," she said, "but it's thin and fine, with a bit of a wave." She tilted her head and studied Lettie's face from all sides. She delved into her bosom again and produced a pair of scissors. "I think we should cut it short, dear, and see how much curl there is. We can always give you a perm."

Not on your life, Lettie thought. "Do you think so?" she asked anxiously.

"Yes, dear, I do. What do you say?"

"Go ahead," Lettie said recklessly, "it can

always grow again."

Just over an hour later she left the salon feeling light-headed. At home she slipped away to her bedroom and studied her image in the mirror. She looked strange. She felt almost naked.

She continued to gaze at the new short hairstyle. She didn't have Christine's blond curls, just soft waves. She looked younger, she realized, surprised and happy. And stylish.

She stepped back and studied herself from head to toe. She would never look like Annabel, or Klara or Christine, but in her heart was a newfound realization: she was pretty too.

Lettie turned away from the mirror and went to the kitchen in search of her mother.

On Monday they closed the doors of the practice at one — everyone was going to the funeral. Lettie went to the service with her parents. The Fourie family had not yet arrived, and only a few people were standing around. It was hot. "You go on in. I'll wait for Klara," Lettie told her parents.

When she came around the corner, Marco was waiting in the shade. A strange apprehension stirred inside her, and she slowed down. He stood looking up at the steeple, at the bell that was steadily tolling. In his dark suit his tall figure appeared sturdier, his shoulders broader. His hair glinted in the dappled shade, and his face looked aristocratic and strong.

She had never seen him like that.

Then he noticed her and his eyes took her in. She saw the momentary surprise on his face — or perhaps she was imagining it. "Lettie," he said, smiling easily. "You look different!"

"I'm wearing a black dress instead of a white coat," she said flippantly. "Hello, Marco."

"You've cut your hair," he said. "It suits you."

There was an unfamiliar reaction in her body. "Let's go inside, it'll be cooler," she said.

She didn't hear much of the service. She was too aware of the man by her side.

Afterward everyone drove out to the farm for the graveside ceremony and refreshments. She went with her parents, and Marco rode with Antonio and Klara. Night was falling when Lettie went home. Lettie guessed one of the Fouries would give Marco a ride.

"The Romanelli boy looks a lot better than when I last saw him," her mom said later, when they were drinking fruit juice under the mango tree.

"Marco?" Lettie replied. "Yes, he's been gaining weight steadily. It's hard to believe one person can find it so hard to gain weight, while others merely glance at a slice of cake and, well . . ."

"His color is a lot better too," said her father. "But he's still painfully thin. And that cough is disturbing, isn't it?"

"Yes," Lettie said neutrally. The conversation moved on to other things.

I mustn't fall in love with this man, she thought as she lay in bed that night. It would be completely unprofessional. Doctors must keep their distance. Besides, it would be just another hopeless crush. Marco was attractive, charming, talented . . .

With a shock she realized it might already be too late.

Luckily she knew by now how to control her stupid, immature heart. She would not allow her dreams to run rampant again and land her in a dark hole.

When Marco arrived for his weekly appointment the next Friday, Lettie had the situation under control. She went through the usual motions. "From now on you may come and see me every second week," she said as she returned her stethoscope to her coat pocket.

"With winter ahead?" he said. "No, we'd better stick to the weekly routine."

"You're the one who made the suggestion awhile ago," she said.

"Well, that was awhile ago," he said. "So, what have you been getting up to that I don't know about?"

"My dad is teaching me to drive," she said. Too late she remembered her decision not to engage in conversation with him again. It had just happened, spontaneously, easily.

And, after all, a doctor had to talk to her patients.

"I want to learn as well," Marco said eagerly. "It's always been my dream, ever since I was a boy, to have my own car. Antonio has an old Fiat he wants to sell. I can pay him in installments. But for that I need a driver's license."

Lettie nearly suggested that the two of them could learn to drive together. Just in time she remembered the professional distance. "Well, we'll see who gets the license first," she said lightly. "See you next Friday."

Suddenly Lettie's weeks were running from

Friday to Friday. And there was nothing she could do about it.

"The town has gone mad," Marco said one Friday afternoon in March as he stepped into the surgery.

She smiled. "Hello, Marco," she said. "How are you? It's the impending election, somewhere at the end of May, I think. It's what all the posters on the lampposts are about."

"And the noise! They drive through the streets in cars, shouting through loudspeakers." He sat down on the chair facing her. "Hello, Lettie, I'm well, thanks. I'm healthy and I've been cleaning my plate. What are they shouting through the loudspeakers?"

"They're advertising tonight's political meeting," Lettie said, trying to focus on the patient, not the man. "The Natte and Sappe will be taking each other on in the town hall. Step onto the scales."

"It's all everyone at school talks about: the election," Marco said, taking off his shoes. "Give me some background."

"You're asking the wrong person." Lettie laughed. "I know next to nothing about politics."

"I'm glad. I have no interest in politics either," he said and stepped onto the scales.

"Hmm." Lettie nodded, studying the numbers.

"Satisfied?" he asked from above.

"Yes, good, just carry on like this. Let's listen to your chest."

"Who are the Sappe and the Natte?" he asked, stripping off his shirt and lying down on the bed.

"The Sappe are members of the United Party under General Smuts, the prime minister. They're pro-British, I think. I'm not sure. Marco, lie still!"

"The stethoscope is cold," he complained.

"Don't be a sissy," she said, pretending to be strict.

He pulled a face and asked, "And the Natte?"

"They belong to the National Party led by Dr. Malan, and they want a republic. And don't ask me anything more, I don't know. You may put your shirt back on."

"Well, just tell me what most people around here will be voting," he said, sitting up.

"National," she replied, "but there are a number of die-hard Sappe, and that's where all the fighting comes from."

"Are you going to the meeting?" he asked.

"Not on your life."

He gave a slight smile and nodded. "Okay,

then I'll see you next Friday," he said.

He left.

Suddenly the surgery was empty.

Irene Fourie would be coming of age during the April vacation, and her parents and brother De Wet were planning a big birthday party on the farm. Klara, Antonio, and Boelie would be coming from Pretoria. And Annabel, who no longer hid her hard pursuit of Boelie, was specially coming for the weekend from somewhere in the Western Transvaal, where she was a journalist. "You can catch a ride to the party with Reinier and me," Annabel said to Lettie on the phone.

The morning of the party Lettie went to Ellen's salon. In the afternoon she took a cold shower so as not to get her hair steamed up and lay on her bed with cucumber slices on her eyelids. She wasn't quite sure why, but it seemed to be the thing to do. She put on a new dress and shoes and added a touch of color to her lips. "I see I'm going to have to keep the shotgun within reach. The young men are going to be queuing up," her dad teased when she joined her parents in the front room.

Less than ten minutes later — in reasonably good time for a change — Annabel appeared in the doorway, dressed in a tight-fitting emerald-green creation. She wore stiletto heels, and sparkling earrings dangled from her ears.

"Gosh, Annabel, you look lovely," Lettie said sincerely.

"Thanks." Annabel looked her up and down. "This rich, earthy shade looks much better on you than those somber colors you usually wear. And you've really lost weight," she said, sounding pleased.

It was the closest Annabel had ever come to giving her a compliment.

They had just passed the church when Annabel slammed on the brakes. "There's something I've been wanting to do for a long time," she said and turned the car around.

"What's up?" Reinier asked from the back.

"I'm going home. We won't be long," Annabel said. "Wait in the car."

"We're going to be late again," he groaned. "Irene said —"

"Irene can wait," said Annabel. "What *we* have to do is much more important."

"We?" Lettie asked skeptically.

"You and I," said Annabel. "Come, here we are, let's go to my bedroom."

Lettie followed Annabel through the quiet house. "Sit," said Annabel. "Hold the reading lamp like this. No, take off your glasses first."

"Annabel, what are you going to do?" Lettie asked anxiously.

"Shape your eyebrows," said Annabel. "These bushy brows have got to go. Since you've evidently decided to do something about your appearance, this is my contribution." She got busy with a pair of tweezers.

"Ouch!" Lettie cried, jerking her head away. "You're hurting me!"

"Sit still," Annabel said strictly. "One has to suffer for the sake of beauty."

Lettie gritted her teeth. "Are you plucking out everything?" she asked after a while. "I don't want to look like a plucked chicken!"

"No, I'm just shaping them." Annabel took a step back to judge her handiwork. "There, one eye is finished. See how you like it."

Lettie put her glasses back on and looked in the mirror. "It . . . makes a big difference," she said, amazed. "But my eyelid is red."

"Nothing makeup can't fix," said Annabel and set to work on the second eyebrow. "Now you just have to get new glasses, with a thinner frame. These black ones are really horrible."

When they reached the car almost half an

hour later, Lettie knew the pain had been worth it. Strange she'd never thought of shaping her eyebrows herself.

"What have you girls been doing all this time?" Reinier asked, annoyed.

"Working on Lettie's appearance," Annabel replied.

"Oh." Reinier sounded surprised. "She looked fine to me."

Irene's twenty-first birthday party was like another wedding reception. The sea of cars outside the barn showed that most people had already arrived. "See? We're late," Reinier said as he climbed out of the car, hurrying ahead.

"Brothers are a pain," said Annabel.

Klara and Christine came to meet them — Klara in a brightly patterned skirt and white satin blouse. Christine was wearing a baby-blue frock with a full skirt and matching shoes. "Hello, you two!" Klara called out cheerily. "Wow, you look smashing!"

It became a merry reunion until the two mommies had to go and care for their little ones. "Come, let's see where Boelie and De Wet are," Annabel suggested.

Boelie was talking to Antonio and a few other men, but when he saw Annabel, he immediately came toward them. "Come join us," he said.

Everyone exchanged pleasantries, saying how good it was to meet again. "You look lovely, Lettie," Antonio remarked.

"Thanks," said Lettie.

Marco was nowhere to be seen. She thought he had been invited as well.

"Can I fetch you a drink?" De Wet asked Lettie and Annabel when he joined them. "Or why don't you come along and see for yourself what there is?"

They went with him to the barn. Inside, the tables were laden with cold leg of lamb, chicken pie, onion salad, curried bean salad, freshly baked farm loaves, and homemade butter. There was a variety of pastries: milk tarts, jam tartlets, *koesisters.*

There was still no sign of Marco.

"How can you watch what you eat when you're faced with all this?" Lettie asked Klara, who had rejoined them.

"Oh, just make the right choice," Klara said easily. "Take a lean slice of lamb, some curried beans, that tomato that was actually meant for garnish. And leave the bread and butter."

"Oh, it's hard," Lettie groaned.

"But worth it, don't you think?"

"Definitely. Where's Cornelius?"

"Asleep. My gran is looking after him. She

doesn't feel up to joining the party."

"I can understand that. Is Marco here?" Lettie asked as casually as possible.

"Yes, he's around somewhere," Klara said vaguely. "Probably outside, at his car. Boelie drove Antonio's Fiat here for Marco. He'll be driving back to Pretoria with us. Marco is so pleased, he's probably still admiring the car." She gave Lettie a conspiratorial nod. "If we're very good with our diet, we deserve something sweet, don't you think?"

Awhile later the band began to play and Lettie sat down on a hay bale. She was used to watching the dancers. She'd perfected the art of being a wallflower.

At the end of the first dance, Antonio asked her for the next one. "I'm not a very good dancer," she warned him.

"That makes two of us," he said, taking her firmly by the hand.

But Antonio danced like a dream. "You wicked liar, you're an excellent dancer," she said.

"So are you." He smiled.

"Oh, and you're a first-class flatterer as well as a liar," said Lettie.

Antonio laughed and twirled her round. "Thanks," he said at the end of the dance, "we'll do it again later."

When they walked back to where Klara and Christine were sitting, De Wet stepped forward. "The next one is mine," he said. "Since you're my wife's doctor, you'll have to stand in for your chubby little friend!"

Back on the dance floor, she noticed Marco on the other side of the room. He was standing near the doorway, talking to one of the young teachers at his school. Lettie looked away.

The band began to play a medley of country tunes. The concertina pulled and pushed, the banjo picked up speed. De Wet sang along in full voice. They whirled around the floor. At the end of the number, Lettie threw her hands in the air. "De Wet, you've danced me off my feet," she said, laughing.

"Time for a drink," he said, laughing as well. "Let's join my lovely wife."

When Lettie looked in the direction of the barn door, Marco was no longer there.

She danced with other men as well: Oom Freddie, reeking of tobacco; Oom Bartel, who held her a touch too tightly; Boelie, who had momentarily escaped from Annabel.

From the corner of her eye, she saw Marco talking to one of the band members and inspecting his piano accordion. Awhile later she saw him dance with Klara and chat with Christine. But the evening was going by and she had not spoken to him yet. It was better this way, of course. She must focus on enjoying herself and forget about him.

She looked around at the partygoers. Reinier had danced with no one but Irene. So that's how it was.

She had dressed with such care, and she thought she looked rather pretty tonight. But he hadn't even seemed to . . .

She admonished herself.

The band struck up a new tune. Marco's deep voice suddenly spoke beside her.

"You've been so busy all night, I haven't been able to dance with you at all."

Her heart leaped as shock ran through her veins. She looked up.

He was standing in front of her, bowing slightly, holding out his hand.

"It's a doctor's duty to dance with her patient," he said, smiling down at her.

"Where did you hear that?" she asked, outwardly calm. "Isn't it the doctor's duty to keep a professional distance?"

Why had she said such a dumb thing?

But Marco merely laughed. "Well, we'll just have to pretend that you're not a doctor tonight. Come," he said easily, taking her hand.

Her heart began to beat wildly.

He swung her into the crook of his arm and began to move easily, in tune with the music.

She was aware of his hand on her back, her hand on his upper arm, her other hand folded in his.

He must be able to feel my heart racing, she thought, mortified.

They danced in silence at first. Then he began to hum along with the familiar tune. She listened, enchanted by his rich voice, lost in a haze of happiness.

When the dance was over, she returned to her seat between Klara and Christine.

He came back to ask her to dance one more time. This time she was prepared. She even managed to joke with him during the dance. When Klara suggested that the men fetch more comfortable chairs — "These hay bales are getting pricklier by the minute" — Marco placed her chair next to his own.

Lettie saw Boelie dance with the bywoner girl, Pérsomi — no longer a girl but a lovely young woman. She was sister to Gerbrand Pieterse, who had died in Egypt before the end of the war, leaving Christine and their ginger-haired son behind. Lettie realized she must stop thinking of Pérsomi as a bywoner. She had done well in school and would soon be a qualified attorney working in the De Vos law firm alongside De Wet.

"What are you thinking?" Marco asked beside her.

"I'm . . . just watching the dancers," she replied.

Then she noticed Annabel's expression across the dance floor. Annabel's mouth was a grim line, her eyes slightly screwed up, her hands clenched into fists.

At the end of the number, Annabel strode across the dance floor, clearly furious. "I'm leaving," she said. "Now. Come." She tossed back her long hair with a movement of her head.

Lettie bent down to retrieve her evening bag from under the chair.

Marco laid a hand on her arm. "Stay," he said.

She looked up. His face was close to hers, his eyes serious, as always, but also tender.

Lettie drew a deep breath. Her heart was beating uncontrollably in her throat. "I came with Annabel and Reinier," she said. "They want to go."

"I'll take you home," he said. His expression was very serious, almost intense.

Lettie licked her dry lips. "Okay," she said softly.

He held out his hand, withdrew it again. "Thank you," he said, equally softly.

Chapter Nine

"Why don't you invite the Romanelli boy for lunch on Sunday?" Lettie's mom said one Friday morning. "It must be lonely for him all on his own in the boardinghouse over weekends."

"Oh, there are other young people at Aunt Gertie's," Lettie said. "The new bank clerk lives there, and the math teacher at the high school." The one Marco had such a long conversation with at Irene's birthday party, Lettie recalled. "But I'll ask him, thanks, Mom."

"We could listen to some music. You said he's fond of classical music?" her dad said.

"I think he'd like that," Lettie agreed.

So it came that they had a visitor after church on Sunday. Lettie's mom had put the roast in the oven long before the service began to be sure it would fall off the bone, and Lettie had laid the table with the crisp, white damask tablecloth, stiffly starched napkins, and crystal wineglasses. They did not have lunch in the kitchen on Sundays.

When Lettie returned to the lounge with the coffee tray, she found her dad and Marco at the cabinet with the leaded glass inserts, going through the record collection. "You have a diverse collection, Doctor," Marco said appreciatively. "I grew up with some of this music, mostly the Italian singers. Some of the others are unknown to me."

"I've been building my collection over the years," said her dad, and Lettie heard the pride in his voice. "What would you like to hear?"

"Here's your coffee," Lettie said behind them and put the tray on the table. The two men turned: one short, round, and bald, the other tall and thin, with thick black hair. "You'll only have time for one or two records. Lunch will be served in ten minutes."

"Could we listen to Tito Schipa?" Marco asked as Lettie left the room. "He's really . . ." She didn't hear the last part of the sentence.

After lunch her mom lay down for a nap and her dad joined them in the lounge. "Italy has produced a number of great masters over the years," he said, selecting a shiny black record with a red label from the shelf. Her dad put the record on the turntable, switched on the gramophone, and carefully lowered the needle. The Victor label spun around.

"We had no electricity when I grew up. Our gramophone had to be wound by hand," said Marco.

"It was the same on the farm," said her dad.

The recording had probably been made sometime around 1910, but from the scratching sounds emerged a pure tenor singing "Santa Lucia."

"Enrico Caruso, the greatest of all tenors," Marco said immediately.

They listened in silence. Marco's eyes were shut, his face relaxed.

"Not only does this man have a golden voice," her dad said when the music stopped, "but there's also a wonderful honesty in his interpretation." Carefully he lifted the record off the turntable and returned it to its sleeve.

"There's music just in his name," said Marco. "Enrico Caruso — six syllables containing all five vowels."

Her dad nodded as he searched for another record. "Do you have anything by Galli-Curci?" asked Marco.

"Oh yes," her dad replied, "but first I'd

like you to listen to this." He handled the next record with care. "This is a copy of Caruso's very first recording — at least, for the gramophone. Evidently he made a few cylinder recordings earlier. This recording was made in a hotel room in Milan in April 1902. Ten recordings were made that day in only two hours."

Her father eased the needle onto the revolving disc, and the piano accompaniment began. The record was very scratched and had an almost flat sound, but the voice was unmistakable.

"In 1902, you say?" Marco asked when the record was finished. "Forty-six years ago? Amazing."

"Back then, records were made of wax, an extremely brittle material that had to be discarded after a while," her dad said, putting the record away. "Thanks to modern technology we are able to preserve this music. Well, I'm going to take a nap as well. You two carry on if you wish."

When her dad had left, Marco turned to her. "It's wonderful," he said. "Can we keep listening for a while?"

"Of course!" Lettie smiled. "Choose what you like."

He spent a long time at the shelf, studying the records one by one, taking a few from the shelf. "What do *you* like?" he asked.

"I love the Neapolitan songs," she said, almost apologetically. "But do play your Galli-Curci first."

At last he chose a recording of Galli-Curci with Tito Schipa, "*Parigi, o cara,*" from Verdi's *La Traviata.* "I hope you'll enjoy it too," he said, sitting down on the soft leather sofa and stretching his legs in front of him.

The sun fell through the open window, where the heavy velvet drapes were almost completely open. A column of light fell on the bright Persian carpet and reached Marco's feet. Behind him the dark wooden wall panels gleamed. To his left, next to the double doors leading to the passage, hung her mother's brand-new painting by Jacobus Hendrik Pierneef — the one she was so proud of.

The music filled the entire room.

When it faded away and the needle kept dragging, making a scratching sound, Marco got up and selected another record from the shelf. He bent down and slowly lowered the needle. Then he sat back down and smiled at Lettie. "Neapolitan," he said.

They listened to Jussi Björling's version of "*Nessun dorma,*" Caruso's cheery "*La donna è mobile,*" Beniamino Gigli, and the bass Ezio Pinza.

Through it all she sat watching him. He didn't notice. He was lost in another world, a different world on the other side of the globe. He leaned with his head against the sofa, his face upturned, his eyes shut. He looked happy. She was glad.

When Marco chose another Schipa recording, Lettie asked, "You like Schipa?"

Marco nodded, his eyes soft. "When I was at university in Turin, a group of us once went to Milan by train, to La Scala opera house," he said slowly. "It was a wonderful experience. We saw *La Traviata,* with Tito Schipa in the role of Alfredo."

"You saw Tito Schipa in the flesh in *La Traviata*?" Lettie asked.

The look he gave her seemed to be sizing her up. Then he nodded slowly.

"You know opera?"

"Oh yes, I know *La Traviata.* I can't believe you actually heard Schipa sing. It must have been wonderful."

"Do you know *Il Trovatore* as well?" he asked.

"The Troubadour? I know it, yes. The story is a bit far-fetched, but the music is heavenly — just very difficult, or so they say. I don't know enough about music to be able to tell. I just enjoy it," she said.

He looked at her with a slight shake of the head. "You know more than enough. I'm so pleased, Lettie," he said seriously.

"Tell me about La Scala, Marco," she said. "It's a dream of mine to see an opera there one day. And . . . you've done it."

"Maybe . . ." He paused, blinked a few times, gestured with his hands. "The theatre has almost three thousand seats. Over the boxes, there's a gallery, the *loggione,* where the poorer people can enjoy the performance. It's where I used to sit with my fellow students. We could still see and hear everything."

She listened to his voice, she looked at the slim hands with the long fingers, and she became aware of his deep yearning for home.

She wished she could put her hand on his arm.

"We went to La Scala only twice in the three years I was at university," he said, a faraway look in his eyes. "We took the train. Milan is about a hundred miles from Turin, and students can't actually afford train tickets."

"Who else did you see perform?" she asked.

"The second time we saw the soprano Pia Tassinari."

He kept talking about shows they attended in Turin. "We were lucky," he said. "In the 1920s, all our best singers went to America, mostly to the Metropolitan Opera House in New York, of course. But the depression brought many back to Italy, especially to northern Italy, where most of them originally came from. That's why we were able to see them back then."

Lettie realized that getting him to talk about his past might be therapeutic. But not now. Later, in the surgery.

At six they had a supper of leftover cold cuts and bread with her parents. "Shall I scramble some eggs?" her mom asked.

"No, no, this is lovely, thanks, ma'am," Marco said.

"Please call me Issie," said her mom.

"Issie?"

"Short for Isabel."

"Isabella." He spoke the name like a melody. "Beautiful," he said and turned to Lettie. "And your full name?"

"Aletta."

"Aletta?" Again the unusual cadence, the unfamiliar accent that changed the ordinary name into a song. "Alét-ta."

When Christine came for her routine checkup early in May, Lettie said, "This baby is going to be born soon. From now on I want to see you once a week."

"Okay," said Christine. She looked up. "Lettie, I'm so afraid."

Lettie's hands grew still. "Why?"

"Gerbrand's birth . . . it was very hard."

"It's always easier the second time," Lettie reassured her. "And I'll be with you all the way."

"Promise you'll come at once when I call you?" Christine's blue eyes were filled with trust.

"I promise." Lettie nodded, smiling. "I'll be at the hospital when you arrive. Just call before you leave the farm."

"Thanks," said Christine. "I think you're the best doctor in the whole world."

Lettie laughed. "I don't know about being the best, Chrissie, but I'll certainly do my very best for you."

"Come for lunch on Sunday," Christine said as she was leaving. "De Wet has asked Marco as well. Maybe he could give you a ride."

"Thanks, I'll ask him," said Lettie.

But during her coffee break half an hour later, she wondered if it was a good idea.

"I think you should start with an exercise program, Marco," Lettie said that Friday afternoon. "I've read a bunch of articles in medical journals that stress the benefits of regular exercise, especially for the heart and lungs."

"Do you think there's something wrong with my heart?" he asked, but she heard the teasing note in his voice.

"What sports did you play before the war?" she persisted.

"I was on my residence's soccer team at university," he said, running his fingers through his dark hair.

"We don't play soccer in the bushveld," she said, shaking her head.

"And I used to row. Our university had a strong rowing club," Marco said, the familiar smile tugging at the corners of his mouth.

"Oh my word, no, we only have the Nile. Once or twice a year it's in flood, but the rest of the time it's almost stagnant, with only a few muddy pools. No, rowing won't work here."

"I see." By now the laughter was clear in his eyes. "Oh, and we used to climb the mountain. I belonged to the mountaineering club."

Lettie began to laugh. "Marco, you're having me on. You know very well the only mountain around here is the one on the

Fouries' farm. And someone who grew up in the foothills of the Alps wouldn't even call it a molehill. But you're still going to exercise, you mark my words."

"You . . . er . . ." He pointed at her face.

Self-consciously she ran her hand over her cheek. A crumb from her sandwich at lunch-time?

"You have a dimple in your cheek when you laugh," he said, sounding amazed.

"Oh?" she said, confused.

He gave a slight shake of his head. "We'll have to see on Sunday if De Wet's mountain can be climbed, or at least explored," he said, getting to his feet. "I believe you're going to the farm with me on Sunday."

Lettie felt her heart contract. "I . . . er . . . haven't decided, Marco."

"Of course you're going," he said firmly. "You have a duty to make sure your patient gets the right kind of exercise." At the door he turned. "See you Sunday after church."

Early on May 24, 1948, just two days before the election, De Wet called, not sounding like his usual charming self at all. "Lettie, I'm driving Christine to the hospital," he blurted.

"I'll meet you there," Lettie said calmly. "And, De Wet?"

"Yes?"

"Calm down. Nothing's going to happen in the next hour."

"Heavens, Lettie, I'm a nervous wreck."

She gave a soft laugh. "Everything will be fine. Trust me."

There was a moment's silence on the other side of the line. Then he said earnestly, "I'm glad you're going to be there, Lettie. Thanks."

"Drive carefully now."

It turned into a long morning. Christine was anxious, unable to relax, no matter what Lettie tried. De Wet paced the waiting room floor like a trapped racehorse. "Go have coffee in town," Lettie suggested.

"No, I'd rather wait here," he said.

At a quarter past three, baby Anna Margaretha was born without any complications. "It's all over and you have a perfect little girl." Lettie smiled.

"Thank you, thank you, Lettie," said Christine. "You're the best doctor in the entire world, and the best friend anyone could have. Can De Wet come in now?"

"Let's put on your bed jacket and brush your hair," the attending sister said, "before I call him."

Soon there was a soft knock on the door. "Come in, De Wet. Meet your daughter,"

Lettie said, stepping aside.

"Look at our lovely little girl," Christine said softly.

Lettie closed the door behind her.

"So the Nats won against all odds?" Marco said when he entered the surgery the Friday after the elections.

Lettie looked up. He was still in the gray pants and white shirt he must have worn to school that morning, though he had removed his tie. His tanned face showed up against the white shirt — *so different from his pallid skin tone when he first arrived,* she thought briefly — and his shoulders were broad and straight under the thin fabric of the shirt.

Lettie drew a deep breath to restore her calm. "Don't tell me you're also going to talk about the election," she exclaimed. "It's all every patient I've seen today has talked about."

"Including Christine?" Marco asked, removing his shoes.

Lettie laughed. "You're right. Christine couldn't care less about politics. All she wants to talk about is her baby."

"How is she?" Marco asked as he stepped on the scales. "Hmm, don't look. I didn't gain any weight this week," he said.

"Both Christine and the baby are well. I saw her this morning," Lettie said. "Marco, you've lost two ounces!"

"Hmm," he said and began to take off his shirt, "but I've gained twenty pounds since arriving here. That's a pound a week. I'd say that's really good."

Lettie shook her head. "You're right. How do you feel?"

"Fine, just fine. Listen to my heart so I can get dressed. It's cold."

She nodded. "You see, it *does* get cold in the bushveld," she said.

"Cold is a relative concept," he said. "When can Christine go home?"

"Probably next Friday. New mothers usually recuperate in the hospital for ten days," she said. "Why don't you pay her a visit? The baby is lovely. Okay, you may get dressed."

"I . . . don't think so," said Marco.

"But you've just complained about the cold!"

"No, I don't think I'll go see her. I don't like hospitals," he said from behind the curtain.

"Oh." Lettie filled out his chart. "I hear you're having an end-of-term concert."

"Who told you?" he asked, emerging from behind the curtain.

"Our receptionist. She's been selling tickets."

"Yes, well . . ." He sank down on the chair at her desk.

Lettie put the chart away. Turning to him, she said, "Marco, I want you to start telling me about the war years."

He looked up warily.

"It would be good for you to talk about it, in your own time," she said calmly. "It'll be therapeutic."

"It will be hard," he said quietly.

"We can do it little by little, every Friday. Just as much as you feel up to."

"You think it's . . . necessary?"

"I don't know if it's necessary, Marco," she said honestly, "but I know it's good to talk about the traumas in one's life. Bad experiences that are suppressed tend to fester."

He was quiet for a long time. "You're right," he said at last, "but I don't want to waste your time."

"I'm your doctor, Marco. I'm responsible for your total well-being. You definitely won't be wasting my time."

She wasn't expecting him to start at once, but he did. "I hid out with a Jewish family in the mountains above the village where I lived. It was the end of June 1940."

Lettie already knew that. Before Marco came, Antonio had talked about he knew, though it wasn't much. Yet she listened quietly.

Marco spoke as if he were delivering a factual history lecture — detailed, but detached. He did not look at her, but through the window behind her back. His eyes gave nothing away. His hands lay folded on the desk between them. Occasionally he raised them to make a gesture.

He told her about the ascent one moonless night, the cave they stayed in, the first icy winter, their food. He explained how frugally they worked with the candles and kerosene, how they wove screens from branches to block the mouth of the cave, how they punched holes in the side of a tin can and filled it with hot coals to get some warmth in the cold winter nights.

"It wasn't so cold inside. Our biggest problem was passing the time." His deep voice spoke calmly. "We cleaned and gathered wood and edible plants and fruits. In summer, of course. The rest of the time we read and talked and made music. At the beginning it was fine." He paused, then looked at his watch. "Heavens, look at the time! Your next patient must be waiting."

"On a Friday you're my last patient,

Marco," Lettie said. "But, okay, we can continue next Friday."

"Did we achieve anything?" he asked skeptically.

"We made a start," she said. "That's important."

But when he had left, she knew they had not yet achieved anything. She also realized that in the half hour or so he'd been talking, he had not mentioned a single name. He'd mentioned facts, but not people — least of all himself.

Sunday afternoons began to shift. After church Marco sometimes had lunch with Lettie's family, and they spent the afternoon listening to music or walking down the town's deserted streets to the common, or just talking in the kitchen. Sometimes they sat reading.

"It says here in the medical journal," Lettie said one Sunday, "that three scientists from the Boston Children's Hospital have managed to cultivate the poliomyelitis virus in a laboratory."

"In Boston?" Marco asked. "Polio has been spreading in America."

"Here too," said Lettie. "And there's no treatment or vaccine. This could be a great breakthrough."

"I don't know the disease at all. We never encountered it," said Marco.

"No, I don't suppose you would have — it's more prevalent in warmer regions, where there's poor sanitation. It's often spread by contaminated water."

"Is it a reasonably new disease?" he asked.

"Oh no, some Egyptian hieroglyphs show figures with one short leg and a club foot. But it was found only in certain areas and not on a large scale. Serious outbreaks of infantile paralysis have only been known since the beginning of this century, especially in urban areas in the summer months. But now it's popping up elsewhere, especially in America."

No matter the subject, their companionship was easy, as if they'd known each other for years rather than a mere six months. Once in a while they drove to Pretoria to visit Klara and Antonio.

More often, Marco picked her up in his Fiat and they drove out to the farm. Gerbrand was always over the moon to see Marco. He was distrustful of Lettie — especially after she'd given him a tetanus shot when a rusty wire had hurt his foot.

After lunch one Sunday Christine, De Wet, Marco, and Lettie sat on the big old veranda in the bushveld sun, making lazy afternoon conversation. Boelie was coming back to the farm, which he'd inherited when his oupa died. De Wet feared strain between Boelie and their father. Annabel had taken a job in London.

"Annabel? London?" Lettie asked, surprised.

"Yes, a two-year contract as an international correspondent for National Press," De Wet said.

"Wow!" said Lettie. "Sounds amazing."

"Hmm, but London is a long way from home," Christine said. She bit her lower lip. "Does anyone want coffee?" she asked hastily.

"No, relax, I'll make coffee in a while," De Wet said lazily.

A few moments later Anna began to cry in the bedroom, and Christine jumped to her feet. "She must be hungry," she said.

"I'll come too," Lettie said, following her down the dark passage.

The room looked entirely like Christine and nothing like De Wet. The walls were painted a light rose, the curtains had a pink floral design, and the big four-poster bed with the lace frill was covered with a pink satin bedspread.

Christine picked up the baby and laid her down on the table for a diaper change. "I feel terrible about what I just said. I wasn't thinking," she said as she sat down to feed the baby.

Lettie gave a slight frown. "What are you talking about? You didn't say anything wrong," she said, sitting down on the edge of the bed.

"Oh yes, I did! I said London is a long way from home. Marco is a long way from home, Lettie. He must be so homesick!"

"Don't worry, Christine, Marco is a grown man. He came here for the climate. He knows he had to get away from the cold," Lettie reassured her.

"You don't think I upset him?" asked Christine.

"I know you didn't."

Christine nodded. "Then I'm glad." She gave Lettie an earnest look. "You and Marco are good friends, aren't you?"

"Yes," said Lettie, "we are."

"Is there something more?"

Lettie shook her head. "No. No, there's nothing more."

"He's a wonderful man," Christine continued, holding Anna upright. "He's attractive, actually quite beautiful, now that he's put on some weight and got a bit of sun on his skin."

Lettie began to laugh. "You can't say a

man is beautiful!"

"Men are beautiful to me," Christine said earnestly. "De Wet is very beautiful, you can't argue with that. And Marco is beautiful too, Lettie. You should look."

She'd been looking a long time. She couldn't help it. Aloud she said, "All right then, they are two beautiful men."

"And Marco is clever and charming." Christine's eyes were fixed on Lettie.

Lettie sighed. "I know all that, Chrissie. But we're really just good friends, wonderful friends." She paused, then said, "And I don't think it will ever change."

Christine sat on her bed, the baby nodding to sleep against her shoulder. Outside a bird called for its mate.

"Lettie," Christine asked softly, "are you in love with him?"

She felt a great sadness drift up like a lazy bubble from someplace deep inside her and lodge itself in her throat. A primal sadness.

She gave Christine a lopsided smile. "Ye-es," she said, "I think I am, a little."

When Christine spoke again, her voice was tender. But it sounded strangely mature. "I know what it feels like," she said. "No one knows, except Klara, but I was in love with De Wet for a very long time, since my school days, even before I left for Egypt. And . . .

then I still missed him. I know that sadness."

Lettie just nodded. She'd been in love before, and she managed to go on with her busy life in spite of the pain. She'd do it again. "I'll be fine, Chrissie, don't worry. Is Anna asleep again?"

"Yes." Christine smiled and got to her feet. "Let's join those beautiful men."

The annual school concert always drew a crowd, but the hall was hardly ever filled to capacity as it was tonight.

"Remember the night you fell asleep onstage?" Christine asked De Wet as Lettie led them to the third row from the front, where she had saved seats. "You were the lead singer and you fell asleep in your chair!"

Lettie joined in the laughter. "Klara was furious!"

"Yes, it was 1938 and I'd stayed up the night before, listening to the election results," De Wet said, "and I'd played rugby that morning. No wonder I couldn't keep my eyes open!"

"Can you believe that was ten years ago?" said Christine. "It feels like yesterday."

Nothing had changed in that time. The hall with its wooden parquet floor, the rows of straight-backed wooden chairs, the stage, the heavy dark-blue curtains — everything looked exactly the same, just slightly smaller than she remembered.

"Your new glasses are beautiful," Christine said.

"Thank you. I had to get new lenses so I thought I ought to get new frames as well. You can get such nice ones nowadays."

The trio took their seats. Lettie was filled with an unfamiliar happiness. She loved her work and her friends. Even Annabel. She might not be tactful, but she gave good advice. She supposed being honest with one's friends was part of good friendship too, even if the truth stung a little.

"Penny for your thoughts," Christine said beside her.

"I'm thinking about Annabel."

"Yes, she used to be here with us. All the years she was your best friend."

Lettie would not go quite that far, but yes, Annabel was her friend.

At a quarter past seven — fifteen minutes late — the principal mounted the three steps to the stage. The audience clapped. He opened the proceedings with a Scripture reading and prayer, welcomed the audience, and thanked an almost endless number of people.

The audience applauded again.

Then the curtains opened and the concert began. There were poetry and piano recitals, solos and duets, a child using a saw as a musical instrument (rather ineptly, but still), and even a dance item or two. It was an ordinary school concert where everyone, regardless of talent, was granted their moment onstage. But the audience enjoyed the show, because it was *their* school and *their* children.

At the intermission the senior girls sold coffee and koesisters on the porch outside.

The choirs performed in the second half. The junior choir sang a number of lighter folk songs, and the senior choir gave a rendition of sacred music. Finally the combined choir delivered two patriotic songs. "It's still the same as when we were here," Christine whispered. "Remember all the hours we spent sitting side by side on these hard seats, Lettie?"

The principal, who was acting as master of ceremonies, appeared onstage and announced, "For our final performance, our senior girls will sing a few popular love songs. I hope you enjoy it, ladies and gentlemen."

The curtains slid open. The lighting was soft. From behind the curtains four Form I pupils were blowing soap bubbles. The bubbles drifted over the stage and up to the ceiling, creating small rainbows before they vanished.

"Oh, how beautiful," Christine whispered.

Six girls in long, flowing dresses with flowers in their hair came onstage. The piano began to play, and the girls twirled round so that their wide skirts billowed around their feet. They began to sing "Can't Help Lovin' Dat Man" from *Showboat,* the musical.

"Lovely," Christine whispered.

Their next song was "Have I Told You Lately That I Love You?" Halfway through the number a violin joined in from behind the curtain.

"Oh!" Christine sighed, ecstatic.

"That must be Marco. I know he plays the violin," Lettie whispered.

"Really?" whispered Christine. "It's beautiful."

"I just love Jeanette MacDonald and Nelson Eddy's movies." Christine sighed when the girls sang "Ah, Sweet Mystery of Life."

"It's lovely," Lettie whispered back. She was smiling, enchanted by the scene. The music had drawn her in. She was glad she had come.

The piano introduced the next song: "Indian Love Call," from the film *Rose-*

Marie. The voices joined in, and the girls held their wide skirts, twirled, and formed a semicircle.

"Wonderful!" Christine whispered.

The next moment a male voice came from behind the curtain, a pure, strong tenor.

Lettie drew a sharp breath and clasped her hands together, her eyes fixed on the stage.

The man stepped into the spotlight. He was wearing a dark dress suit and a crisp white shirt. His tall figure was proud and erect.

"It's Marco!" whispered Christine.

Slowly he crossed the stage to the center. His voice carried all the way to the back of the hall.

The girls faded into the background.

Marco's voice filled the hall.

The audience was captivated.

Slowly Lettie let out her breath and looked down at her hands. She felt totally defenseless, as if she were being torn apart, exposed.

No, she thought, *no, please.*

She'd been in love before, but never like this.

She closed her eyes, tried to shut herself off, no longer able to look at him.

But his voice reached every hidden corner

of her heart.

Applause erupted.

Lettie opened her eyes. Around her people were clapping and cheering, jumping to their feet, shouting, "Encore! Encore!"

"Lettie, you're crying!" Christine said, dismayed.

"No, no, it's just . . . it was so lovely," said Lettie, brushing her hand over her eyes. "Chrissie, I . . . my head aches and I'm tired. I'm going to leave now. Will you tell Marco . . . ?" She made a helpless gesture with her hands.

Her friend nodded. She understood. "Go," she said. "We're leaving as well, just as soon as we've spoken to Marco."

Dear Lord, Lettie prayed on her way home, *why did You bring this man all the way from Italy to this town?*

Quietly she slipped in at the back door of her parents' house and tiptoed to her room. She could hear them listening to music in the living room.

How could she ever listen to that music again without seeing him?

She curled up under her duvet.

How could she continue with a normal friendship? After tonight, it would be impossible.

She buried her face in her pillow.

She didn't know how they could continue being nothing but friends, but she knew she could no longer be his doctor. She could no longer trust herself to be professional.

Early the next morning the phone rang. Lettie jumped out of bed. She didn't want her father to wake up unnecessarily. He'd been looking tired recently.

But there was no emergency. It was Klara's excited voice. "Christine called last night, in the middle of the night!" she said. "She told us about the concert and Marco's singing. Since then, there's been no stopping Antonio. We're leaving for the bushveld in an hour to see the concert tonight. Can you believe it?" She was so excited that she was virtually stammering. "I'm calling to ask you to get us tickets, Lettie. Christine reckons the hall will be bursting at the seams tonight, because the bushveld has never seen anything like it. And get yourself a ticket as well. You're coming with us."

"I'll get the tickets, but I've already seen the concert," Lettie protested.

"Well, you simply *have* to come with us tonight," Klara said firmly.

"Ask Christine. She really —"

"No, Christine has to look after her own kids and Cornelius," Klara said. "Thanks,

Lettie, see you tonight!" Before Lettie could say anything else, she ended the call.

So it happened that Lettie was sitting in the hall yet again, in the fourth row from the front. The hall was packed, with no room for the proverbial mouse — the bush telegraph had done its job. Children were sitting on the floor in front of the stage, and people were standing in the open doors and at the windows.

Lettie steeled herself against emotion. When the girls in their pretty dresses with flowers in their hair sang "Indian Love Call," the strong tenor came from behind the curtain again, and again the audience gasped.

Marco appeared in his dark suit and white shirt, his dark hair combed back, his face lit up by the spotlight.

A collective sigh went through the audience.

Lettie watched, saw everything, drank it in to remember it later.

To her left a movement caught Lettie's eye. She turned her head in Antonio's direction. His aristocratic face was raised, the strong profile outlined in the stage lighting that reached their seats. His gaze was fixed on his brother on the stage.

Tears were rolling down his cheeks uncontrollably.

Lettie averted her eyes.

When the concert was over, the people stood talking outside the hall, as if they were reluctant to leave.

"That's the brother of Antonio Romanelli, the man who helped build the bridge," a lady said. "Do you remember when Antonio sang 'Funiculì, Funiculà' in the church hall?"

"Well, this Italian is even better," a second lady said. "He's a fine figure of a man, isn't he? Just so painfully thin!"

"I've never seen the hall so full for a school concert," the principal said, rubbing his hands together with pleasure.

At last the cold chased the people back to their homes.

"Could we have coffee at your place?" Antonio asked Lettie. "We have to leave early tomorrow morning and I'd like to spend a little time with Marco. I know it's presumptuous, but the farm is too far and —"

"No, no, of course you're welcome," Lettie said at once. "We can catch up all night."

"We won't do that." Antonio laughed. "I'll come with Marco. He should be here soon. You girls go ahead in our car."

Would this night never end?

Her kettle was just boiling when Marco drew up at the back door. Klara laughed. "I see he knows his way around. He heads straight for the kitchen."

She put her arms around her brother-in-law. "Marco, you were fabulous tonight," she said sincerely. "Why didn't you go on? It was the highlight of the evening, the people were carried away."

"I didn't want to risk having a coughing fit," Marco replied.

Klara laughed. "I was so proud of you!"

"Thank you," he said. "I still can't believe you drove all the way from Pretoria."

"It was worth every mile," Antonio said seriously. "I'm glad we did."

"You were really good, Marco," Lettie said cautiously. She turned and filled the bag with coffee grounds. She poured boiling water on top and pushed the coffeepot to a cooler spot on the stove. Then she busied herself with the cups, fetched cookies from the pantry, and filled the sugar bowl.

The other three talked nineteen to the dozen, laughing and making up for lost time.

At last she was forced to sit down next to Klara, on the only vacant chair.

She knew Marco was watching her across

the table. From the corner of her eye she saw the slightly worried expression on his face. But she avoided his eyes as much as possible.

Tonight, especially, avoidance was better than the alternative.

At last everyone left.

She got into bed.

Sleep eluded her.

"Daddy," she said on Monday morning as they were driving to the hospital, "I think you should take over Marco Romanelli's care."

"Why?" her father asked, frowning.

"Well, I think he should talk about his wartime experiences. It was a traumatic time for him. He's told me about the years they spent hiding in a cave in the Alps and about the two camps, one in Italy and one in Poland. But we don't get to the crux of the matter. He might be more willing to speak to an older person, a man. Besides . . ." She hesitated a moment. "We've become good friends and . . . I don't think it's a good idea for me to treat him."

Her excuse sounded feeble.

But her father nodded. "Okay," he said. "I suspect he might find it easier to speak to you after all, but we'll see. I can take over his medical care. He comes on Friday afternoons, doesn't he? I'll ask Mrs. Roux to reserve that spot in my diary."

But on Thursday her father was feeling unwell, and by Friday morning he had come down with the flu.

"You stay in bed," Lettie said firmly. "I'll reschedule our patients."

She drove her father's big old Hudson, first to the hospital, then to the surgery.

At the surgery she and Mrs. Roux went through the appointments. "Please call Marco Romanelli at the school and tell him not to come today," said Lettie. "Just make sure he gets the message."

She worked all day without taking a break. Patiently she listened to every real and imagined complaint, prescribed medication, gave advice, and scheduled follow-up visits.

Mrs. Roux brought a sandwich and coffee at lunchtime. "I spoke to Mr. Romanelli himself. He'll call on Monday for a new appointment," she said.

Thank heaven for small mercies, thought Lettie and continued working. The sandwich soon curled up in the dry bushveld air, and the coffee grew cold.

It was almost dark when the last patient left the surgery. "I'll just complete the chart, then I'll lock up. You go along home," Lettie told Mrs. Roux.

She had just begun when there was a knock on the door. "Come in!" Lettie called out.

The door opened. She glanced up briefly.

He was standing in the doorway.

Her heart jumped.

"Are you very busy?" he asked.

"No. Yes. But come in, sit," she stammered.

He turned, shut the door, and sat down at the desk, his slim hands folded on the desktop between them. They looked pale. She hoped he wasn't ill.

"Lettie, I have a problem," he began, "and I want you to help me right away. But first you must promise to be absolutely honest."

She struggled to contain her thoughts, to control her heart. "Of course I'll help. Are you feeling unwell? Is it a medical problem?"

"It's partly a medical problem, yes," he said seriously. "The part I want you to be absolutely honest about is purely medical."

"Okay, Marco." She felt herself regaining control. "You have my word."

He ran his hand over his hair in the gesture she knew so well. Then he folded his hands on the desk again and drew a deep breath. "There's this girl . . . woman . . . I've become very attracted to," he began slowly. He looked down at his hands, then up and past her, through the window, at the dark night outside.

Lettie felt herself grow cold.

"The woman doesn't know. I haven't said anything. First I wanted to come and ask you."

Lettie felt her throat close up. "Ask . . . what, Marco?" She forced the words past the lump in her throat.

"I have to be certain about the state of my health, Lettie. I can't tell a beautiful woman that I like her, that I would like to be in a relationship with her, if I know I'm not in good health."

Lettie sat motionless for a moment, her entire being frozen. Then her professionalism kicked in. "So far you've come through the winter unharmed, Marco," she said tersely, her voice steady. "When a person's lungs have suffered as much damage as yours, of course there's no guarantee that the pneumonia won't return. But I think it depends largely on the climate. Will you . . ." She paused briefly. *The woman must be from around here, how else?* "Do you intend to stay on in the bushveld?"

"It's the plan," he said.

"The climate here is good for you. Your digestive system will always be sensitive, but you've learned how to cope with it. The body is a wonderful creation — it gradually heals itself." She felt her mouth go dry. "So, yes, I'd say you aren't facing any serious health issues," she concluded.

Her thick tongue licked her dry lips.

He nodded, still not looking at her, still gazing through the window.

She had to know. "Marco, does this woman share your feelings?"

His eyes were still fixed on the window, his expression serious. "Yes, she feels the same."

She forced a smile to her stiff lips. "Then you should speak to her, Marco. I . . . hope it works out for you."

He turned his face to her, his eyes gentle, clear. "Lettie, it's you. You're the woman I'm speaking of," he said simply.

Her heart stopped. Her brain froze.

Then breath rushed back into her lungs and her heart began to race. "Marco?"

He got up and came around the desk.

She looked up at him.

He folded his beautiful hands around her face.

"Lettie, will you . . ." He shrugged, then gave her a wide grin. "Will you come to the movies with me tonight?"

Chapter Ten

Lettie lay in bed, snug under her duvet.

Tonight she'd be unable to sleep.

Everything felt unreal.

She had driven home in a daze. "I'm going to take a bath. I don't want supper tonight, thanks, Mom," she had said on entering.

"Are you coming down with the flu as well?" her mother asked, worried.

"No, I'm going to the movies," Lettie said.

"The movies? But aren't you exhausted?"

"Not at all."

She thought long and hard about what to wear. At last she chose a soft cream woolen dress with a matching coat. She brushed her hair until it shone, applied her makeup with care, and put on her new glasses with the delicate gold frame.

She studied herself in the long mirror in her parents' bedroom and was pleased with the result.

At a quarter to eight Marco knocked on the door. He stood in the doorway, tall and straight in his dark suit. Lettie drew a slow breath: he, Marco Romanelli, had come to fetch her, Lettie Louw, for a date, *a real date.*

He came in to greet her parents. Although they were clearly intrigued, they refrained from asking questions.

In the intimate space of the car he turned to her. "Now I can say what I've wanted to say so many times before: you look lovely, Lettie."

"Thanks, Marco."

Could a woman tell a man she found him lovely too? She knew nothing at all about dating and men. She was twenty-seven, and this was her first real date.

She felt odd, awkward in her new role. But delighted, absolutely delighted.

The movie wasn't very good. It was an amateurish black-and-white Western dating back to prewar times. The chairs in the city hall were hard, the projector got stuck, and the drinks Marco bought during intermission were lukewarm.

Yet it was the best night of her life. All through the show, Marco's arm rested on the back of her chair. Occasionally he touched her neck, and after a while he drew her closer so her head rested on his shoulder. It was not a very comfortable position, but she did not move away.

When he pulled up in front of her home, he walked her to the door, but he refused her invitation to come in for coffee. "Tomorrow is a workday, and you must get to bed. Thank you for a wonderful evening, Lettie."

He put his hands on her cheeks, raised her face, and gently kissed her on the lips before turning and walking to his car.

She closed the front door, and the exhilarating wonder of being in love filled her entire being. With her fingertips she touched her lips.

Saturday morning arrived gray and cold, but the song in Lettie's heart did not fade. She drove to the hospital, then on to the surgery.

At eleven Mrs. Roux brought her a cup of tea. "Mr. Romanelli called," she said. "I promised him you'd return his call as soon as you had a moment."

Last night's joy that had been slumbering all morning broke through the surface. "Will you get him on the line, please?" she asked, trying not to give anything away.

A minute later his mellow voice came on the line. It went straight to her heart before it registered in her mind. "Did you sleep well?" he asked.

"Not a wink," she said.

He laughed softly. "Can I keep you awake again tonight?"

Her heart leaped. "Of course. Would you like to come for supper?"

"I'd like that, thanks. I want to speak to your father."

"My father? What about?"

"I want to ask his permission to court his daughter — it's how we do it in Italy," he said.

"Oh." She laughed self-consciously. "Oh, all right then."

The gray day was almost unbearably bright.

They ate in the warm kitchen. The room was filled with the aroma of lentil soup and freshly baked bread with homemade butter. "No wonder Esau gave up his birthright for this," Marco remarked. "It's delicious, thanks, Issie."

After supper Lettie helped her mom with the dishes while Marco talked to her father in the bedroom. "Marco is a nice young man, and handsome too, but like Dad said, he's not in good health. And . . . he's not one of our own, no matter how hard he tries to fit in. Are you sure you're doing the right thing, Lettie?"

"Yes, Mom, I'm sure," Lettie said firmly.

"I just don't want you to get hurt," her mom said.

Pain is never far away; it counteracts the joy, Lettie thought. *As long as the joy outweighs the pain.* "I know, Mommy," she said. "I know."

As they sat alone in the living room later that evening, things seemed suddenly awkward between Lettie and Marco, as if their former easy camaraderie had belonged to two other people. The deserted street was suddenly emptier, the heavy leather furniture creakier, the paintings on the walls blander.

"Tell me about school. What did you do this past week?" she asked.

He gave her that slow, amused smile, as if he knew a joke the rest of the world didn't. He seemed relaxed, oblivious of Lettie's insecurity.

"It was just another week of trying to instill a love of English poetry in children who hate English and who live to play rugby and hunt impala in the veld. I read *Romeo and Juliet* and told them stories from ancient Greek and Roman mythology and taught them to express themselves in a civilized manner."

She was also smiling now, slightly more at ease. "According to Mrs. Roux, all the schoolgirls are in love with the handsome teacher with the beautiful voice."

He made a dismissive gesture. "Yes, well . . . Lettie, I really don't want to talk about school."

"Fine, what would you like to talk about?"

"About us, about where we are and . . . yes, about us."

She was silent for a moment. If that was what he wanted to talk about, she decided, maybe she could ask him. "Marco, on Friday afternoon, when you . . ." *Could it have been only yesterday?* "Yesterday, when you came to see me, you said the woman feels the same."

"I was right, wasn't I?" She saw the hint of a smile on his lips, the twinkle in his eye.

"How could you have been sure?"

He looked at her thoughtfully. His eyes were gentle, but serious. "I've felt it for a while, just as you must have known how I feel. There was a connection between us from the start — no, more than that. I felt we understood each other. I was immediately attracted to you. You're a beautiful person, Aletta."

Warmth flooded her. "I didn't know you felt the same," she said.

"I wanted to wait before I said anything, make sure my health was good enough. I actually wanted to wait until after the winter. But then . . ." He hesitated.

"Then?" she asked.

"At the concert . . . I knew something was wrong, and I couldn't understand what. I could accept that you were feeling unwell on Friday evening. But Saturday night it was clear you were avoiding me. I couldn't imagine what I'd done to upset you."

"And that's what made you come and speak to me?"

He shook his head. "No, it was because of what Christine said."

"Christine?"

He sighed. "Sunday morning I drove out to the farm," he said. "I was confused, lonely. I needed to get out of my room at the boardinghouse. I wanted to take a walk in the veld. De Wet and the rest had gone to church. When I returned to my car, Christine came out to invite me to lunch. She asked if something was wrong, and I told her I didn't know what I had done to upset you over the weekend. She said, 'You men are all the same, you're so dumb!'

"I didn't understand then, but the more I thought about it, the clearer it became. It's a man's duty to speak up. When, after all these months, I still hadn't said anything, you must have assumed . . . well, that there was nothing. I really didn't want to make you unhappy, Lettie."

"I'm over the moon right now."

"Well, sit here beside me then," he said, patting the sofa.

She got up self-consciously and sat down beside him. Everything was awkward all over again.

He reached for her and drew her closer. She felt the rough fabric of his jacket against her cheek, she smelled the soap he had used in the shower before he came, and she saw the fine dark hairs on the back of his long fingers. "This is where I want you," he said, sounding content.

"Shall I put some music on?" she asked.

"No, talk to me."

She heard the sound of his voice, felt the inner peace caused by his nearness. *I could grow old with this man,* she thought.

"Tell me about your week," he said. "You must have been very busy with your father at home."

She laughed softly. "My week was much the same as yours, Marco, only different. I was busy, yes, especially on Friday." Another thought struck her. "I asked my dad to take over your care, Marco. I think it's the right thing to do."

"So Mrs. Roux told me. But I'd rather be your patient," he said.

"I don't think it's a good idea," she replied.

He was silent, then he said, "Fine. I understand."

"I think you should continue telling him about the wartime years. It could be therapeutic," she said. "It's important that you get to the heart of the matter."

There was another long pause. "Lettie, I do understand why it's important, but if I must, I'd rather talk to you. At best it won't be easy. And it's harder talking to an outsider." He stared into the distance, his expression grim. "We don't have to do it in office hours, but I'd prefer talking to you. It might be easier."

"We can try . . . I don't know," she said hesitantly. "Please talk when you feel the time is right. I can't tell you when."

He turned to her and stroked her cheek with the back of his free hand. "You're not just beautiful, you listen and understand," he said.

She nestled against him. It still felt strange, yet so right, so natural.

"When you're sitting with me like this, I'll find it easier to talk than when you're facing me across your desk," he said. He pulled her closer and gently kissed the top of her head. "I don't know what else to say, Lettie. I'm not hiding anything from you."

She paused. On the windowpane the shadows of the bare branches moved in the light of the full moon. "See the beautiful patterns the branches create on the windowpane? Do you see, Marco?"

"Yes, I see." His voice was rich and calm, like deep red velvet or mellow wine.

"What did you find beautiful when you were in the mountains, Marco?"

"The stars, the nights, the silence," he said.

"Tell me," she said.

He described the beauty of the surroundings, the wonder of living so close to nature, day and night. He spoke of the snow, the streamlets when the snow began to melt, the first Alpine flowers in spring.

No people.

"And worst of all?" she asked. "I don't mean the cold, or the moment the soldiers found you. Something that happened in your little group."

He thought long and hard. "It was . . . yes . . ."

He fell silent, but kept stroking her hand while his thoughts went back on the long, hard road into the past.

She waited.

"When the old lady died," he said at last.

"What was her name, Marco?" she asked gently.

"Mrs. Rozenfeld." At last the nameless characters were brought into the light. "They were the Rozenfeld family. They're all dead now."

The silence was complete, as if the universe were waiting.

"Tell me about them."

Bit by bit the story came out, more easily after a while, but still slowly.

When he fell silent, she sat without moving. This person she was falling in love with had gone through waters she had only skimmed the surface of in her lifetime.

She was about to get up to make coffee when he said, "But that isn't what I remember most clearly. My most haunting recollection is of Ester asking for an apple one night when I was going home to pick up provisions. But there was not a single apple to be had in the village. 'I have such a craving for an apple,' she said when I returned empty-handed.

"I wish I could have brought her the apple," he said very softly. "I still think of it . . . many nights."

■ ■ ■ ■

It was much later when Lettie got up to make coffee. Her parents were asleep. She and Marco had their coffee in the kitchen. "It's time for old men to leave and pretty girls to go to bed," Marco said, getting to his feet.

She still found it incredible that she could be the pretty girl he was referring to. She walked him to his car in the backyard.

At the screen door he turned to her. "Thanks for tonight. It was good. And, Aletta, thank you for" — he shrugged — "listening."

He took a step toward her, opened his arms, and wrapping them around her, held her against him.

An intense joy spread through her body. She put her arms around his neck and raised her face to his. She felt his arms tightening around her, felt his urgency as his warm mouth closed over her own.

Heat flooded her body, accompanied by an unfamiliar tingling sensation.

He held her a moment longer, then let her go. "Good night, Aletta," he said and turned away.

She put the latch on the screen door and

gently closed the back door.

This, she instinctively knew, was the indescribable joy brought about by the love between a man and a woman.

The following weekend, after Lettie's father had taken over Marco's care, Mrs. Roux said to Lettie, "Aunt Gertie from the boardinghouse called to say someone should take a look at Mr. Romanelli. He's not well."

"Is it his stomach? Something he ate?" Lettie asked.

"No, I reckon it's the flu. Aunt Gertie says he has a very bad cough."

An icy fear grabbed hold of Lettie, threatening to choke her. "I'll go," she said. "Thanks, Mrs. Roux."

With a heavy heart she drove to the boardinghouse. Marco couldn't afford to get the flu. He was far from strong.

She pulled up at the boardinghouse, opened the gate, walked up the cement path, and climbed the three steps to the wide veranda with its shiny red floor. She knocked on the green front door.

Aunt Gertie led her down the long passage to room 5. From the kitchen came the smell of frying onions. "It's so strange that you're a doctor now," Aunt Gertie said, making small talk. "You were always a smart girl, but to be a doctor?"

She knocked, opened the door. The smell of friar's balsam hung in the air. "I've steamed him," Aunt Gertie said.

Marco was asleep under the duvet. Lettie put her hand on his forehead. It was burning. Lettie closed her eyes for a moment. *Dear God,* she prayed, *please help him.*

Marco opened his eyes and smiled. "Aletta?" he said, gripping her wrist.

He's making no effort to hide his love for me, she thought self-consciously. It was clear that Aunt Gertie had noticed. "How do you feel?" Lettie asked, gently withdrawing her hand.

"On top of the world, now you're here."

He seemed not to care that Aunt Gertie was in the room! Lettie felt her cheeks flush. "Marco! Be serious! You're burning up. Does your throat hurt?"

"My throat hurts, my muscles ache, my nose is blocked. You have your work cut out for you," he teased.

When he laughed, it brought on a fresh coughing fit. It racked his chest, and he doubled over, then struggled to sit up, gasping for breath.

"See why I'm worried, Doctor?" Aunt Gertie asked.

Lettie nodded. "I'm glad you called. I

need a few extra pillows," she said, helping Marco to sit up. "We must try to keep him in an upright position, even when he's sleeping."

When the coughing had subsided, he leaned back, exhausted. "Sorry," he said, his eyes closed.

She held a glass of water for him to drink. "Do you have a headache?" she asked.

"No, but my head feels fuzzy."

Aunt Gertie returned with a pile of pillows of different shapes and sizes. "See what you can use, Lettie," she said.

"Thanks, we'll manage now."

"Tell me if you need anything, boiling water, whatever."

"I will. Thanks, Aunt Gertie."

"I still can't believe you're a doctor," Aunt Gertie said on her way out.

Lettie closed the door and turned back to Marco. "Now please tell me how you really feel," she said seriously.

"Terrible," he answered. "Common-cold terrible."

"I know exactly what you mean," she said, smiling as she fluffed up the pillows behind his back. "Let's take a listen to that chest."

"It won't be good," he warned her. "And warm up that cold metal thing before you hold it against my skin."

She laughed softly and rubbed the stethoscope with her hand. "Okay, lie back so I can listen."

She listened, made him lean forward, and pressed the stethoscope against his back. He was still painfully thin, his spinal column clearly visible under the skin. Carefully she pushed him back against the pillows and pulled up the duvet.

"So?" he asked, serious at last.

She took his hand from under the bedding and folded her fingers around his wrist. "Your chest hurts, but at this point I'm not too worried about your lungs," she said. "Just stay in bed and keep warm. Your heart rate is slightly elevated."

"It would be normal if your father were holding my hand," he teased again.

"Marco!" she said. "Don't talk like that, especially not in front of others. Aunt Gertie's the unofficial news broadcaster in town."

"There's no one else here at the moment," he said, giving her a tired smile. "Besides, people will have to get used to the fact that their lovely doctor is no longer available."

Despite her anxiety about him, she was flooded with joy. "Open your mouth so I can take your temperature," she said.

He lay back against the pillows with the

thermometer under his tongue. His face was paler than usual, and his thick dark hair was tousled. Lettie said, "I'm going to prescribe a cough syrup that might make you sleepy. I'll ask Aunt Gertie to steam you again. It's good for the chest."

"She steams up the whole room. I feel as if I can't breathe." He spoke past the thermometer.

"Don't talk," she said. "I'll tell her not to overdo it. Stay in bed. Don't go out in the cold air, even if you're warmly dressed." She removed the thermometer from his mouth.

"What does it say?" he asked.

"It's a bit high — a hundred degrees Fahrenheit," she said. "You can take Disprin every four hours to bring your temperature down. It will make you feel better as well. But whatever happens, you're not to get up."

He lay watching her with a smile on his lips. "You look ravishing in your white coat, you know?" he said.

"Marco! How can I do my job if you keep . . . well . . ."

"Keep doing what?" he teased.

"Making eyes at me," she countered.

He laughed softly. "Just wait till I'm back on my feet," he said, "then you'll . . ."

But the laughter went over into a second

coughing fit. She helped him sit up and rubbed his back until the worst was over. "Take the medicine now and lie back," she said, measuring out a dose of the cough mixture. Then she dissolved two Disprin in a glass of water and held it to his lips. "I'll send my father to take a look at you tomorrow."

He shook his head. "I'll be good, I promise," he whispered. "It's good to have you here."

"Okay. Try to sleep now."

He lay back, exhausted, his forehead sweating, his hands ice-cold. "Will you stay awhile?" he asked, his eyes closed.

"I'll stay until you fall asleep, Marco, and I'll come back tonight. By next week you'll be up and about again," she said, stroking his tousled hair.

He smiled, took her hand, and pressed it to his lips. "Aletta," he murmured.

She stroked his hair until she was certain he was sleeping. Then she closed the door softly, gave instructions to Aunt Gertie, and drove home in her father's big old Hudson.

As she drove past the church, fear had a firm grip on her heart.

Marco improved over the weekend. His cough still rattled but his temperature had come down. But early on Tuesday morning Lettie received a call from a very agitated Aunt Gertie. She spoke so loudly that Lettie had to hold the receiver away from her ear.

"Marco had such a bad case of the chills in the middle of the night that I nearly called you," Aunt Gertie shouted.

"I'm on my way," Lettie said.

She put her head around her parents' door. Her father was still in bed. "Aunt Gertie called," she said.

"I heard," said her father. "Do you want me to come along?"

"No need, I'll fetch you later."

When she walked into Marco's room, she could see he was gravely ill.

"Let's take your temperature," she said, slipping the thermometer under his tongue. She placed her hand on his forehead. He was very warm. "Does your chest hurt?" she asked.

He nodded.

She took the thermometer out and looked at the reading. His temperature had shot up to a hundred and two degrees. A cold realization gripped her.

She took out her stethoscope. "Do you have trouble breathing at times?" she asked, examining him.

He nodded again.

She straightened up and stroked his hair. "Marco, I'm going to admit you to the hospital," she said.

"No! Please don't!" he exclaimed. "I want to stay here, in my bed, where it's nice and warm. Aunt Gertie can look after me."

She shook her head. "You need more care than she can provide, Marco," she said seriously. "Can I pack a few things? Pajamas? Toiletries?"

"Pneumonia?" he asked softly.

She nodded. "I'm afraid so, Marco. But if we treat it without delay, we can stop it in time."

He lay back against the pillows, his eyes closed. "I hoped . . ." He fell silent.

When she laid her hand on his brow, it felt cold and clammy. "You'll feel better soon enough," she tried to comfort him. "I'm taking you in now, then I'll fetch my dad at home for a second opinion."

"Is he back to working a full day?" he asked, his eyes still shut.

"Half day," Lettie said as she packed his bag, "but he's back on his feet. Come, put on your warm coat and we'll go. Here, take the scarf as well, and wrap it around your nose and mouth to keep out the cold air."

■ ■ ■ ■

It was a typical small-town hospital, built in the years when the Spanish flu had taken its toll among the inhabitants of the bushveld. The rooms were big and cold with wooden sash windows overlooking the water pipes in the courtyard. The walls were painted white, and the polished linoleum flooring went halfway up the walls. The beds were high and hard, the starched sheets had perfect hospital corners, and the gray blanket was covered with a light-blue bed-spread.

Lettie managed to have Marco admitted to a double room. She turned down the bedspread and drew the stiff sheet up to his chin. "Fetch more blankets, please, Nurse," she said. "He's warm now, but before you know it he'll have an attack of the chills."

When the nurse had left, Lettie bent down and kissed him gently on his burning forehead. "I'll be back soon," she said softly.

He nodded. "Thanks," he said.

With a heavy heart she picked up her father at home. "I'm worried, Daddy. His chest doesn't sound good," she said.

At the hospital, her father listened to Marco's chest, then looked up at Lettie. She knew from his expression that the news was not good. "Pneumonia," he said. "In the early stages, fortunately." He gave her a small smile. "Continue with the current treatment, Doctor," he said. She could hear the underlying pride in his voice.

Lettie nodded. "Sister," she said to the nurse, "let's begin with antiphlo immediately. Make certain you reheat it every four hours. Keep the patient warm and his body temperature as constant as possible. If his temperature goes up, whatever you do, don't give him a sponge bath. Have him take two Disprin every four hours. And we'll start treating him with M&B 693 immediately."

The sister made notes. "And for the cough?" she asked.

"Let's try Mist Expect Stim," Lettie said. She turned to her father. "What do you think?"

"Yes, I agree."

When everyone had left the room, Lettie lingered. "You'll soon feel better," she tried to encourage him.

"Please explain in plain English what you're planning to do to me?" Marco asked, smiling feebly.

"We're going to put a hot poultice on your chest, Marco. It's called Antiphlogistine, antiphlo for short. It's a sticky paste that's spread on a piece of linen the size of your chest and covered with a thin layer of gauze to keep the concoction away from your skin."

"How do you get it warm?" he asked.

"The sister heats it in the sterilizer," Lettie replied. "Don't worry, she'll take care not to burn you. The poultice is kept in place with what's known as a many-tailed bandage tied across your chest."

"And the medicine?" he asked.

"M&B 693? Sulfanilamide, to fight the infection. You might find the big white tablets hard to swallow, especially if your throat hurts. But try your best."

"I will."

"And the cough mixture is Mist Expect Stim, short for Mixture Expectorant Stimulant. It will help loosen the phlegm when you cough."

She noticed he was very tired. "Try to sleep," she said.

"Will you stay with me?" he asked, reaching for her hand.

She took his hand in both her own. "I'll stay awhile, Marco, but then I must get back to the surgery. You'll soon start feeling better. Just get some rest."

He closed his eyes.

■ ■ ■ ■

Marco did not get better. The next morning his temperature was still a hundred and two degrees. "The Disprin lowers the temperature slightly but it simply goes up again," Lettie said when she came back from the hospital to take her father to the surgery. "He's getting worse, Daddy."

"If only we could get hold of some penicillin," her father said. "But I don't know where, or how we'd get it here."

"I'll call Antonio," Lettie decided. "He told me to let him know if Marco's condition deteriorates."

"He could try to get hold of penicillin in Pretoria or Johannesburg, but I doubt he'll be successful." Her father shook his head. "It's very hard to get one's hands on."

"Antonio will find it," Lettie said firmly. "I know him. I should have asked him last night."

That same day Antonio managed to find the penicillin. On Wednesday afternoon he traveled to Johannesburg to fetch it, then he and Klara drove all night with the precious ampoules packed in cotton wool. He dropped Klara and Cornelius at her parents' farm and came straight to the hospital. "Where is he?" he asked when Lettie met him in the foyer. "Sorry, good morning, Lettie," he added apologetically.

She smiled. "Hello, Antonio, I'm glad you've arrived safely. Come," she said, taking the parcel from him. "Thank you. This penicillin's a miracle cure. It's going to make all the difference."

"How is he this morning?" asked Antonio, his voice raw with anxiety.

"No worse than yesterday," she said. "The hot poultices and the medication are helping, but he's still gravely ill. I'm so thankful for this."

Quietly she pushed the door open.

Marco was lying against a stack of pillows, his eyes closed. At the sound of the door, he opened his eyes. "Aletta," he said, smiling and holding out his hand.

Then he noticed Antonio behind her. "Tonio?" he said, surprised.

Antonio took two steps to the bedside and embraced his brother.

Lettie closed the door and went to the nurses' station to prepare the injection.

Later that morning Lettie joined Antonio and Klara for a cup of tea in the cold waiting room with the upright chairs. Marco was asleep. The first dose of penicillin had been introduced to his bloodstream to fight the disease.

"He looks very uncomfortable," Antonio said anxiously.

"We must keep him in an upright position as much as possible. He must never lie flat on his back, not even at night," Lettie explained.

"But why are those things under his legs?" asked Klara.

"Oh, those are donkeys — to keep him from sliding down in the bed," Lettie replied. "A donkey is just a pillow rolled in a sheet and inserted behind the patient's knees. The tails, the two ends of the sheet, are tucked firmly under the mattress to keep the donkey in position."

"Heavens, Lettie, I'm sick with worry," Antonio said, running his hand over his dark hair the way Marco was apt to do.

"Will you tell us exactly what's going on, Lettie?" Klara asked. She kept stirring her tea. Round and round went the spoon. "We know he's got pneumonia and one can" — she glanced at Antonio — "get very sick, but what exactly does it entail?"

Lettie nodded. "It's an infection of the pulmonary alveoli and the surrounding tissue that sometimes affects patients whose immunity has been compromised after a heavy cold or flu. If it's not treated in time, the alveoli could deteriorate to such a degree that the lung capacity diminishes. It could have serious consequences. Nowadays we can treat it with penicillin. And we diagnosed Marco early, which also helps. I believe he'll start getting better now."

"I saw him reach for you with his hand," Klara said cautiously, "and you stroked his hair. Is there . . . I don't know, something between you?"

Lettie nodded slowly and bit her lower lip. "Yes, there is," she said softly. "I didn't sleep a wink last night. I . . ." She shook her head. "I'm so terribly worried about him."

She felt Antonio's strong arm around her. "You're doing your best, we know," he said, "and your best is more than enough." He held her at arm's length. "I'm so glad, Lettie. I couldn't have wished for anyone better for my brother."

"It's not that serious between us," Lettie protested, blinking and fighting to regain her composure.

"I know," Antonio said softly. "It's never that serious."

Lettie spent another night at Marco's bedside, this time with Antonio sitting opposite her. "We can't both stay awake all night," said Lettie.

"I had a few hours' sleep this afternoon," said Antonio. "Why don't you lie down on the other bed and try to sleep? I'll wake you if he needs you."

"Wake me at one. He must get his next shot at a quarter past," Lettie said.

"Can't the night sister give it to him?"

"No, I want to do it myself," she said firmly. "After that, I'll stay awake and you can sleep."

The minute her head touched the hard pillow she was asleep.

She was woken by a movement next to her and sat up hastily. It was nearly midnight.

"He's come out of the rigor, Doctor," the night sister said as she removed the blankets from Marco's bed.

"But just a little while ago he was shivering and shaking," Antonio said anxiously.

"It's what the fever does. His temperature will be very high now," Lettie said. "Marco, we're going to take your temperature, okay?"

But Marco seemed unaware of his surroundings. He was restless and wouldn't open his mouth. "Under the arm?" the night sister asked.

Lettie nodded and stroked Marco's hair

to calm him.

"If only the fever would break tonight," the sister said, handing Lettie the thermometer.

"He should start reacting to the penicillin after the fourth dose," Lettie said softly. She looked at the thermometer and shook her head.

"High?" asked Antonio.

"Very. I don't want to give him any more Disprin — his stomach . . ." She sighed. "We can wipe his face with a moist facecloth. It should bring some relief. And . . . Antonio, we must pray."

"I've been praying all night," Antonio said. "It's all I've been doing — praying."

Hot and cold spells succeeded each other the rest of the night with increasing intensity. Neither Lettie nor Antonio slept another wink. At a quarter past one Lettie gave Marco his fourth penicillin shot. "The body is fighting hard now. The fever is combating the infection, that's why he's having such a hard time," Lettie explained when Marco began to shiver and they piled the blankets back on. "Nurse, please fill the hot-water bottle with boiling water again."

"Lettie, will he make it?" Antonio asked, his eyes and voice filled with fear. "He's so terribly ill."

"If the fever breaks, he'll make it," Lettie said. "There's nothing more we can do for him."

"And if it doesn't break?"

"That's not an option," Lettie said quietly.

At times Marco fell into a fitful sleep, just to wake with a start and struggle to sit up. "Aletta," he said, bewildered.

"I'm here, Marco," she said calmly. "Look, Antonio is here too."

Marco stared at them, then sank back onto the pillows, his face a fiery red.

At other times he would wake and cough uncontrollably. They raised him to a sitting position, lifted his arms to help him breathe, rubbed his back. He gasped for air.

"Lettie?" asked Antonio, on the verge of despair.

"He'll make it," she said softly.

At four in the morning Marco opened his eyes. "I'm thirsty," he said calmly.

Both Lettie and Antonio jumped to their feet. Lettie laid her hand on his forehead. "How do you feel?" she asked.

He gave her a faint smile. "Parched," he said.

She looked up into Antonio's dark eyes, so similar to Marco's. "The fever has broken," she said.

The eyes looked back at her anxiously. “It means he’ll get better?”

“Yes, Antonio, he’s going to get better,” she said. “We can give thanks.”

She poured some water from the jug and held the glass to Marco’s lips.

Chapter Eleven

Marco's recovery was slow — one step forward and two steps back — but he was gradually getting stronger. "Antonio brought only one course of penicillin," Lettie told her father on Friday evening. "I hope we won't need a second."

"The medication will last until Monday," her father calculated. "No, I think a single course will do the trick."

On Saturday afternoon Marco was feeling so much better that De Wet and Christine joined Antonio and Klara during visiting hours, and even Boelie popped in. They sat in the sterile hospital room, their banter and laughter brightening the white walls and warming the gray day outside.

Lettie perched on a hard bench at the head of Marco's bed. He did not let go of her hand. Klara and Christine sat on the second bed, their legs swinging. Antonio, De Wet, and Boelie sat on the straight-backed hospital chairs the nurses had hastily brought in.

"The treatment here is first-class," Marco said, smiling. "My doctor might have something to do with it." Gently he touched her cheek.

"I'm so happy Lettie and Marco are together." Christine sighed contentedly.

Everyone burst out laughing. Lettie felt her cheeks flush. "Christine!" she said, mortified.

"I'm serious!" Christine protested. "Here we are, the three of us together again. Only Annabel is missing."

"You're right," Klara agreed, laughing. "We're all happy, we just didn't have the guts to say it out loud." She turned to Boelie. "What do you hear from Annabel, Boelie?"

"She writes that it's quite warm in London," Boelie said, sounding distant.

"That's not very romantic," Klara remarked.

Her brother gave her a cool look. "No," he said, "it isn't."

"The next time everyone is together again, maybe at Christmas, we should play games!" Christine said. "It's always such fun."

"That's a good idea," Lettie said.

"A very good idea," De Wet agreed. "Remember that night during our varsity days, Lettie, when the two of us wiped the floor with your little friends over here?"

She remembered, and after all the years she suddenly realized it no longer hurt. "They never stood a chance," she teased.

"If Lettie was on your team, I can well believe you destroyed your opponents," Marco said.

"And I was stuck with the rest of the girls," Boelie pretended to complain.

"Boelie, you're looking for trouble!" Klara said. "We weren't bad, we just didn't get the hands."

"Never mind," Lettie said, "next time we'll play Monopoly, and it'll be every man for himself."

"Don't put De Wet in charge of the bank," Boelie said, "or there'll be all kinds of shady transactions."

"It's called financial strategy," De Wet said seriously.

"If you're going to argue before we've even begun to play, count me out," Christine said.

The conversation ranged between stories about the kids, the dry winter on the farm, and Antonio's latest project in Pretoria, interspersed with De Wet's witticisms. When the bell rang at four to announce the end of visiting hours, everyone got up to take their leave. "We'll come and say good-bye before we leave for Pretoria tomorrow, and Antonio will come tonight," Klara said, stooping to kiss Marco's cheek.

"That would be nice." Marco smiled.

When everyone had left he said, "That was great. You have wonderful friends."

"But now you're exhausted, aren't you?" Lettie asked worriedly.

"I am," he said, closing his eyes. "Stay with me awhile, won't you? They won't kick you out."

When the August winds were chasing clouds of dust over the dry scrubland and the farmers were gazing at the sky for signs of the first rain clouds, Marco turned thirty-two. "Shall I invite a few friends for supper at my parents' home?" Lettie asked the week before. "I do know how to cook, you know."

Marco looked at her with that familiar amused smile. "I believe you can do anything," he said, "but I want you all to myself that night. I'll book a table at the hotel."

"Hmm, let me think," she said, playing along. "The hotel serves tomato stew on Tuesday nights. It might be a bit stringy and greasy, but otherwise it could be nice, thanks, Marco."

"No à la carte?"
"Not at our hotel, no."
"Tomato stew sounds lovely," he said.
On Friday afternoon she went shopping for a new dress. "I believe you and that Italian teacher with the splendid voice are a couple?" said Miss Pronk. "It's incredible. You were such an odd, plump little ugly duckling. And now you're beautiful, a true swan."
Lettie began to laugh. "Annabel de Vos might be a swan, Miss Pronk," she said, "but there's not much swan in me! I think I'll take the red one, please."
"Child, you're beautiful! Gorgeous!" Miss Pronk persisted. "In this deep-red frock, with your rosy cheeks and shiny hair, you're going to take that Italian's breath away."
Tuesday afternoon Lettie had her hair done. "My dear, I hear you're heading for the altar with that handsome Italian," Ellen said. "What shall we do today? A little henna?"
Lettie laughed. She realized she was laughing a lot nowadays. "I'm not about to get married, Ellen, and I don't want to change my hair color. Just trim the ends and set it in soft curls," she said.
At half past seven she joined her parents in the living room. The deep-red frock fell

in soft folds over the curves of her body, her hair was done in soft curls, and her complexion was glowing. Her father shook his head. "Lettie, you're becoming more beautiful by the day."

"I hope you have a wonderful evening, my darling," her mom added.

Lettie smiled. "We're going to eat stew in the hotel dining room, but I'll be with Marco and that means it will be a perfect evening."

Marco was tall and slim in his dark suit, his shoulders broad under the tailored jacket. He stopped in the doorway and looked at her. "You look wonderful, Aletta," he said.

"And you," she replied, "are unfairly handsome, Marco Romanelli. Congratulations on your birthday. I hope —"

His laugh began deep in his belly. He folded her in his arms and held her close. "Aletta, there's no one like you," he said and kissed her lips.

She was laughing too. "Your mouth is red," she said, "and you've smeared my lipstick. But it was a lovely birthday kiss!"

He held her even closer. "Now everyone can see you belong to me," he said. "Thanks for my kiss."

"Come in, we have gifts for you." She took

his hand and led him into the living room.

"You really didn't have to," he protested.

Her parents came in to offer their congratulations. "Open Lettie's gift first," her father said.

"Okay," Marco said, somewhat hesitantly.

"Behind you. On the table, under the sheet," Lettie instructed, smiling.

Marco turned and slowly lifted the sheet to reveal a gleaming, brand-new gramophone.

He put out his hand and stroked the dark wood. Then he looked at Lettie, his eyes almost defenseless. "How deeply you understand me, Aletta," he said, opening his arms.

She walked into his embrace. "Open it," she said.

He raised the lid of the wooden cabinet, smiled, and shook his head. "A gramophone," he said, amazed. "Music in my room."

"Let's find out if the sound is satisfactory," her dad said, handing him a parcel that clearly contained a record.

Marco shook his head again. "You're so good to me. Thank you," he said simply. He tore off the wrapping paper and nodded. "I should have known, Doctor," he said, shaking her father's hand. He turned to Lettie's mom and kissed both her cheeks.

"The gramophone is plugged in, you can try it out," Lettie's dad said, clearly excited by the prospect.

Carefully Marco put the record on the turntable and lowered the needle. From the dark wooden cabinet came the clear voices of Amelita Galli-Curci and Tito Schipa in a duet from *La Traviata.* "Recorded at La Scala," Lettie's father said proudly.

"The sound . . . listen to the quality, it's incredible," Marco said in a near whisper.

They listened in silence. Marco put his arm around Lettie again and drew her to him. "Aletta," he said softly, overcome by emotion.

When the music died down, Marco returned the record to its sleeve. "Thank you very much, Doctor, Isabella — this is really special," he said.

"Well, the two of you must get going, or you'll be late for your dinner," Lettie's mom said, dabbing at her eyes with a handkerchief.

When they arrived at the hotel, Marco took Lettie's elbow and steered her up the steps and across the wide veranda with the wicker chairs. Instead of turning left to the dining room, he led her up the wooden staircase to the top floor. "Where are we going?" she asked uncertainly.

"Don't worry, I'm not planning to seduce you," he said, laughter in his voice.

I'm afraid I'd be easy pickings for the handsome Italian by my side, she thought, but she kept her thoughts to herself.

Marco opened the door to one of the rooms. Lettie stopped in the doorway.

The curtains were drawn and there were candles everywhere. In the middle of the room a table had been set with a snow-white tablecloth, gleaming silverware, sparkling wineglasses, and a centerpiece of white daisies, red candles, and green cat's-tail.

"Marco?" she said, surprised.

He smiled and pointed at two easy chairs in the corner where there was a small table with two glasses of dark-red sherry. "Shall we enjoy an aperitif?" he asked, his eyes dancing.

"Marco, you're unbelievable," she exclaimed, smiling back at him. "It's lovely, thank you."

"I would have liked a little mood music, but the facilities are limited," he said. "Now that I have my own gramophone, however . . . Lettie, it's a very generous gift and such good quality, it must have cost you a fortune. I hope you didn't use all your car savings?"

"There's enough left for my little Volkswagen," she said proudly.

"Then you earn a lot more than I do," he said, laughing. "I can't tell you in words how happy I am about my music."

There was a knock on the door and a waiter entered, pushing a trolley. Marco pulled out her chair and opened a bottle of red wine. "Are the two of us going to finish the bottle?" she asked, laughing.

"I only have a birthday once a year," he said, filling her glass to the halfway mark.

He lifted the lids of the serving dishes.

"It's not tomato stew," Lettie said slowly. "It's . . . Italian food?"

He nodded. "May I dish up for you?" Deftly he transferred the pasta to her plate.

She watched him in silence: the thin, dark face with the straight nose and the mouth with the ready smile, the thick, glossy hair, neatly combed back, but already escaping to fall over his forehead, the slim hands with the long fingers spooning pasta strings onto her plate. She didn't have to see his eyes to know exactly what they looked like: dark, sensitive, intense at times, at other times full of fun.

Her gaze took in the flowers, the candles, the greenery on the table — the colors of the Italian flag, it dawned on her. How could it be that this incredible man had fallen in love with plain Lettie Louw?

She took the first mouthful and lowered her knife and fork. "Marco, who made this food?" she asked, tilting her head sideways.

"Why? Is something wrong?" he asked anxiously.

"It's delicious! No one here can cook like this!"

He smiled faintly. "I'm glad. I made it, Aletta, here in the hotel kitchen."

"You?" she asked, surprised. "I didn't know you could cook like this! When did you make all this lovely food?"

"Last night, and this afternoon. The pasta is homemade. I made it myself, Sunday morning."

She took another mouthful. "It's very different from the macaroni we buy at the store," she said appreciatively. "I'm afraid you're a much better cook than I am."

"I can't make lamb and roast potatoes like your mom," he warned her, his dark eyes dancing with mirth.

"You cook like your mom, I cook like mine. How does that sound?"

He looked at her, suddenly serious. "I love you, Aletta," he said.

It was the first time he had said the words. She felt each word, she felt a reaction start deep inside her. *I am experiencing the deep-*

est happiness a woman can know, she thought.

"I love you too, Marco," she said.

"Did you enjoy last night?" her mother asked the next morning at breakfast.

"It was lovely, thanks, Mommy," Lettie replied.

Words would always fall short.

Saturdays were never busy, so Lettie went to the surgery on her own. Her father was gradually turning over his patients to her. Only a handful of grumpy old-timers and stiff-necked middle-aged gentlemen refused to be tended to by Lettie. "Don't take exception, my girl," said Oom Kallie from the other side of the mountain, "but it's not decent for an old man to see a female doctor. The nurses in the hospital are bad enough."

She filed away the last patient charts, locked the door of the surgery, and walked to her car.

He was waiting for her. He had parked his Fiat in the shade of the jacaranda tree behind the surgery, next to her father's big old Hudson. When he saw her, he got out of the car and came over to meet her. He bent down to kiss her and took her doctor's bag. "Hello, Lettie," he said cheerfully. "What are we doing this afternoon?"

She laughed. "I have no idea. What do you have in mind?"

On Saturday afternoons in the past she used to wash her hair and . . . well, spend the afternoon reading, or something.

But now there was someone who wanted to spend his Saturday afternoons with her.

"Let's head out to the reservoir and go for a walk in the veld. We can watch the sun go down."

"Let me take my dad's car home first, and I'll pack a basket with sandwiches and fruit," she said.

"Sounds good. And change into something you can walk in."

She laughed again. Laughter came so easily when she was with him. Her entire being was filled with laughter. "Yes, this gray skirt and white blouse certainly won't do."

He smiled. "You're lovely," he said, closing the car door.

You're lovely you're lovely you're lovely, the wheels sang on the tarmac all the way home.

You're lovely you're lovely, her hands sang as she made the sandwiches.

You're lovely, her heart sang as she changed her outfit.

They drove out to where the town reservoir lay between two hills. It had been built during the depression as part of a government project to create jobs for thousands of poor white people. Marco stopped near the dam wall. They spread their blanket in the sparse shade of a thorn tree and put down the picnic basket.

The dam wasn't very big, but neither was the town. The water lay dark and sparkling, the low hill on the far side scattered with stones. There was no wind. Dappled shade fell on the blanket, and the earth basked in the lazy winter sun.

"The last time I had a picnic like this was in Italy," Marco said pensively, "before the war."

Instinctively she knew she should seize the opportunity. It might not present itself again. One puzzle piece was still missing. In all their conversations he had never mentioned the name of Rachel Rozenfeld. It was Antonio who told Lettie that Marco had been engaged to a beautiful Jewish girl who died in the prison camp shortly before the end of the war.

She decided to speak. "With Rachel?" she asked as casually as possible.

He looked up sharply, his eyes very dark. Then his features softened. "Yes," he said, "with . . . Rachel."

Lettie took his hand in her own. "Tell me about her, please, Marco."

He brought both their hands to his mouth, pressed her hand to his lips. "Aletta," he said, shaking his head.

She waited.

Then he began to speak. He gripped her hand as if he were taking her along with him on the difficult path. She stroked his hand and walked beside him every step of the way. They both knew it wasn't easy for her either.

He spoke at length, with long silences between the words. He dug deep to find small slivers of memory. He cut to the bone.

Words may fall short, Lettie realized again, *but they're all we have.*

"She was so hopeful the last time I heard from her. Occasionally someone managed to smuggle a letter into camp," Marco said. His fingers gripped Lettie's hand. "She was so brave. She never lost hope, not even when her sister died. Then, around Christmastime, she was gone as well."

They sat in silence. Long after he had stopped talking they kept sitting, Lettie's fingers gently caressing his hand.

"Antonio told me she was a beautiful girl," Lettie said after a while.

Marco turned to her, his gaze honest,

exposed. “She was beautiful, yes,” he said, “with dark hair and rosy cheeks. And she was hardworking and courageous.” He took a deep breath. “But today I know what it means to have a soul mate, someone who is my intellectual equal, who feels music the way I do, who understands without my having to explain.”

She watched him calmly.

“Aletta, you’re beautiful. I love you like I’ve never loved anyone before and never will again.”

His words flooded her brain, washed over her body, and entered the chambers of her heart where they were anchored, to be remembered and cherished in years to come.

She put out her hand and stroked his cheek. “Thank you, Marco. You understand . . . with a deeper understanding than words can convey.”

He drew her to him. “Look at the sun on the water, sparkling like thousands of diamonds,” he said. “It’s going to be a beautiful sunset. The dust is turning the sun red.”

What lay in the past would remain there. In front of them, the sun was lighting up the water.

But before the sun touched the hilltops, she said, “It’s getting chilly. I think we should go home."

"You're right," he said.

He got up, pulled her to her feet, and took her in his arms. His arm slid down her back and he pressed her to him. "Heavens, Aletta, I miss you," he said.

She reached up and touched his cheek. She nodded. She understood.

Their Sunday visits to the farm became sustenance for the rest of the week — for all of them. They barbecued or made dinner, sometimes they ate cold cuts and salads, and occasionally in winter it was hot soup and fresh bread.

What Lettie loved more than that was the conversation, the camaraderie, the sharing of small worries and joys.

"Where's Boelie?" Marco asked one Sunday when Boelie hadn't joined them.

De Wet shook his head. "He was here this morning, then he took off up the mountain, as irritable as a bull at the sight of a red rag," he said.

"He wasn't in church this morning," Christine said.

"I wonder what's the matter," Marco said, frowning.

De Wet shook his head again. "He's probably at loggerheads with my dad again. I knew from the start they wouldn't get along, but I hoped they'd get past their differences. It can't go on like this."

"What will you do?" asked Marco.

"I wish I knew," said De Wet. "What I do know is that Boelie is a brilliant farmer, much better than my dad. If given the opportunity, he could become the most successful farmer in the district."

"He's managing our farm as well," said Christine.

"He has great ideas. He dreams big, but he's also practical," said De Wet. "I love listening to his schemes."

"So we each have our own talents," said Lettie.

"It's the wonderful thing about life," said Marco, "that every person is unique."

Driving back to town in the late afternoon, Marco asked, "How do you feel?"

"Fine," Lettie answered, surprised. "Why?"

"You didn't eat much at lunch, and you didn't want cake with your coffee this afternoon."

She gave an embarrassed grin. "I need to lose some weight," she said apologetically.

He frowned. "Why?"

She sighed. "Marco, look at Christine.

She's beautiful . . ."

"Lettie," he said earnestly, "you're every bit as beautiful as Christine. And more capable and much smarter."

"Nonsense, Christine is perfect!"

"You're even more perfect," Marco said seriously. "Promise me you'll never change, Aletta. You're beautiful, feminine, soft. I love holding you, feeling your softness against me — you're all woman. Don't get any thinner, promise?"

She knew where that came from, but if it was how he truly felt, she would understand. "If it's important to you, Marco, I promise." She nodded.

"It *is* important. Very important."

She reached out and touched his cheek. "I promise," she said. Then she gave a soft laugh. "It's one promise I won't find hard to keep."

He nodded contentedly and put his hand on her knee. He didn't say anything more — he didn't have to.

That evening they sat in his room at the boardinghouse listening to the new records he had ordered. Caruso was singing. The red label said *Gramophone Concert Record.*

They sat facing each other on the only two chairs in his small sitting area, while the master of all tenors sang "*Mattinata,*" and "*Ave Maria.*"

Sunday evenings are made for missing your loved ones, especially if they're far away, Lettie thought.

Then Tino Rossi sang "*Oh Mon Papa.*" Marco sat motionless, his eyes closed.

When it ended he got up slowly, bent over Lettie, and gently kissed her forehead. "Lovely, isn't it?" he asked before he chose the next record.

"Beautiful." She smiled.

Beniamino Gigli began to sing "*Mama.*"

Lettie watched Marco in silence. *I've found my mate,* she thought, *my Adam, created for me.*

"Do you miss your parents, Marco?" she asked when the music faded.

He gave her a sad smile. "Yes, I often think about them, especially on a Sunday like today. But I know I'll go back to see them one day. And I want to take you along." He gave her an earnest look. "Lettie," he said, his eyes very dark, "I want so very badly to ask you to marry me."

She looked into his dark eyes and she understood. "If you asked me to marry you, Marco, and I said yes, I'd be the one person on earth who would know exactly what she was letting herself in for." She paused before continuing. "Besides, consider the alternative."

"Not getting married?" he said.

She smiled, nodding slowly. He always understood.

He returned her smile and reached for her with both hands. "Aletta, who knows exactly what she's letting herself in for, would you consider being my wife?" he asked.

Chapter Twelve

Marco Romanelli, the Italian with the golden voice, and Lettie Louw, daughter of Dr. and Mrs. Louw, tied the knot on a bright Saturday in mid-December.

But before that could happen, Marco, like Antonio before him, had to be confirmed in Lettie's church. "I can't marry you to a Catholic man in our church, Lettie. The Catholics are our sworn enemies," the minister had said. "But I will recommend to the council of elders that the Italian be instructed in our religion, as we did with his brother before him."

The Romanelli brothers conferred at length during the weekend when Antonio and Klara came for the engagement party. It was a difficult decision for Marco — even more difficult than the decision to leave his country and his people, he told Lettie earnestly. But getting married at the registry office wasn't an option for either of them.

The blessing of the church was essential.

Three years earlier it had been a difficult decision for Antonio as well, so he knew best how to give Marco advice. They headed up the mountain and only came back when the sun had nearly gone down.

That night Marco spoke to Lettie. "Antonio says all the church will basically ask of me is to declare that I believe in God the Father and Jesus Christ the Son and the Holy Spirit, that I believe in the Holy Christian Church, the Forgiveness of Sins, and the Resurrection. I believe all those things already, I have for years. You know, Aletta," he said, pensively caressing her hand, "I always wondered how Antonio could give up the Catholic Church so easily. But now I understand. He gave me the answer from God's Word itself, from the book of Ruth."

"Where you go I will go, and where you stay I will stay. Your people will be my people and your God my God," said Lettie. "God's Word always has the answers. We must just look for them." Marco nodded.

"You love me very much," Lettie said softly.

"Yes, Aletta, I do. I'm willing to be confirmed in your church."

They would get married in the same church

as Klara and Christine, the church where they were all baptized and confirmed. The reception would be held in the Fouries' barn, and the entire community became involved. Miss Pronk offered to make Lettie's wedding gown for free. Ellen suggested Lettie grow her hair so they could style it in curls and adorn it with fresh flowers.

Neighbors promised chicken pies and roast lamb and trays with stuffed eggs and rainbow sandwiches. Patients came bearing bottles of beetroot salad and curried beans and onion salad, stewed quinces and yellow peaches. The farm ladies brought bushels of fresh fruit, crates of vegetables, even a ten-gallon canister of thick cream.

"These people are just like the folk from my village in Italy," Marco said late one afternoon.

"I don't know where to put everything in this heat!" Lettie's mother sighed.

"I'll get Boelie and De Wet to take everything to the farm. The pantry is big and it's cool," Aunt Lulu said. She was managing the wedding like a military operation, and everything was going according to plan.

"My mom is in her element," De Wet said when he arrived to pick up the supplies.

The week before the wedding, the women worked from dawn to sunset, stuffing and marinating legs of venison, baking dozens of koesisters and scores of milk tarts and brandy tarts, polishing the brass and silverware until everything sparkled.

Klara and Antonio came from Pretoria. Antonio worked side by side with Marco and Boelie, and in the evenings De Wet came to lend a hand. They cleared out and cleaned the barn, hauled big logs down the mountainside for the fires outside, fetched tables and chairs from the church and the school for the reception. Through it all, there was constant banter and laughter.

Klara had to take special care of herself, as her second baby was due in April. "But no one is supposed to know," Aunt Lulu told Lettie's mother in a conspiratorial whisper.

The men lined the walls with hay bales and the women covered them with snow-white sheets collected from all the neighbors. They set out the tables and chairs and pushed the wagon into a corner to serve as a makeshift stage for the musicians. "It's beginning to look like something," Christine said late on Thursday afternoon, her face streaked with dirt.

"Tomorrow Pérsomi will start with the table decorations. She's very good with flowers," said Aunt Lulu. "She wants to cover the walls with willow boughs and large sheaves of sunflowers. I think it will look stunning."

But Lettie didn't get to see Pérsomi's artistry right away. On Friday she and Marco were banned from the premises and instructed to rest. They were also strictly forbidden to see each other again before the wedding. "It's going to be a long wait until Saturday afternoon," Marco said. "I love you, Lettie Louw."

"It's the last time you'll be able to say that," she told him with a smile.

"That's why I'm saying it, Miss Genius," he said, laughing.

That night Lettie lay in the bedroom that had been hers all her life. *For the last time,* she thought. *Tomorrow is my wedding day. Tomorrow night I'll be Aletta Romanelli, wife of Marco Romanelli.*

She still found it hard to believe it wasn't a dream.

"It's strange, the way our paths crossed in the end," Marco had said Thursday, stirring his coffee when they had a moment alone in the kitchen.

"Years ago my mom told me life sometimes leads you along a strange crooked path, but in the end it will always take you where you're supposed to be," she replied.

He looked at her strangely for a moment. "Your mother said that?" he asked, shaking his head.

"Yes," she said, smiling. She wondered why he found her mother's words so remarkable. "And I believe it's true."

The church was a fairyland with masses of white arum lilies from the damp, low-lying areas on the farms and old-fashioned white rambling roses from all the gardens in town. The church was packed. Everyone was there. The majestic tones of the organ launched into the "Wedding March," and Lettie and her father walked slowly down the aisle. At the altar Marco was waiting for her, dressed in a dark suit with a white rose pinned to the lapel.

The minister read from the Bible, prayed, and delivered his message. The congregation sang a hymn to the accompaniment of the organ.

Then the bridal couple turned and looked up at the gallery. Klara and Antonio had asked to sing to them, but no one knew what the song would be.

The organ began to play. In her clear, strong voice Klara sang "The Lord's Prayer" in Afrikaans. It was so beautiful, so moving, that all the ladies fumbled for their handkerchiefs.

Then the organist turned up the volume, and in his rich tenor voice Antonio sang the same song in Italian. Lettie felt Marco stiffen beside her and draw a deep breath. Klara's rendition had been lovely, but Antonio's was in a different class — a class to which only his elder brother might possibly aspire.

But then Antonio's voice grew thick, then thinner. In the middle of the lyric it faded and died.

The next moment Klara took over, and a few notes later Antonio joined in again. Together they completed the hymn, Klara singing in Afrikaans, Antonio in Italian.

When the bridal couple turned back to the pulpit to take their vows, Lettie saw that Marco's eyes were brimming with tears.

Outside the church, the guests were crowding around to congratulate the bride and groom. "No, no," De Wet protested, trying to create order, "you can do it on the farm, all night long. There'll be more space — and plenty of food and drink."

The cars filed through the church gate, heading for the farm.

When at last they were alone in their wedding car — Annabel's father's shiny, brand-new black Buick Super, driven by her brother, Reinier — Marco turned to Lettie. "You look more beautiful today than I have ever seen you look, Mrs. Romanelli," he said earnestly.

"Thank you, Marco. It's the happiest day of my life." She took his hand and pressed it to her cheek.

All the way to the farm they sat close together in the back of the big Buick, their fingers with the shiny new rings entwined.

The wedding car stopped at the entrance to the barn. The guests formed a guard of honor and applauded. The newlyweds got out and walked through the arch they formed with their arms: Marco, tall and handsome in his dark suit, and Lettie, radiant in her pure-white satin gown with not a frill in sight.

The fruit punch and orange cordial were ice-cold, and the year-old sheep and suckling pigs were on the spit. The interior of the barn had been transformed into a reception hall of note.

De Wet was master of ceremonies and soon had the guests roaring with laughter at his quips. Antonio proposed a toast to Marco and Lettie. The guests enjoyed his witty anecdotes, delivered in English. He turned to Marco and addressed him in Italian, speaking earnestly. Marco nodded, that familiar smile on his lips. Subsequently Antonio turned to Lettie and, in faultless Afrikaans, welcomed her to the Romanelli family. The guests cheered and clapped and got to their feet to drink to the health of the bride and groom.

Then it was Marco's turn. He delivered a brilliant speech, emotional at times. He even said a few words in Afrikaans. The men nodded approvingly, the women sighed contentedly, and the young girls gazed at him, entranced.

Marco and Lettie opened the dance floor to the tune of Tchaikovsky's "Waltz of the Flowers" from *The Nutcracker.* They were soon joined by De Wet and Christine, with other relatives and friends following suit. Antonio and Klara remained seated. A pregnant woman was required to behave with decorum. But the second dance found Antonio on the dance floor with the new Mrs. Romanelli.

The party took off. The band gave it their best, the tables groaned under the weight of the loaded platters, and the guests ate and danced and had fun.

Much later in the evening, Lettie left the party to change into her going-away outfit.

Miss Pronk had been adamant that it was an unmissable part of every wedding. Klara and Christine accompanied her to Klara's childhood bedroom, where Lettie changed. "It's been a wonderful wedding, Lettie, and you look absolutely stunning," Klara said, leaning back. "What a pity I couldn't dance. Thank goodness it's temporary."

"Do you realize the three of us are almost sisters now?" Christine said excitedly. "And if Boelie marries Annabel, we'll be well and truly related."

"I don't think a marriage between Boelie and Annabel would work," said Klara. "They're both hard nuts to crack."

"And when Lettie has babies, our kids will all be friends," said Christine.

Lettie laughed. "Hold your horses!" she cried.

Together the three friends walked back to the barn.

When the school reopened early in January 1949, Lettie returned to the surgery. "I suppose we'll have to order a new sign that says 'Dr. Lettie Romanelli'?" Mrs. Roux asked on her first day back at the office.

But Lettie shook her head. "My professional name will remain Dr. Lettie Louw," she said.

■ ■ ■ ■

In January 1949, Pérsomi Pieterse joined Annabel's father and De Wet as an attorney's clerk in the firm De Vos and De Vos. Their offices were two doors to the left of the surgery, along the veranda. Only the pharmacy separated the lawyers' offices from the doctors' rooms. Lettie sometimes saw Pérsomi in the early morning when she came to work, or late in the afternoon when she was walking home.

"Pérsomi is a great asset to the firm. She's worked here during her vacations and she's brilliant," De Wet said one Sunday afternoon when Lettie and Marco ate with the Fouries out at the farm.

Lettie saw Boelie glance up quickly before he carried on eating.

"She and her mom have left the bywoner home and moved into our townhouse. Boelie lent a hand," said Christine.

"Much more convenient, I'm sure," Lettie said.

"Aunt Jemima is going to look after Gerbrand after school in the afternoons until De Wet finishes work. She's his ouma, after all."

"Don't tell me the little scamp is going to

school next year!" Marco bridged the slight awkwardness. He laughed. "I bet they won't know what hit them."

"Surely he's not *that* naughty," Christine said uncertainly.

"No, no, he's just lively. He's a lovely little boy," Marco said quickly.

"This onion salad is delicious, Christine," Lettie said. "Have you heard from Klara lately?"

"De Wet's ouma made the onion salad, and Klara says it's hot and she's feeling rather uncomfortable," Christine said without stopping to breathe.

"How she's going to handle another baby I truly don't know," said Boelie. "Cornelius is a handful, I saw it at Christmas. Klara runs after him all day."

"You said the same thing when Christine was pregnant with Anna," De Wet reminded him, "and she's doing all right."

Boelie raised an eyebrow but said nothing.

"All kids are demanding," said Christine, "but they're also adorable. Annabel wrote to me as well. She says she's well."

"Yes, she writes to me too. She says she's fine, but I think she's homesick," said Lettie.

Boelie sighed, and Lettie had no idea what it meant.

■ ■ ■ ■

Klara and Antonio's little girl was born in April and was given Klara's mother's name: Lulu. "Marco and Antonio's brother, Lorenzo, and his wife, Gina, also had a little girl," Lettie told Christine on Sunday.

"That's wonderful news," Christine said, trying to get another spoonful of porridge past Anna's lips. "When are you and Marco planning to start a family?" Her hand flew to her mouth. "Sorry, Lettie, I shouldn't have asked."

Lettie laughed and covered Christine's hand with her own. "We're friends, Chrissie," she said. "You can ask me anything." Her expression grew serious. "But I don't know if we'll have children. Marco's health isn't good."

"But . . . he looks healthy!" Christine cried, dismayed. "I didn't know he was ill."

"He's healthy now, but I'm scared of the approaching winter," said Lettie. "If only we could keep the pneumonia at bay for a few years, I'd feel a lot better."

"I think his health will continue to be good this winter," Christine said. "I'll get Boelie to bring you a pocket of oranges every week to boost his immunity."

■ ■ ■ ■

Unfortunately it wasn't quite so simple. When the weather turned colder, Marco wore the turtleneck sweaters Klara's ouma had made for him. "If you can just keep his chest warm, Lettie," Klara's ouma said, "and a spoonful of lemon-and-honey every morning does wonders for the immunity."

They went for a walk every day, never early in the morning but late in the afternoon, when the bushveld earth was still warm from the heat of the sun. They ate Boelie's oranges and grapefruit, avoided closed public spaces, and stayed home in the evenings.

But at the end of June, the monster that regularly sneaked into the surgery found its way into Marco's chest. Lettie had him admitted to hospital without delay. She ordered the prescribed amount of penicillin, and they began to apply hot poultices to his chest. "This time we've nipped it in the bud," she reassured Antonio on the phone.

By mid-July, when Klara and Antonio and their young family arrived on the farm for baby Lulu's baptism, Marco was back on his feet — much thinner than at Christmastime and very pale, but overjoyed to see his brother and the children. And when he addressed Cornelius in Italian and the boy replied, he couldn't contain his excitement. "The child is a genius!" he told Lettie. "And Lulu is the most beautiful baby I've ever seen."

"Blood is thicker than water!" Klara laughed. "It's high time you had some of your own, brother-in-law, so you can see what these little angels get up to at night."

But when Lettie brought up the subject of children, Marco shook his head. "No, Aletta," he said firmly. "I'm not taking the chance of leaving you behind to raise my children on your own."

In December, Christine and De Wet hosted Christmas at the farm. All the Fouries were there, as well as Lettie's parents, Marco, and Antonio.

On Christmas Eve everyone gathered to sing carols around the Christmas tree in the front room. Irene was at the piano, Boelie played the guitar, and the rest joined in the singing. All the Fouries were good singers, except their mother, Lulu, who was a Fourie by marriage but sang heartily just the same. "My mother-in-law always makes the rest of us who can't sing feel better," Christine said to Lettie in the kitchen, laughing. "You know I can't sing at all!"

This year the ranks of the Fouries were bolstered by the strong tenors of the two Romanelli brothers, and Lettie and her parents joined in with gusto.

But after a while seven-year-old Gerbrand could no longer bear it. "Are we still getting our presents tonight?" he asked his dad.

De Wet held up both hands. "This young man feels we should hand out the presents now," he said. "I suppose you want to read the nativity story first, Dad?"

"Yes," Klara's father said. "Irene, fetch the Bible."

They listened again to the age-old Christmas story. They held hands and bowed their heads, and Lettie quietly gave thanks that her husband and parents had been welcomed into such a family.

They exchanged gifts, small tokens of love. For the past months Marco had been spending his evenings carving toys. Cornelius's gift was a truck with wheels that could actually turn. He got down on his knees at once and pushed the car all over the floor, shouting, "Vroom! Vroom!"

"Cornelius, say thank you to Oom Marco!" Antonio said.

The child looked up at Marco. *"Grazie,"* he said and carried on playing.

Marco laughed. "It's enough reward that he's enjoying it so much," he said.

Baby Lulu's gift was a dolls' house with four rooms. "Marco, it's any little girl's dream!" Klara said, overcome.

"She's still too young to play with it," he said apologetically. "You'll have to keep it until she's a little older. My mother-in-law made the curtains and carpets. Next year I'll make some furniture."

"Thank you, Aunt Issie," Klara said.

De Wet and Christine's Anna got a doll's cradle with bedding made by Lettie's mom. De Wet tried to engage the little girl's attention. "Look, this is for your baby." But she was more interested in the cookie in her ouma's hand.

Gerbrand got a rifle. "To hunt lions," Marco said.

Gerbrand immediately took aim at the ginger cat, asleep in the corner. "Pow! Pow! Pow!" he shouted, and Lulu burst into tears.

Klara's mother stepped in. "Come, let's eat. Once these kids really start playing, we'll never manage to feed them."

That night in the guest room, Lettie had a long, earnest conversation with Marco. "We can't live our lives in the shadow of death, Marco," she said.

"But we must make responsible decisions, long-term decisions," Marco said. "To have a child is a commitment for the next eighteen years. It's a very long time for a man who's — let's admit it — living on borrowed time."

"I want you to stop thinking of your life as borrowed time, Marco. We all live on borrowed time. Take that young family in the car crash last weekend. They didn't know how much or how little time they had. None of us knows."

But he shook his head slowly. "Aletta," he said.

"We both love kids, and we're not getting any younger," she continued. "I believe we're denying ourselves a great deal of happiness by not starting a family. Think about it, that's all I ask."

He put his arms around her and drew her close. "I'll think about it," he promised.

She waited until she was absolutely certain. She lived with the wonder for a few days, held it safely inside her, cherished its presence in her body.

Then she spoke to the man she loved. They lay in bed, covered by only a sheet, for the nights were still very warm. The light was out, the glow of the half-moon and the bright bushveld stars reflected in the windowpanes. "We're going to have a baby, Marco," she said.

She felt him stiffen, heard him draw a sharp breath. "Are you sure, Lettie? Have you seen a doctor?"

She began to laugh. "I *am* a doctor, Marco."

He sat up. She looked at the outline of his movements as he ran his fingers through his hair. "Shouldn't you see . . . another doctor?"

"There's no need," she said calmly. "Everything is a hundred percent normal."

He lay back against the pillows and held out his arm. She moved closer, snuggled into her place. He held her tightly. "Are you sure?" he asked again.

"I'm sure," she said. "Our baby will be born mid-October."

"I have to wait that long?"

She laughed softly. "That's how long it takes, yes."

He lay motionless for a while, stroking her arm. *He's processing the miracle,* Lettie thought.

"I want you to stop working at once," he said suddenly.

"Why?" she asked, surprised. Then she laughed and raised herself on her elbow to look at his face. Her finger followed the contours of his classical profile. "I'm not sick, Marco, just pregnant."

"Oh." He thought awhile longer. "But you'll have to get in a partner immediately."

"You're right, I'll have to get a partner. The practice can easily support two doctors, and now that my dad is almost completely retired, I'll have to look around for someone else regardless."

They lay in silence for a while. "Marco, how do you feel about the news?"

"It feels strange," he said. "I think I'm happy, but it's just such a foreign thought."

She understood, because she knew him. He needed time to let the realization sink in and develop. In his own time he would share with her the joy of parenthood.

Just before they fell asleep, Marco said, "Heavens, Aletta, I hope we made the right decision."

"We did, Marco, we did."

In May, Fanus Coetzer joined Lettie in the practice. In his interview he was frank with Lettie and her father.

"Doctors," he had said, "I'm going to lay my cards on the table so there won't be any misunderstanding later. I'm fifty-two, divorced, with three grown children, and I'm a recovering alcoholic. But I've always been a good doctor. I lost everything I had, but I made a decision to turn my life around. I'm starting from scratch. I undertake to be the best doctor I can be."

In August, with Christine's third baby due any moment, Lettie was grateful for the extra pair of hands. And Fanus was indeed a good doctor. But it was Lettie herself who carefully laid Christine's second baby girl in her arms.

"She's lovely," Lettie said, stroking her friend's blond curls. She bent over the infant's wrinkled little face. "Hello, baby Lulani, welcome to the best extended family in the whole world."

Then she turned for the door. "I'll call De Wet," she said.

Evenings after supper were the most peaceful time of day. "It's going to change pretty soon," Christine and Klara warned Lettie. "Better enjoy it while you can."

When the washing up was done, Lettie joined Marco in the living room. She sat down carefully in the deep armchair and picked up a medical journal from a side table. "This year, 1950, has seen major progress in the field of science," she said, shifting in her seat to find a more comfortable position. The reading lamp bathed her in a soft glow.

At the table Marco looked up from his stack of papers. "I know about the groundbreaking heart surgery earlier this year. The first human aorta transplant, wasn't it?"

"Yes, with the worldwide increase in heart conditions, it was probably the most important development. There was also the discovery of hepatitis A, of course. And I've just been reading about a breakthrough in the synthesis of penicillin, which could lead to the development of more antibacterial medicines."

"Penicillin seems to be a miracle cure, able to cure every disease," Marco said, stretching his tall figure.

"Oh no, not at all. It's ineffective against poliomyelitis," Lettie said, her eyes fixed on the article she was reading. "For centuries infantile paralysis was restricted to children between the ages of six months and about four. Now the average age of children who contract the disease has risen to nine, and a number of patients over the age of fifteen have even been diagnosed." She frowned, shaking her head. "It says here that the paralysis is worse in the older children."

Marco got to his feet. "And there's still no treatment for it?" he asked.

"I doubt there ever will be," Lettie said. "The paralysis is permanent. The young patients never fully recover. But there's been some progress in the development of vaccines. One is presently being used in the Congo and Poland. Just how effective it is, we'll have to see. The disease is turning into a pandemic."

"There have been more local cases as well, not so?" Marco asked, crossing the floor to her chair, where he bent down and gently kissed her forehead. "I'm going to make coffee, or I won't stay awake to grade this pile of papers. Would you like some hot milk?"

She looked up guiltily. "Sorry, I'm keeping you from your work," she said.

He smiled. "No, Aletta, I find everything you tell me interesting — much more interesting than the standard eights' essays."

All day she'd been aware of a vague discomfort — the onset of the contractions she had so often described to other women. In the morning she had tea with her mom without letting on, in case it was a false alarm.

By the time Marco came home from school in the late afternoon, she knew it was time. She greeted him, then said, "Our baby will be coming sometime tonight or tomorrow morning."

He froze, his eyes nearly popping. "Where's your bag?" he asked without returning her greeting.

She began to laugh. "Marco, let's have tea first. My mom has sent you a lovely milk tart. We don't have to —"

"Lettie, I don't know anything about having babies, so we're leaving for the hospital this minute," he said.

"And I know everything about having babies," she said, still laughing. "We're going to sit and have our tea."

But when another contraction came halfway through her cup of tea, he jumped up, leaving his half-eaten milk tart on the plate. "Come," he said firmly.

"Please don't speed," she said when they turned into the street. "This baby is still hours away."

Later he sat on her bed, puffed up her pillows, and held the glass when she wanted water. "Please go to bed, Marco. I'll tell the sister to phone you when I go to the delivery room."

"I'm staying," he said. His tie was crooked, and he had run his fingers through his normally neat hair so often that it was completely disheveled.

"This is a great learning opportunity," she said awhile later. "In the future I'll know exactly what women endure when I deliver their babies."

"Shouldn't we send for Fanus?" Marco asked. "It's getting late."

"The sister will call Fanus as soon as I'm taken to the delivery room," she said calmly.

When the night sister decided the time had come, Marco was dispatched to the waiting room. "I love you, Aletta," he said stiffly.

She smiled. "I know. Everything will be fine. It's a big adventure."

But by four o'clock the next morning, when their baby girl was finally born, the great adventure and the learning opportunity were very far from Lettie's mind. Giving birth was hard work, she realized, painful work. She was soaked in sweat, parched, exhausted. But when she heard that familiar first cry, pitiful yet strong, she was the happiest woman on earth.

"Call my husband," she told the midwife, "and leave the baby for a while. You can bathe her in a moment."

"Doctor?" Sister Gouws asked uncertainly. Allowing a husband to see his wife and child in such a state was totally unheard of!

"Fanus, fetch Marco," Lettie said firmly.

Her colleague laughed. "Do as she says,

Sister. She's the boss," he said.

Lettie reached for the baby, still wrapped in towels, and took her in her arms. *Our very own little baby,* she thought, *mine and Marco's.*

She heard him at the door and looked up.

Marco stopped in the doorway. His face was ashen, his dark hair hung low over his forehead, and dark shadows cupped his eyes.

"Meet your daughter," she said and held out the bundle to him.

He approached as if treading on holy ground. He stroked Lettie's damp hair, his eyes never leaving the small face in front of him. Then he reached out with both hands and picked up the baby carefully, as if she were extremely fragile. "Isabella," he said.

After a while he looked up, his eyes defenseless, uncertain, questioning. "I already love her so deeply," he said, shaking his head in total awe.

Lettie nodded. "She's our little girl," she said.

Ten days later Lettie was discharged. Baby Isabella was strong and healthy, with rosy cheeks and dark hair. Her eyes were beginning to focus and seemed to gaze at the world with amazement.

Her cradle was on Marco's side of the bed. During her first night at home, he got up at hourly intervals to make sure she was breathing. "Marco, get some sleep, you're going to be exhausted tomorrow," Lettie scolded after a while.

"Tomorrow is Saturday," he said. "And she's so tiny, anything could happen to her."

"She's a healthy baby, nothing's going to happen," Lettie reassured him.

And when at the age of six weeks she gazed into her father's dark eyes and the little rosebud mouth widened into a smile, Marco looked up and said, "Now I know we made the right decision, Aletta."

He left the room and returned with the marble statuette of the Virgin and Child Isabella's grandfather Giuseppe had made. "I'm giving it to her, Lettie, so she will always know she is special," he said.

"Lettie," her mother said the day before Christmas, "please run through all the kids' names again. There have been so many babies, my mind's in a whirl."

Lettie laughed. "Mommy! There aren't that many! De Wet and Christine have Gerbrand and the two girls, Anna and Lulani. Klara and Antonio have Cornelius and Lulu. That's all."

"Doesn't Klara have another baby as well?" Her mother frowned.

"There's one on the way, but not until June. Then they'll also have three."

Her mother frowned. "Heavens, Lettie, these young parents are irresponsible!"

"No, Mommy," Lettie protested, "it's not a bad idea to have your children close together."

"Don't you get any ideas," her mother cautioned. "Daddy and I love taking care of Isabella in the mornings when you go to the surgery, but we're too old for another one!"

Around Isabella's first birthday, Annabel returned from abroad, her contract at an end. Almost immediately she staked her claim on Boelie. She clung possessively to his arm the first Sunday they were all together on the farm.

"Heavens, the yard is swarming with kids." Annabel laughed, tossing back her long, silky hair. "Is this what happens when I leave you without supervision?"

"Yes, you're falling behind." Christine laughed. "Are you coming to the kitchen?"

"No, thanks, I'll stay here. I'm useless in the kitchen," Annabel replied.

The kitchen was in its usual state of chaos. "I was going to make a salad, but —" Christine began.

Gerbrand rushed in from outside. "I'm starving, Ma," he said.

"Take a cookie," said Christine. "Wait, no, don't take a cookie, we're about to eat . . ." But the boy was already through the door with three cookies in his hand.

"Pass me the tomatoes and onions. I'll make the salad," Lettie said. "I notice Annabel is all over Boelie."

"Isn't she!"

"I thought there was something between Boelie and Pérsomi," Lettie said. "We saw them at the movies a few weeks ago. They didn't see us, but they looked cozy."

Christine shrugged. "De Wet and I thought so too, but we were clearly mistaken. Or maybe something happened. I don't know." She leaned forward slightly. "De Wet thinks Pérsomi is a much better match for Boelie than Annabel. He and Pérsomi have been colleagues for almost four years, so he should know."

Lettie smiled. Christine would always believe De Wet knew best, even if the whole world disagreed with him.

But then again, De Wet was probably right. He usually was.

Leonora Maria Romanelli was born in June

1952. "If it's another girl," Lettie had said beforehand, "we should name her after your mother."

"If it's another girl," Marco had said, stroking her hair as they sat together at home, "I'd like to call her Leonora."

"From *Il Trovatore*?" she asked.

He smiled, his eyes gentle. "Yes, Miss Know-It-All, from *Il Trovatore.*"

Now, in the hospital, he was studying the wrinkled little face in the bundle of towels. "She looks nothing like Isabella," he said, amazed.

"She's her own little person," said Lettie.

He nodded. "Papa's little Leonora," he said in Italian. "When you're a little bigger, Papa will play you your own opera, okay?"

Early in October, just two days after Lettie had gone back to work, Annabel came to see her. Lettie had seen the appointment in the register for one o'clock. It was later than Lettie liked to stay, but it might be an emergency, she thought.

"I'm going to be home a little later than usual," Lettie told her mom on the phone. "I don't think I'll be able to fetch the girls before two."

"Don't worry," her mom reassured her. "Leonora is asleep and Isabella is in the garden with her oupa — I think they're looking for fairies."

At a quarter past one Annabel walked into the surgery. "Sit," Lettie said. "How are you?"

Annabel peeled off her gloves and took a good look at the room before she sat down on the chair opposite Lettie. "So this is where you hide out by day?" she said.

"Actually, I work mornings only. I usually go home at one," Lettie said pointedly. "How can I help, Annabel?"

Annabel shrugged. "I've been feeling a bit out of sorts lately," she said. "I think you should take a look."

"Okay, tell me how you've been feeling."

The more symptoms Annabel listed, the more Lettie's suspicion was confirmed. How she was going to break the news to her friend, she didn't know.

"Why don't you get undressed, and I'll take a look," Lettie said, but she knew a physical examination wasn't really called for.

Dear Lord, give me strength for what lies ahead, she prayed when Annabel sat back down again.

She looked at the girl who had been her friend since childhood. Annabel looked back confidently, almost defiantly.

Lettie drew a deep breath. "Annabel, there's absolutely nothing wrong with you. You're pregnant," she said, without mincing words.

"Impossible," Annabel said calmly.

"There's no doubt."

"I'm incredibly shocked," Annabel said, but her eyes were triumphant. "I'd appreciate it if we could keep it quiet."

"What happens in here stays within these four walls, I promise," Lettie said seriously. "But you'll have to tell Boelie as soon as possible."

"Yes, now he'll have to marry me," Annabel said and got up. "I must go. I have an appointment at the hair salon."

Long after she had left, Lettie remained seated behind her desk. She felt cold inside, numb. She recalled Annabel's words at a Voortrekker camp a lifetime ago: "See, Lettie, that's how you treat men. If you stroke their egos, they'll eat out of your hand."

It was an extravagant wedding with too many flowers, too much liquor, too many long-winded toasts, too many caterers specially imported from Johannesburg, and too much food.

It was not like the modest farmer Boelie at all.

■ ■ ■ ■

The year 1952 also heralded the worst outbreak of infantile paralysis in the history of the United States. By the end of November, nearly sixty thousand cases had been reported, more than three thousand young patients had died, and a third of the total number of patients had suffered permanent damage as a result of the disease.

But Lettie told Marco about a radical new discovery in the field of medicine. "Did you know that a lens has been developed that one can wear directly on one's eye?" she said one evening when Isabella and Leonora had been bathed and put to bed. "It's called a contact lens."

Marco gave his slow smile. "Interesting," he said, nodding. The smile remained in place. "And do you know who first had the idea of a lens like that centuries ago?"

"Probably the Italian genius Leonardo da Vinci." Lettie teased in return.

"Bingo, Miss Know-It-All! Leonardo da Vinci."

"Really?" Lettie said, surprised. "I was just pulling your leg."

"Da Vinci was the first man to describe the concept of a lens that is in direct contact with the eyeball and takes on its shape," Marco said, nodding.

"Well, aren't you Italians something else!" Lettie responded. "As soon as those lenses become available, I'll be first in line to get them and be rid of my glasses forever."

"Aletta," Marco said, suddenly serious.

"Yes?"

"Forget it. You're perfect the way you are." He held out his hand to her. "I think we should go to bed as well. What do you say?"

She smiled. "Yes, Marco, I think so too," she said, taking his hand.

"I hope this child is a boy so Boelie can produce the heir and get it over with," Annabel said to Lettie during her next visit. "De Wet and Christine don't seem capable of doing it, and I don't plan on going through all this drama a second time."

Lettie laughed. "In three, four months you'll have forgotten everything. Boy or girl, the baby will be a pure joy."

But Annabel held up her perfectly manicured hand. "One is quite enough for me, thanks very much."

Cornelius Johannes Fourie — Nelius for short — was born on Van Riebeeck's Day 1953.

And after many painful hours of coaxing and encouraging, Lettie could finally say, "You have a perfect baby boy, Annabel."

Annabel lay pale and exhausted against the pillows. "I'm so glad," she said, her eyes shut.

"Can I call Boelie now?"

"No, I'm exhausted. Just hand me a glass of water," Annabel replied.

When Isabella heard they were going to the farm on a Sunday after church, she was always overjoyed. "Gerbrand will show me the baby cows," she said excitedly, "and Anna —"

"Calves," Lettie said automatically.

"— calves and Anna will play with me."

"Tata, tata," Leonora said, equally excited. "Tatatata."

Pérsomi often drove out to De Wet's farm on Sundays, and a firm friendship had developed between the quiet law student, Lettie, and Christine.

"My folks are moving to Margate," De Wet said one Sunday during lunch. Pérsomi glanced up, frowning.

"Margate?" Lettie asked. "Why do they want to leave the farm?"

"Boelie and my dad can't live on the same farm anymore," De Wet said. "Christine and

I have been expecting it for a while."

"And now, with Annabel also in the picture . . ." Christine shook her head. "Lettie, you and I know her, we've come to understand her over the years. But my poor mother-in-law is having a hard time."

Pérsomi didn't say a word. Her face was a closed book. Lettie wondered again what had gone wrong between her and Boelie.

Later, when they were alone in the kitchen, Lettie asked Christine, "How are things between Boelie and Annabel? I worry about them."

Christine shook her head. "We're also worried, Lettie. De Wet and Boelie live on neighboring farms, but they seldom come here. When we do see them, there's always tension. De Wet misses the brother he used to have."

At the end of summer, when the days were getting cooler, Annabel came to the surgery alone. Her face looked like thunder.

"Hello, Annabel," Lettie said calmly, "what can I do for you this morning?"

"You can tell me it isn't so," Annabel said and began to strip off her clothes.

It was on the tip of her tongue to ask what she was talking about, but one look at Annabel made Lettie swallow her words.

Very soon she saw that it was indeed so. "You're pregnant again, Annabel," she said calmly. "Congratulations."

"Impossible!" said Annabel.

"That's what you said the last time as well," Lettie said, still smiling, "and here you are — a married woman."

"I've been taking precautions," Annabel said.

"Precautions are never a hundred percent effective. It might be a shock at the moment, Annabel, but when you get used to the idea and the baby you're carrying becomes a reality, you're going to be overjoyed."

"No, Lettie, you don't understand," Annabel said. Contrary to her nature, she seemed on the verge of tears.

Lettie got up and came round the desk. She crouched next to her friend and put her hand on Annabel's arm. "Don't worry, my friend," she said gently, "everything will work out, you'll see."

Tears streamed down Annabel's cheeks. "No, no, it won't!" she cried and gripped Lettie's hand. Then she closed her eyes and drew a deep breath. "Sorry," she said, letting go.

Lettie got to her feet and handed her a tissue.

Annabel looked up, apparently back in control. "Can we do something about this, Lettie?"

Shock waves ran through Lettie's body. Her mouth went dry. "What exactly do you mean?" she asked stiffly.

"You know very well what I mean. I don't want this baby."

Lettie took a moment before she spoke, tight-lipped. "No, Annabel, nothing can be done. The topic will never be raised again, not between these four walls, and not outside of them either."

Lettie drove home with a heavy heart. She had a throbbing headache and her shoulders and neck were tense and stiff. The revulsion she still felt after Annabel's insinuation had formed a lump in her stomach.

She steered the car through the open gate of the brand-new home Antonio had designed for them. The garage doors stood open as if to welcome her. There were delicate rainbows in the fine mist of the sprinkler that was watering the newly planted lawn. The old trees threw long shadows over the driveway and the patchy lawn and the colorful flower beds.

Slowly Lettie began to relax.

Isabella heard the garage doors close and

ran out. Behind her followed Leonora, her small arms wide open. "Mama! Mama!" they cried.

Lettie gathered up her two little girls, hugged their soft figures, and walked into the house that was filled with the smell of Marco's thick tomato sauce simmering on the stove.

"Marco," she said, putting down the girls and walking into his embrace, "we have a wonderful life."

He gave her a skeptical look. "You clearly have no idea what my day was like," he said.

"And mine," she said, with feeling, "but then I came home."

Chapter Thirteen

"Who are those scientists from Boston you told me about?" Marco asked one evening when the two of them were reading in the living room. Soft music was playing in the background. Their daughters were in bed. Marco was reading the paper while she was engrossed in a medical journal.

"The ones who cultivated the polio virus in a lab?" she asked. "Enders and Robbins and . . . I think Weller?"

"It says here in the paper they're being awarded the Nobel Prize in medicine for their research."

"Wonderful. Cultivating that virus was an incredible breakthrough."

"According to the same article, there have been serious polio outbreaks all over the world. I wonder why it has suddenly become such a dreaded disease," he said.

"I'm not sure," she said, frowning. "In theory it should have been on the decline with improved sanitation and hygiene. I think somehow the natural immunity of the world's population must have diminished. Infantile paralysis is highly infectious."

He folded his newspaper and set it aside. "There's something else I want to discuss with you," he said.

"Yes?"

"Antonio called today. They're planning to go to Italy for about three weeks, to visit my parents and brother. He wants to know if we want to go with them."

Lettie smiled. "How wonderful! Of course. When do they plan on leaving?"

"They don't want Cornelius to miss school, so they want to go during the July vacation. It's summer in Italy, a lovely time of year."

"We can afford it," Lettie said, "and I think it would be marvelous for your parents to meet their grandchildren."

Marco was silent for a while, then he said, "Of course I'd love to go, but I think we should plan it for the same time next year. The children will be a year older. Especially Leonora is very young for such a long journey."

"But surely Antonio and Klara are going by air."

"Yes, but it's still a three-day trip. You

spend the first night in Kampala, the second in Cairo, and on the third day you arrive in Rome. Then it's another day on a bus or train to Turin, where you have to rent a car."

"I didn't realize it was such a mission," Lettie said.

"There's another reason," Marco continued. "My parents' home is small. It has only two bedrooms, so both families can't stay there. Lorenzo's in-laws have a big villa higher up the mountainside, but I think both Antonio and I would prefer to stay in our childhood home if we go back."

"Yes, I can understand that," said Lettie.

"My parents are getting older and I know Mama. She'll want to spoil us and cater to all our needs. It might be a bit overwhelming if we descend on my parents with five kids in tow."

Lettie began to laugh. "And they can be so wild and uncontrollable when they're all together! Marco, I'd love to meet your parents and see where you grew up. But I think you're right, we should wait."

"Next year we'll go. I promise," he said.

That winter, shortly after Antonio and his family had left for Italy, pneumonia clawed its way back into Marco's chest. It hit him harder than before, completely eroding his resistance and leaving him doubled over with pain.

Lettie immediately resumed the treatments that had helped him in the past. She hired Sister Greyling, a recently retired nursing sister with years of experience, to care for him by day. She herself spent each night at his bedside.

This time it took a second course of penicillin before Lettie was satisfied that Marco was on the mend.

With Marco in the hospital, the children became unruly. Especially Isabella missed her papa terribly. "I think you should take her to see him," Lettie's father suggested.

"Marco is still very weak, Daddy," Lettie replied.

"The child is worried about her father. She's too young to understand. I think she'd feel better if she could speak to him."

"If you think so," Lettie agreed uncertainly. "I'll see how he feels this afternoon and fetch her. But Leonora must stay."

On their way to the hospital she tried to prepare the child for what was waiting. "Papa is very sick. He's in bed," she said.

"I know, he has pneumonia and he coughs," Isabella replied earnestly.

"Yes, that's why he has to sit up in bed, even when he's sleeping. If he's asleep when we get there, we mustn't wake him."

"I want to speak to Papa," the child said.

"If he's awake, you can, Isabella. Papa has a tube in his arm to help make him better, and sometimes there's a mask over his nose to help him breathe."

The child sat up straight in the passenger seat next to Lettie, her legs dangling, her feet in white socks and shoes. "I want a red ribbon in my hair," she had insisted before they left.

She seemed to be pondering something. "Can Papa talk?" she asked after a while.

"A little, but only when he's awake," Lettie replied. "And not too much, or he'll start coughing."

"I know," Isabella said.

They walked down the shiny hospital corridor together, the child at Lettie's side, her shoulders straight, her head held high.

When they reached the ward, Lettie took Isabella's hand and quietly opened the door. "Papa's asleep," she whispered. "We must be quiet."

Isabella nodded seriously. She let go of her mother's hand and walked to the bed. But her eyes were level with the mattress.

"Come, Mommy will lift you up so you can see Papa," Lettie said, bending down.

She sat on Lettie's arm and looked at her

father for a long time. "Why does Papa look so funny?" she whispered. "His face is funny . . ."

"It's the color of the illness, Isabella," Lettie said softly. "It has a smell too."

She breathed in. "Yes, I smell the illness," she said.

"Papa will soon be well, then he'll play with you again and tell you stories."

"And sing songs," the little girl whispered. "Mommy will make Papa better."

"It's Mommy's work, my love. But Mommy can't do it alone. Actually, it's Jesus who makes Papa better. That's why we pray for Papa every night."

"And every morning. Oupa prays for Papa in the mornings when we eat our breakfast," she said seriously.

Slowly Marco opened his eyes. The gaunt face blossomed, the eyes shone. "Isabella," he whispered hoarsely.

The little face broke into a smile. "Papa!" she said happily and held out her arms.

"Come to me," he whispered, making a slight movement.

"Wait, careful," said Lettie. "Come, Mommy will pull the blanket down, then you can sit here, in Papa's arm."

"The one without a tube," Isabella said and carefully moved closer to her father.

She put out her hand and stroked his face. "Papa, you look like a pirate. You must shave," she said.

Marco smiled. "Yes, I must." He beckoned feebly with his other hand. "Aletta?"

She came round the bed, sat down, and took his hand in her own. "Your little girl wanted to see you. We won't stay longer than five minutes," she said.

He nodded. "Leonora?"

"Our youngest is fine," Lettie said. "She's being spoiled rotten by my parents. We'll have to go back to a strict routine when everyone is back home again."

"As long as the children are happy," Marco said.

"Leonora misses Papa when we go to bed at night," Isabella reminded Lettie.

"Tell her Papa will be home soon," Marco said.

The next moment he was overcome by a coughing fit. Lettie lifted the child off the bed, then held him upright, handed him his handkerchief, rubbed his back, and gave him a sip of water when at last the coughing subsided. She rearranged the pillows behind his back and he leaned back, exhausted, his eyes shut. "Papa is going to rest now. We must go," Lettie said.

"I want to kiss Papa good-bye, but not on

his cheek, it's too scratchy. I want to kiss his forehead," the child said firmly.

Lettie picked her up. She leaned over and kissed her father's brow.

Marco lifted his hand and stroked her hair. "*Ciao,* Isabella," he whispered.

"*Ciao,* Papa," said the clear little voice.

Isabella held Lettie's hand as they walked back down the long corridor to the entrance. It wasn't something that happened often, for the child was fiercely independent. "Papa is sick," she said somberly.

"Papa is getting better. Before long he'll be fit as a fiddle," Lettie tried to reassure her.

"I know," said Isabella.

In the car on their way back home she said, "When I grow up I want to be a doctor and make people better."

"That's a good idea," said Lettie. "Or you can be a teacher, like Papa, and teach children to be clever."

The child gave it some serious thought. "Or a fireman, then I can slide down that long pole," she said.

Lettie laughed. "You can be anything you wish," she said.

When the two of them walked into her parents' home, her father asked, "And?"

"You were right, it was the right thing to

do, for both of them," Lettie said.

September 1954 arrived dry and hot. The rains had not yet come. The flowers Mrs. Roux put in the waiting room for Spring Day had wilted by noon.

At one, just as Lettie was getting ready to leave, the phone rang. "Dr. Ismail wants to speak to you," said Mrs. Roux.

"Put him through," said Lettie. Yusuf Ismail was an Indian physician with a surgery on the main street in town. He did most of his work at the non-white hospital. Occasionally they exchanged opinions on difficult cases, and sometimes he called to ask her to assist during an operation.

"Dr. Louw?" came the familiar voice over the line.

"Yusuf Ismail!" she scolded. "How many times must I tell you my name is Lettie?"

"And how many times must I tell you if I call you Lettie, the Boers in the vicinity will stone me to death?"

"You're just as obsessed with politics as the rest of the folk around here." Lettie laughed. "How can I help?"

"I've got bad news. I've just diagnosed our first case of infantile paralysis."

Lettie felt a shock pass through her body.

"Where, Yusuf? Who's the patient?"

"A five-year-old black boy admitted to the non-white hospital yesterday. I'm afraid he's too far gone. They brought him in from a farm in the district, but it's too late. I wanted to send him to Pretoria, but the ambulance can't take him until tomorrow."

At the white hospital two ambulances were on standby, Lettie knew. But the law decreed that no non-white person was to be transported in an ambulance reserved for whites.

"Yusuf!" she said helplessly. "Have you informed the authorities?"

"I've been battling for more than an hour to get the call through to Pretoria," Yusuf replied wearily. "And Dr. Maree has been out in the district all week. I can't reach him."

Lettie knew that Yusuf didn't have the luxury of a receptionist who could tell the operator it was an emergency, that this call to the state department in Pretoria should get priority.

"Listen," she said, "I'll get Mrs. Roux to phone Pretoria. She's very efficient, she'll set all the wheels in motion. The non-white hospital will probably have to be quarantined at once."

"Yes, and I wouldn't be surprised if I got more cases very soon, specifically from the area the child is from," said Yusuf. "This disease spreads like wildfire."

"Let's hope most people from that community have a natural immunity against the disease," Lettie tried to encourage him. She had to choose her words carefully. Her colleague was quick to pick up any discriminating insinuation, whether one meant it or not. "I still think people from urban areas are more susceptible to the virus."

"I hope you're right," said Yusuf. "I'll keep you posted."

The disease spread rapidly through the district. There were new cases on a weekly basis, the victims chiefly black children. The limited facilities of the non-white hospital were hopelessly inadequate. Women were choosing to give birth at home for fear of being infected; Yusuf Ismail drove miles in his small Ford Prefect to deliver babies or tend to children with feverish bodies and anxious eyes.

"I simply can't help everybody," he told Lettie one afternoon when she phoned to ask how he was doing. "I don't have the necessary equipment, and the medication the government provides is the bare minimum. I hear you've also diagnosed a case."

"Two, actually, a little boy last week and

another five-year-old boy this morning. That's why I'm calling," Lettie replied. "They're both from the Boggoms River district. I suspect the water might be contaminated. I notified the authorities, but I suppose they're going to want to fill out forms in triplicate and get approval before anything will be done."

"I wish the people would seek help sooner, then at least we can treat the symptoms," Yusuf said despondently. "By the time they get to me, it's often too late. And of course there are so many superstitions and traditional remedies and medicines . . ."

The line grew quiet. "We do what we can," Lettie said. "I fear our region is the perfect breeding ground for the virus: it's hot, the water supply is often inadequate, and whatever the source, it's used by too many people . . ."

"If only we had a vaccine." Yusuf sighed.

For a while after Lettie put the receiver down, she sat motionless. The child she had diagnosed that morning had upset her. The ambulance had taken him to Johannesburg, accompanied by Sister Greyling.

But it was a four-hour drive, and there was very little even Sister Greyling could do for him along the way.

Lettie sighed and picked up her doctor's

bag. She was glad to go home.

At the beginning of October, Boelie and Annabel's daughter was born. *Baby Fourie,* said the label on her bassinet in the hospital nursery. "We haven't decided on a name yet," Boelie said, looking grim.

Six days later he sat opposite Lettie in her surgery, his face pale with worry. "She doesn't even want to breastfeed," he said desperately and ran his fingers through his hair.

"This baby won't be the first to be raised on formula milk, Boelie. Neither is Annabel the first new mother to react this way. Female hormones can be very volatile after pregnancy and birth. Baby blues is a common occurrence."

Boelie shook his head. "It's not natural for a mother to reject her baby so utterly. She hasn't held her even once. She's a perfect baby, isn't she, Lettie?" His dark eyes pleaded for reassurance.

"She's a beautiful little girl, Boelie, and she's thriving on the formula milk. There's no need to worry. Annabel will come round, you'll see. Just give her time."

Boelie shook his head. "I hope you're right. I sincerely hope you're right," he said heavily. There were dark smudges under his eyes. He got to his feet and picked up his hat from the corner of her desk.

At the door he turned. "You know, Lettie, sometimes the mistakes we make are irreversible," he said.

He closed the door without saying good-bye.

Every day more people came to the surgery and the list of house calls grew longer. Every common cold or slight flu symptom was regarded with suspicion. "Doctor, are you sure it's not polio?" The voice would choke to an eerie whisper, forced past the fear.

"There's an entire family in the waiting room to see you," Mrs. Roux said one sweltering Thursday morning in early November. "It's a mister and missus, just so you know."

"Show them in," Lettie said, smiling. Over the years Mrs. Roux had developed her own cryptic code to supply the doctors with information about the patients.

Mr. Viljee entered: fat, pompous, brazen. Behind him came Mrs. Viljee: fatter, more pompous, even more familiar. A string of children trooped in, sniffing, fiddling, clambering.

"How can I help?" Lettie asked formally, trying to keep her eye on the swarming kids.

Mr. and Mrs. Viljee made themselves at home in the two chairs reserved for patients while the children explored the surgery. "Hang on, no, you can't play with that," Lettie protested. She turned to the father. "Is there someone I need to examine?"

"We've brought them for a thorough checkup," he said, leaning back smugly in his chair. "We're not taking any chances with this polio thing. We're not that type."

"You want me to examine all of you? Is one of the children sick?" Lettie asked.

"What do they look like to you? Do they look sick?" Mrs. Viljee demanded, sounding aggressive.

"You want me to examine them all to make sure they're healthy?" Lettie got up and lifted a child off the bed. "No, leave those books on the shelf," she said.

"There's nothing wrong with my kids," Mrs. Viljee said firmly.

"In that case I don't understand what you want from me," Lettie said as patiently as possible. She removed an instrument from a child's grasp. "No, don't touch this," she said. "And mind your shoes on —"

"I've already told you we've brought them all for a thorough checkup in case they've got polio," Mr. Viljee said impatiently.

Lettie picked up the bell on her desk and

rang it vigorously. The children froze, the door opened, and Mrs. Roux said, "Yes, Doctor?"

"Mr. and Mrs. Viljee and the children will wait outside, and the children will come in one by one to be examined," Lettie said firmly.

"We're staying," Mr. Viljee said, equally firmly.

"One of you may stay. The other must wait with the children."

Mrs. Viljee took offense. "If all my children aren't welcome here, we're leaving! Come!" She marched to the door. "I'm not going to be pushed around by a young upstart who thinks she's smart just because she has a so-called education. 'Don't understand what you want from me'! I ask you!"

The children trooped out behind her, sniffling and looking offended.

At the door Mr. Viljee turned. "And don't even think about sending us a bill. I'm not the type to be pushed around. You've chosen the wrong man to mess with, missy. You don't know James Viljee!"

A moment later Mrs. Roux peered around the door. "For heaven's sake," she said, "what just happened here?"

"I'm not quite sure myself, but I think I may just have lost a large number of patients," said Lettie.

"Doctor, what were you thinking?" Mrs. Roux asked, smiling. "Would a nice cup of tea be any consolation?"

Lettie's phone rang the next morning. "Mr. Pistorius, the principal of the high school, is on the line," Mrs. Roux said.

"Did something happen at the school?" Lettie asked worriedly.

"I'm not sure. He just said he wants to talk to you."

"Okay, put him through," Lettie said.

As it turned out, nothing had happened at the school. As high school principal and chief elder in the congregation, Mr. Pistorius said, he was speaking for the entire community in their deep-rooted desire to approach Dr. Louw to inquire whether she might perhaps find time in her hectic schedule for an information session on the dreaded disease infantile paralysis, which was fast turning into an epidemic both countrywide and locally and was leaving members of the community paralyzed with fear, so to speak . . .

Here the principal lost track and stumbled over his own rhetoric and long-windedness.

"It sounds like a good idea," Lettie said warily. "Maybe we could arrange for the

Department of Health —"

"The community owes you a debt of gratitude for agreeing despite your hectic schedule," he continued. "The event will take place Monday night — a fortnight from today. It's hard to find a time and date to suit everyone. There's the prayer meeting on Wednesdays, town council meeting on Tuesdays, church council meeting on Thursdays, and then it's the weekend. And if one happens to serve on all those councils —"

"Mr. Pistorius, what exactly do you want me to do?"

"Oh, if you could address us on the dreaded disease — no longer than about forty-five minutes, please, then there should be ample time for questions — we would highly appreciate it."

"A forty-five-minute information session!" Lettie gasped. "Mr. Pistorius, I'm a doctor, I'm not —"

"My deepest gratitude, Dr. Louw, for the years you've been a pillar of the community. We appreciate —"

"No, no, I think you're confusing me with my father. He's retired, so —"

"Well, thank you once again, Dr. Louw. Good bye."

Slowly Lettie replaced the receiver. "Shall I send in the next patient?" Mrs. Roux asked from the doorway.

"Yes, send him in," Lettie said, dazed.

That night when the girls had gone to bed, she said to Marco, "Your principal asked me today to deliver a lecture on infantile paralysis during an information session."

He smiled, amused. "How long did he take to ask you that?"

"My word, the man is pompous! I'm sure he wasn't that bad when I was at school. But worst of all, I didn't agree to do it, he just presumed I would. I really can't do it, Marco. I'll call him tomorrow and tell him —"

"Of course you can do it, Aletta," Marco said calmly. His smile reached his eyes. "You should hear him tie himself in knots when he speaks English!"

"Marco!" she scolded. "Why haven't you told the poor man you understand Afrikaans? Put him out of his misery?"

Marco laughed. "He can do with a little practice," he said.

"Oh goodness, you two," Lettie said the next Sunday afternoon as she and her friends were making salad in the kitchen. "I know how to take care of people's health issues. But speak in front of all those people! Klara and Annabel can do it, yes. Or you,

Pérsomi, you do it every day in court. But I really don't know if I *want* to do it."

"I know how you feel," Christine said. "I could never do it. Why can't Fanus Coetzer do it? Or your dad, or Yusuf Ismail?"

"My dad isn't up-to-date with the latest developments. He's a full-time oupa these days," Lettie said, shaking her head.

"I wouldn't trust Dr. Coetzer after five in the afternoon," Pérsomi said tactfully, "and Yusuf won't be allowed to enter the school hall. I think it's very important that people get the right information, and I think you're the person to do it, Lettie."

"Well, that's it then. A good thing you're so smart," Christine said. "Why don't you ask De Wet to help you? Of the lot of us, he's the one who knows best how to address an audience."

Lettie smiled. It was heartening to witness Christine's blind faith in her husband's abilities. *Pérsomi could also help me,* she thought. *She's making a name for herself as the best litigator in the district. Or I could ask my husband. Marco has no problem speaking to a large group of people.*

"Start by telling the people what infantile paralysis is and where it comes from," Marco suggested when she began to work on her lecture.

"I want to keep it as short as possible. I only want to say what is absolutely necessary," Lettie explained.

"The people are there to be informed," he said. "You have the knowledge, Lettie. I think you owe it to your audience to give them the facts as fully as possible."

"Go on to explain the symptoms," Marco said, "so they will recognize the disease, then tell them what the treatment entails."

"It's not quite that simple," Lettie said worriedly. "The symptoms resemble those of ordinary flu, and there's no treatment." She shook her head. "There's already such hysteria around the disease, I can't tell people that!"

"You have to be honest, Aletta," Marco said seriously. "But you can offer them hope by telling them about the progress being made in medical research."

"They'll know that. It's been all over the papers and the news."

"Not everyone reads the papers or listens to the news on the radio," he said calmly. "Let me help you write your lecture."

"You'll have to write it in Afrikaans. Bushveld folk don't understand English," she said.

"No, *you're* going to write it, in Afrikaans. I'll just be lending a hand."

On the appointed Monday night Lettie dressed with care. She gave extra attention to her makeup. "If you know you look good, it gives you confidence," Pérsomi had said the day before.

She stepped back and inspected herself in the full-length mirror. Isabella appeared in the doorway behind her, fresh from her bath and in her pajamas, her dark hair neatly brushed. "You look pretty, Mommy," she said.

"Your mommy is beautiful, and tonight she'll show everyone she's not only the best doctor, but also an orator of note." Marco put two-year-old Leonora on the double bed and began to dry her hair with a towel.

"Marco, don't tease, my nerves are shot," Lettie said.

"Mommy looks pretty, Mommy looks pretty," Leonora echoed her older sister, squirming out of her father's grasp.

"Come, you're going to Oupa and Ouma now. Mommy and Papa are going to the school," Marco said.

"Are you going to sing, Papa?" Isabella asked.

"No, Mommy is giving a talk," Marco replied, and gathered them in his arms. "Lock the door, Lettie, please?"

■ ■ ■ ■

There was a sizable audience in the hall, chiefly parents and grandparents anxious to protect their children against the dreaded disease. *They're here to learn. They're scared,* Lettie realized. *Marco was right, I can help them.*

But when she found herself on the stage after the meeting had been opened with a long prayer, in which the reverend pleaded with the Lord to keep the children safe, after the headmaster's verbose welcome, and after various procedural arrangements had been announced by the mayor, Lettie stood looking out over a sea of faces. For a moment she panicked, then she remembered Marco's advice. "Take a deep breath and look them in the eye."

She took a deep breath. "Infantile paralysis, or poliomyelitis, is an acute viral infection, an inflammation of the gray matter in the spinal column, that is easily spread from one person to the next, orally or through contact with fecal matter. Poor personal hygiene and contaminated water contribute to the increase in reported cases."

She felt herself grow calmer. The audience looked back at her impassively. "That's why washing our hands is so important, and boiling our drinking water when we're not sure how clean it is," she ad-libbed.

The audience remained unresponsive.

She looked down at her notes. "The first clinical description of infantile paralysis was provided by the English doctor Michael Underwood in 1789. Later, the disease was known as Heine-Medin disease because of the work of doctors Jakob Heine and Karl Oskar Medin in the 1840s and 1890s respectively. The polio virus was isolated by Karl Landsteiner in 1908.

"The disease later became known as infantile paralysis because it affects mainly children," she continued. "Though infantile paralysis, or poliomyelitis, has been endemic for thousands of years, epidemics were unheard of until the nineteenth century. It has become one of the most feared children's diseases of the twentieth century."

The next time she looked up from her notes, she looked for Marco. He was smiling and nodding encouragingly. *He thinks I'm doing okay. He's proud of me.*

She continued more confidently. "Polio causes no symptoms in people with natural immunity — and that's ninety percent of patients — although those patients can spread the virus."

Lettie remembered that Marco had told her to use her hands. She raised her hand and pointed at her lips. "The polio virus enters the body through the mouth and attacks the first cells it finds, those in the throat, for instance, or the mucous membranes in the intestines. That is why the first symptoms are a sore throat or an upset stomach, and of course a high temperature — the body's way of fighting the virus."

She looked down at her notes again. "In about three percent of cases the virus ends up in the central nervous system, and the patient may contract nonparalytic aseptic meningitis, which leads to severe headache, backache, fever, vomiting, and lethargy. In only *one* percent of cases" — Lettie was careful to stress the word — "the virus destroys the motor neurons, which leads to muscle weakness and paralysis.

"The incubation period averages six to twenty days, but it could be shorter or longer."

She glanced up at her audience. The people were gazing at her, attentive now. Here and there someone was frowning or nodding anxiously.

She took a sip of water, and her eyes sought out Marco's. She was getting to the worst part now. He was smiling and nodding. Next to him sat Christine and Pérsomi. Christine smiled at her, but Pérsomi was listening attentively.

"There is no cure for poliomyelitis," Lettie said as emphatically as possible. "Treatment merely serves to relieve some of the symptoms, like pain, and to prevent complications, like infections in the weakened muscles. Exercises and an improved diet are prescribed to restore as much function as possible to the affected muscles. Long-term rehabilitation includes physical therapy, braces to prevent deformity or fractures in weakened limbs, corrective shoes, and sometimes orthopedic surgery.

"In case of paralysis of the respiratory muscles, an iron lung is used to help the patients until they are able to breathe independently again, usually about two weeks from the onset of the paralysis."

A hand went up in the audience. "Yes?" Lettie asked.

"Can you please explain what an iron lung is?"

"An iron lung is a kind of cylinder in which the patient is placed so that only the head remains free," Lettie tried to explain. "It pressurizes the patient's chest, forcing out air. Then the pressure is relieved and the lungs are inflated again. Almost like doing artificial respiration with one's hands."

Another hand went up. "Is there an iron lung in our hospital?" a man in the third row asked.

"Oh no, it's a very expensive and highly specialized piece of equipment," Lettie replied. "The nearest iron lung is at the Johannesburg Children's Hospital."

"And without it a child with breathing problems will die?" the same man asked.

"It's possible, yes." Lettie nodded. "Without the iron lung the patient can suffocate, or contract pneumonia. Five to ten percent of patients who contract the paralytic form of the disease develop respiratory problems, and about four percent of those don't survive. Usually only an arm or a leg is affected, sometimes both arms or legs. But at the first signs of further paralysis the child is taken to Johannesburg by ambulance."

Another hand went up. "Is there no other treatment?" a lady in the front row asked.

"Other long-term treatment includes hydrotherapy, massage, and passive exercise," Lettie replied. "There's a lady in Australia doing research on various kinds of physical therapy, but the results have not been published."

"What are the chances of a child with a slight degree of infantile paralysis recovering completely?" another lady asked.

"The paralysis is often temporary," Lettie replied. "Nerve impulses are sometimes restored after a month, and complete recovery might occur in six to eight months. Muscles have the ability to recover completely, even if half the original motor neurons have been lost. But if the affected nerve has been completely destroyed, it can't be regenerated. Paralysis that remains after a year is usually permanent.

"The good news," Lettie said, folding up her notes, "is that scientists have developed several vaccines that are currently being tested to fight the polio virus worldwide. I hope that in about three years our children will all have been vaccinated, which will protect them the same way the vaccination against smallpox does."

"But this doesn't help us in the next three years," someone said loudly from the middle of the audience.

"No," Lettie agreed, "but it's hope for the future."

When they drove back to her parents' home to pick up the girls, Marco said, "I was very proud of you tonight, Aletta. I know it wasn't easy, but you did a really great job."

"I'm glad you think I was okay," Lettie

said with a smile. "One thing I can tell you: I'd rather do ten complicated operations than get back on a stage to speak to so many people again!"

Early in February 1955, Leonora woke one morning feeling out of sorts. "She feels warm," Marco said worriedly.

An icy fear gripped Lettie. She laid her palm on Leonora's forehead. *Steady,* she told herself, *every parent expects the worst at the slightest sign of a sniffle.* But for the first time she was able to put herself in the shoes of a parent entering her surgery with a sick child.

The child's skin was warm under her cool hand. "Her temperature is slightly raised. It's not serious. I don't think it's anything much," Lettie said.

"Are you sure?" Marco asked.

She saw her own anxiety in her husband's eyes. She reached out with her hand and gently stroked his cheek. "I'll ask my dad to keep an eye on her today, but I really don't think there's anything to worry about."

But all morning fear kept gnawing at her. She phoned home twice. "She's not well, but she's asleep now," her mom said. "Daddy agrees it's just a touch of flu. There's no need to worry."

And when she picked up the girls just after one, her dad said, "No, Lettie, it's just old-fashioned flu. In a day or two she'll be herself again."

She got up a few times during the night to check on the child. Leonora was still warm, but her condition didn't seem serious. Marco also returned a few times, saying, "She's warm and restless, but she's asleep."

The fever stayed around for three days, not growing worse, but not improving either. "Just keep her quiet," Lettie told her parents. "We don't want to take any chances."

When she fetched the girls in the afternoon of the fourth day, her mom said, "Leonora is definitely getting better. She even ate something today. We kept her quiet, but Daddy says in a day or two she'll be as right as rain."

Relieved, Lettie drove home. "No," she told Marco that evening, "I don't think we should give her a proper bath. I'll just give her a sponge bath. Let's wait until her temperature is normal before we bathe her again."

She got up in the night to make sure the child was okay. Leonora was still warm, but she seemed to be sleeping more peacefully.

"She's getting better," she whispered to Marco.

The next morning Lettie was up early. She made porridge and coffee, and sandwiches for Marco and herself. After a while Isabella woke up and came into the kitchen, bleary-eyed. "Leonora is still asleep," she said and got up on a stool to eat her milk and rusks.

"Still?" Marco asked when he joined them in the kitchen, freshly showered and neatly dressed.

"Yes," Lettie said. "Would you like some porridge?"

Leonora began to cry in the bedroom. "I'll go," Marco said and got to his feet.

He hurried down the passage.

"Wait, Isabella, don't stir your porridge with the sugar spoon. Look, now there's porridge on the spoon. Mommy will give you another —"

"Lettie?" Marco was standing in the doorway. His voice sounded strange.

Lettie turned.

Their child was limp in his arms.

Tears were rolling down his cheeks.

"She can't stand," he said.

Chapter Fourteen

"She can't stand."

The words entered through Lettie's ears and reverberated in her mind.

The words cut through her.

". . . can't stand . . ."

The words cut her to pieces.

Her legs gave way, and she sank down on the nearest chair.

"Mommy?" her eldest said.

". . . can't stand . . ."

Then the meaning got through to her.

Marco was still in the doorway, the child sobbing in his arms. She got up, her mouth parched.

She took three steps to reach her husband and child, three endless steps.

She reached out and took Leonora from Marco. She was warmer than an hour before. She clasped the child to her bosom. "There, there, my darling, there, there."

"Is it . . . ?" Marco asked, his voice raw.

Lettie acted on instinct. She ran her fingers over the child's left leg. "Can you feel that?" she asked.

The child nodded.

Lettie tapped gently on the knee. The natural reflexes were missing. "Can you tell Mommy where it hurts?" she asked.

"My legs hurt," the child sobbed. "And my head."

Lettie looked up into her husband's dark, anxious eyes, brimming with tears. She nodded slowly. "Probably, yes."

He took the child from her again, carefully, gently clasping her to his chest. "Papa's little princess, Papa's beautiful little girl," he said over and over in Italian.

"Don't cry, Papa," the child replied in Italian. "It's not so bad."

"Leonora," Marco said softly.

Lettie drew a deep breath and forced the words past the large lump in her throat. "I think we should take her directly to Johannesburg," she said.

Marco looked up and nodded. "Yes," he said, his voice stronger now. "But let's first say a prayer."

"Mommy?" Isabella's small voice jolted Lettie back to reality.

She looked down. Her eldest daughter's face was filled with alarm, her eyes fearful, her lips trembling. Lettie picked her up and wrapped her arms around the child. "Leonora is ill. Papa is going to say a prayer for her," Lettie said.

"Okay," said Isabella.

Marco knelt, his youngest still in his arms. Lettie knelt beside him, her arms protectively around their eldest daughter.

Marco began to pray, deeply, earnestly, in his mother tongue. Lettie bowed her head. She didn't understand everything, but she felt a deep sense of peace settle over her.

My child has polio, she told God wordlessly in her own language. *You know I am helpless. With all my years of training and experience, I can't help my own child. We place her in Your hands. Please help me make the right decisions and give her the right support.*

And have mercy on us.

When Marco said amen, he got up. He had found some peace as well, Lettie noticed.

She put out her hand. He opened his arm and held her against him. "Come, Isabella," he said softly.

The little girl leaned against their legs. She put out her hand and stroked her little sister's leg. "Don't worry, Leonora, Jesus and Mommy will make you better," she said earnestly.

Lettie shook her head. "Heavens, Marco," she said.

He nodded, but his shoulders were square. "You think we should take her straight to the Johannesburg Children's Hospital?"

"Just as a precaution," Lettie said. She tried to think straight. "I should go with her in the ambulance, to make sure she's comfortable and calm. She needs a firm mattress, and I can apply hot poultices to her legs for the pain."

He nodded. "Shall I stay with Isabella?"

"I think it's best. She's going to need you," Lettie said. "I'm going to give Leonora a shot for the pain. It's going to get worse as the day goes on. I'll arrange for an ambulance."

"Will you manage on your own?" he asked worriedly.

She shook her head. "I wish with all my heart you could be with me, Marco. But it could be weeks, and you have to be at school. And we have two children. It's important that we don't upset Isabella too much."

He nodded and stroked her hair.

She fetched her doctor's bag, gave the little girl a shot. She was so small and was crying so bitterly. Then she phoned Mrs. Roux.

"Don't you worry about a thing," her receptionist replied. "I'll take care of everything. The ambulance should be there any minute."

She called her parents. "We're on our way," her dad said.

"We don't want to upset the children too much," Lettie warned him.

"I understand," he said.

Marco had put Leonora on the double bed. "Lie still, my little princess. Papa will stay here with you," he said softly. "Isabella, don't get up on the bed, sit here on the carpet."

"My parents are on their way," Lettie said. "I have to pack."

"No, your mother can pack. Sit here with us awhile, just until your folks arrive."

She sank down on the carpet beside Isabella and rested her head on her husband's knee. He stroked her hair. She reached out and took Leonora's small hand into her own. Isabella climbed onto her lap. With her free hand she hugged the child against her. "You're right, Marco," she said heavily, "it could be three, four weeks before we're together like this again."

He kept stroking her hair. "We'll soon be reunited. Even four weeks isn't that long," he said.

"What's waiting for us and our little girl?" she asked, feeling lost.

"I don't know," he said softly. "But we'll get through this, Aletta, now and in the years to come. The four of us have got each other."

Lettie's parents arrived. When the ambulance drew up at the door half an hour later, Lettie's bag was packed. "Just buy what I've forgotten," her mom said, flustered.

Lettie took leave of her family, then picked up Isabella and held her tightly. "You're staying with Papa, and with Oupa and Ouma. Mommy is going with Leonora. But we'll be back as soon as Leonora feels better. Mommy loves you very much."

"I know," Isabella said. "Make Leonora better quickly."

She put the child down and stepped into her husband's embrace. His strong arms closed around her protectively. She leaned against him for a moment. She could hear his heart beat through the coarse fabric of his shirt. "I love you, Aletta," his beautiful voice said simply.

"And I love you, Marco," she said.

Then she turned and climbed into the back of the ambulance. Leonora lay waiting, her eyes filled with apprehension.

The driver shut the door.

Through the window Lettie watched her family grow smaller on the sidewalk: her dad, bent and old, with his arm around her gray-haired mom's round figure. And Marco, tall and straight, their eldest daughter on his arm. They kept waving until the ambulance turned the corner.

Then Lettie focused her attention on her sick child.

On their way to the hospital, Leonora's temperature began to rise and she was in tears again. Everything hurt: her head, her neck, her body. Her legs were very, very painful. "Take the hurt away, Mommy," she pleaded.

When they had crossed the Pienaars River, she fell asleep.

Lettie leaned back, exhausted, and closed her eyes for a moment.

A sudden realization flashed like a lightning bolt through her heavy heart.

The early symptoms of paralytic poliomyelitis, she knew, included high temperature, headache, stiff back and neck, muscle atrophy, loss of reflexes. Paralysis would progress for two or three days and be complete by the time the fever broke. So far only Leonora's legs were paralyzed, but the disease would run its course.

Spinal polio was the most common kind of paralytic poliomyelitis. It attacked the part of the spinal cord responsible for muscle movement, including that of the limbs and the intercostal muscles. The infection caused inflammation of the nerve cells, so the muscles stopped receiving signals from the brain, becoming passive, weak, and finally completely paralyzed.

Leonora began to whimper again. Lettie leaned over her. She was very hot. "Mommy's here, sweetheart," she said, placing her cool hand on the little girl's burning forehead.

"Mommy, it hurts," the child sobbed.

"Where does it hurt?" Lettie asked.

But the child just kept sobbing, "It hurts."

She couldn't give Leonora another shot, not even to bring the fever down. Lettie felt helpless. She poured fresh water into the hot water bottle. "Come, Mommy will put this on your legs. It will make the pain a little better."

"No, no!" cried the child. "It hurts!"

It was a long way to Johannesburg. They still had the last part of the Springbok Plain to cross, then they had to navigate the traffic in Pretoria before they could tackle the last thirty miles to Johannesburg.

What she feared more than death itself

was bulbar poliomyelitis, which affected the muscles of the diaphragm, making it difficult for the patient to breathe. It left small children helplessly trapped in an iron lung, sometimes for weeks or even months on end.

Tears began to roll down Lettie's cheeks. She no longer tried to hold them back. She succumbed to her grief for her perfect little girl who was crying with pain and who was facing an uncertain future.

The next moment she felt a small hand on her knee. "Don't cry, Mommy," Leonora said.

She dropped to her knees beside her child, one arm protectively over the hurting body, the other hand wiping the damp, dark hair from the warm forehead. "Mommy loves you so much, Leonora."

"You're crying, Mommy," the child repeated.

"Yes, sweetheart, I'm crying because you're in pain. Mommy doesn't want you to have pain."

"Mommy must take the pain away," the child said.

"Maybe that's why Mommy is crying, Leonora. I can't take the pain away." How could she explain?

There was a strange anxiety in the child's

eyes, a fear of the unknown. "My legs can't stand," she said.

Lettie nodded, still stroking the small forehead. "I know."

Marco would have known the words to say, Lettie knew. Marco would have made up a story about the king's messenger who had had a fall.

"Leonora, you have a sickness that has put the pain in your body, that has made your legs weak and tired — paralyzed them. Your body is putting up a big fight. That's why you're so warm. It's your body's way of fighting the sickness. Do you understand?"

"No."

Lettie licked her dry lips. "We don't always understand everything," she said. "I'm going with you to a hospital, where I'll stay with you. There's a very clever doctor at the hospital and he's going to help Mommy make you better."

"Jesus will help too," the child said.

The lump in Lettie's throat grew huge. "Yes, what's most important is that we remember it's by the grace of God that we are able to travel by ambulance to a fully equipped hospital in Johannesburg," she said, speaking over the child's head.

"Papa will come to see me," the child said.

"No, sweetheart, Papa must stay with Isabella, or poor Isabella will be all alone. The two of us will miss Papa very much, but we'll soon be back with him, I promise. You must always remember that Mommy and Papa love you very much."

The child began to cry again. "What's the matter, my sweet?"

"It hurts!" she said. "It hurts!"

"There now, my love, Mommy will move the hot water bottle. Is that better?"

When the ambulance finally drew up at the children's hospital and Lettie got out stiffly, she knew that this journey alone with her child had been necessary. For her, and maybe for her child as well. Just before they arrived, she had given Leonora something for the pain. She would need it during the next hour or two. Lettie felt stronger. She knew what was waiting, but she had found the strength to handle it.

Klara and Antonio were waiting in the foyer. Lettie walked into their embrace.

They all turned to the little girl on the stretcher. "Look who's here, Leonora," Lettie said cheerfully.

"Oom Tonio and Tannie Klara," the child said. "My legs hurt and they don't work."

Lettie saw Antonio turn away to hide the tears that were rolling down his cheeks.

How the brothers took after each other!

Klara took the child's hand, smiled, and said, "Your papa told us you're not well, so we came at once to give you a kiss." She leaned over and kissed the little girl's forehead.

"Is Papa here?" the child asked, perking up.

"No, my love," Klara said, "he called us on the phone."

"Oh, I thought he was here." Her eyes searched for her mother. "Mommy," she cried, "the hurt is coming back!"

"Lettie, let me introduce you to Dr. Erasmus," Antonio said. "He's the pediatrician who has come to examine Leonora. My sister-in-law, Lettie Romanelli — or Dr. Lettie Louw."

So the next part of the journey began, through administration and forms, through corridors to examination rooms and children's wards, through a battery of tests. Leonora clung to her mommy, sobbing with exhaustion and pain and fear.

Somewhere amid the chaos Klara brought tea and an egg sandwich and remained strong when everything became too much for Lettie.

"They can't *do* anything for her," Lettie said softly. "She's so tired, so scared. Can't they just leave her alone?"

Klara rubbed her back. "I'm sure they're just doing what they have to. I . . . don't know what to say, what to do."

"Just stay here," Lettie said wearily. "It means so much to me that you're here, Klara."

Late that afternoon Leonora finally lay in a white hospital bed — a lively little girl imprisoned between high white rails, her dark, damp hair spread on the white pillowcase, her body a small mound under the white covers. "Lettie, Antonio is coming to fetch me in a while. I have to go home," said Klara.

"Of course," Lettie said.

"I'll come again tomorrow, in my own car."

"No, you don't have to —"

"I'll be here," Klara said firmly. "Where will you sleep tonight? Shouldn't we take your luggage —"

"I'm staying with Leonora," Lettie said.

"You can't sleep here, and you need to rest. You must keep up your strength," said Klara. "There's a hotel down the street. We'll reserve a room for you and drop off your luggage. At least you'll have somewhere to take a shower and a nap."

"Okay. Thanks, Klara," Lettie said. She

was suddenly bone-tired, too worn out to argue.

In the early evening the specialist sat down with Lettie at Leonora's bedside. "It's easier to explain when you're talking to a colleague," Dr. Erasmus began with an apologetic smile. "But it's also harder, because you know we're so totally helpless."

"Yes," Lettie said.

"Dr. Louw, so far Leonora's torso has not been affected. The right leg is slightly less affected than the left one. Of course, the paralysis could still spread during the next day or so before the fever breaks, but based on what I've learned about the disease during the past few years, I believe Leonora has it in a less severe degree."

"I'm so grateful," Lettie said softly.

"I also believe the chance of her developing bulbar polio is reasonably slim."

"It's my worst fear," Lettie said, nodding.

"The possibility is not excluded, of course," Dr. Erasmus hastened to add, "but it's unlikely. We've done every possible test, and for the next few days we're just going to keep her calm and under observation. We'll give her pain medication and a light sedative at night to make sure she sleeps."

Lettie nodded again.

Dr. Erasmus gave her an earnest look. "I

want you to get a good night's sleep tonight."

"She's my child," Lettie said.

"That's the mother in you talking, Dr. Louw," said Dr. Erasmus. "The doctor in you knows very well that your little girl is going to sleep peacefully tonight, that she'll be in the hands of people who work with infantile paralysis every day, and that she will need a rested mommy tomorrow morning. Am I right?"

Lettie sighed and stroked the sleeping child's hair. "You're probably right," she reluctantly agreed.

"Do you have somewhere to stay?"

"My brother-in-law has booked me into a hotel down the street."

"Would you like to make a phone call?"

"I'd like to call my husband," Lettie said. "I see there's a public phone booth in the corridor."

"It'll take hours to try and get through from a phone booth to an operator in the bushveld," Dr. Erasmus said. "I'll ask reception to place the call for you. They'll send for you." He gave a slight smile. "They'll do it for Dr. Louw, if not for Mrs. Romanelli."

Lettie managed a smile too. "Yes, it usually works, doesn't it?"

■ ■ ■ ■

When the receptionist summoned Dr. Louw fifteen minutes later, Leonora was still asleep.

"Marco?" Lettie said into the receiver.

"Lettie?" She heard the effect of the long wait, and the doubt and fear in his voice.

"She's okay," she said immediately.

"And how are you?"

An overwhelming weariness took hold of her and she closed her eyes. What she wouldn't give to be with him now, calling the two little girls for their bath. "I'm fine, just exhausted. But we're okay. Please don't worry."

"I'll stop worrying when the two of you are back home again," he said seriously. "Have you seen the specialist?"

She told him everything: about the findings, the tentative good news, the difficult two or three days ahead. It felt like sharing a heavy load, like halving the weight she had to bear. *Dear Lord, thank You, thank You for this man,* she prayed wordlessly.

She spoke to Isabella as well. "Papa stayed with me all day. We played," the child gushed. "Tomorrow he's going back to school and I'm going to stay with Oupa and

Ouma. Is Leonora better? When are you coming home?"

And thank You, dear Lord, for my bouncy little girl, who puts the warmth back into my cold heart, she prayed as she walked down the long corridor, back to the room where her sick child lay.

She pushed the door open. Leonora had woken up and was crying bitterly.

Lettie hurried to her bedside. "No, no, my sweetheart. What's the matter?" she asked, leaning over the small figure.

The child clung to her. "You were gone," she sobbed. "I want to go potty, Mommy!"

"Mommy's here, Mommy's here," Lettie soothed her. "It just feels as if you want to go potty, Leonora. There's a little tube that takes your wee-wee away so you don't have to go to the bathroom."

"You were gone, Mommy," the child cried again.

"I spoke to Papa on the phone," Lettie said, calmer now. "Papa says he loves you, and Isabella says —"

But the child began to cry even harder. "I want my papa," she cried.

"No," Lettie said softly but firmly, "crying like this won't do any good. It will just make you feel worse. Papa can't come right now. Papa is at home with Isabella. Would you like me to tell you a story?"

Only when Leonora had been asleep for several hours and the night sister told her at eleven that she really should get some rest herself was Lettie able to tear herself away from her child's bedside and get into one of the waiting taxis in the parking lot. Antonio had already made all the arrangements at the hotel, and Klara had unpacked her suitcase and put her clothes away.

Her body ached with exhaustion. The moment her head touched the pillow, she was fast asleep.

Four days later she was able to report to Marco that the possibility of their daughter's recovery was increasing. "Her right leg might be temporarily paralyzed, but it's not certain. Cells that have lost function can begin to repair themselves after about six weeks," she explained, "and Dr. Erasmus thinks it might be what's happening with Leonora's right leg."

"And the left one?" Marco asked, still anxious.

"The left leg may have suffered permanent damage, Marco, but it's too early for a prognosis."

After a while he asked, "Lettie, is Leonora suffering?"

Pain shot through her. How do you tell a father who is far away that his little girl cries helplessly at times, that her mommy prays endlessly for the pain to disappear? How do you tell him about the fear in her eyes when the sister enters the room with a syringe or the doctor lifts the blankets away from the soft little body? How do you tell your life partner that you wish you could take the child's pain on yourself, that you wish everything was just a nasty black dream and that the sun would rise on a normal day tomorrow morning?

"Yes, Marco, she's in pain," she answered slowly. "We give her medication, but it's only partly effective."

His groan sounded as raw as her heart felt.

"I miss you terribly." The words came from deep inside her, finding their way over her lips.

"Do you want me to come to Johannesburg?"

She wanted it more than anything in the world. "No, no, it's really not necessary. I just want to talk to you."

"Oh, Aletta." He missed her too, she could hear it. "Tell me more."

Lettie took a deep breath. "When I look at the other children, I know we're actually blessed. Leonora is out of danger, and she won't have to lie trapped in that terrible iron lung. She has full use of her arms, and one day she should be able to walk again. More than half the mothers here can't tell their husbands the same thing tonight."

"I'm grateful too, Lettie. When will you be home?"

"It's impossible to say. They're moving Leonora to the children's ward tomorrow. She'll be put on a course of penicillin to prevent infection in the weakened muscles. At some stage they'll start her long-term treatment. I don't know what lies ahead. It all depends on the progress she makes."

She listened to the news from home, to the good wishes from people who were praying for them. He recounted the stories Isabella told when he fetched her at her grandparents'.

She just listened to his voice. His voice, the man he was, was what she would take back to their gravely ill daughter in the hospital bed.

When Leonora was admitted to the children's ward, which she shared with nine other young polio patients, their daily routine changed drastically. Leonora soon realized there were other children whose legs were also paralyzed. Some couldn't even use their arms. She realized they felt the same pain she was feeling. A few hours after being admitted, she was sitting up against the pillows, talking to the little girl in the opposite bed.

Young as she was, she understood. "That little girl is very sad. Her mommy isn't here," she whispered to Lettie.

The other moms in the ward soon discovered Lettie was a doctor. She became the one who had to explain in detail what was happening to their children and what they could expect.

Every other morning Klara came all the way from Pretoria to see how they were doing. The first day she came, she brought a soft teddy bear with a bandaged leg. "His leg hurts too," she told Leonora.

"Does he have polio?" Leonora asked.

"I think he just has a sore leg," Klara replied.

"No, he's paralyzed," the child decided. From that moment the bear got exactly the same treatments she did. The sisters even had to give him injections. At night the bear slept in Leonora's arms.

But when the pain got too bad, she forgot about the bear.

Klara brought a coloring book and crayons to pass the long hours, but at times it was too painful for Leonora to sit up. Klara also brought some of her own children's storybooks for Lettie to read aloud. "I'm a hopeless storyteller," Lettie admitted.

Antonio often came in the evenings. When he entered, Leonora clapped her hands, overjoyed. Antonio always had to tell a story. "I'm not as good as your papa," he said, laughing, but he tried his best.

"What language does the man speak?" one of the other moms asked one night after he had left.

"Italian," Lettie replied. "My husband is Italian. Antonio is his brother."

"And this little girl speaks Italian and Afrikaans?" she asked, astounded.

"That's how she's growing up," Lettie said.

"Papa tells better stories than Oom Tonio," Leonora said. "I wish Papa could tell me a bedtime story."

About a week after Leonora had been moved to the children's ward, Dr. Erasmus called Lettie to her bedside. "Look," he said and tickled the sole of her right foot with a feather.

Lettie clearly saw a slight reflex movement in the leg. She felt as if she were witnessing a biblical miracle of old. The greatness of the tiny movement shocked right through her.

"There's definitely some activity," he said, "but we'll only know in a week or two whether we can hope for a full recovery."

Leonora's left leg remained inert.

That evening Lettie could hardly wait to share the news with Marco. "What exactly does it mean?" he asked.

"It's a start," she admitted. "There's still a long, hard road ahead."

"Even a crooked path has a starting point," he said philosophically.

"You won't believe how she's grown in the past ten days. There's a little girl of about seven here, a headstrong child who had to start with physical therapy today. The doctor came to speak to her and her mother while I was having lunch. When I returned, Leonora gave me a lecture on the importance of exercises," Lettie said, laughing. "I doubt she even knows what the word means."

"When does Leonora start with exercises?"

"I'm not sure, but I don't think we're going to stay that long. I miss you too much. I can't be alone much longer."

"I'd love you to come back," he said immediately, "but we must do what's best for

Leonora."

"I can treat her at home. We can hire Sister Greyling full-time for the next month or two. I'll ask Dr. Erasmus about the treatment tomorrow, what massage techniques and exercises he recommends. Then I think we're coming home."

"I'll fetch you," said Marco. "The house is empty without you, Lettie."

"I think it will be better if we come by ambulance," said Lettie. "Leonora should be kept still and preferably flat on her back. Let me get all the details and we can discuss it tomorrow night."

"I miss you, Aletta."

She was silent for a moment. Then she said, "You know, Marco, when I'm having a really hard time during the day, I just have to remember that I'm going to talk to you again in the evening and things immediately seem more bearable."

The next night she reported, "We must keep her on a special diet to build muscle and boost her immunity, with enough calcium to strengthen her bones. She'll have to start with physical therapy soon, initially two short sessions per day."

"Is there a physical therapist in our town?" Marco asked.

"I know Sandra Havemann worked as one years ago. I'll find out if she's willing. What's wrong with your voice, Marco?"

"I'm fine. Must be the line."

"Oh." She was getting to the most difficult part. "Leonora's right leg should recover completely. Dr. Erasmus is quite confident about that. But her left leg has suffered serious damage, Marco. She'll have to wear braces to prevent the leg from breaking or bending."

"Ah, no." She could hear his pain. Her heart went out to him, but she had to persevere.

"It looks as if the damage might be permanent, Marco." It was hard to break the news to him, but at the same time it was a relief to share her grief.

There was silence on the other end of the line. Then he asked, "But she'll walk again?"

"Our little girl should walk again. She might need surgery on the leg and foot, but only in about ten years' time."

"Oh, Lettie, I feel so sorry for her."

"Marco, you're hoarse."

"I'm fine, really, Lettie. Don't worry."

But long after he had ended the call, a vague anxiety gnawed at her.

The next night, a Friday, there was no reply

when she phoned home. She asked the operator to call her parents' home. Twenty minutes later she heard her mother's voice on the line.

"Mommy, is Marco there?"

"Yes, they're having supper here and spending the night." Her mother had a tendency to bellow to make sure she'd be heard over the great distance. "Marco is a bit out of sorts. Daddy thinks the strain of the past few weeks is getting to him. He has an appointment with Fanus Coetzer tomorrow morning just to be on the safe side. He's bathing Isabella at the moment. Would you like to speak to him? Oh, here he is now."

"Hello, queen of my heart, how are you doing?" The beloved voice sounded almost cheerful.

"I'm fine," she said. "Why are you so jolly?"

"We've been having fun, Isabella and I." He laughed. "Your mom bought some bubble bath and I'm sporting a Father Christmas beard."

"And the bathroom is sopping wet, I suppose," she said, laughing as well. It was so normal there — so far removed from here. She pulled herself together. "Marco, Leonora had her first massage session on her left leg today."

"And how did it go?"

Lettie hesitated before she said, "She's a brave little girl."

He understood at once. "Was it very painful?"

"Yes, Marco, it was, but it has to be done. How are you feeling? You still sound hoarse."

"I'm fine, just a little tired. I have a bit of a sore throat. Your mom is spoiling us with supper tonight, and then I'm going straight to bed."

"What time is your appointment tomorrow?"

He laughed softly. "Nine o'clock, with your colleague, Miss Know-It-All."

"I'll phone around noon to hear what he said."

"Aletta, I'm just tired and worried, that's all."

"You're seeing the doctor anyway and I'm calling tomorrow," she said firmly.

When she finally got through the next afternoon after waiting almost half an hour, there was no reply at their home. It took her another half hour to get through to her parents. "Marco has just left," her dad said.

"What did Fanus say?"

"Just a sore throat and exhaustion. He gave him a shot of penicillin just to be on the safe side. Marco has gone to pick up some clothes for himself and Isabella. They're spending the rest of the weekend here."

Lettie nodded. She was glad Fanus gave Marco a shot, even if there wasn't much wrong with him. "So Ouma is spoiling them some more?"

"You'd better believe it! There's roast lamb in the oven."

"How I wish I could be there!" Lettie sighed.

"Marco says you and Leonora might be coming home at the end of next week," her dad said.

"It all depends, Daddy. If everything goes according to plan, yes. We're terribly homesick. How's Isabella?"

"She also has a bit of a sore throat and the sniffles. She and Marco probably picked up the same bug."

"You'd better get them well before I come home with Leonora next week," said Lettie.

"I'll do my best, don't worry."

"And give them my love. I'm not going to call again tonight. It's almost impossible to get hold of the operator on weekends. I'll talk to them both tomorrow night."

■ ■ ■ ■

Sunday morning broke clear and cloudless, with doves cooing in the lush green trees and church bells pealing across the city as Lettie walked the few blocks from the hotel to the hospital. It was good exercise, and it cleared her head.

She planned to get a wheelchair and take Leonora out to the garden. The weather was perfect, with not even the slightest breeze. Klara and Antonio were coming in the afternoon. They had promised to bring their daughters to spend some time with their cousin.

Lettie went up the steps and made her way to the ward where Leonora lay. There was the usual bustle just before breakfast.

The child lay watching the door with anxious eyes, her bear clasped tightly in her arms. She was waiting for her mommy. "The hurt didn't come last night," she said the moment Lettie reached her bedside.

Lettie leaned over and kissed her forehead. "I'm so glad. How's your little bear?"

"He's a bit scared, so I'm holding him tightly. I don't want to eat the porridge."

"I know, but you must," Lettie said, sitting down on the chair beside the bed, her back to the door. "I think —"

"Dr. Louw?" someone said behind her.

"Yes?"

"There's a phone call for you at reception."

"Thank you," Lettie said and got to her feet. "Mommy will be right back, Leonora."

She hurried down the hospital corridor. Who on earth could be phoning so early? She picked up the receiver. "Lettie speaking," she said.

"Lettie?" Her father's voice was gray.

Fear took her breath away, nearly choked her. Isabella? Her mother?

"It's Marco," her father said.

"What about Marco?"

"The ambulance has just left for Pretoria. Yusuf Ismail is with him. Lettie, he has polio."

She sank down next to the telephone.

The receiver fell out of her hand.

Her mouth broke open.

Soundlessly.

Antonio was there, his face a strange gray color. Klara was there, looking appalled. "I'll go to Leonora," she said.

Leonora?

. . . diminished immunity increases the severity of the disease . . .

"Drink this, Dr. Louw," someone said.

"Come with me, Lettie," she heard Antonio say. "I'll take you to the General Hospital in Pretoria. That's where they're taking Marco. Klara will stay here with Leonora."

They drove through the streets.

. . . the older the patient, the more severe the paralysis . . .

She heard her own voice speak. "Marco's lungs are too weak."

She heard snatches of the words Antonio was saying: ". . . be strong . . . have faith . . . specialist . . ."

She knew the hospital.

"Lettie, this is the specialist who will look after Marco when he arrives," Antonio said.

"My husband has diminished lung capacity," she heard herself say. "He gets pneumonia every year."

"We'll see what we can do, Dr. Louw."

. . . the chances that the respiratory muscles will be paralyzed increase tenfold in adult patients . . .

"He won't be able to go into an iron lung, it won't work."

"Let's be optimistic, Dr. Louw. Here, I want you to drink this."

Antonio was beside her through it all.

The paralysis ran its inexorable course.

The specialist shook his head. "It's affecting the entire body," he said.

"The heart muscle?" she heard Antonio's strange voice ask.

The specialist nodded. "Yes, I'm afraid so."

Antonio walked beside her back to the white room.

A whisper: "Tonio?"

"I'm here, Marco." Antonio spoke Italian. His voice was strong. Hastily he wiped his eyes and moved into Marco's line of sight. "Mama and Papa sent a letter. They're both well. The mountains are white under their blanket of snow. Mama is baking focaccia and biscotti and making minestrone. Papa got an order from America for a hundred statuettes."

A peaceful expression spread over Marco's face.

"Aletta?" he mouthed soundlessly.

"I'm here with you, Marco," she said, gently stroking his face. "I'll stay, I won't leave you."

"Leonora?" His eyes were wide open. Not afraid, but intensely focused.

"Leonora is doing very well, she's recovering rapidly. Soon she'll be a healthy little girl again, running and playing outside in the sun with Isabella. And Isabella is fine, just missing her papa."

Marco closed his eyes. "Lettie, I love you," he whispered almost breathlessly.

Tears were streaming down Lettie's face. "And I love you, Marco Romanelli," she said.

Marco fell into a deep, peaceful sleep from which he did not wake.

PART FOUR: WANDERING

Chapter Fifteen

Day after day Lettie followed the path laid out for her. Where it was leading, she did not know.

She walked the path back to her empty home.

She followed it through the funeral in town and the burial at the farm. The school choir sang and sounded hollow without Marco's voice to accompany them.

She let the path direct her to the normal Sunday dinners at the farm, where she tried not to notice Marco's missing chair, the missing place setting. Tried not to let her anger show. Anger at how normal everything was, when it could no longer be normal. Anger toward God. Fury at His mistake.

She let it carry her into the comforting arms of her family, who grieved with her but did not seem to rage.

Sister Greyling — Tannie Bes, the children called her — came early in the mornings to stay with Leonora. Isabella spent those hours with her grandparents. At noon her oupa took her home to Tannie Bes. Lettie tried to be home from the surgery by two, but sometimes it just wasn't possible.

Sandra Havemann came every afternoon for Leonora's physical therapy. Her right leg was growing stronger. Leonora could move her toes and her reflexes were good.

But every movement, every touch, was painful. The little girl burst into tears every time she laid eyes on Sandra. "Mommy!" she cried and held out her skinny arms to Lettie.

The physical therapy was necessary to prevent further muscle atrophy and to strengthen muscles that had not worked for months. Lettie tried to explain it to Leonora in the simplest way. But while she was trying to encourage her, to explain, or to distract her with stories and games, her heart was crying with her child. And all the time she knew: Marco would have done it so much better.

The gaping pit of his absence remained. At times she was drawn right down to the bottom. At times the climb to get out again was just too steep.

After story time in the evenings Lettie sat in

the living room, reading. She did not play music anymore.

She ordered every piece of literature published worldwide on infantile paralysis. She informed herself of every possible bit of progress, every new treatment, every speck of hope.

The vaccine developed by Jonas Salk of the University of Pittsburgh in 1952 was introduced to the world on April 12, 1955, Lettie read in a medical journal one evening. After only three doses, 99 percent of patients were immune to the polio virus. The remedy had the potential to contain the spread of the disease worldwide.

It was wonderful news: the hope the world had been waiting for.

But for some it had come too late.

Sometimes it became too much for her. She was simply too involved.

"Why don't you play in your room for a while? Look, Mommy has brought you each a puzzle. Isabella, build yours here on the coffee table. Leonora, you sit over there."

Two pairs of excited dark eyes looked back at her.

"I'll bathe you in a while and then I'll tell you a story, okay?"

She closed the bedroom door behind her.

Only that morning a thirteen-year-old patient had said to her, "The thing about this illness is the paralysis. When muscles are paralyzed, they're paralyzed, and it doesn't matter how much you exercise, nothing works. It just hurts. It makes you feel helpless, and no one understands, because they think you're giving up."

"But you won't give up, will you, Jacques?"

"I don't know, Doctor," he said, sounding very mature. "I feel I might as well give up, because I can't do what I used to. Polio isn't for sissies, my dad says."

"No," she said, "it's for the strong-willed."

"Strong-willed people who know what it means to lose all their dreams," he said with a bitterness not befitting his age. "My dream was to play fly-half for the high school's first fifteen. At junior school I played for the first team in standard four and five. I was good, everyone said so. I was set on making first team in standard eight. My dream was to play rugby for the Springboks one day. Now I can't even walk without crutches."

"I know, Jacques," she said. "I think you've probably always lived by the motto 'I can.' Now you'll have to learn to say 'I'll try.' "

The boy shook his head. "I don't want to," he said. "I don't want to be like this."

"You could get rid of the crutches, but only if you continue with the physical therapy and the exercises," she said earnestly.

"And will I play rugby again?" He sounded almost defiant.

"Maybe you can try again one day. I believe in holding on to your dreams, but you also must be realistic." She was speaking around the truth, she realized, half dazed. She must come straight out with it. "I don't believe you'll make the first team, Jacques. I think what you must strive for is to learn to walk again in the shortest time possible, maybe even to run, so that one day you can teach your sons, who might inherit your talent, to play in the first team."

What consolation was that for an Afrikaner boy of thirteen?

She sank down on her knees beside her bed.

People came to her for advice, for help, for hope.

She didn't even have a solution for her own child.

Her eyes were brimming with tears — lately it had been happening quite often.

She knelt quietly, allowing the tears to fall.

Chapter Sixteen

In time her path widened, began intersecting the paths of others who were not part of her daily routine.

It was early morning, windless and humid. When Lettie finally got away from the school and drove to the surgery, the cicadas were screeching shrilly.

Marco, she said in her thoughts, *our eldest daughter started school this morning.*

It was beginning to get easier, having these conversations with him. She still wanted to share things with him.

I wish you could have seen her dressed in her navy-blue uniform and shiny new shoes, the brand-new satchel with her playtime snack in her hand. You would have been so proud of her, Marco. She was the only child who didn't cry. She wanted to know why the others were. I tried to explain. I said maybe they weren't used to their mommies leaving them.

She said, "That's not a very good reason."

Oh, Marco, I nearly cried myself at that. But you'd be proud to know that I left without shedding a tear.

Lettie parked her car under the jacaranda tree behind the surgery. *One thing I can tell you, my love — you would not have been able to say the same!*

At other times it was less easy to talk to Marco — the pain of missing him was just too much.

Like when Leonora took her first steps.

At the age of one, it was into her papa's arms.

When she had to learn to walk again at four, the safety of her papa's arms was no longer there.

"The right leg is strong enough," Sandra Havemann had said, "but we can't risk letting her stand on her own without braces to protect the left one."

So Lettie and Leonora went to Johannesburg to see the specialist and then to have a special shoe made.

The braces were heavy, the shoe hard. Everything hurt all over again. Every small movement was accompanied by tears. There was so much courage, so much effort, and so little success.

It was so much easier to tell Marco about

Isabella learning to read or winning at athletics or singing a song at the eisteddfod.

She asked Antonio to advise her on having a cottage built adjacent to the house. At Lettie's request, Sister Greyling agreed to live there and work for her family full-time.

In the winter of the following year, when Isabella could read her sister storybooks from the library and Leonora was getting along reasonably well in her heavy shoe and iron braces, Annabel walked into Lettie's surgery one morning.

"Good morning, Annabel," Lettie said. "Cold, isn't it?"

"Yes, let's talk about the weather if there's nothing else to say," Annabel said, peeling off her gloves.

Oh, heavens, are we in a mood again? Lettie thought briefly. "How can I help you?" she asked.

"I'm not sick," Annabel said, sitting down to face Lettie, "and I'm definitely not pregnant again."

"Good," Lettie said.

"You never forgave me for that day, did you?" Annabel's eyes were defiant.

"It's in the past," Lettie said. "That's not why you're here."

"No," said Annabel, "it's not. I've come

to tell you Sapa has offered me a two-year contract in a senior position."

Lettie frowned. Sapa — the South African Press Association? Surely that wasn't a job Annabel could do from here. "In Joburg?"

"No, London."

"London?"

"Yes, London, England," Annabel answered curtly. "I've worked there before."

"But . . . that was before you were married, before you had kids," Lettie said.

"It's a wonderful opportunity, the kind that doesn't just fall into one's lap."

Lettie felt her disbelief growing. "But . . . your kids? What does Boelie say?" she asked to gain time. Was Boelie thinking of leaving the farm?

Annabel was silent for a moment. "You have no idea what it's like in our home, Lettie, or you might understand. And Boelie is one thing, but I also haven't told my father yet. That won't be easy."

Her father wasn't at all well these days.

"I have to get on with my own life. Parents can't expect their children to put their lives on hold for their sake." Annabel leaned forward slightly, her voice insistent — almost as if she was asking for Lettie's approval. "I need to get away, Lettie. My life with Boelie is unbearable. And Boelie won't be the first father to raise his kids on his own."

Lettie's heart sank. "Well, it's not forever."

Annabel gave her a brooding look. "I'll probably stay longer if I can," she said. "I want to get away from everything. Are you shocked?"

Outside, a go-away bird was calling its mate: *Kweh! Kweh!* "Are you thinking of divorce?" Lettie asked, evading Annabel's question.

Her friend shook her head. "No, I'm not that stupid. As a journalist I'm not going to be earning much, and I've always been used to a certain standard of living, which I'm not about to give up. Boelie is a wealthy man. I gave him an heir, and it's his duty to take care of me financially. If I'm the one who walks out of the marriage, especially if I leave the kids with him, I'll get nothing."

Lettie felt the same revulsion of three years ago rise up in her. "Shouldn't you be thinking of Boelie as well?" she asked.

"So he can run off and marry the first by-woner girl who comes along and looks at him like a lovesick puppy?" Annabel asked bitterly. Lettie had no doubt she was referring to whatever had formed between him and Pérsomi all those years ago. "So *she* can inherit the Fourie millions? No thanks,

I'm not that stupid."

Lettie looked at the beautiful woman sitting opposite her. Nelius was only four. Lientjie had just turned two. "Annabel, do you really think it's best?"

"Yes, Lettie," Annabel said, elegantly easing her gloves back over her long fingers. "I've made up my mind." She got up. "I just came to say good bye. For what it's worth."

Just before Annabel reached the door, Lettie said, "Why did you really come here today? If you'd already made up your mind?"

Annabel turned. For a moment she looked almost vulnerable. "Maybe I just wanted you to understand. You were the closest I ever had to a sister. And when we were young, your home was always my refuge. Your mom . . ."

She shrugged, turned, and left the room without a backward glance.

So Boelie raised his children alone, just as Lettie raised hers on her own.

In January 1958, Leonora started school. Lettie did her best to prepare the child for what was waiting. "It's not like Sunday school. There are many children," she tried.

"You're going to like it. You'll have lots of

friends," Isabella chipped in.

But afterward Lettie drove to the surgery with a heavy heart. *I left a very brave little girl at school this morning, Marco, surrounded by a crowd of inquisitive children.*

She didn't cry. But this time I did.

"The child is very musical," Leonora's teacher said at the end of the first school term. She was an older lady who had years of experience with small children. "Have you considered having her take music lessons?"

"She's very young," Lettie said hesitantly.

"She's a bright child, Dr. Louw, and I think it would be stimulating. It would distract her. And it would be something she can do that other children can't."

Lettie thought for a moment. "And if Isabella wants to take music as well?"

"Isabella must be treated on her own merits. She has many talents, of which music is one. It should be developed, yes. Your husband was musical, if my memory serves me right?"

Lettie smiled. "Yes, they get the music from Marco — definitely not from my side of the family!"

So the search began for a good second-hand piano — something as rare as hens' teeth, Lettie soon found out. The girls began to take lessons two afternoons a week. Leonora sat at the piano for hours, tinkling out tunes with two fingers. "Are you practicing your pieces or just playing tunes?" Lettie wanted to know.

"No, Mommy, I'm practicing, ask Tannie Bes."

Do you know, Marco, the music is back in our home? Lettie said in one of her imaginary conversations. *I took out your gramophone and records and showed the kids how it works. They love some of the records, especially the Neapolitan songs. After a while Isabella said, "It's Papa's music, I remember."*

I was so glad she remembered.

"Isabella punched a boy today. She knocked him out," Leonora said one winter's evening at supper.

Lettie felt herself grow cold. "Isabella did . . . what?"

"She punched a boy. His nose bled," Leonora said, eating a large spoonful of soup.

Words stuck in Lettie's throat.

She looked at Isabella. "He was asking for it," the child said defiantly.

"You . . . punched a boy?" Lettie asked, filled with disbelief.

"Mommy," Isabella said and pulled back her shoulders, "that boy is in my class and he's a real bully. He pushed Leonora during break without any reason at all, and she fell. So I hit him." Her lips were pursed in a severe expression.

Dear Lord, give me wisdom, Lettie prayed. Her heart ached for her broken daughter who was pushed over on the playground. If she were there, she would probably also have wanted to punch the boy. "Couldn't you just have talked to him?" she asked feebly.

"So he and his friends could laugh at me?" Isabella asked, still defiant.

Lettie shook her head. "No matter what the situation is, a girl should never raise her hand against someone else," she said, frowning. "Anyway, who taught you to do that?"

"Oom Boelie," the child answered instantly. "He was showing Gerbrand, but then he said we girls, Anna and Lulani and I, must watch as well. You must be able to defend yourself, Oom Boelie said. Gerbrand says Oom Boelie was a very good boxer a long time ago."

Lettie shook her head in dismay. "Boxing is . . . a savage sport. And it's only for men, definitely not for little girls." She thought for a while before she spoke again. "Isabella,

I understand that you were angry with the bully who pushed Leonora, but violence is never the answer. I never want to hear again that you raised your hand against another child. No matter what happens, you don't hit other children. Is that clear?"

There was an obstinate silence.

"Isabella?"

"Yes, Mommy, but —"

"Isabella!"

"Yes, Mommy, I understand." The stubborn expression was still in her eyes.

But it was not the end of the story. At lunch on the farm the next Sunday, with everyone gathered around the table, Anna spilled the beans. "At break on Tuesday a big boy pushed Leonora and she fell. Then Isabella punched his lights out," she said loudly.

"Wow!" De Wet and Boelie said simultaneously.

"Lights out?" Boelie added.

"His nose bled," Leonora said smugly.

"His nose bled?" Gerbrand asked, impressed.

"We've already —" Lettie began. But no one was listening. Everyone's attention was focused on Isabella.

"He was asking for it," Isabella said firmly.

"Seems like it, yes," said Boelie. "How did

you do it?"

"Quick left, straight right, go for the nose, just like you showed us, Oom Boelie," Isabella said.

"Wow!" said Gerbrand. With his right hand he made a fist and punched the palm of his left hand.

"He fell flat on his back in the dust — *oof*!" Anna demonstrated, waving her fork in the air.

"No, wait, Anna, you're throwing your food around," Christine protested.

"I said —" Lettie tried again.

"Well done!" Boelie exclaimed, holding out his hand. "Shake, Isabella!"

"Boelie!" Lettie said, shocked. "This is completely wrong! I told Isabella it's quite unacceptable for girls to resort to violence. Now here you are, praising her behavior?"

The children's eyes flashed from one grown-up to the other.

"Moms and dads educate children in different ways," Boelie said firmly. "I agree girls shouldn't resort to violence. But even a girl, maybe especially a girl, should be able to defend herself."

He looked at the children and spoke earnestly. "Tannie Lettie is right, you should always try other ways to solve your differences first. But if nothing else works . . ."

"Talking won't work with Willie," Isabella said firmly.

"I believe you. I've known a few boys like that in my time," Boelie said. "But your mommy is right, Isabella, you'd better not hit a boy again."

"She won't have to," Anna said. "When Willie was lying on his back in the dust, lights-out, Isabella said, 'If you tell the principal I hit you, I'll tell him how you pushed my little sister on purpose.' She told him! Just like that!"

"Could Willie hear her when he was lying there . . . lights-out?" De Wet asked, amused.

"He wasn't completely lights-out, Daddy. He could still hear." Anna put the matter to rest.

Christine planned a surprise party for Boelie on the weekend of his fortieth birthday. Though it was Christine's idea, Pérsomi ended up making all the arrangements. Planning had never been Christine's strong suit, and Pérsomi seemed to want the job.

The whole family was there. Klara and Antonio came from Pretoria for the weekend. Even Irene came all the way from Pietermaritzburg. And because Irene was there, Annabel's brother, Reinier, came too.

It turned into a lovely evening around the

fire. When the meat came off the *braai,* the men put thick logs on the coals to make the flames flare up again. The kids played until they were exhausted and fell asleep in their mothers' laps or at their feet. "I'll fetch a few blankets, it's getting cool," Christine said.

Boelie and Antonio fetched their guitars, and everyone joined in a spontaneous sing-along.

Tonight she was missing Marco in a strange way. The pain was less intense, but she longed for his presence, wished he could share in the happiness of the moment.

"Everyone sings so well," Leonora said beside her.

"Come sit in my lap," Lettie said, "and we can sing too."

But after the next song the child looked at her with a smile. "You can't really sing, Mommy," she said, amused.

"You little scamp," Lettie said, laughing. "I know I don't sing very well. You don't have to tell me!"

Leonora bent double with laughter. "You sing out of tune," she said. "But don't worry, sing if you want to."

There you have it, Marco. You always used to smile when I joined in the singing!

When the child had fallen asleep in her

lap, Lettie looked at her friends in the soft firelight. Next to her sat De Wet and Christine. The two of them were never far apart. Klara and Antonio sat opposite them, next to Boelie, who was bent over his guitar. Irene's head was resting on Reinier's shoulder.

Next to her sat Pérsomi, with young Lientjie in her lap, covered by a blanket. The child had fallen asleep. Pérsomi was stroking the child's hair, her eyes on the dancing flames.

Boelie's eyes were on Pérsomi and the sleeping child. His dark eyes were filled with pain.

"The oral polio vaccine that was refined for mass usage last year is now being used worldwide," Lettie read in her journal. In South Africa as well, children were lining up to get the round white lozenge with the pink drop of liquid on it.

"Some kids went back in the line for another sweet," Isabella said at supper that night.

"My teacher said I could just have the sweet without the drop, because I've already had polio," Leonora said.

Leonora was a slight figure in her heavy

boots, but on the inside she was every bit as strong as Isabella. Mercifully she was a little more tactful.

When Leonora was in standard seven and Isabella in standard nine, the school decided to stage an operetta: a romantic story with lyrics written to the music of a selection of Strauss waltzes.

Auditions were compulsory for all pupils. The girls queued up, hoping to get a part. The boys had to be coerced into attending the auditions, "or they won't be allowed to do sport," Isabella said at supper that evening.

"And how did it go?" Lettie asked.

"Great," Isabella answered. "Leonora will definitely get the lead, everyone says so. She sings better than anyone else."

But the next afternoon Leonora was quiet. She withdrew to her bedroom, where she sat listening to music.

Lettie was immediately suspicious. "Isabella, what happened?" she asked, placing a glass of milk in front of her daughter at the kitchen table.

Isabella's dark eyes burned with fury. "You won't believe what that old cow did, the horrid beast! Katrien got the lead. Katrien, who can't sing for toffee, is supposed to mouth the words while Leonora sings from behind the curtain! Behind the curtain! With her talent! Mommy, I . . ." Isabella was so indignant, she nearly choked.

Lettie felt as if someone had poured a bucket of ice-cold water over her. She sank into the chair beside Isabella.

"Mommy, the teacher announced it during short break in the presence of everyone who had come to hear about the auditions. There were lots of kids, boys as well."

The pain increased. "Then what happened?"

"When everyone had left, Leonora stayed behind to ask why she couldn't sing the lead. The old cow told her it was a romantic role, the heroine is supposed to move lightly across the stage, the audience mustn't feel sorry for her. Besides, the teacher said, Leonora was going to carry off all the prizes at the eisteddfod again, so that should be enough for her.

"Then Leonora said — and I'm so glad she said it! She said she won't sing from behind the curtain."

My child, my brave child, Lettie's heart wept. "What will happen now?"

"The old cow sent for me at long break. I thought she was going to tell me to get Leonora to sing from behind the curtain, which I wasn't going to do anyway. But she said she wants *me* to sing the lead, so I told her to shove the operetta."

"Isabella!"

"I know, Mommy. But I was angry. I was so angry I couldn't think straight. I'm sorry. They're probably going to call you in because of what I said. But I'm not sorry I said it."

"Oh, Isabella," Lettie said, shaking her head. "And don't call Mrs. Griesel an old cow."

"Yes, I know. But have you *seen* her?"

How could she channel an active volcano's boiling lava? Lettie wondered as she went upstairs and knocked on Leonora's bedroom door.

"Come in," Leonora answered her mother's knock.

She was sitting on her bed, her legs stretched out in front of her. She had taken off her shoes. There was music in the background.

She smiled at Lettie, her eyes calm. Gentle, like Marco's eyes. "Isabella told you," she said.

Lettie sat down beside her, and the child snuggled up to her. "How do you feel?" Lettie asked, putting her arm round her daughter's thin shoulders.

"If you ask me, Isabella has thrown away

her chances of being head girl next year," Leonora said seriously. "I'm sorry about that, but I'm glad she had a go at Mrs. Griesel."

"I want to know how you feel about what happened to *you,*" Lettie said.

"I'm sad," Leonora said slowly, "but I understand what she was saying. I know she's right. You can't have a lead singer limping around onstage."

She fell silent. Lettie waited. She knew her youngest. Leonora was considering her next words.

"That's what hurts most," she said at last. "I wanted to study music after school, you know, singing and piano and violin."

"You can still do it," Lettie said.

"I know. But I wanted to be a singer. And I wanted to sing opera — in Vienna and London and Italy, like Mimi Coertse. I wanted to be Leonora in *Il Trovatore,* onstage in La Scala.

"I know I must let go of the dream. My left leg will always be one inch shorter than the right one, even if I get that operation at the end of the year. They're just going to fix the bridge of my foot. But people will always notice my deformity, especially onstage. I'll still study music, yes, but all those roles I was going to sing were just pipe dreams."

"My dream was to play rugby for the Springboks one day," a boy once told Lettie.

What could she say to her own fourteen-year-old now?

"You don't have to say anything," the girl said calmly. "Just stay here with me. I just wanted to tell you: that's what hurts most."

In January of Isabella's matric year, Antonio had the idea to take all five Romanelli children to Italy in June. Cornelius had done his year of compulsory military service, and he and Lulu were both starting their studies at university. Marié — Klara and Antonio's youngest daughter — was in standard nine, with Leonora in standard eight.

"The kids will only get busier," Antonio said. "My parents would love to see Marco's daughters again. Last time I took them, they were eight and ten."

"Where will everyone sleep?" Lettie asked. "Or are you going to stay in Lorenzo's mountain house?"

"*Villa,* I'll have you know, not *house.*" Antonio smiled. "Cornelius and I might sleep there, but the girls can sleep in the back room at their grandparents' home. It'll be more fun. We really should do it this year, my parents are getting on."

On their return, the girls couldn't stop talking. "Oupa Giuseppe took us hiking in the mountain, and one night we all slept in a cave," Isabella said, bubbling. "The mountain is like nothing you've ever seen, Mommy. The cliffs — it's incredible! Oom Tonio said next time he'll take us in winter and teach us to ski."

"And what did you enjoy most, Leonora?"

"Ouma Maria taught me to cook a whole lot of dishes. I'll show you," Leonora said. "And Oupa Giuseppe played the violin for me. Oupa and I made music for hours. Music is the way we talk to each other. It's easier for him."

"Oom Lorenzo and his children came for a weekend. His kids are proper windbags —"

"Isabella!"

"Sorry, Mommy. But to say they're full of themselves is putting it mildly. If you could meet them, Mommy . . ."

"Oom Lorenzo says people will think I'm his daughter, because we have the same walk," Leonora said, smiling slightly.

"And the sunsets —" Isabella began again.

"Mommy, the people in that village —" Leonora interrupted.

Lettie began to laugh. "Wait! One at a

time, I can't keep up!"

"Next time you really should come along, Mommy," Isabella said urgently. "To see for yourself. Promise?"

Lettie nodded. "Yes, one day I'll go," she said slowly.

The Sunday before Christmas in 1968, the family sat around the table as usual, in De Wet and Christine's big dining room. Everyone was there, even Klara and Antonio, who had come from Pretoria for the holiday. The young people had their own table on the veranda. They could no longer be considered children. Even Lientjie was in high school.

Out of the blue Boelie announced, "My divorce was finalized last Monday."

Everyone sat frozen in disbelief. Boelie? Divorce? It was unthinkable.

Only Pérsomi showed no reaction, Lettie realized. She glanced at De Wet and noticed that he didn't look surprised either. He must have handled the divorce proceedings.

"And . . . Annabel?" Christine asked slowly.

"Annabel met someone else, a colleague," Boelie said. "She's the one who asked for a divorce."

"She . . . ?" Lettie began, but fell silent.

"How do you feel about it, Boelie?" Klara asked, frowning.

All eyes turned to Boelie. His dark eyes looked straight back at them. He addressed everyone around the table. "I made peace with it years ago. I'm just relieved it's over without the kids suffering too much damage."

There was an awkward silence.

"Oh," Klara said at last.

De Wet got up and went to the kitchen.

Then Boelie dropped a second bombshell. "Yesterday morning I asked for Pérsomi's hand in marriage," he said, gazing at the lovely woman sitting opposite him, smiling gently. "And she agreed."

There was a moment's silence, then pandemonium broke loose. Heads shook in disbelief, and there was much talking and laughter. The youngsters came in from outside. Glasses were handed out, and De Wet and Gerbrand popped the champagne corks. Everyone was patting Boelie's shoulder. Lientjie smiled broadly, her arm round Pérsomi. "Daddy told us last night," she said, beaming. "Do you know how hard it was not to give the game away?"

Two months later Pérsomi walked down the aisle in a classic white wedding gown.

Behind her followed Lientjie, conscious of all the eyes on her, but chic and proud in her floor-length light-blue evening gown. At the pulpit Nelius waited beside his father, smartly bow-tied for the occasion.

When the "Wedding March" began to play, Boelie turned. He stood motionless, watching Pérsomi come down the aisle. Only once did he shake his head slightly, as if in total disbelief.

"I'm going to cry," Lettie whispered to Christine, who was standing beside her.

"I'm already crying," her friend said, sniffling. "It's so beautiful."

"Oh, what a beautiful wedding! I want to get married in our church one day," Isabella said.

"You will. It's where both of you were baptized and where Papa and I got married," said Lettie.

"I'm going to ask Oom Tonio to walk me down the aisle," Isabella dreamed on.

"Oom Tonio will cry," Leonora warned her.

"Your papa would have cried too," Lettie said.

"I don't remember much about Papa," Leonora said.

"I do, but it's more his music I remember," Isabella said.

"I'm glad Oom Boelie married Pérsomi. It's so romantic." Leonora sighed.

Now Pérsomi will be in charge of the Big House, Lettie thought. *Life certainly leads some people down strange paths.*

All people, actually.

The reception took place in the barn of the Big House. And when Leonora and Antonio serenaded the bridal couple at the reception, Lettie knew Marco would have been proud. *Your princess has walked her crooked path all by herself,* she told him.

And next year Isabella will be studying medicine at Tukkies. She didn't want to hear of going to Wits. When she graduates, she wants to join me in the practice.

She felt Klara's hand on her arm. "That was beautiful," Klara said.

Lettie nodded. "Heavenly. Italian heavenly."

Klara smiled, her eyes gentle. "Do you still miss Marco?"

"I think of him often," Lettie said slowly, "and very often I wish he could have been here to share the joy his beautiful girls bring me. Like tonight. Yes, I miss him, but I have a full life nonetheless."

"I've always wondered — I still do when I see someone like you who lost the love of her life at an early age — whether the pain always remains so intense."

Lettie didn't really know how to answer her friend. Words were so feeble, so inadequate. "The first few years I often dreamed of Marco at night, and it would ease the loneliness for a while. Though sometimes it made the thin scab fall off, and then the pain was worse. But after so many years the pain isn't really there anymore. My memories are happy ones. I loved a wonderful man."

She paused, then continued, "I had the strangest feeling tonight, Klara. When Antonio sings, I always see Marco in him. Tonight, with Leonora by his side, the feeling was especially vivid. Suddenly I noticed that Antonio is turning gray — in an attractive way, I must add — but there's gray at his temples."

"We're all getting older," Klara said, smiling, "older and a little heavier!"

"We're getting older, yes, and heavier," Lettie said softly. "But I'm lucky: my beloved has remained slim, his hair is still dark, he's young, and he's handsome. Marco stayed behind in 1954. He'll never grow old."

Chapter Seventeen

It was a cool autumn evening, not yet cold enough to light a fire in the fireplace but with a nip in the air.

The bean soup was simmering on the stove, the delicious aroma filling the kitchen. Lettie was expecting Leonora and Danie for dinner. They would probably spend all evening discussing their upcoming wedding. It was exciting, wonderful to see her youngest daughter's rosy cheeks and shiny eyes. But Leonora was a perfectionist, and no matter how Lettie and Danie tried to reassure her that everything would go perfectly, Leonora wanted to be sure the smallest details had been attended to.

She wondered what was keeping them.

That very moment Leonora's car turned into the driveway, followed by a second set of headlights. *It must be Danie,* Lettie thought and gave the soup a final stir.

"Mommy?"

Something in her younger daughter's voice made her look up at once.

Both her daughters were standing in the kitchen doorway. She knew at once that something was terribly wrong. "Where's Danie? What's the matter?"

But she knew. She recognized the signs. "Who?" she asked softly.

Isabella took her by the arm and led her to a chair. She didn't want to sit. She remained on her feet.

"Anna and Tannie Christine were in a car accident, in Pretoria," Isabella said.

They were there for the birth of Lulani's first baby, Lettie remembered.

She waited, surprisingly calm.

"Mommy . . ." Leonora stopped, uncertain how to go on.

"It's Christine," Lettie said.

Her daughters nodded, their eyes on her. *They want to spare me the pain.* But no one can keep the people they love from suffering pain. Pain is part of life. Like death is part of life.

"Christine died in the accident?" she heard her own voice ask.

Her daughters nodded again.

She sank down slowly on a kitchen chair. Isabella knelt beside her. Leonora sat down on another chair. They took her hands.

"Mommy, I'm so sorry," Leonora said.

"And . . . Anna?" Her mouth was dry.

"She only has minor injuries. Tannie Christine died on impact."

Still she was filled with that peculiar calm. "Please get me a drink of water," she said.

Isabella jumped up. Lettie heard water running from the tap into a glass. She drank the cold water.

Leonora stroked her arm.

She thought about her friend, about their friendship that had lasted from their school days over so many years. And about De Wet. She knew what he was going through.

"Oom Boelie took Oom De Wet to Pretoria," Isabella said.

After a while Danie came. And Albert, Isabella's husband, came as soon as his hospital rounds were over. They ate the thick bean soup and fresh bread. They drank coffee.

"How do you feel?" Albert asked worriedly.

Death no longer held any fear for Lettie. Marco had gone to a better place so many years ago. Sometimes she thought she was the only one who still remembered him. She and Antonio — they thought of him. Her mom had gone almost ten years earlier, and shortly afterward her dad. Now her friend had gone.

How *did* she feel?

"My heart aches," she said slowly, "and I know tomorrow and next week will be even worse. My heart aches for De Wet. And for Christine's children. Right now their pain is raw."

She paused. "I'll be fine," she said calmly. "But right now I'd like to be alone."

She got up from the table and went to her bedroom.

On a Sunday afternoon three years later, Lettie drove out to the farm with Antonio and Klara. "I think we'll start moving in next week," Klara said excitedly. "We've been planning to retire in my hometown for so many years, and now we're about to move into our new home. I can hardly believe it."

"And I can hardly believe you're going to be living so close to me," Lettie said. "What a treat!"

Lettie had a bowl of salad in her lap, and Klara had made dessert. "If we don't plan ahead, there'll be nothing but meat on the table at De Wet's," Pérsomi had said sometime in the months following Christine's death.

As they were crossing the Pontenilo, Antonio said, "When the move is over and everything is in place, Klara and I are planning to go to Italy. We wondered if you'd like to come, Lettie?"

Lettie sat quietly in the backseat. Italy. After all these years.

She had the money. Isabella and Albert had taken over her medical practice. She no longer had any excuse for not going.

Maybe she'd been afraid all these years: afraid of meeting Marco's parents, afraid of seeing their pain. Because they had lost a child, and it was a pain that never went away.

But his parents were gone, both of them.

Maybe she'd been afraid that the village Marco had always described, the village in the foothills of the mountain, would open up her own wounds.

But the wounds had healed a long time ago. There was no longer even a scar.

"I think I'd like to, thanks," she said slowly. "When are you planning to go?"

"We haven't really decided," Antonio said. "Definitely in the European summer, for a few weeks."

"And what are you planning to do?"

"Tour Italy," Klara replied. "There are a number of places I still want to see. And of course we'll visit Lorenzo, probably go to their mountain villa. It's a lovely time of year in the village. It's beautiful there."

Lettie smiled.

"I can show you where Marco and I lived, where we went to school," Antonio said, "and we can visit the university in Turin. Okay, here we are. Please help me keep De Wet's dogs from jumping up on my car!"

At lunch their intended tour was mentioned again. "Gosh, it sounds lovely." Pérsomi smiled. "There are so many places one learns of at school — I remember our teacher telling us about the hills around Rome where a she-wolf raised Romulus and Remus. The pictures of the Tower of Pisa, Hannibal crossing the Alps with his elephants . . ."

"I saw Rome when it was flattened by bombs, at the end of 1945," De Wet remembered. "It was when I went to look for Antonio. It was terrible, the destruction of centuries-old cathedrals and castles."

"I wish you could see it now, De Wet," Klara said. "The Italians have rebuilt everything."

"Why don't you all come?" Antonio asked suddenly. "The six of us. We can put our heads together and work out an itinerary that suits everyone."

There was silence around the table while they looked at each other. "How long do you plan on staying?" De Wet asked.

"A month, three weeks. We haven't really decided yet," Klara replied.

"I haven't retired like the rest of you. I won't be able to go for a month," Pérsomi protested.

"*Your* problem," Boelie said drily. "If I can leave the farm in Nelius's hands, surely you can leave your firm in the hands of Lettie's son-in-law for a week or three?"

"Yes, well, I suppose Danie could manage," Pérsomi said thoughtfully.

"And he's got that new lawyer — Bertrien or something, doesn't he?" De Wet added.

"Bertrien de Goede," Pérsomi said. "She's very new. And very young."

"As you once were," De Wet said. "She's plenty capable. She just needs confidence."

"Do you feel like coming, De Wet?" Klara asked.

"Yes," De Wet said after a while. "Yes, I think I'd like to go."

"You've just radically improved your own record for quick decision making," Boelie remarked.

The women cleared the table and made more coffee. At four, still sitting at the table and making their plans, they cut the milk tart Pérsomi had made and ate it.

When Lettie phoned her daughters that

evening, they were equally excited about the idea. "It's just so expensive!" she said to Isabella.

"Ma! You have plenty of money. For goodness' sake, use some of it!" Isabella dismissed her qualms.

"I'm so glad you're going to do something for yourself," Leonora said sincerely. "All your life you've sacrificed everything for us. Now it's your turn."

That night Lettie lay in bed a long time, sleep hovering at the door. *I'm going to Italy,* she thought. *I'm going to take a tour of Italy, with my friends.*

Inside her was an excitement such as she hadn't known for years. She felt young again, she thought, amazed. Young and carefree and adventurous. And almost absurdly excited.

Part Five: Destinations

Chapter Eighteen

On this hot summer morning, the streets of Rome were teeming with people and bicycles and buses and honking cars. Furious taxi drivers shouted at motorists, cyclists rang their bells, and buses pushed their way over to the sidewalks, then simply swung back into traffic, cutting off approaching cars.

"Heavens, are there no traffic rules here?" Boelie asked.

Antonio laughed. "That's why we're chiefly going to be walking or making use of trains," he said. "Even taking a bus is nerve-racking."

Pérsomi was walking at Lettie's side, her beautiful face filled with awe, her tall figure elegantly clad in light slacks and a cool blouse.

Ahead of them walked Klara and De Wet, talking animatedly. Klara was wearing a bright-blue summer frock, comfy sandals, and a wide-brimmed hat. The three of them all had splurged on a new wardrobe for the trip. Every so often you could hear her laugh at one of De Wet's remarks. "De Wet is in top form," Pérsomi said to Lettie.

She was glad she had taken regular walks over the past two months. Despite the jet lag, she felt fit and young and raring to go after a quick shower at their hotel that morning.

Klara and De Wet stopped to study the buildings across the street.

Lettie looked as well. A centuries-old building of gray granite blocks was squeezed between two modern structures — one of dark-green glass and steel, the other ornately decorated, the worn plaster covered with a pink base coat, the balcony railings painted electric blue.

"Those three are really mismatched," Klara said.

"Like three disgruntled women who ended up together in a queue," Pérsomi said.

"We'll never get to the Colosseum if you stand and stare at every building," Boelie called impatiently from up front. "Are you coming?"

"We're on vacation, Boelie. You're not going to hurry us along," Klara said firmly.

"Maybe we *could* walk a little faster," Lettie said quickly. Because when Boelie and Klara crossed swords . . . "Antonio says the Colosseum is still blocks away."

"I hear Rome is known as the world's biggest open-air museum," De Wet said when Lettie caught up.

"I tried to read up on all the places we're going to visit," Pérsomi said, "but there's just too much information."

At last the Colosseum loomed in front of them — the largest amphitheater ever built, constructed at the time of the Roman Empire and dating from the first century. "It's seen as one of the greatest examples of Roman architecture and engineering skill," Antonio explained.

"It's not exactly in good nick," Boelie said. "Their engineers might not have been so skillful after all."

"Boelie! It's two thousand years old!" Klara said. "Besides, it was mostly damaged by earthquakes."

"In another two thousand years it won't be here anymore," Boelie predicted.

"There's a Latin expression we learned at school," Antonio said. *"Quamdiu stat Colisæus, stat et Roma; quando cadet Colisæus, cadet et Roma; quando cadet Roma, cadet et mundus."*

"What does it mean?" Klara asked.

"As long as the Colossus stands, so shall Rome; when the Colossus falls, Rome shall fall; when Rome falls, so falls the world."

"I think Rome and the world are safe for now," De Wet said.

"What I find most interesting," Antonio said, "is that the large audiences that flocked to the Colosseum created a need for people to be able to leave the stadium hastily. The solution was much the same back then as the one architects employ today. There are eighty numbered exits. Only two of the original numbers are still visible, 23 and 54."

"Yes, look!" said Pérsomi, pointing. "You can still see it over there: XXIII. Real Roman numerals!"

"The past is merging with the present," Lettie said, amazed.

"The last time I was here," said De Wet, "I stood looking at these gigantic structures and I tried to imagine the cheering crowds, almost like when the Springboks and the British Lions square off at Loftus."

"I don't know about springboks," Lettie said, smiling, "but I know there were more than just a few lions in this arena."

After climbing to the top, they had coffee, then walked down the Via Sacra, the oldest street in Rome. They passed under the

Triumphal Arch of Constantine, and Antonio explained that it was the way taken by the emperors when they entered the city in triumph. He explained the meaning of the friezes around the arch and told them the story of Constantine's victory over Maxentius. He pointed at the stone and marble work and said the arch had served as the finish line for the marathon event at the 1960 Summer Olympics. Antonio was in his element. This was his heartland, and old buildings were his passion.

They ate large slices of pizza at one of the many sidewalk cafés. They sank their teeth into the soft topping, they tugged at the tough crust, and long threads of cheese dangled down their chins. "It's quite hard to eat this with decorum," Boelie said as he wound a string of cheese back around his pizza slice.

"You won't find *pap en wors* in Italy." Antonio smiled.

"No, no, I like the pizza. It's just strange," Boelie said.

That afternoon they visited the Pantheon, the temple commissioned by Marcus Agrippa for the ancient Roman gods. They examined the colossal granite columns, listened to Antonio's explanation of how the concrete dome with its central opening to the sky was built. After almost two thousand years, he told them, it was still the world's largest unreinforced concrete dome. "Now that's what I call engineering skill," Boelie said.

"It reminds me of the Voortrekker Monument," De Wet remarked. "It also has a domed roof with an opening. And a marble floor, and even the arch motifs over the entrances."

"Yes, Moerdyk was strongly influenced by Italian architecture," Antonio said. "I helped build the church in our town many years ago. I think the main reason I was hired was because I'm Italian," he said, laughing.

"What are we doing tonight?" De Wet asked as they were walking back to their hotel.

"Dinner and bed," Klara answered firmly.

"I vote for an early night as well," Lettie said.

"Us too!" Boelie said. "Pérs and I couldn't sleep a wink in those cramped plane seats."

"I was too excited to sleep anyway," Pérsomi confessed.

"For goodness' sake, you're behaving like a bunch of senior citizens," said De Wet.

"Easy for you to talk," Lettie said. "Your arms and legs were all over the place on the trip over. I had to perch in a corner of my seat like a finch all night."

"You could have woken me," De Wet said.

"What do you mean?" Klara said, laughing. "She tried, but you just carried on snoring!"

"I don't snore!" De Wet protested. "Lettie, do I snore?"

The others burst out laughing. "De Wet, is there something we should know?" Antonio asked.

"Come on, no, I mean . . ."

But the laughter and banter didn't stop. It wasn't often that De Wet was caught on the wrong foot.

"Did you ever see the movie *Roman Holiday* with Audrey Hepburn and Gregory Peck?" Antonio asked the next morning at breakfast.

"Yes, sometime around 1953 or '54," Lettie replied. It was one of the last movies she had seen with Marco. They had traveled to the neighboring town because Marco wanted to see it so badly. On their way back, he couldn't stop talking, not about the storyline or the acting, but about the places where the scenes had been filmed. "One day I'm going to show you all those places, Lettie. That's a promise," he had said.

"We're going to see many of the well-known landmarks in that movie," Antonio said. "Including the Trevi Fountain. And if we have enough time, the Spanish Steps as well."

It's still so unreal that I'm actually here, Lettie thought as she followed the others. This morning she was wearing a silky summer dress and her new sunglasses. Those were a novelty too. "Now that you're wearing contact lenses, you should buy some stylish dark glasses," Leonora had said. "You look lovely in this pair, very mod. Go ahead, Ma, buy them."

"You girls are bankrupting me!" Lettie had said before giving in.

Rome was bustling, with cars and buses rushing past. Street vendors kept trying to fob off cheap mementoes, and the air was filled with the smell of freshly baked focaccias and biscotti and the garlic-and-onion aroma of cannelloni and ravioli sauces.

"Everything smells so delicious," Lettie said as she fell into step beside Antonio. "I'm really pleased I came along."

"Then I'm happy too," Antonio said. "I wanted to show it to you."

The Trevi Fountain was built at the junction of three roads. According to legend, around the time of Christ, the Romans discovered a source of fresh water with the help of a maiden.

"The scene is depicted on the facade of the fountain," Antonio explained. "This water was diverted to the Baths of Agrippa in ancient times and for more than four hundred years provided Rome with water. Invaders later destroyed the aqueducts, but during the Renaissance, the Roman custom of building a beautiful fountain at the end of an aqueduct was revived, and the Trevi Fountain in its present form was built."

"Engineering skills again," Boelie said.

"Maybe the waterworks, yes, but the beautiful fountain was definitely not designed by engineers," Antonio retorted.

They studied the finely chiseled white marble figures among the rough rocks. "The last time I was here I remember thinking this was probably what the friezes on the Voortrekker Monument would look like," De Wet remembered.

"If you throw a coin in the fountain, you'll be sure to return to Rome," Klara said. "Believe me, it works. Antonio and I always throw in our coins and we always come back. De Wet, did you throw money into the fountain the last time you were here?"

He gave a lopsided smile. "I did," he admitted. "Three coins."

"See, it works!" Klara said triumphantly.

"Then I'll put in three coins as well," Lettie said and scattered her coins in the water. "I hope I get three return trips to Rome in exchange!"

"That's what you think!" Antonio said with a knowing smile.

"Oh! Well, what does it mean then?" Lettie asked.

"Wait and see," Antonio said enigmatically.

When she turned, De Wet stood looking at her with a smile. "You know!" she said. "Come on, De Wet, tell me!"

"It's money in the water," De Wet said drily.

De Wet had been rather quiet all morning, Lettie realized and gave him a sharp look. She hoped he wasn't coming down with something.

"I remember Anita Ekberg in *La Dolce Vita* falling into this fountain," Pérsomi said. "I read somewhere that the scene was shot in winter. Evidently Anita could stay in the cold water for hours, but the actor playing opposite her . . ."

"Marcello Mastroianni, wasn't it?" Klara said.

"Yes, Mastroianni. Not even a wetsuit under his clothes could keep him warm. It was only after he'd finished a bottle of vodka that they could shoot the final scenes."

"I heard that the name of the character Paparazzo — the photographer who worked with Mastroianni, remember?" Antonio began.

"Yes, I remember Paparazzo," Klara said.

". . . that his name is where the word *paparazzi* comes from, used all over the world to refer to pushy photographers," Antonio continued.

"Hmm, interesting," said Pérsomi.

"They also say," Antonio continued, "that the name itself comes from the Italian word *papataceo,* which refers to a large, pesky kind of mosquito."

Lettie nodded. "Strange that a single supporting character in a single movie gave rise to a word that's used all over the world. But it's rather apt, I suppose: pesky mosquito."

De Wet was still gazing at the water cascading down.

The group split up to catch their preferences. Lettie walked beside De Wet as he strode down the street. "Tell me if I'm going too fast," he said.

"Don't worry, I'll complain," she said, smiling. "Are we going somewhere in particular, or are we just walking?"

He was silent for a moment, then he said, "Actually, I'm retracing my footsteps, Lettie."

She understood at once. That was probably why he had been so quiet all morning. "You were here with Christine once," she said.

He nodded. "I hope you don't mind. If you wish . . ."

"No, I'd like to come along," she said. She had never found the right moment after Christine's death to talk to him about her. For the first few months he isolated himself. Then he carried on as if he had left his sorrow behind.

They walked in silence — the easy silence between old friends who have come a long way together. Now and again they talked about trivial things. At a market stall they bought each of their daughters a scarf.

De Wet shook his head. "I don't really know why I wanted to come here," he said.

The trees formed a green roof overhead. The sun made lacy patterns on the sidewalk at their feet.

He was quiet for a long time. Good experiences become precious memories, Lettie knew. Unhappy events are painful to remember.

"When we first saw each other after the

war, she said if I'd ever had any feelings for her I should just leave her alone," he said.

They passed a shop. De Wet stopped. "There was a different shop here during our visit. I bought a red ball for Gerbrand," he remembered.

"How did you feel when you first saw Gerbrand?" Lettie asked.

He shook his head slowly. "It was a terrible shock to me. Not only that there was a child — that too, of course — but especially that Pérsomi's brother was the father. I knew Gerbrand well. I grew up with him, played rugby with him . . . never mind. Heavens, Lettie, I still can't imagine Gerbrand . . . that Christine . . ."

He fell silent.

"Yes, I understand," Lettie said.

"It's by the grace of God that I managed not to hold it against the child," he said. "To me he was just a lovely, lively little boy. But if I'd got my hands on Gerbrand . . ."

He stopped and turned to her. In his eyes was a strange glow, a deeper pain than she had ever seen in him before. "I've never said this to anyone before, Lettie, but what he had done to my Christine . . . If I'd got hold of that man, I swear I would've killed him."

She put her hand on his arm.

He closed his eyes, shook his head. "I suppose I shouldn't have said that."

"That's what friends are for," she said.

He set off again with long strides. A moment later he stopped at a sidewalk kiosk and turned to her, his old self again. "Can you face eating pizza for lunch?" he asked with a smile. "I'm starving."

"Me too," she said. "When in Rome . . ."

He rewarded her with a belly laugh. "You're lovely," he said before buying an enormous pizza.

"Do you think we'll manage to eat this entire thing?" Lettie asked.

"We'll feed the rest to the birds," De Wet said.

At the next park they came across, they sat down on a bench. De Wet unwrapped the pizza and put it between them. "Lunch is served, signora," he said gallantly.

She laughed and dived in. As she had predicted, they couldn't finish the pizza. "You should have bought the medium instead of the large!" she said.

"I was so hungry then, I could have eaten an ox," De Wet said, tossing bits of pizza on the grass.

A squirrel with a thick bouncy tail approached. De Wet threw down a trail of crumbs right up to his shoe.

"I'm pretty sure you're not supposed to

feed the animals," Lettie said, stretching her aching feet in the sun.

"Hmm," De Wet said and threw more pizza crumbs on the grass.

"Thanks for coming with me today, Lettie," he said. "It couldn't have been very interesting for you."

"I enjoyed it," Lettie said. "Christine was my best friend for many, many years. And . . . sometimes it's good to talk."

"If one is lucky enough to find someone who can listen," De Wet said earnestly.

"Tonight we're going to paint the town red. I refuse to let you old-timers go to bed with the chickens again!" De Wet said when the friends met in the hotel foyer that evening.

"Who's your old-timer?" Pérsomi laughed. She was wearing a simple deep-red frock, and her dark hair was done up in an elegant chignon.

Boelie's hand was around her waist. There was a smile on his face.

After all these years they're truly happy, Lettie thought.

"Why don't we walk down the street and see what we find?" Antonio suggested.

It was a warm summer's evening. The streets were crowded with people laughing and calling out to each other. They crossed a square where age-old statues stood bathed in the soft glow of modern streetlights. The moon drifted through the fleecy clouds, and musicians played on street corners.

The evening is going to my head. I'm getting drunk on the lukewarm night and the music and the moon above.

At an open-air restaurant Boelie stopped. "This looks like a nice place," he said.

"And they're playing good music," De Wet agreed.

"You two have seen there are steaks on the menu." Klara laughed, her eyes twinkling with mirth. "That's why you want to go in here."

"I could do with a steak as well," Antonio said at once. "We all could."

"And a bottle of good wine," Boelie said.

"Or two," De Wet agreed.

"Do we ladies have a choice?" Pérsomi asked, amused.

Boelie gave her a surprised look. "No," he said.

Some things would never change.

Inside, the staff moved two tables together to make room for them all. The tables had red-checkered tablecloths and candles stuck into potbellied wine bottles. The men ordered large steaks, the ladies a variety of Italian dishes. Antonio beckoned to the waiter and ordered two bottles of wine. After a while the man returned with six long-stemmed wineglasses laced between his fingers.

They ate and drank and laughed at De Wet's quips.

On a small stage at the back of the restaurant, a few older gentlemen were making cheerful music on a violin, guitar, and accordion. They were playing Italian folk songs, some with captivating tunes that soon had the friends swaying from side to side, some with a pulsating rhythm that set their feet tapping and their shoulders shaking.

Some of the diners began to sing along, raising their glasses and clapping their hands.

Antonio joined in the singing. "Shall we order another bottle of wine?" he asked from his position at the head of the table.

Lettie laughed. "Gosh! My head is spinning already."

"Yes, go ahead," De Wet cried. "Tonight we're dancing on the tables!"

Antonio jumped to his feet and held out his hand to Klara. "Do you see a dance floor anywhere?" she protested, laughing, but getting up just the same.

"That's what the street is for!" Antonio cried exuberantly.

De Wet also got up and turned to Lettie. His green eyes glistened, and his silver hair fell over his forehead. "Let's show these Italians a thing or two!" he said.

Laughter bubbled up inside her. She felt young and carefree. She looked up at him. "Why not?" She threw out the challenge.

The musicians moved among the tables, playing a fast, wild folk tune. More couples began to dance on the sidewalk. Passersby stopped and applauded.

They danced round and round. De Wet went faster and faster. Lettie clung to him for dear life, her feet flying over the uneven sidewalk. "De Wet!" she protested, laughing. "We're going to land on our backsides in the middle of the Eternal City!"

He looked down at her laughing face. "You're so beautiful, Lettie. Do you realize I could easily fall in love with you here in the Eternal City?" he asked, overflowing with happiness.

Shock jolted through her body.

No. No.

"De Wet, don't!"

"Okay," he said with a strange smile.

He danced on as if nothing had happened.

Chapter Nineteen

She spent a long time in the shower. The water poured over her face and down her neck. The soap foamed at her feet.

She washed her hair, and the bubbles ran down her body.

She washed away the night's events.

The words remained.

All night long sleep eluded her.

Because a few unthinking words, a few frivolous words in the jolly spirit of the evening, had stripped away forty years in a matter of seconds, leaving her naked and exposed.

At breakfast Antonio announced, "We're going to visit the Vatican City. The men must wear long pants and the ladies should put on frocks, or we won't be allowed in."

"We'll die in this heat," Boelie complained.

"It's no worse than the bushveld, and

there we used to go to work in long pants every day," De Wet said.

"Not all of us," Boelie replied.

"I'll put a pair of your shorts in my handbag," Pérsomi said. "Then you can change as soon as we get out."

Lettie forced herself to eat the light continental breakfast. She chatted with Klara. She asked Antonio about their activities for the day. She shared a joke with Boelie and Pérsomi. "Imagine!" she said. "This morning I asked the girl who cleans our rooms if she had slept well. 'Grazie, signora,' she said. 'But *scusami,* in Italy we do not ask the other person what they do in the night.' "

Boelie laughed. "De Wet, just listen to the lecture Lettie got from the chambermaid this morning."

But at that moment the waiter brought their coffee and Lettie was saved from having to tell De Wet the story.

She avoided looking at him.

She had told herself over and over the night before that he wouldn't even remember, that it had just been a passing remark, he hadn't meant anything by it, he'd had too much wine and was talking through his neck.

Still, she couldn't look at him.

After breakfast she exchanged her pantsuit for a dress but took no special care with her appearance.

They boarded a bus for the Vatican City, which lies on a hillside. Lettie hastily sat next to a stranger and looked through the window at the scenery. They crossed the Tiber and walked the last few hundred yards to the high walls surrounding the smallest sovereign state in the world.

As they were crossing St. Peter's Square, Pérsomi fell into step beside her. "Lettie, what's wrong?" she asked, frowning. "Did you and De Wet argue?"

She shrugged and said, "He said something last night that upset me."

"Does he know he upset you?"

"No, no, he doesn't know."

Pérsomi shook her head. "I think he knows. I know him, and he's not himself either this morning. He was already having coffee when Boelie and I entered the dining room, and that says a lot."

"It's not serious. It's probably nothing. I mustn't be so sensitive."

"So, here we are," Antonio said, stopping in front of a towering obelisk. To the left was the enormous St. Peter's Basilica with its domed roof, to the right a series of tall columns.

"This obelisk looks more Egyptian than Roman," De Wet said.

Lettie's eyes automatically went to him when he spoke, but only for a moment. In that half glance, however, she had taken in his tall figure, still slim and athletically built like when they were at school together. It was enough to make her heart shrink.

"It's originally from Egypt, you're right. It was brought to Rome sometime in the first century," Antonio said. "This is the place where the apostle Peter is said to have been crucified with his head downward, then buried. His grave is said to be directly underneath the high altar in the cathedral. The obelisk probably survived after the fall of the Roman Empire because of its proximity to St. Peter's grave. Come, let's take a look inside."

They mounted the steps and walked past the colossal eighteen-foot statues of St. Peter and St. Paul to the front of the biggest cathedral in the world. They looked up at the ornate vaulted ceiling. They crossed the shiny marble floor. They paused at the tall statues.

"Look," Pérsomi said, almost whispering, and motioning with her head, "there's Michelangelo's statue of Mary, with the crucified Jesus on her lap."

"The *Pietà,*" Lettie whispered, amazed. For a moment she forgot everything else and hurried to the statue in its large glass display case.

She looked up at the sculpture. What she was looking at here, she suddenly realized, was the stone Michelangelo spent two years carving and shaping and sanding to become the Virgin and Son.

Just like her children's oupa had extracted a much smaller Virgin and Child from a piece of marble.

The moment felt almost sacred.

"Lettie?" she heard a soft voice say behind her.

The moment splintered.

She pretended not to have heard, turned to Klara, and said, "I always thought it was much bigger."

She had no idea what Klara replied, and it didn't matter.

She was being childish. She couldn't avoid De Wet for the rest of the vacation, not even for the rest of the day. There was a lump in her stomach, a spasm in her back that shot up into her neck, and a threatening headache. She licked her dry lips.

In the Sistine Chapel they craned their necks to look at the painted ceilings twenty meters above them. "We're just in time to see it," Antonio said. "The chapel is going to be restored. Work starts next year and it will be closed to the public for up to ten years."

"Then we'd better take a proper look," Boelie said. "Do you think they'll repaint the ceiling as well?"

"Boelie! You philistine!" Lettie said, smiling.

"Evidently Michelangelo lay on his back when he painted it." De Wet spoke next to her. "It's high, isn't it?"

"Yes, very," Lettie said, moving on.

If she didn't do something about this tension, she thought as she gazed with unseeing eyes at the scenes above and around her, she was going to get the grandmother of all headaches. Moreover, the vacation she had looked forward to so much was going to turn into the great-grandmother of all nightmares.

"Let's buy a few loaves and some cheese and cold cuts and fruit and picnic in the Vatican gardens," Klara suggested when they were back outside in the bright sunshine. "Antonio and I have never been there, and they say it's lovely."

"Don't forget the beers," Boelie said at once. "I'm parched."

"I don't think we'll be allowed to take beer in," Antonio said, "but we might find coffee somewhere."

"The men will do the shopping. You ladies may go," De Wet said. "We'll come and find you."

"We'll meet you at the radio offices," Antonio hastened to add. "The gardens are too big to go in search of you."

For a moment Lettie considered telling them she had a headache and was going back to the hotel, but she decided against it. She didn't want to draw attention to herself, and so far only Pérsomi had noticed that something was wrong. Besides, there was a good chance she'd get lost in this strange city.

She took a painkiller from her handbag and swallowed it dry.

In the beautiful gardens she managed to relax. It was quiet. They strolled along the paths, admiring the lush vegetation. Klara lingered at a statue, while Pérsomi and Lettie walked on. After a while they sat down on the edge of a fountain to wait for her.

"It's so lovely here," Pérsomi said, dipping her hand in the water. "My eyes are so tired of looking at man-made things."

"I want to take a look at that peculiar flower over there," Lettie said.

"Just stay on the paths, or Romulus and Remus's she-wolf might eat you," Pérsomi said, smiling.

Lettie wandered off. She had to be alone for a while. She pressed her fingertips to her temples. Around a corner, screened by plants, she paused for a moment. What was happening to her? How could it be that a few words had turned her into a lovesick teen?

But she knew.

"Lettie?"

She swung around.

De Wet was standing a few steps away, his eyes guarded. In his hand he held a single flower. He held it out to her. She stood motionless, looking at him.

"I'm sorry, I was out of order last night," he said. "I crossed a line, I know."

Still she stood motionless.

"I didn't think before I spoke. I must have had one too many."

She waited. He gave her a lopsided grin. "Take the flower, please, and tell me I'm forgiven."

She smiled in spite of herself. "De Wet, where did you find this flower?" she asked.

"Picked it, over there," he admitted.

"And if they arrest us because you stole a

flower from His Holiness the Pope's garden?"

"Then we'll have a wonderful story to tell the folks at home." He smiled, more at ease now.

She put out her hand and took the flower.

"Forgiven?" he asked.

"As long as you behave," she said.

But Lettie knew: the chemical reaction of so many years ago was unquestionably back.

Their train to Venice was leaving early in the morning. Lettie slept reasonably well and felt much better when she woke up at daybreak.

She took a shower, washed her hair, and put on a deep-blue pantsuit and a crisp white blouse. She was ready for anything. The matters of her heart were under control. Lettie was still feeling positive and strong when she opened her bedroom door and dragged her heavy bag out into the corridor.

"Here, let me help," De Wet said behind her. "Did you sleep well?"

Despite her best intentions, her heart jumped at the sound of his voice. She pulled herself together, took a deep breath, turned calmly, and said, "Like a baby, thanks, De Wet. And you?"

They walked down the corridor to the elevator. On their way down, she looked him in the eye and chatted easily — like in the old days.

But a treacherous realization had lodged in her mind: De Wet, who had been late even for his own wedding, had been standing in the corridor, waiting for her to come out.

The station was a hive of activity.

People were calling out to each other at the top of their voices, arguing loudly about the price of tickets and fighting with the conductor for better seats.

"When I look at this chaos, I'm truly grateful Antonio can speak Italian," Boelie remarked.

Antonio managed to find them six seats in the same compartment. He and De Wet stood inside the compartment while Boelie handed them the luggage through the window. "Thank goodness the men are here to haul those heavy bags," Lettie said.

"Yes, they can be useful at times," Klara said with a smile.

Lettie was about to say Klara sounded just like Annabel but stopped herself in time. Mentioning Annabel's name in Pérsomi's presence was still a sore point.

When at last they got tucked in, the bags were stacked on the overhead luggage racks and under the seats. De Wet raised himself from the seat where he was reclining and motioned to Lettie to sit next to him.

She gave him a friendly smile but sat down next to Boelie and Klara instead, facing him.

You're not catching me off guard again, she thought. *I follow my own path. Alone. The way I like it.*

By afternoon, after hours of taking in the beautiful scenery through the train window, a delicious lunch in the dining car, and even a short nap in the straight-backed seats, Lettie's defenses began to crumble.

Somehow they always ended up together.

And there were small things: the way he looked at her when she was talking, the way he leaned over her to open the window, his genuine interest in what she was reading, his participation in a conversation about something she found interesting.

He's a proper Casanova, Lettie decided as the train slowly drew into the last station.

"We're in Venice!" De Wet said, his green eyes dancing with excitement.

And good friends or not, she thought somewhat helplessly, *I'm so weak that I fall for his charm every time.*

■ ■ ■ ■

The taxi dropped them off at their hotel — the *Hotel Casanova,* Lettie read on the ornate sign.

Well, if that isn't an omen, she thought.

They signed in, three Fouries and three Romanellis.

"Mrs. Romanelli?" The man at reception asked the same question his colleague in Rome had asked. "You speak Italian?"

"My husband was Italian," Lettie explained in her best rusty Italian, "but he passed away. I don't speak much Italian, I'm afraid, but I do understand it."

And, just like in Rome, Lettie was given the best room.

The Piazza San Marco was abuzz with people in the late afternoon. Large swarms of pigeons were pecking up crumbs at pedestrians' feet, fluttering up, and landing ten yards farther.

The square was dominated by the Cathedral of St. Mark's at the eastern end — a large white building with a series of domed roofs.

De Wet walked ahead of Lettie, deep in conversation with Pérsomi. They were completely at ease in each other's company, just as they should be, Lettie noted. There was a time when she had been able to walk with him that way, relaxed, cracking jokes. Less than a week ago, in fact.

She turned to Klara. "It looks almost Oriental, all these domes and turrets," she said.

"I agree. There's a strong Oriental influence, probably because of early trade connections with the East," Klara said.

She and Klara stood looking at the round-arched portals and the patterned marble slabs. Antonio joined them, pointing out the finer details of the architecture, explaining the bronze Horses of St. Mark, guiding them along the Merceria.

"The most wonderful shops are here," Klara said enthusiastically. "You can buy everything here, from —"

"Tomorrow," Antonio interrupted. "We'll do some shopping tomorrow. Now I suggest we find somewhere to eat."

Talk as she might, Lettie was constantly aware of De Wet.

She listened with half an ear to Antonio's description of the houses lining the street and dating from the early sixteenth century.

"The history of Europe is so much older than our own," Pérsomi said. "In the early sixteenth century Bartolomeu Dias had only just sailed around the Cape."

"You remember your history well, don't you?" said De Wet.

"I had an excellent teacher," Pérsomi said, smiling at Klara.

Klara laughed. "It was 1488," she said.

"The year you were Pérsomi's history teacher?" De Wet teased.

"Who would have thought, when I was Pérsomi's schoolteacher, that one day she would be my sister-in-law?"

"*I* would have thought," Boelie said seriously.

There was a short, awkward silence before Antonio said, "There's a popular restaurant quite close by, the Caffè Quadri. It might be a bit pricey."

"We're only young and in Venice once," De Wet said cheerfully. "What do you old-timers say?"

"This youngster says let's spend the money our young wives are earning," Boelie said, putting his arm around Pérsomi's shoulder.

De Wet turned to her. "Lettie?"

"Do I count as one of your old-timers?" she asked.

"Definitely not," he said, laughing. "Caffè Quadri, here we come!"

■ ■ ■ ■

During the meal De Wet was his old charming self — actually, he and Lettie had a lovely conversation. She felt like herself again. Well, almost.

Back at the hotel, the women sat in the deep armchairs of the luxurious lounge and ordered tea.

"Is De Wet making eyes at you, Lettie?" Klara asked after the waiter left, tilting her head as she spoke. She sounded suspicious, almost disbelieving — as if she had just made a great discovery.

"Definitely not. It's your imagination," Lettie hastened to reply.

"*I* think he is," Pérsomi said calmly, leaning back in her chair. "I know him, and if he's not making eyes, he's definitely paying you a great deal of attention."

Lettie drew a sharp breath. "You're both mistaken. He's just being friendly, enjoying his vacation," she protested. "And remember, the rest of you are married couples, so it's only natural that we'll be paired off."

"Okay," Pérsomi said, "if you say so."

But if it turned out to be true, if it was more than just casual attention so that even her friends were noticing . . . Lettie simply couldn't face the pain that kind of frivolous game would inevitably lead to. The sooner she put a stop to it, the better.

The next morning the weather was sunny, the sky was cloudless and blue, and the Adriatic sparkled in the distance.

They chattered cheerfully as they crossed the square to the Merceria, Klara's street with the marvelous shops. "We'll meet at eleven at this sidewalk café," Antonio said, pointing. "Klara and I are going to a toy shop lower down."

"I want to show Boelie something I thought we might buy for Lientjie," Pérsomi said and took Boelie's hand.

Lettie didn't want De Wet to feel obliged to spend the day with her. Turning to him, she said, "I want to look at handmade lace. I doubt you'll be interested."

"I'll come with you anyway," he said easily. "Maybe we'll spot a Ferrari or Lamborghini going for a song."

"Yes, or an orangutan." Lettie laughed.

De Wet stopped to gaze at a display of Venetian glassware and jewelry in a shop window. He turned to look at her with those exceptional green eyes. "Help me pick out something typically Venetian for the girls, please?" he said. "I'm not very good at that kind of thing."

His eyes are really something special, almost exactly like Klara's. She nodded. "Maybe I could buy something for my daughters too," she said as they entered the shop.

They looked at ornate wine decanters and fine glasses, at smoky glass bowls, at porcelain figurines. "No, it's all too fragile. We still have a lot of traveling ahead of us," Lettie said.

"You're right," said De Wet.

They opted for colorful necklaces made of different types of glass beads. They took care to pick something special to suit each daughter — bright multicolored beads for Anna ("Yes, they go with her personality," he said), a chunky deep-red string for Isabella ("It'll make her look very Italian"), a smoky-blue one for Lulani ("She has Christine's blue eyes"), creamy beads with small hand-painted roses for Leonora ("She'll always be our little rosebud"). The saleslady carefully removed the ones they selected from among the rest.

"Which one do you prefer?" De Wet asked, poring over the multitude of strings lying on the counter.

She put out her hand to point at a string she had noticed from the start: light-blue glass beads richly decorated in a fine floral design. "Hand-painted," the saleslady said in broken English.

"Buy it," De Wet encouraged her.

She picked up the label and looked at the price. She laughed. "Oh no, it costs an arm and a leg," she said, carefully replacing the necklace. "I'd rather buy a variety of small mementoes. Here in Venice I want to buy some lace. I've heard it's best to go to one of the smaller islands where the women still make the lace by hand. Even there I think it might be exorbitantly expensive."

"Well, let's pay for our purchases then," he said, turning away.

She paid for her two strings, and the saleslady put them in satin bags with pictures of St. Mark's Cathedral. She stepped outside to wait for De Wet.

They had only walked a few paces when he stopped in his tracks. "Here," he said, unceremoniously handing her a satin bag.

For a moment she wondered whether he wanted her to put it away in her handbag.

Then it hit her like a bucket of cold water. Slowly she opened the bag and looked inside.

It was the expensive beads.

She looked up at him. His green eyes looked back expectantly.

Suddenly she felt incredibly vulnerable. His eyes . . .

She shook her head. "De Wet, I'm sorry, but please don't," she said, holding out the bag to him. He shoved his hands into his pockets.

"Lettie," he said somewhere between solemnity and good humor, "it's only a string of beads. It's" — he shrugged nonchalantly — "worldly goods." He smiled, somewhat embarrassed, his eyes on her face. "Go ahead. Take the stupid thing!"

She hesitated before she replied. "Thanks. It's truly beautiful. But . . . please don't, De Wet. It's . . . awkward."

For a fleeting moment there was a strange expression in his eyes. Then he nodded slowly. "Fine," he said, completely serious now. "I understand."

But he didn't retrieve the bag.

They met up with the others and walked to the Rialto Bridge, the oldest of the three bridges across the Grand Canal. They boarded a waterbus and traveled the length of the Grand Canal. They looked at the buildings on either side of the canal, dating from the thirteenth to the eighteenth centuries and reflecting the wealth and prosperity of Venice at the time.

Lettie struggled to focus on Antonio's stories. After a while she sat down by herself in the front of the waterbus and looked out over the wide canal. There was a light breeze in her face and hair, and the dark wavelets lapped softly underneath the boat.

Slowly she felt her composure return. De Wet had behaved normally after the morning's incident. He'd been spontaneous and friendly as usual.

And it was what she wanted, she knew with complete clarity. She wanted their relationship to be uncomplicated — without unnecessary problems or pain.

She felt as if a heavy load had rolled off her shoulders.

Sometime later De Wet's voice drew her attention. "We wondered where you were. We were afraid you might have fallen overboard."

She laughed. "You don't get rid of me that easily," she said and rejoined the rest of the group.

"Boelie, tonight you'll *have* to serenade Pérsomi," De Wet teased as they headed to where the gondoliers were waiting in their brightly colored boats. "If you allow one of those Italians to go first — you know what they're like — you might as well wave your pretty young wife good bye!"

"I'm lucky to have my own Italian to sing to me." Klara played along. She pretended to give a deep sigh. "But you're right, De Wet, I'm afraid Boelie will have to sing."

"All I can sing is 'The Lion Sleeps Tonight,' and that certainly won't do," Boelie said with feigned seriousness. "Pérs, maybe the two of us should go to the movies instead."

Pérsomi laughed. "Tonight it's you and me and that gondola."

Tonight it's De Wet and me and that gondola, Lettie thought. But it no longer made her nervous, because things were back to normal between them. She was looking forward to an enjoyable evening in the company of an old friend.

And that was exactly how it turned out. The two of them reclined in the soft seats. Below them the dark water slowly moved past, while above them the sky changed color and the first stars appeared.

"The stars on the farm are so much brighter," she said.

"Yes, I'm afraid the air over here is polluted," he said. "But on the farm we don't have thousands of lights reflected in the water. Don't you think it's beautiful?"

"Lovely," she said.

"Me sing?" the gondolier asked. "Or me play?" He pointed at his violin.

"Lettie?" De Wet asked.

"Sing, please," she told the gondolier. To De Wet she said, "Mediocre singing is a lot better than mediocre violin playing."

"Smart," he said, leaning back.

The gondolier sang softly, rowing at a leisurely pace. It was a lingering melody, a lullaby of days gone by perhaps.

"Heavenly," Lettie sighed, leaning back.

"Why don't you close your eyes? It might be even more heavenly," De Wet said next to her.

"And miss seeing these stars?" she said.

They sat in silence, occasionally pointing at something or sharing a thought from the past. The Italian night with its unfamiliar northern stars softly enfolded them.

"Me sing opera?" the gondolier asked after a while.

"No, carry on with what you're doing, it's beautiful," De Wet said, his head tilted back.

"You like?"

"Yes, we like," said Lettie. To De Wet she whispered, "We're probably in for a hefty tip."

"Hmm," said De Wet. "A good thing you're a rich doctor."

"Hmm," Lettie said, too lazy to protest.

"Row, row, row your boat, gently down the stream." The familiar song from her nursery-school days popped into Lettie's head. But she kept silent. She didn't want to break the spell. The stream in the song had turned into a dream.

"We here," the gondolier said much later.

"Lettie," De Wet said softly.

Slowly she opened her eyes. "Maybe you can use your charm to bargain with him," she said.

His face wore a puzzled frown. "What are you talking about?"

"The tip."

He burst out laughing. "I nearly said you're lovely again, but I've been told to behave." He held out his hand to help her out. "Thanks, Lettie, it was a wonderful evening."

"It was an unforgettable evening, De Wet. Thank you," she said sincerely.

"You said you wanted to go to an island where they make lace today," De Wet said when he met her for breakfast. "Would you mind if I tag along? Boelie and Pérsomi want to take another trip to the farms in the district and" — he smiled — "I'm kind of up to here with Venetian architecture."

"You're welcome to come along, De Wet."

They boarded a ferry to the island of Burano, walked through narrow alleys flanked by tall, brightly painted houses, and stopped at numerous stalls selling hand-blown glass and lace. "It's easy to buy the girls presents, but I never know what to buy Gerbrand," De Wet said. "I'm not good at buying gifts. It used to be Christine's department."

"I still have to find something for my sons-in-law," Lettie said.

"I haven't even given my sons-in-law a thought," De Wet said, "not to mention the grandchildren."

"Okay, Gramps," Lettie teased. "I'm glad we're not all as old as you!"

"We'll talk again when you have grand-kids of your own," he said, his green eyes gentle.

Most of the lace on the island, they soon found out, was made commercially. The handmade lace was too expensive to market economically. "Well, I suppose that means I can buy a tablecloth anywhere," Lettie said, somewhat disappointed. "Even tray cloths are so expensive."

"May I buy you a handmade cloth, plee-eease?" De Wet asked, his face screwed up like a small boy's.

"No, De Wet, you can't," Lettie said, smiling.

"Then can I buy you something to eat instead?"

"Fine," she agreed, laughing. "Let's find something to eat."

They found a tiny café with a menu in an Italian dialect Lettie didn't understand. The chubby woman behind the counter didn't speak any English. "We won't have any idea what we're ordering," De Wet said, looking dubious.

"We can always order two different dishes and share," Lettie said. "That way we're halving the risk."

While they were waiting, De Wet popped into a shop across the street to look for something for his daughters.

Lettie read on a sign outside the café that Leonardo da Vinci visited the island in 1481. At the time, the women had been making lace for decades, a skill they had learned at the time Cyprus ruled over the island. Da Vinci bought lace for the chief altar of the Duomo di Milano, the Milanese Cathedral, and so introduced the beautiful lace to the rest of the world.

"Read what it says here," she said when De Wet returned with a large bag in his hand. For a moment she was tempted to ask him what he had bought, but she controlled her curiosity.

"Hmm, interesting," he said when he had finished reading.

"Marco was a great admirer of Da Vinci," Lettie said, smiling at the memory. "He traced nearly everything back to Da Vinci, even contact lenses!"

"Did you know Da Vinci had trouble reading and couldn't spell at all?" De Wet asked.

"No," Lettie said, "Marco never said anything about that."

They ate the food that was placed before them on the rough wooden table in large pasta bowls. De Wet's order was plain pasta with cheese, while Lettie had a few pieces of seafood in her dish.

"You may have some of my prawns, but it will cost you," she teased him.

"Hey, who tipped the gondolier?" he countered.

"Okay, that's worth three prawns," she said and put half her prawns on his pile of pasta.

Repacking her bag later that evening, she thought about the day. It had been another lovely day, just as she had hoped it would be.

De Wet hadn't uttered a wrong word,

didn't touch her once, not even when he took her parcels to carry them. They were two old friends again, who enjoyed spending time together.

It was exactly what she had wanted.

And yet . . .

She sank down on her bed beside her half-packed bag.

Suddenly, bizarrely, she felt as if she had lost something.

Chapter Twenty

The train took them to Milan, the city of La Scala opera house. Lettie found it strange to think that more than forty years ago Marco also traveled to Milan by train for a performance in La Scala.

In the compartment the other four laughed and joked. De Wet seemed to be in a world of his own, only occasionally taking part in the conversation.

It made her strangely unhappy.

She soon discovered that the easy familiarity that had existed between them the day before had, for some reason, disappeared. He did not sit beside her, nor did he offer to help her with her luggage.

They arrived in Milan at lunchtime. "We'll register at the hotel before we visit the Milanese Cathedral," Antonio said.

Lettie smiled and tried to catch De Wet's eye. *You were right, another church,* she wanted to say to him. But he was not looking at her.

All roads led to the Milan Cathedral, or so it seemed to Lettie. Once there, all roads seemed to lead around the cathedral.

They stood some distance away to get the full picture. "Gosh, this is what I call a frosted Christmas cake," Boelie said.

"I like it — it looks like delicate lacework," Lettie said.

"To me it looks like a castle in a fairy tale, one in which the princess is locked in the tower," Pérsomi said.

"I also think it's a bit extravagant," Klara said, tilting her head to study the building. "It's very Gothic, isn't it, Antonio? It doesn't seem typically Italian."

Antonio launched into a historical explanation of the cathedral's mishmashed style. De Wet remained silent.

"You can climb up to the roof to get a better view of the sculptures," Antonio said.

"Oh yes, I want to do that," Pérsomi said at once.

"All right then," Boelie said, smiling, "we'll climb. Are you coming, De Wet?"

"Yes, okay," De Wet said and fell in behind them.

He did not look in Lettie's direction. He did not invite her along.

■ ■ ■ ■

That evening she took the clothes hanger with her long evening gown from the wardrobe. Lettie was going to a performance at La Scala — a dream come true. What Marco — or her father — would have given to be a part of this experience!

She had bought the evening gown specially for this occasion. She vowed not to allow anything or anyone to spoil the evening for her.

Lettie applied her makeup carefully and took time fixing her hair. Then she picked up her evening bag and went downstairs to the foyer.

She saw De Wet from a distance. He was standing with his back to the staircase, talking to Klara and Antonio. He wore a dark dress suit that fit his tall figure like a glove. His hair gleamed silver in the light of the chandelier.

Lettie paused for a moment to look at him, then she continued down the stairs.

She saw Klara notice her. She saw De Wet turn to look at her. Just for a moment she saw the admiration in his gaze. Then a veil dropped over his face.

Antonio came to meet her. "Lettie, you

look stunning," he said sincerely.

"It's my La Scala gown," she replied, taking a playful twirl. "You don't know how many years I've been dreaming about this evening."

There was a strange expression in Antonio's eyes as he smiled at her and nodded. For a moment she feared he would burst into tears. But he swiftly regained control.

La Scala was a large, stately building from the late eighteenth century. "It looks like a city hall," Boelie said.

"A grand city hall," said Pérsomi.

"Yes, the one in Durban," Klara agreed.

"I'm sure the acoustics will be a lot better," Lettie said as they walked through the elegant foyer to be shown to their seats.

Antonio had reserved seats in the front row of one of the opulent boxes, and they had an unobstructed view of the entire stage and the orchestra below.

They filed in to take their seats: Pérsomi and Boelie, then Klara and Antonio. De Wet stepped aside, and Lettie sat down next to Antonio. De Wet moved in beside her.

The interior of the building was as large and impressive as the exterior. Lettie took a deep breath. She wanted to etch every moment into her memory.

The members of the orchestra entered. The audience clapped.

The curtain went up.

She was drawn into a world she had first been introduced to through sound in her childhood home in the heart of the bushveld. The world of Enrico Caruso and Beniamino Gigli and Tito Schipa; of Bach and Mozart, Beethoven and Mendelssohn; of *La Traviata,* of *Il Trovatore* — of Leonora's dream that would forever remain a castle in the air.

The music swept her along. She was oblivious of her surroundings.

When the lights came on for intermission, she looked up, surprised. "I was in a different world," she told De Wet apologetically.

"I noticed," he said, smiling. "Are you enjoying it?"

"Incredibly. And you?"

"Yes, Lettie. It's a . . . yes, you're right, it's an incredible experience."

In the bright light she looked up and smiled. "Up there is the loggione," she said, pointing. "Marco told me that's where they used to sit when they came here as students."

He looked up and nodded. "It's probably cheaper up there," he said. "You're thinking of Marco tonight."

"Yes, but my memories are happy ones," she said.

He smiled, almost sadly. "Yes, I know."

When the lights went down again and the music began, Lettie became aware of De Wet's arm on the backrest of her seat. *He's just making himself comfortable,* she told herself and tried to bring her focus back to the events on the stage.

But she was constantly aware of his arm.

The world she had been so engrossed in suddenly became a small, artificial world on a stage.

She imagined she felt his arm touching her back. She sat motionless.

Then she heard him give a soft sigh. Removing his arm, he folded his hands in his lap.

The atmosphere had changed. The magic world on the stage could not enchant her again.

It was late when they reached their hotel. "No, I don't think I'll have coffee," Lettie said, excusing herself. "I'm going to bed. See you all in the morning. And thanks, Antonio, for arranging this wonderful evening."

"It was a pleasure," Antonio said, smiling. "I'm glad you enjoyed it. Sleep tight."

Lettie had barely closed the door when there was a knock. When she opened, both Klara and Pérsomi were standing in the corridor. "May we come in?" Klara asked.

Lettie stepped aside, somewhat surprised. She had clearly said she was tired and wanted to sleep.

Inside the room, Klara turned to her. "Lettie, sit. Let's talk."

Lettie shook her head, confused. "Talk? What about?"

"You and De Wet."

Lettie looked at her friend in silence. *I'm tired, my very soul is exhausted, and I don't have the strength for this.* She sank down onto the bed. "There's nothing . . ."

"There isn't nothing, Lettie," Pérsomi said calmly, sitting down beside her. "You're like a coiled spring, De Wet is going around like a bear with a sore head, and neither of you is happy. Klara and I think it's unnecessary."

Lettie felt the last of her energy drain from her body. "It's really nothing . . ." Suddenly the tears began to flow uncontrollably. "I'm so confused," she said.

"Do you want to talk about it?" Pérsomi asked gently.

Lettie shook her head. But the words came anyway. "I don't know what's happening. I don't even know what I want."

There was a long silence. From outside came dim street noises. Inside, there was the dull drone of the air conditioner.

"How do you feel about him, Lettie?" Klara asked.

"I don't know. I'm . . . afraid of him." She surprised herself when she spoke the words. *Afraid? Of De Wet?*

Klara sat down on a chair. "Why?" she asked, astonished.

"I don't know. He's . . . oh, Klara, he's your favorite brother, I know, but he's always been a Casanova, always ready for a good time. I know. And I can't . . . Not now . . ." She stopped, as if words failed her. How could she explain?

"De Wet is no more a Casanova than Boelie," Pérsomi said firmly. "We worked in the same office every day for more than thirty years. We worked together on numerous cases, often traveling to Pretoria on business. I'm not aware of a single occasion when he even looked at another woman while Christine was still alive. And goodness knows, he had plenty of opportunities. The young law clerks, the female interns, women who came to seek his aid with contracts or divorce — heavens, I wish you could have seen how shamelessly some women came on to him."

"My son-in-law has told us how women of all ages chased after De Wet," Lettie said quietly.

"He's attractive and charming. It's not his fault women find him irresistible," Pérsomi said. "But he's not a good-time guy, Lettie."

"When he was young he had a different girlfriend every week."

"That's not true either," Klara said seriously. "He always loved Christine, but he never had the courage to tell her. And then . . ." She shrugged. "Then it was too late. He could have spared everyone a great deal of misery if only he hadn't been too afraid to speak up."

Lettie kept shaking her head. "I . . . I'm just so confused, I really don't know . . ." She fell silent. How could she explain something she didn't understand herself?

"What are you afraid of, Lettie?" Pérsomi asked again.

There was a long silence before she replied, "I'm afraid . . . of what's inside me. I'm no different from all the others. And my life, the way it is now, the way it was before I came on this vacation, is good. I'm happy. I don't want to stir things up, I don't want . . ."

She took a deep breath, tried to think clearly.

"I've been alone for more than twenty years," she said, more for her own benefit than her friends'. "I'm not used to having someone around me. I have everything I desire: my beautiful home and garden, the town where I have spent my entire life, my friends. My two daughters and their husbands live close by. It's where I plan to see my grandchildren grow up."

She drew an almost gasping breath and tried to put her thoughts in order. "Isabella and Albert have taken over my practice — the practice started by my father. Leonora and Danie . . . Oh! Why would I want to complicate my life?"

"You don't want to take a risk," Klara said.

"There's no reason to," Lettie answered. "But there are many reasons not to. And don't tell me, 'He who hesitates is lost.' There's nothing I want to gain. I'm content with things the way they are."

"You don't think, if things work out between you and De Wet, the future may have great happiness in store for you?" Klara asked.

"But I *am* happy," Lettie said. "And besides . . . Oh, Klara, be realistic. Why on earth would De Wet be interested in me in the long run? And don't tell me I'm smart — no man looks at a woman because she's smart. I'm . . . just plain old Lettie. Actually, I'm too exhausted to think."

Klara got up and went over to the mirror. "Come here," she said.

Lettie got up listlessly.

"Look in this mirror and tell me what you see."

Almost indifferently Lettie glanced at her image in the mirror. "I see you and me," she said.

"Look at yourself," Klara ordered. "What do you look like?"

"Tired," Lettie said.

"Come now, Lettie," Klara said sternly. "As a child and a teenager, you were overweight, and you wore thick spectacles. What do you look like now?"

"A little thinner, but certainly not slim," Lettie said.

Pérsomi joined them. "Lettie, you're a beautiful woman, and now that you're wearing contact lenses, everyone can see your extraordinarily beautiful eyes," she said honestly. "And your complexion is like velvet."

Lettie remembered her mother's words, which had been no consolation to her at the time: "Your complexion is a bit oily, but it means you won't have wrinkles when you're older."

"I think Klara is right," Pérsomi said, still looking at Lettie in the mirror. "You don't look at yourself objectively."

Klara turned away from the mirror and sat back down on the chair. "I just want you to think carefully, Lettie," she said. "De Wet might not be as self-assured as he appears. We all wear masks. Maybe he finds it hard to say how he really feels, I don't know. Men think and act differently from us women."

"I think," Pérsomi said slowly, "you're afraid he's just amusing himself with you. I doubt very much that's true."

"I don't know if that's what I'm afraid of," Lettie said slowly. "Maybe, yes, I'm afraid I'm just a distraction for him while he's on vacation."

"No, you're not," Pérsomi said.

"I suppose I'm most afraid of myself," Lettie admitted reluctantly. "I . . . don't want to take a risk."

"Well, first you must decide how you feel and what you want to do," Klara said and got to her feet. "Then you must be honest with De Wet. But it can't go on like this."

Pérsomi gave her a reassuring smile. "Right now you need to take a bath and relax. Try to get some sleep, it's very late. Everything will look better in the morning."

The morning did not bring the new perspective Pérsomi had promised.

Lettie showered, then went down to the dining room. She could do with a cup of coffee.

She saw De Wet the minute she entered. He was sitting alone, apparently having had the same idea. She poured her own cup and went to his table.

He got up immediately and pulled out a chair for her. "Good morning. Did you sleep well?" he asked gallantly, but there was a guarded expression in his eyes.

She sat down facing him and put her cup on the table.

She looked him in the eye. "De Wet," she began, then shrugged helplessly, "I'm sorry I'm spoiling our vacation."

"No, it's me," he said at once. "I'm so confused."

She took a sip of the hot coffee. "I'm confused too," she said softly.

He looked up, nodded slowly. "Yes, Lettie, I know."

They drank their coffee in silence.

"We mustn't spoil the others' vacation as well," he said.

"I know," she said.

They carried on drinking their coffee.

They were walking through the Porta Ticinese, the old city gate of Milan, first built in the sixteenth century. De Wet and Lettie walked side by side, seemingly at ease in each other's company.

They were heading for the Santa Maria delle Grazie, the Holy Mary of Grace church, where the mural of Leonardo da Vinci's *Last Supper* could be found in the convent.

"You say Marco was impressed with Da Vinci?" De Wet asked.

"Oh yes," Lettie said. "Apparently Da Vinci was incredibly versatile. I've told you he was the first to describe the concept of a contact lens. He even designed a kind of helicopter."

"I remember learning at school that he was an artist and sculptor and scientist or mathematician, or something," De Wet replied. "I don't remember the exact facts."

"There's more. I know he was also an architect and an engineer," Lettie said.

"Boelie and Antonio will find it hard to believe that one person could be both," De Wet said, laughing.

At last they stood in front of the *Last Sup-*

per, one of the most reproduced paintings the world has ever known. "I never imagined it would be so big," Pérsomi said, surprised.

"I didn't know it was painted on a wall. I thought it would be on canvas," Boelie said.

They stepped closer to examine the details. "See the oranges on the table?" Antonio asked.

"Yes?"

"Well, it's a historical error. Oranges were brought to Europe from India in the fifteenth century by Dutch sailors. The events in this painting date back one thousand four hundred years earlier."

"Interesting," said De Wet.

They studied the apostles, and Antonio identified each of them by name. "The building was damaged during the war," he said. "In August 1943, the Allied troops bombed the church and convent. Large sections were destroyed, but some of the original walls survived, among them the wall with the mural of the *Last Supper,* because it had been protected with sandbags."

"War is a terrible thing," Pérsomi said with feeling.

"Terrible," said Antonio, nodding in agreement.

There was a moment's silence. *Each of us was influenced in some way by the war forty years ago,* Lettie thought. Antonio was a soldier and was taken prisoner. Boelie was interned. Pérsomi lost her brother, Christine the father of her unborn child. And through Christine, De Wet was connected to the war. Through Antonio, Klara's life was completely changed.

And my own life too. Marco never would have come to South Africa if the war hadn't ruined his health. He probably would not have died so young if not for the damage his lungs sustained during the war.

"The painting is disintegrating, isn't it, Antonio?" Klara broke the silence.

"Yes, the wall has deteriorated and the base under the paint is disintegrating," Antonio answered. "Ongoing restoration is carried out, but ultimately it's just a question of time."

"Well, then it's a good thing we're seeing it in time," Boelie said and turned away. "I wonder if there's any coffee around here."

"Boelie!" Klara and Lettie said simultaneously and began to laugh.

The next morning they were off to Turin, scarcely a hundred miles away.

Lettie hurried off to buy an English magazine at a kiosk on the platform. When she rejoined the others, there was a vacant seat next to Klara, and one next to De Wet. He motioned for her to sit next to him, his gaze almost daring her to refuse. They both remembered what had happened the previous time.

She gave a slight smile and sat down beside him, facing Klara and Boelie.

"Thanks," he said gallantly, his eyes twinkling.

"My pleasure entirely," she answered, matching his tone.

Antonio began to tell them about the Shroud of Turin — according to legend, the cloth the body of Christ was buried in.

Lettie became aware of De Wet's arm sliding behind her back.

She sat motionless.

". . . preserved in the cathedral of St. John the Baptist," she heard Antonio say.

"Sounds very Catholic to me," Boelie said.

"Is there any evidence that the shroud is authentic?" De Wet asked, resting his hand on her shoulder.

She gave a quick sidelong glance at the others. She didn't want them to notice, especially Boelie, who could be merciless.

"Last year a group of American scientists examined the shroud . . ."

She tried to move away.

". . . but they could find no evidence of

fraud and called it a mystery," Antonio said.

De Wet's grip on her shoulder tightened.

"A mystery? That's not very scientific," De Wet said, taking part all too innocently in the conversation.

"No, definitely not," Antonio said. "There are many varying opinions about the shroud."

"Relax," De Wet said very softly, close to her ear.

"Will we be able to see it?" Boelie asked.

She leaned back slightly in an effort to relax.

"No, the shroud is only on display to the public every twenty-five years," Antonio answered.

"That's better," De Wet said softly.

"What's better?" Pérsomi asked, frowning slightly.

"That they take such good care of the shroud nowadays," De Wet answered calmly.

"Oh," Pérsomi said, looking confused.

"Now, what are we going to be seeing in Turin besides churches?" Boelie asked, rubbing his hands together.

"Well, there's a lot to see, but I'd like to show you the university where my brothers and I studied," Antonio said tentatively. "But if you'd rather . . ."

"No, let's go see your university," De Wet

said immediately. "The rest of us all went to the same university in South Africa. It would be interesting to visit yours."

Lettie turned to him. "Wait a minute! I went to Wits, not Tukkies!" she protested.

"Philistine!" Boelie said.

Seldom had a hundred miles passed so quickly.

Lorenzo came to meet them at the station. They would be staying with him and Gina.

Lettie was shocked when she saw him. He looked even more like Marco than Antonio did. Something about his manner also reminded her of Marco — the smile that plucked at the corners of his mouth before it turned into a proper smile, the way he tilted his head when she was introduced to him.

It felt very strange.

But his eyes were completely different from Marco's eyes.

"Aletta!" he said, opening his arms wide. "At last I meet Marco's Aletta. Welcome, welcome!" He kissed both her cheeks.

Marco's Aletta? That felt strange too.

Lorenzo kept up a lively conversation in fluent English while they walked to his car. Lettie walked behind him, noticing he was not as thin as Marco was, and his walk was completely different, a bit ungainly on the wooden leg. He had arranged for one of his colleagues to come to the station as well. Lettie, Klara, and Antonio drove with Lorenzo while the rest got into the other vehicle.

They drove through the city and up a hill, where castle-like houses clung to the hillside. "Lorenzo has a very grand home. His wife is also very grand," Klara warned the two of them.

Lettie laughed softly. "Thanks for the warning. Shall I put on some lipstick?"

"Definitely," Klara said.

On their arrival, Gina took the ladies on a tour of the house and garden. She struggled with English, so she kept switching to Italian, which Klara had to interpret. "Luncheon will soon be served," Klara said, her eyes dancing with mirth, "then we'll take a nap, and at four coffee will be served. But if you two would like to do something else . . ."

"Sounds right to me," Pérsomi said at once. "I think I'll take my nap at the pool."

The men had disappeared and did not join them for lunch.

At around half past three Lettie went outside to find Pérsomi basking in the sun. "Careful you don't burn," she warned.

"The sun is my friend," Pérsomi said. "Are the men back yet?"

"No," Lettie replied.

She had not laid eyes on De Wet since they arrived in Turin. She found herself looking for him all the time.

She shook her head slowly.

"Why are you shaking your head like that?" Pérsomi asked with a slight smile.

"I'm in love and I don't know what to do," Lettie said without thinking.

Pérsomi looked at her calmly. "Sit down," she said and moved up so that Lettie could sit beside her on the towel. "What's bothering you?"

"Everything," Lettie said and sank down beside Pérsomi. "Pérsomi, I'm really, well, attracted to him. But now I think, what if it . . . yes, like you said, 'works out'? I can't just marry a strange man!"

"Strange man? De Wet?"

"Yes, well, you know what I mean. And if it happens . . . do I give up my home and live in Christine's? It's unthinkable."

Pérsomi was quiet for a long time before she spoke. "I moved into the Big House when I married Boelie — a place where as a child I felt nothing but mortified. Even more, I moved into Annabel's home. Do you realize what that required of me?"

Lettie had never given it a thought. "But you were younger! I'm too old for all this," she protested. "Teenagers fall in love, or students in their twenties — not women with married daughters."

"Love doesn't ask one's age," Pérsomi said seriously. Lettie waited. Pérsomi always chose her words carefully.

"I've given a lot of thought to what you said the other night: that you're content with your life the way it is at present, that there's no reason to take risks," Pérsomi said. "You're right, there isn't. I understand. I was alone for a very long time as well. My life was ordered. I was happy.

"But . . . I don't know how to say this without sounding corny, Lettie, but it's better not to be alone. You already know the value of that happiness. You've had it before. Don't let it pass you by. It's a rare and precious thing." Pérsomi shrugged. "That's all," she said, a little self-consciously. "But I wanted to say it to you."

That night dinner was served in Lorenzo and Gina's elegant dining room, with maidservants carrying in one course after another.

Lettie sat opposite De Wet. When she looked up, she saw the happiness in his expression, the joy of being with friends.

"You won't believe what Antonio did in his second year," Lorenzo began with yet another anecdote as he filled up their glasses.

Lettie became aware of a movement under the table. De Wet was playing footsie with her like a lovesick teenager. She looked straight at him, flooded with warmth and happiness.

He was taking part in the conversation, but when he caught her eye, he smiled and winked.

After dinner the ladies retired to a different room, where coffee was served. They struggled for a while to keep the conversation going, then gave it up and decided to turn in.

In an adjoining room Lettie heard the men's raucous laughter.

I saw so little of him today, Lettie thought as she lay in bed. *I miss him. I know it.*

And there is a greater happiness. I know that too.

She curled up and pulled the sheet over her head.

The uncertainty remained.

After breakfast they took a bus to the university. They took a walk through the botanical gardens on the banks of the Po. They paid a visit to the Castle of Valentino, the seat of the Architecture Faculty of the University of Turin.

"Did you have your lectures here?" Boelie asked, impressed.

"Yes, here in this building I sweated blood," Antonio said, clearly proud.

"And I thought the Old Arts building at Tuks was impressive," Pérsomi said.

But to Lettie none of the old buildings, the historical streets, the exotic plants held any interest. She had eyes only for the tall man with the silver hair and green eyes.

Lorenzo and Gina announced that they were taking their guests to a restaurant that night. "We'll have to dress up," Klara said. "My sister-in-law moves in high social circles."

"Surely not evening gowns?" Pérsomi asked.

"No, but definitely the little black number with real pearls," Klara teased.

But when the time came to get dressed, Lettie left her own black dress hanging in the cupboard and took out one of her old favorites. It felt easy on her body, familiar.

For a long time she stood with the string of Venetian beads in her hand. It matched the dress perfectly.

She bit her lower lip and fastened the beads around her neck.

The heavy handmade beads lay cool against her warm skin. She looked at herself in the mirror. Her fingers stroked the beads one by one.

Then she turned and left the room.

De Wet noticed the beads at once. His eyes met hers, and they were filled with joy.

He was in his dress suit again. Christine was right so many years ago. After all this time he was still a beautiful man.

Klara noticed the beads as well. "Lettie, they're gorgeous! Where did you get them?" she asked, touching the fine mosaics with her fingertips.

"Venice," Lettie said vaguely.

She looked up to see Pérsomi watching. Her friend knew where they had come from, Lettie realized at once. Pérsomi gave a slight nod of approval.

Gina was clad in a tight-fitting black dress. She had taken her hair up in a chic roll. Around her neck was a string of large, perfectly round white pearls. She was an aristocrat and she looked the part — the only daughter of the Baron and Baroness of Veneto, granddaughter of the rich Baron

Veneto from before the Great War.

The restaurant had thick carpets, soft, deep chairs, and crystal chandeliers that bathed the room in soft light.

The headwaiter knew Signore and Signora Romanelli well and led them to a table in a corner.

Gina sat between De Wet and Boelie and talked nonstop to De Wet, who was charming in return.

Lorenzo talked them through the menu, suggested certain courses, and ordered wine.

After they'd had their starters, Gina accompanied the ladies to the powder room. "I've never been in such a grand ladies' room before," Pérsomi whispered to Lettie as they returned to their table.

On a small stage a gray-haired gentleman was playing soft music on a gleaming Steinway.

"Gina says he's a superlative singer," Klara interpreted.

"Do you mean to tell me you know that big Italian word?" Lettie asked, surprised.

"No, I'm simply going with the ambience," Klara said, her eyes dancing with mischief.

After the main meal, the musician began to sing. *He really does have a superlative voice,* Lettie thought, enjoying their inside joke. His style was not operatic, but light. He did a few jazz numbers, a few others that sounded like country music, everything in Italian. "Interesting music for a top-class Italian restaurant," she remarked to Antonio, who was sitting beside her.

"The American influence is everywhere," he replied. "Lorenzo says he'll take requests, if you'd like to hear a Neapolitan song."

"No, this is lovely," she assured him.

The dessert was so elegantly served that Boelie asked, "Where does one begin to eat this concoction?"

"Start at the top," Klara said. "But mind it doesn't hop out of your plate. The crust is quite hard."

Lettie proceeded with caution, taking care not to disgrace herself in a strange country in the company of the in-laws she had only just met!

She saw De Wet get up to talk to the musician, then saw the man nod before carrying on.

"You have two beautiful daughters. I was amazed at how good their Italian is," Lorenzo said beside her.

"It's thanks to Antonio. He speaks Italian to them," she replied.

"I believe Leonora is very gifted," Lorenzo

continued.

"Oh yes, she's very musical. She gets it from the Romanellis," Lettie said.

Before Lorenzo could reply, De Wet touched her shoulder. "Dance?" he said.

She felt a rush of happiness. "Excuse me," she said to Lorenzo.

De Wet pulled out her chair and led her to the dance floor. They joined the other swaying couples, moving to the gentle rhythm of the melody.

They had not danced since their second night in Rome — the night the Eternal City changed color forever.

He was close to her, his body against her, his arms around her.

She was breathless. Time stood still. Eternity had frozen in a second.

The melody became familiar, though the language was not. De Wet's melodious voice crooned in her ear. In her head she sang along. "And afterwards we drop into a quiet little place and have a drink or two . . ."

De Wet held her away from him and gave her an inquiring look as he sang the words quite clearly. "And then I go and spoil it all by saying something stupid like 'I love you.' "

She understood and spoke without thinking. "Maybe not quite so stupid."

He stopped in the middle of the dance floor and looked down at her, his green eyes inscrutable. “I know, Lettie,” he said. “But do you know it too?”

The words entered through her ears and went straight to her heart.

“We can’t stop in the middle of the dance floor in this grand place,” she whispered anxiously. “Everyone is looking.”

His soft laugh came from deep inside. He leaned forward slightly and pulled her closer. “Let them,” his deep voice said.

His arms went around her. His feet and body began to move in time to the music again. He was still singing, and his voice added to the enchantment of the silvery evening in that strange, magnificent space.

“And though it’s just a line to you, for me it’s true . . .”

Chapter Twenty-One

All the villagers knew Antonio was coming home. At the first sharp bend in the steep road they saw a bunch of brightly colored balloons tied to a rock.

Antonio was leading the way in Lorenzo's big car. With him were Klara, Boelie, and Pérsomi. Lorenzo and Gina were joining them later for the weekend. In the meantime the maidservants would cater to all their needs in the stone villa.

Behind Antonio came De Wet and Lettie in a bright-red Dino Ferrari. "Your Italian dream was to see an opera in La Scala. Mine was to drive a Ferrari up a mountain pass," he had admitted to her, slightly embarrassed. "I'm going to rent a Ferrari for a few days and drive up to Antonio's village. Will you come with me?"

He was as excited as a little boy at the prospect.

"If you promise to drive carefully," she

said, playing along.

"I'm going to drive fast," he warned her. The excitement made him feel young and adventurous. "And you'll have to tie a scarf around your hair," he added. "It's a convertible."

"I haven't said I'd come," Lettie protested, laughing.

"Wait until you see the car. You'll pay me to come," he said with confidence.

The road to the village was narrow and steep, with hairpin bends and low stone parapet walls. At the next bend Antonio stopped again and handed Klara the balloons. "We have to take them along for the village kids," he explained. "They'll be waiting for their balloons at the square."

After negotiating the sharpest bend of all, Antonio stopped for balloons again. "This is Giuseppe's bend, named after my father," he explained. "It's where he found my mother. She was just a child, a refugee from somewhere in France. He took her to his parents' home. It's one of the happiest stories of the village," he said, smiling fondly.

All the people of his childhood were long gone, Antonio had said the night before: the village doctor, Father Enrico who was also their teacher, the Baron of Veneto, even Tia

Sofia, old Luigi, and their only daughter. And of course the grandchild who had laid down his life for his country in the war.

That was one of the saddest stories of the village.

When they came round the last bend, the village unfolded before them.

The villagers had never been rich. The houses were cramped and built right on the streets. The church was simple, the square small and unadorned. The children were waiting. They chased after the balloon-filled car like mountain goats.

The big stone villa high on the mountainside immediately caught the eye. It had a magnificent view of the entire village.

Even higher up, across the Ponte Bartolini, the ancient bridge across the Bartolini River, lay the castle. It was in ruins, with only the thick stone walls still standing firmly where they were erected centuries before.

At dusk, so Klara said, courting couples went up to the castle to cuddle and kiss in the shadow of the walls.

Antonio drew up in front of the stone villa. They all got out and stood admiring the view. Below them lay the valley with its fields and orchards and marble quarries, where the stone carvers were still removing chunks of rock from the belly of the mountain, and the cliffs and deep ravines, shaped over centuries.

"It's breathtaking!" Lettie said, amazed.

The road leading up to the village was visible only in places. "Just look at the winding road that brought us here," said De Wet.

"And the mountain!" Pérsomi said breathlessly. "Tomorrow I want to climb it, all the way to the top."

Antonio laughed. "All the way to the top isn't an option," he said, "but we can definitely go some way up the mountain early tomorrow morning. We can easily reach the first cave. You old-timers all look reasonably fit to me."

"We *are* fit," Pérsomi said. "And those who can't keep up can wait on the path, and we'll meet up with them on the way down."

Boelie groaned softly. "Next time I want to get married, please remind me not to pick a young wife."

"Oh, Boelie, you poor man," Klara teased him.

"That level piece of ground over on the side where the sun goes down is where we used to play soccer," Antonio said, pointing. "And down there was the doctor's house. His son, Pietro, lives there now. He's quite a renowned writer in Italy."

"He's the one who found Marco in a hospital in Rome and brought him home," Lettie remembered. "I'd like to meet him."

"You will. You'll meet everyone in the village," Antonio said. "No one is persona non grata around here."

"That house on the other side of the square was where Antonio's family used to live. A young teacher and his wife rent it from Lorenzo at present," Klara said.

"On that small patio in front of our home, the men gathered on Saturdays to play chess and talk about politics," Antonio said. "My father and Don Veneto and Father Enrico and the doctor, later also Mr. Rozenfeld. They drank the wine Father Enrico made, and my mother cooked for them: pasta con ragù, cannelloni, ravioli, minestrone soup, sometimes polenta, simmering slowly in a cast-iron saucepan."

"For goodness' sake, you're making me hungry," Boelie said.

Antonio laughed out loud. "Boelie, I'm never traveling without you again," he said. "Let's go see if the maidservants cook as well as Gina said."

At dusk Lettie and De Wet headed up the path. They crossed the Ponte Bartolini and walked past the level ground where Antonio used to play soccer with his friends, past the centuries-old bell tower to the remnants of the stone walls that were once a castle.

They stopped there to look up at the walls towering over them, at the steep cliffs higher up the mountain. "I hope we don't have to climb those cliffs tomorrow," Lettie said somewhat anxiously.

"I'm sure there'll be a path," said De Wet. "See the path the water has carved through the rocks over the centuries?"

"This is a truly beautiful part of the world," Lettie said, sitting down on the warm rocks.

De Wet stood admiring the view before he sat down beside her. "I was serious last night when I asked if you knew that I meant the words I was singing," he said.

She felt her inner being grow quiet. The time had come.

"I'm not stupid, De Wet," she said.

"I've never thought that, Lettie. Naive, maybe, at times, but without a doubt one of the smartest women I know."

She was quiet for a long time. He was waiting for an answer, but she didn't really know what the question was. "There are many things I'm unsure about," she said after a while.

"Then we should talk. There are things I want to know as well."

"I don't know where to begin," she said.

"At the beginning," he suggested.

She gave it a moment's thought. "De Wet, how do we know this thing between us won't blow over when we get home? We're here, in the most romantic setting in the world, we're on vacation, we're with people we love. But reality is back home, not here. Who's to say . . ." She stopped, uncertain how to go on.

"This is no holiday romance for me, if that's what you mean," De Wet said.

"I know. I just wanted to be sure."

"Is it because this is Marco's home?" he asked kindly.

"No. No, strangely enough, it's not. We never had this village in common. This is where he loved Rachel, and I . . ." She didn't know how to complete her own thought.

She sat quietly, waiting for him to continue.

"I've given it a lot of thought, Lettie. I'd like to spend the rest of my life with you." He smiled somewhat sadly. "You know, when young people get married, they believe they'll grow old together. It didn't work out for you and Marco or Christine and me."

He regarded her fondly. "But I hope the two of us will grow old together. I love you, Lettie."

She pressed her hands to her warm face. "It's the first time you've said it," she said softly.

"Is it?" he asked, almost surprised. "But I . . . yes, well . . ."

She laughed softly. "I love you too, De Wet."

"It makes me very happy to hear you say it," he said, feigning relief. "It makes the road ahead more even."

They sat in silence for a while, the moment almost too big for them.

"Your turn," she said. "What are you unsure about?"

There was a long pause. "Actually, there's something I'd like to discuss with you," he said.

"Yes?"

"I've been playing with the idea for a while, but it depends on what you think, of course . . ." He hesitated, then started over. "Boelie and Nelius want to buy my farm. They've been farming it for years, after all. Gerbrand will never farm — flying is all he's ever wanted to do, and my sons-in-law have no interest in it either. I'm considering selling to Boelie, giving the kids their share, and having a smaller, more modern house built in town — in that new neighborhood where Antonio and Klara live."

He fell silent.

"Yes?" she asked. She began to add up the implications. A brand-new, modern home . . .

"That's all. How would you feel about it?"

She would probably have to sell her home, but it also meant she wouldn't have to . . .

"In the end it's your decision," she said hesitantly. "And your children's."

"You threw three coins into the Trevi fountain, remember?"

She gave him a puzzled look. "Yes?"

"One coin means you'll return to Rome one day. I believe you will. Two coins mean you'll find love in Rome." He began to smile. "I believe you have. Do you agree?"

She smiled too. "And the third coin?"

He shrugged. "Three coins can mean either divorce or marriage," he said, his green eyes twinkling.

"Well, divorce certainly isn't an option," she said.

"But marriage is." He looked directly at her, his gaze suddenly very serious. "That's why I want you to make this decision with me. Lettie, will you marry me?"

Suddenly she didn't have to think anymore. The answer was clear. "Yes, De Wet, I'd like that very much."

His face broke open in a smile. "Then I'm going to kiss you now," he warned her, his eyes dancing with mischief.

"I thought you never would. I —"

But he didn't allow her to finish the sentence.

"Shall we tell the others?" he asked, much, much later.

"No, let's keep it a secret for now," she said.

He laughed softly. "If we go back now, they'll know at once. Your eyes are sparkling like a young girl's, Lettie."

She laughed, embarrassed. "We should speak to our children first," she said.

"You're right," he said. He laughed again, looked deep into her eyes, and began to croon: "If I should live forever, and all my dreams come true, my memories of love will be of you . . ."

"That's my favorite song at the moment!" she said, amazed. "How did you know?"

He threw back his head and laughed. "I guessed. I've known you for years, remember?" he said, getting to his feet. "Come, we have to get back, it's almost completely dark."

Hand in hand they walked down the narrow path that wound its way back to the villa.

AUTHOR'S NOTE

Thanks to everyone who comes to me with a story — all my historical novels are based on true stories people have told me.

Thanks to NB Publishers, and specifically Etienne Bloemhof and Eben Pienaar, for their help in publishing all three of the books in the trilogy.*

Thanks to Jan-Jan, who virtually has a research library in his apartment. I only have to ask, "Jan-Jan, please lend your mother a book on the persecution of the Jews in Italy during the Second World War," and he will produce a variety to choose from.

Thanks to my cousin Leonie Nel, who contracted a severe degree of infantile paralysis at the age of three. The pain suffered by the character Leonora, the giving

* Published in the United States as *The Girl from the Train, Child of the River,* and *The Crooked Path.*

up of her dreams, and the ultimate acceptance of her new body with its limitations were based on what Leonie experienced in her own life. Thanks as well to various other polio victims for snippets from their own lives that I could weave into my story.

Thanks to Dr. John Pauw, who practiced in the 1950s and could supply me with background information. And especially to my mother, Alida Moerdyk, who worked as a nursing sister and can describe to me the exact treatment and medicines for any disease, such as pneumonia. What a blessing that, at the age of eighty-eight, she still has the same quick mind she had as a young working woman in the 1940s and '50s!

Thanks to my pharmacist daughter, Madeleine, for her proofreading, very useful feedback, and especially help with medical terms and concepts.

As always, a very special thanks to my good friend and ex-colleague Elize Gerber, not only for proofreading the manuscript, but also for being my soundboard and writing partner.

Thanks to good friends who understand, even during vacations: Suzette and Christo, Fanie and Wourine.

Thanks to my husband, Jan, for his help

with classical music and especially for continuing to love his writing wife.

If I have a gift, it is a pure blessing — the greatest thanks go to my heavenly Father.

— Irma Joubert

BIBLIOGRAPHY

Battaglia, Roberto. *The Story of the Italian Resistance.* London: Odhams, 1957.

Delzell, Charles F. *Mussolini's Enemies: The Italian Anti-Fascist Resistance.* Princeton, NJ: University Press, 1961.

Gilbert, Martin. *The Holocaust.* New York: Holt, Rinehart and Winston Publishers, 1985.

Hall, Walter, and William Davis. *The Course of Europe Since Waterloo.* New York: Appleton-Century-Crofts, 1951.

www.health24.com: "Polio"

www.cloudnet.com: "The History of Polio"

www.bmj.com: "A Calculated Risk: The Salk Polio Vaccine Field Trials of 1954"

www.politicsforum.org: "Mussolini's Italian Concentration Camp for Slovene, Communist, and Jewish Prisoners," by James Mayfield (Chairperson, European Heritage Library) www.holocaustresearchproject.org: "The Destruction of the Jews of Italy"

DISCUSSION QUESTIONS

1. Which character did you most relate to and why?
2. How do you see Lettie acting as her own person throughout the novel?
3. Lettie struggles with body image for a significant portion of her life. How do you see her resolving that and moving forward?
4. Lettie is a strong female character. She forges her own path in medicine, keeps her name professionally, and is eventually a single mother. How do people react to this strength of character throughout the novel?
5. Lettie suffers some intense personal disappointment. How do you see her finding the strength to persevere through these situations?
6. How did Lettie and Marco's personal experiences before they met one another allow their relationship to flourish and deepen in the way that it does throughout

the novel? How different would their relationship have looked had they met before they faced those difficult times?

7. Have you, like Lettie later in her life, ever found yourself afraid to take risks for happiness because you might disrupt the status quo? What happened in that situation?
8. There are many ways that love is played out in relationships throughout the story. Young love, soul-mate love, convenient love, a marriage without love, and more. Some of these loves are faithful; some are difficult. Whose love story resonated the most with you? With whom did you identify most strongly? What parts of the marriages in the book stood out to you and why?
9. In a world of vaccinations that are readily available, it can seem odd to think that this was not always the case. Did you learn anything about polio and the vaccination for that disease that you hadn't known before?
10. How have you seen love and life worth experiencing in your own life? What are the crooked paths on which you have found yourself?
11. Pérsomi and Boelie have a story told in more detail in *Child of the River.* Have you

read this book? What did it add to your experience of this story?

12. The political backdrop of South Africa at the time of the novel is one in which the apartheid legislation was being formed. How does this affect the lives on the characters?

ABOUT THE AUTHOR

International bestselling author **Irma Joubert** was a history teacher for thirty-five years before she began writing. Her stories are known for their deep insight into personal relationships and rich historical detail. She's the author of eight novels and a regular fixture on bestseller lists in the Netherlands and in her native South Africa. She is the winner of the 2010 ATKV Prize for Romance Novels.

Facebook: irmajoubertpage

The employees of Thorndike Press hope you have enjoyed this Large Print book. All our Thorndike, Wheeler, and Kennebec Large Print titles are designed for easy reading, and all our books are made to last. Other Thorndike Press Large Print books are available at your library, through selected bookstores, or directly from us.

For information about titles, please call:

(800) 223-1244

or visit our website at:

gale.com/thorndike

To share your comments, please write:

Publisher
Thorndike Press
10 Water St., Suite 310
Waterville, ME 04901